THE ABSENCE

THE ABSENCE

Bill Hussey

Bloody Books

www.bloodybooks.com

Bloody Books is an imprint of Beautiful Books Limited.

Beautiful Books Limited
36–38 Glasshouse Street
London W1B 5DL

ISBN 9781905636464

9 8 7 6 5 4 3 2 1

A catalogue reference for this book is available from the British Library.

Cover design by Ian Pickard.
Typeset by Ellipsis Books Limited, Glasgow
Printed and bound in the UK by CPI Mackays, Chatham ME5 8TD

For Graeme Hills, reader of first drafts
and a dear friend.

Prologue

- May 2006 -

Darkling I listen; and, for many a time
I have been half in love with easeful Death

Ode to a Nightingale, John Keats

In her dying hour, the old woman listened.

'. . . as the heatwave continues, meteorologists have warned of possible droughts across the Lincolnshire Fens.

'And in other news: police are still searching for missing schoolboy, Thomas Ray Jennings, from the village of Potter's Drake. In a fresh development, Inspector Michael Innes confirmed today that he *has* interviewed convicted child-killer, Muriel Elizabeth Sutton. Inspector Innes stressed to reporters that Mrs Sutton is not a suspect in this case. It is possible, however, that she saw Thomas on the day of his disappearance. Mrs Sutton lives alone in an isolated property not far from where Thomas went missing.'

Alone? The old woman's lips thinned until they spread like a scar across her face. No, no, Mr Radio Reporter, sir, in all her long years she had never once been '*Alone*'.

'In 1972, Muriel Sutton was convicted of the brutal murder of her twelve-year-old sister, Alice Daecher. She spent the next sixteen years incarcerated in Gannet's Rest, a psychiatric hospital for the criminally insane. No longer considered a danger, Mrs Sutton was released in 1988 and returned to Daecher's

Mill, the family home she had shared with her sister. Since then she has led a quiet life, but the case – once dubbed 'The Fenland Horror' – continues to provoke reaction in nearby Potter's Drake. Mrs Joan Deekwater, a longtime resident, had this to say:

'I remember it well, though t'were thirty or more years back. My God, *how* that little girl died . . . But, no, I don't think the old lady has anything to do with this kiddy goan' missin'. Don't stand to reason. She's nowt but a frail little thing now, all twisted up wi' art'ritis. And anyway, she'd never hurt another child. You only have to look into those eyes of hers to see it, plain as day. Muriel Sutton's haunted by what she did. Haunted bad.'

Muriel Sutton, haunted – *haunted bad* – switched off the radio and turned back to her work. She made two corrections and then nodded, as if satisfied. Her Last Will & Testament had not been a lengthy document but the writing of it had taken some time. The light in the study was poor and a draught, singing through the wood-wormed window, had convulsed her writing hand into an arthritic claw. Such disabilities and distractions, however, did not account for the slow scratch of her pen. Rather, it was the questions, repeated often in her mind:

Can I do this? Can I bring them here? Innocents. Children . . . Her *children . . .*

Had anyone known the secret history of Muriel Sutton, they might have asked why such questions concerned her. After all, since her return from Gannet's Rest, she had brought many 'innocent' guests to Daecher's Mill. Every few years a stranger would be invited to step inside these walls: to drink a glass of water, to have a bite to eat, to take the weight off their weary feet. Muriel would stand back from the door and watch them trot into the slaughterhouse; watch until the shadows consumed them, made them hollow . . .

True, the invitation was always hers, but it had *never* tripped easily from her lips. Indeed, in those first months after her release from Gannet's Rest she had refused to bring strangers here. Even when the cries pierced the attic walls, she had not wavered. After years in an asylum, screams in the night were as lullabies to Muriel Sutton. And so, for a long time, she endured the whispers, the scratching of fingernails behind the walls, the faint sound of a child crying. Such noises drew her often to the crumbling outskirts of her sanity, but they could be borne. She could even cope with the smell that sometimes wafted down the stairwell. That ghostly stink of burnt hair and cooked flesh – yes, even *that* her mind could withstand. As long as the dead thing ('Not thing' the psychiatrists had insisted, 'you didn't murder a thing – it was your SISTER') remained within the attic, all might be well.

It was a cold, moonless night when her SISTER broke free.

At first, Muriel had not known what had woken her – a mouse behind the wainscot, perhaps, or the call of a marsh bird from the dunes. Blinking the sleep from her eyes, she had felt her heart cramp in her chest. Darkness softened and the figure beside the bed became more distinct. It stood over her – a child-form – tears streaking the crusted mask that was its face. Muriel drew back. Her breath shortened into gasps. She ought to have known that doors and locks could not hold it. Perhaps the creature had, in fact, only been kept at bay by her own faltering will. Now, as she felt one fire-flayed hand caress her cheek, that will gave way. Alice's head rolled back and a few ragged sobs, like those of a starved dog, rose from her throat. The crying tore at Muriel Sutton. In her mind's eye, she saw herself shamble across the outskirts of sanity and into the wastelands beyond. Accepting this, she pulled back the bedclothes and allowed her dead sister to climb up beside her. Flesh, hot and tacky, clung to Muriel's skin. Melted lips whispered in her ear.

'*Please don't deny me* again. *Please don't murder me* again. *You can't stand by and watch me starve. Your own sister. Your own Alice.*'

Muriel, lost in the wastelands, heard her own voice on the wind.

'All right,' she answered. 'I'll bring them. Strangers. God help me, I'll *feed* you.'

Muriel tried not to think about the last eighteen years – almost two decades, in which she had, at intervals, provided nourishment for the presence in the attic. Instead, she sat back and reviewed her testament. Cramped into the top half of a single sheet of paper sat a few formal words. At their insistence a gift was bestowed upon a family that, as far as she knew, did not deserve it. Who in this world *could* deserve such an inheritance?

Muriel dashed her signature across the bottom of the testament. She sealed the paper in an envelope, addressed it 'Nightingales – care of Cuttle', and reached for her cane. Arthritis shrieked along her shank and spine as she got to her feet and hobbled into the hall. By the time she reached the foot of the stairs her face was tucked in with pain. The old murderess grasped the banister. She filled her lungs and felt the agony ebb. *Smother it,* she told herself, *soon you must play your hand and you must have your wits about you. The thing –* SISTER *– must not see fear in your eyes. Must not suspect . . .*

'*Muriel? Where are you? What are you doing down there?*'

Muriel's thoughts flew like a shadow before her. They took her up into the winding unlit summit of the house. They unlocked the attic door and threw it wide. They harried her into the nursery bedroom and forced her to look upon the occupant of the rocking chair. The child-figure giggled.

'*You're bringing them, aren't you, Muriel?*'

'Yes.' The word sizzled between her teeth. 'Yes, one last time.'

'*And they'll stay, won't they?*'

'They'll stay.'

'*You promise?*'

'They'll stay always . . . But first you must keep *your* promise to me. I'm too old, too tired to do this anymore. You have to let me go. You have to give me peace. You have to make it as it was before.'

'*Of course I shall grant your wish, but I shall always keep you close.*' Again, that liquid laughter echoed down the stairwell. '*Now come and claim your reward. I shall give it to you, if you kiss me.*'

Her freedom for a kiss. Her life long ago for a kiss. It was a small enough gesture. All she had to do was to put her lips to the creature's face. A face that she knew – o so very well. Muriel had, after all, moulded each fire-blighted feature with her own hands.

'*Yes.*' The voice continued. '*They will stay always. For ever and ever and ever.*'

Muriel climbed the stairs. With every step the arthritis coiled in her hip like a ball of hot wire. She ignored the pain. Soon she would be beyond it.

'They'll look after me when you're gone, Muriel. They'll feed me when I'm hungry. Here, inside my tabernacle of Water and Shadow, they will lay their offerings upon my altar. And, in each Darkness, I shall take what is mine.'

I

- JUNE 2006 -

A Drawing of Nightingales

Study me then, you who shall lovers be
At the next world, that is at the next spring;
  For I am every dead thing,
  In whom Love wrought new alchemy.
    For his art did express
A quintessence even from nothingness,
From dull privations, and lean emptiness;
He ruin'd me, and I am re-begot
Of absence, darkness, death: things which are not.

A Nocturnal Upon St Lucy's Day
John Donne.

One

The temperature in the school gymnasium had reached a brain-frying thirty-five degrees, but Joseph Nightingale was no longer there. Joseph Nightingale was memory-bound . . .

In his dream, the past reached out to the boy and reclaimed him. Stifling summer switched to frosty autumn and he was back in the car. His breath whitened the air. His hands curled around the steering wheel. Streetlights zipped by, bright exclamations on the black page of the night. The smell of her filled his senses: a perfume of vanilla and sandalwood. To scare her, just a little, Joe gunned the engine. He glanced left and smirked. Parental disapproval, forming awkwardly now as he progressed further into manhood, crumpled the brow of his passenger.

'Keep it under fifty, smart arse.'

'Aye, aye.' He saluted and toed the brake. 'Don't worry, I know this car.'

'He passes his test a fortnight ago and he knows *this* car.'

'Hey, I'm a prodigy.'

'You're a cheeky little bastard.'

'Language, mother.'

'But I love you.'

Joe turned right onto the lane that bisected the woodlands. There were no streetlights here and the trees ahead shadowed the road. He slowed to forty. Leaning forward, he kept a careful eye on the pocked tarmac picked out by the headlights. Fear skimmed the surface of his thoughts, like a stone skipped across a lake. He would never admit it, but driving this car made him nervous. This artfully restored, flame-red machine that rammed his heart into his throat at every switchback corner. His dad had been right: it was too crude and twitchy a beast for a kid to master. He should have agreed to a modern motor with ABS brakes and those safety features that took all the thrill out of driving. But Joe had been adamant: it was the '67 Triumph Spitfire or nothing.

In his peripheral vision, he saw his mother move the crystal ball in her lap.

'Hey, careful.'

'Jesus, Joe, it weighs a tonne.'

'Cost a tonne, too.'

'Yeah, well I hope she's worth *your* extravagance and *my* crippling leg cramp.'

Joe had to acknowledge that it *was* an expensive gift, but Samantha Jones was worth every penny. As soon as he saw the ball glinting at him from the craft shop window he knew that he had to buy it for her. He had even risked running late for his Jericho College interview, scrabbling around the unfamiliar town for the nearest bank and withdrawing some of his college savings. His mother hadn't protested. She had just trailed after him, tapped her watch and exhaled audibly. She *had* complained a little when, fearful of breakage on the journey home, he had insisted on her carrying the heavy orb in her lap, rather than entrusting it to the boot. His pulse quickened now as he watched her balance the ball on her thigh. It flashed in the light of the moon. Hollow at its middle, it wasn't strictly speaking a crystal ball at all. Those were used for divination and were solid rock (rose quartz, obsidian black), the owner of the shop – a woman who smelled of incense and, very faintly, of weed – had told him. This, on the other hand, was a healing orb. The glass was less than an inch thick, the centre filled with 'a positive karmic force'.

Joe's mother found her cigarettes and replaced the gift in the bowl of her lap. Anticipating the fumes, Joe opened the driver window a crack. Night air, full of the promise of winter, whipped into the car. He shuddered. A match flared. By its light, his mother appeared in the windscreen, a disembodied head racing in front of the car.

'Don't tell Bobby,' she said, drawing on the cigarette. 'You know how he goes on about me smoking.'

'I won't,' Joe promised, 'but only if you spot me a tenner 'til Friday. The ball's wiped me out. Deal or no deal?'

'Deal. So what is this girlfriend of yours? Some sort of Earth Mother or Wicca Queen?'

'Neither. She's just a little tapped.'

'Hmm.' Janet Nightingale gave her son an appraising look. 'Explains a lot . . . Jesus, Joe, it's freezing, put the heaters on.'

'They don't work. Had to hold my hands on the glass to clear the frost before we left. Nothing works: heaters, fag lighter, radio. Cool, eh?'

'*Oh my darlin' – Oh my darlin' – Oh my darlin', Clementine.*'

'What are you doing?'

'Singing. I'll be your radio.'

'Cheers. I think.'

'*Now she's gone and lost forever . . .*'

'Mum, please.'

'*. . . awful sorry, Clementine.*'

Urgent action was required: a burst of AC-DC, Bowie, even Busted. Anything to stop her singing. Joe reached for a tape. He raked through a dozen or so, tossing the rejects back into the glove compartment. Finally, he found the mix tape that Samantha Jones had recorded for him. He held it up and read the label. She'd dotted the 'i's' with heart-shapes.

'JOE!'

The boy's heart snapped into a gallop. His eyes fixed on the road ahead. What he saw there sank that skimming stone of fear once and for all.

'*Mum . . .*'

Afterwards he would say that the trunk had appeared out of nowhere. That was how he remembered it. One minute the road was clear, the next the tree lay there like a twisted arm reaching across the division of the forest. Doubt remained, however. They had visited three university campuses – it had been a long, long day – he had been very tired . . .

Joe wrenched the steering wheel right. Tyres locked and screamed. The burn of rubber stung his nostrils and, in the rear-view mirror, he saw tails of blue smoke twist into the air. He braced himself – stomped the brake to the floor – but the car careered across the road, missing the felled tree by inches. Despite his pumping the brake, the speedometer remained at forty as they left the blacktop and hit the mass of bracken that bordered the road. The foliage was no match for the Triumph. The raised front bumper tore through it with a percussive thud. Then, for a moment, forward momentum ceased. In the same instant, Joe experienced a sensation of weightlessness, as if he had left his stomach back on the road. He could hear the drone of the engine, the hiss as the front wheels span in midair. The interlude seemed dreamlike – a horror story cut short. Then, very gently, the nose of the roadster dropped. Joe felt his stomach slam back into position. The car pivoted through forty-five degrees and, with a groan from the chassis, started its descent.

Through the windscreen, Joe saw the depth of the gully below and his bladder gave way.

'*Muuu . . . !*'

The seatbelt cut down the word in his throat. He heard his

collarbone crack like a dry twig. Flares of pain danced before his eyes but he remained conscious.

The Triumph sheared a path through the undergrowth, swatting branches aside as it went. Torn from its fitting, the nearside wing mirror spiralled into the air. It hit the windscreen, shattering the glass into spider web fractures. Particles exploded into Joe's face. Beyond the blood pounding in his ears, he could make out the shriek of rending metalwork. Piece by piece, the twitchy beast was coming apart.

They continued to fall, and now the smell of petrol flooded the car. Joe's fear ratcheted up a notch as he detected a whiff of something else: superheated metal, ready to burn. The forest bed filled the windscreen.

Joe twisted his neck, tried to look at his mother. In these final moments he needed reassurance. Forgiveness. Her face turned towards him and he saw . . .

'Mum?'

A different kind of terror slipped into the boy's mind. Cold – terribly *cold* – it supplanted the white-hot dread of the accident. What he saw in his mother's face he would later put down to shock, hers or his own: a perfectly rational explanation that he never wholly believed.

Her face was empty.

There was no horror written there, no anticipation of pain or death. No fear for herself or for her son. There was nothing. Her face seemed to Joe a lifeless canvas of flesh. A canvas that was soon to be torn to shreds.

As Joe watched, gravity plucked the healing orb from his mother's lap. It caught the moonlight and blazed, solid and whole for the last time. The impact came, the ball shattered. Joe closed his eyes against the spray that jetted across his face. In his mouth, he tasted the hot iron of blood.

Joe sprang back in his chair. His eyes snapped open. As dream and reality moved against each other, the latter slotting the school gymnasium over the interior of the Spitfire, Joe imagined his hands wet around the steering wheel. He couldn't understand why his fingers passed through it, why pens, pencils and examination papers flew off the dashboard. Looking down, he saw dog-eared car mats transmute into floorboards.

A finger tapped his shoulder.

'Are we keeping you awake, Mr Nightingale?' The invigilator glanced down at Joe's answer paper. 'There are two hours of the examination remaining. In the words of the divine Warren Zevon, sleep when you're dead.'

The invigilator marched off between the desks. Embarrassment and the terror of the dream added to the heat that burned through Joe's body. He slipped a hand under his shirt and felt the puckered flesh of his left shoulder. He didn't want to relive any of it, but some treacherous instinct motivated his fingers. They traced the topography of the seven-month-old scar.

Joe tore his hand away. He gathered up his papers and glanced at his fellow examinees. There were a few tuts and smirks, to which he held up a hand in apology. They all soon settled again. Only one among them did not slump back over her work. Samantha Jones. Joe had been watching her, on and off, throughout the English Lit exam. He had found her concentration and the jig of her pen a little intimidating. Now she was biting her nails, chewing through the bitter polish which she applied daily to curtail the habit. A smile fluttered her lips. Joe stared and the smile died.

Stupid. It was all so stupid. He should talk to her. He should . . .

Feet clattered in the corridor outside. Joe looked through the gym windows. He saw the hurtling form of Miss Rawlston, Oberstgruppenführer of the PE department. She ran down the glazed concourse which connected the gym to the school. In other circumstances the spectacle of this middle-aged woman, hair unkempt, breasts swinging and knocking against each other like the balls of a Newton's cradle, would have been comical. What made it far from humorous was the sound coming from her mouth. Projected in one shrill note, Miss Rawlston's scream made every pen in the examination hall shiver to a stop.

Two

The art teacher had barely ten years on the boy that sat before him. In fact, while Bobby Nightingale had managed to lose all traces of acne before his last birthday, Mr Fleet ('Greg' to those students who attended his after-school role play games) still had a dog's collar of zits erupting around his throat.

'Look, Bobby, going off the boil after your mother's . . . accident was to be expected,' Greg Fleet said, searching through the GCSE art submissions on his desk, 'but you've gotta start making an effort again. Your work last year was good. Brilliant, in fact. That Schwitters-influenced piece was well beyond what I would expect from a pupil of your age. Dada at fifteen? Fantastic. But this . . .'

Mr Fleet held up Bobby's latest project. The art teacher's expression made it look as if someone had just wafted a week-old turd under his nose.

'What's wrong with it?'

'There's no theme.' Fleet sniffed and handed the painting to its creator. 'No skill, no ambition. It's just paint slopped onto a page. What's it supposed to be?'

'It's surreal. It's not supposed to *be* anything.'

'Don't bullshit a bullshitter, Bobby. All you've done here is throw crap at a canvas and call it "*Downwind*". Well, I for one wouldn't want to be downwind of *this*. Look, I'd like to help you. I think you could be a really good painter, but carry on like this and I'd be wasting my time. You listening?'

'Yes. Try harder. Got it.'

'Jees-*us*. Okay, here endeth the lesson. Now, sod off, and take that rubbish with you.'

Bobby stuffed *Downwind* into his backpack.

'Hey, one more thing,' Fleet said. 'Are you coming to Role Play Club tonight? We haven't seen you for a long time. Your buddy Matt still comes, you know.'

'Yeah. Sorry. I think I've kinda outgrown it.'

'Outgrown dragons and elves and enchantment spells? What are you, eighty?'

Bobby shrugged and slung the backpack over his shoulder.

'What about the stuff?'

Greg Fleet picked the bag of confiscated cannabis resin from the table and dropped it into his desk drawer.

'Don't worry about that. I'll keep it to myself this time. Go on, get going.'

A single thought occurred to Bobby as he closed the door behind him: *do these fucking teachers* ever *have to buy their* own *shit?*

Mr Fleet's intervention for the sake of Art had excused Bobby Nightingale from second period maths. Trigonometry was the order of the day and as sine, cosine and tangent were about as comprehensible to him as a David Lynch movie translated into Arabic, Bobby decided to skip the final half-hour of the lesson. In any case, it was much too hot to worry about triangles; today was made for better things. Sneaking outside via the concourse fire door, Bobby searched his pocket. He took out his Union Jack Zippo lighter and a ready-rolled spliff. Before firing up he looked over towards the gymnasium.

In his panic, the lighter fell from Bobby's hand.

It was school policy that, in the summer months, come hell and high water, all games lessons *must* take place outside. This being the case, Bobby had not expected the gym to be in use. He had forgotten about the A Level exams. He thrust the joint back into his pocket and checked to see if he had been observed. Pupils were arrayed the length of the room, heads bowed like wilting flowers. It took a minute or two to pick out his brother.

Joe was leaning against the climbing wall, his eyes closed. Not a good sign. The Old Man would be royally pissed off if Joe messed up his exams. Things being how they were, other parents would cut the kid some slack, but not Richard Nightingale. Even before the accident he had been a tough old bastard, but the loss of his wife had hardened him into a blunt, heavy presence. On one of the rare occasions that the Nightingale brothers spoke about what was happening to their family, Joe had given his opinion on their dad's behaviour. He said that the Old Man acted as he did because he didn't want the boys to wallow in self-pity. Richard Nightingale had always believed in strength of character and a stern work ethic. Grief had been allowed only a short sojourn in the Nightingale household, and then it was back to work and school.

Hurried footfalls drew Bobby's thoughts away from his home life. The eyes of the kids in the gym snapped in his direction. He felt exposed, stripped bare by their gaze. It took a moment for him to realise that *he* was not the object of their fascination. Miss Rawlston, the PE teacher who, if playground gossip was to be believed, kept her husband trussed up in the cellar with a rubber ball stuffed into his mouth, tore along the concourse.

She was screaming.

The games mistress saw Bobby and came to a halt.

She's lost it, Bobby thought, as he stepped reluctantly into the concourse. *The cops have found her torture dungeon. They've put her husband into an abused animal sanctuary, and she's lost it. Simple as.*

'Are you all right, Miss Rawlston?'

The ogress shook her head. Her mouth gaped, clamped shut, gaped again.

'What's happened?'

Tears welled and her body gave way to one long tremble.

'Miss Rawlston?'

'Blood.' The word exhaled between gasps for air. 'Changing room. Boy – Hurt – So – So much *BLOOD*.'

Bobby turned and raced back towards the main school building. He did not heed the cries telling him to stop. Later, he would wonder if he had known what waited for him in the locker room. Of course, there was no way that he *could* have known. There had been no signs beforehand, nothing . . . Except that wasn't quite true. A few days ago, the kid had come looking for him. Bobby recalled that paste-white face, those red-rimmed eyes – '*Please, Bobby. Please help me* . . .' He had promised to do what he could, to use his influence, and then he had promptly forgotten the pleas for him to intervene. Other concerns, petty and selfish they seemed afterwards, drove Matthew Linton from his thoughts.

Bobby threw open the changing room door.

Steam roiled and fogged the air. A steady thunder of water rattled from beyond the entrance to the showers. Otherwise everything was quiet, still. Football boots and sweat-stained shirts, odd socks and empty deodorant cans littered the benches. Bobby's gaze moved on through the steam clouds. His eye ran along the gutter which stretched across the shower entrance and his stomach lurched. A stream of pink water was frothing and bubbling in the drain. Bobby's legs felt weighted, but he shambled forward. He splashed through the tinted water, turned and looked down the length of the shower room. In the far corner he saw . . .

RED.

A fragment of hell composed of red.

It filled Bobby's mind so that, for a moment, he could see nothing beyond that horrific, captivating colour. There were traces here of the paintings he revered. He recognised the flowing, pooling red of the dancer's dress from Edvard Munch's 'The Dance of Life'; the smeared and clotted red of Goya's 'Saturn Devouring His Son'; the firework red of Franz Marc's 'Fighting Forms'. Reds of many shapes and shades, all of which drew the eye. They gleamed in stark relief against the white-tiled floor, they flecked and smattered the walls. Bobby thought he could even taste redness on the air. The colour burned his throat, bowled into his gut and smouldered there.

Bobby took a step forward. Then another, and another, until he found himself standing inside that little piece of hell. He slipped on the wet floor and landed hard on his tailbone. Shockwaves crackled along his spine but he soon forgot the pain. As his vision cleared, he saw that he had fallen within inches of the blood-soaked boy. In the close confines of the shower room they sat opposite each other, like children about to play pat-a-cake. If he reached out he might touch cold dead skin. His feet scrabbled and, using the heels of his hands, he managed to propel himself backwards. In that crab-like shuffle he got as far as the gutter. He stopped there, unable to go further, and stared back at the corpse.

Matthew Linton sat slouched against the wall, his head listing to the right. The shower overhead was on full and pelted the kid with boiling water. Water which streamed down his face and muted the vibrancy of the blood. The school uniform he wore was drenched through, the shirtfront freshly dyed. Matt's mouth hung open, and his tongue, with the tip bitten through, lolled over a set of pinkish teeth. The kid's hands lay open at his sides, palms up, as if to say 'hey, what can you do?'

Bobby tried to draw himself away, but again felt the tug of an invisible chain. The tug of *RED*.

There was more to see.

An old-fashioned cut-throat razor glinted from where Matt had dropped it.

'You stupid fucking fuck,' Bobby roared. 'Why didn't you . . .'

I came to you. I did. The words might have come from Matt Linton, so real did they sound in Bobby's head. *You promised you'd help but you didn't. Hey, don't mess yourself, it's okay. Nothing matters now.*

Bobby's eyes focused on the gash cut into Matt's throat. It looked like a second mouth: two grey lips that formed a crooked smile.

You're not to blame, old friend. It's all so okay. Shit happens.

Three

Joe shouldered his way through the crowd. He reached the midpoint of the throng and stopped dead. His brother, drenched to the skin, was being led out of the locker room. Joe tried to call out but Bobby's name died in his throat. The boy's expression – hideously blank – reminded Joe of his own face staring back from the bathroom mirror. How often had he seen that expression in the months after his mother's death? How often had he read in its emptiness the story of his misery?

Trembling, Joe took out his phone and tried to call his father.

Standing outside Room 14 of the Castle Lodge Hotel, Richard Nightingale reached into his pocket and switched off his phone. Then he took a breath and slipped the keycard into the automated lock. Almost as soon as the green LED lit up, Susan Keele emerged and pinned him to the jamb. Her mouth pressed hot on his. Fingers travelled well-traversed routes down the length of his torso. It was all he could do to edge them into the room and close the door. Two weeks apart and she was hungry for him. The raised eyebrows of the elderly couple entering the room opposite – the smirk of the maid vacuuming the corridor – meant nothing to her. She crushed her lips against his neck and Richard felt himself grow hard against her. Why not? One last song from the bedsprings, what was the harm in that?

'Stop.'

'We haven't even started yet,' she giggled.

'No, just stop.'

Attempts at a smile, an effort to convince herself that he was joking, wrinkled the corners of the woman's eyes. The smile faded and she stood away from him.

'What is this? I thought . . .'

'We can't. I can't. Not anymore.'

'But she's gone, Richard. It's been seven months and she's gone. Janet's dead . . . I was going to meet your boys. We've waited so long.'

Richard shook his head. 'It's over. It was just an affair – nothing – and now it's over.'

Susan Keele stood dumbfounded. She reached out to Richard but he pushed her hands away.

'Why?'

Richard shrugged. 'The only thing I know is that I don't want you anymore. Are you listening, Susan? I don't want you.'

Susan tore off her robe and crammed it into the tote shoulder bag on the bed. Richard remained by the door and watched her dress. The clumsiness of her movements aroused him. When she hitched up her knickers, tearing the band and leaving the cleft of her arse exposed, he felt the strain of his erection. He wanted to grab her by the hips, to push her onto the bed and run his tongue along the curve of her spine. He wanted to snap away her bra and cover her nipples with his mouth. As clothes were yanked and tugged into place, he longed to tear them from her. He wanted these things so much he almost convinced himself that the urges were born of love.

'You say you don't want me.' Her eyes narrowed. 'Your prick tells a different story.'

Hard words, but it was just an act. In her face, Richard

could see the pain begin to bite. To stop himself reaching for her, he pressed his hands under his arms.

Susan Keele stood at the door, back to him, bag in hand.

'I love you. I love you so much . . . Say something. Please, God, just say *something* before I go. This, it makes no sense. Can't we talk? Can't we just . . . ?'

'No. Goodbye, Susan.'

Richard paid his bill and left Castle Lodge. It was a short walk from the hotel on Beaumont Fee to his gallery at the junction between Danesgate and Steep Hill. Once there he moped about in the back office, made a couple of calls and placed an order for a job lot of Monet, Rembrandt and Jackson Pollock prints. Exhausting all other distractions, he decided to pick the boys up from school. He left the gallery in the hands of Miss Marchant, his manager, and stepped out onto Steep Hill.

It was the beginning of the summer season and Lincoln's precipitous medieval streets were choked with tourists. Richard joined them, squeezing a path through the crowd. He was jostling at the centre of a party of overweight Americans (*'Jeepers, this sure is a climb' – 'Yup. Christ knows why those Limey assholes had to build all their old shit on hills.'*) when he looked up and felt a familiar thrill. Pinnacle by pinnacle, the holy grail of the hill emerged from between the clustered shop fronts.

The Cathedral Church of Remigius and St Hugh. Majesty wrought in stone. Rarely a week passed that Richard did not visit the Minster. It wasn't that he was a religious man, far from it, but he was a devout worshipper of beauty. Whenever he stepped beneath the cathedral's great west façade, he felt an indescribable stirring. Logic told him that it was nothing more than a chemical reaction within the brain, or a set of learned responses, yet it felt like it went to the very pit of him. Every part of the cathedral – the rose windows, the cavernous nave, the shadow-filled cloisters – spoke to something within the man. This aesthetic sensibility had been with Richard since birth but it was an enfeebled aspect of his personality. He knew that he could crush it easily beneath the dark thoughts which plagued him. Thoughts dominated by his late wife.

During the early years of their marriage, when he had taken pleasure in showing her the books and paintings and buildings that he loved, he had gifted Janet Nightingale a piece of his soul. He had only realised the importance of that gift in later years, when his wife had vanished; a disappearance that had not been physical but spiritual. After she had given birth to Bobby, their second son, the lights had gone out of her eyes. Richard's beautiful, soulful girl was gone and what was left behind was a husk. It had looked and sounded and moved like Janet, but contained only a memory of her. It was a thing of desolation, of emptiness, of *Absence*. And wherever Janet – the real Janet – had gone, she had taken part of Richard with her.

No, he would not think of it.

The gallery owner picked up the pace. He strode past antiquarian bookshops and tearooms. Resisting the lure of the cathedral, he took a left onto Drury Lane. He found his Mercedes E-Class saloon sporting a parking ticket, which he added to the stack in the glove compartment. Then he roared onto Union Road and took the sweep of the A46 south and out of town.

Richard could still smell Susan Keele on his clothes. He opened the window and sprayed his shirt with car deodoriser. It was no good; her scent clung to him. They had been sleeping together for four years. Four years of hotel rooms and weekend cottages. Janet had known, of course, but had never said a word about it. Desperate for some hint of emotion, Richard left evidence of his assignations around the house. He watched as she read the bar bills and credit card statements, even the love notes. That blank, inscrutable face never shifted. Not a hint of pain or rage. Until the kids came home, there was nothing to be got from her. God, she had frightened him.

Even now, seven months after her death, Richard could not shake that fear.

His phone vibrated. He pushed a button on the hands-free kit.

'Mr . . . itingale . . . ?'

'Speaking.'

'My name is Cuttle. . . . Solicitor . . . village of . . . Drake. . . .'

'Sorry, you're breaking up. Can you repeat that?'

'. . . great pleasure to inform you. . . . inheritance. . . . legacy . . .'

'Legacy? I can't hear . . .'

'The late. . . . Sutton. . . . millhouse . . . Daecher's Mill.'

'Hello?'

'It's just waiting for you.'

The phone went dead.

Richard depressed the brake and the Merc came to a standstill. Half a mile of traffic wound down the hill before meeting a gridlocked roundabout. While he waited, Richard checked the phone's call log but the last number had been withheld. A legacy. Sutton. The name had a familiar ring about it . . . Probably some kind of mistake. He glanced at his watch and tapped out his frustration on the steering wheel. With all the pace of a semi-comatose snail, the traffic moved forward and stopped again.

The atmosphere in the car felt close. Richard pumped the air-conditioning down to fifteen degrees but still the heat throbbed at his temples. His tongue stuck to his palate and the first tremors tingled his fingers. Through a constricted throat, he felt the call of his stomach: *chink chink – you need a drink.*

Flashes of something red diverted Richard's attention. He looked up.

A child, sitting on the back seat of the Ford Fiesta in front, had turned to face him. She was dressed in a bright red rubber raincoat. The hood had been pulled down and only her mouth could be seen. Richard smiled and waved. For a long time the girl remained stock-still. Then her head crooked to one side in a sudden, birdlike movement. Grinning, she leaned forward across the parcel shelf. Richard stared. His hands tightened around the steering wheel. A rill of sweat trickled along his cheek and ran into the stubble around his jaw. His eyes widened as the girl's smile split across her face.

Thin, bloodless, her lips drew back to reveal a row of cement-grey teeth. The kind of teeth one would expect to see in the head of a ninety-year-old. The upper and lower incisors were broken and appeared as pointed as the canines. As Richard watched, a stream of dark fluid dribbled over the child's lips and down her chin, frothing as it passed between those ragged teeth.

The sky darkened. A finger of cloud had reached in from the south, its path mirroring the stretch of the carriageway. With the sun blocked out, a hundred or more sparkling windscreens dimmed. The effect was like a string of fairy lights being switched off. Rain pattered against the Fiesta's rear window. Within moments it had strengthened into a thunderous downpour. It hadn't rained in weeks but Richard took no notice of the deluge. Through the bullets of rain he watched as a pair of long-fingered hands reached up to the raincoat's hood. They grasped the edges, ready to pull the hood back and expose the face beneath . . .

The phone rang and Richard jumped. When he looked

back, the girl was gone. Sunshine blazed through the clouds and set about scorching the rainwater off the blacktop. The kid had probably ducked behind the back seat. Either that or he had imagined her. Perhaps the heat had got to him. The heat and the call of his stomach – *chink chink*

The voice that came through the hands-free speakers was not that of the last caller.

'Mr Nightingale?'

Richard's breath felt like a desert wind in his throat. 'Yes?'

'My name is Inspector Walter Smith. I'm phoning about your son.'

'Joe? What's happened?'

'Not Joseph. Your other son. Bobby.'

'Is he all right? Where is he?'

'Calm down, sir. Bobby's fine. A little shook up, no doubt, but he strikes me as a strong lad. The fact of the matter is there has been a death at the school. A young boy. Your son discovered the body.'

'Who was it? The kid, I mean.'

'His name was Linton. Matthew Linton.'

Richard nodded. He had some vague recollection of the name.

'We need you to come and collect Bobby,' DI Smith continued. 'Then accompany him to the station. A few procedural questions, you understand? How soon can you be here?'

Richard pulled onto the hard shoulder.

'Ten minutes.'

'That's fine. Drive carefully, sir.'

Richard sped along the breakdown lane, car horns trumpeting against his progress. He forgot all about the mysterious phone call and the little girl with the broken teeth.

Four

'Okay, Bobby, we don't want you to go into a lot of detail. We have Miss Rawlston's statement and that covers most of our questions. Just tell us what you saw when you went into the changing room.'

Seated beside his son, Richard felt Bobby tremble. He wanted to put his arm around the boy but refrained. The detective inspector sitting opposite smiled through the bracken of his beard, in what was clearly supposed to be a gesture of reassurance. Richard did not feel reassured and was pretty sure Bobby didn't either.

'If you feel able to describe it to us, just a little, it *would* help,' said DI Smith. 'You see, Bobby, we have to be sure that . . .'

'I didn't touch him.'

'Did you pass anyone in the corridor?'

'No.'

'And I believe that, before you found Matt, you were with Mr . . .' Smith flicked through his notebook. 'Fleet. The art teacher. He tells us that you're a very promising painter. I do a bit of that myself. Sketching mostly. Can never get hands right. How do you do ha . . . ?'

'He was dead. His throat was cut. There was a razor in his hand. Near his hand. Left hand. It was an old fashioned sort of thing. Matt was left-handed.' Bobby's brow crumpled. 'Whose razor was it?'

'We believe it belonged to his father. Now, Bobby . . .'

'There was no-one else there. He was . . . white. Real white. There was a lot of blood. *Red* . . . He, Matt, he killed himself. I don't know why.'

As he spoke, Bobby laid his hands flat upon the desk. Richard wondered whether it was to stop them shaking.

'Okay, Bobby. That's okay, that's just fine. Can we get you a drink? Tea? A coke?'

'I want to take Bobby home now.'

'Of course, Mr Nightingale. We understand what a shock this must have been. If Bobby needs to see a counsellor, well that can be arranged.'

'That won't be necessary. I just want to get him home.'

'There are a few more questions.'

'Then get on with them. Quicker this is done, quicker the boy can put it behind him. Quicker he can forget it ever happened.'

The smile behind the beard never wavered.

'Of course. Just as you say. Now, Bobby, can you tell us a little bit about Matthew?'

'What d'you mean? Can't his parents do that?'

'Sure. But you were his friend. Kids tell their friends things they'd never tell their folks. You know that.'

'I haven't hung around with Matt for a long time.'

'Why was that?'

'No reason. We started liking different things. We knew each other from Warhammer.'

'Warhammer?'

'Role play. Fantasy role play games.'

'Dragons and knights. That sort of thing?'

'I grew out of that stuff. Matt didn't.' Bobby's tongue clicked in his mouth. 'It was the only thing we were both into. When I quit there wasn't any reason to still hang out together.'

Spittle flecked Bobby's lips. The kid wiped it away on the back of his blazer cuff.

'That's fine. Relationships change as we grow up, I know that,' said DI Smith. 'I've just got one last question and then your dad can take you home. Had Matt spoken to you in the last few weeks? Maybe there was something worrying him. Maybe he'd come to you to talk about it.'

'I told you, we weren't . . .'

'Friends. Yes, you said. And that wasn't my question.'

A bluebottle landed on the desk. It buzzed, testing its wings in case this new terrain proved inhospitable. In the silence that followed DI Smith's question, the insect waddled towards the oasis of sweat left by Bobby's palms. It put out feelers, tasting the perspiration.

'Matt didn't come to me. I don't know anything.'

Dinner was not a communal meal in the Nightingale household. Richard, who often worked late, ate alone. The boys sometimes shared meals: pizzas and takeaway curries consumed in silence in front of the TV. They had not eaten as a family since November of the previous year, when Janet Nightingale had died in the passenger seat of her son's low-slung roadster. If she had been the glue that held them together, then it was a thin sort of adhesive. Just how thin none of them had realised until the pot was empty and they had started to come apart.

Joe made a few rounds of ham and mayo rolls and brewed a pot of coffee. He carried a tray into the sitting room and set it down in front of his brother. Bobby had been flicking between Hollyoaks and the local news. For a split second, the face of Matthew Linton appeared onscreen: a happy child, losing his puppy fat and showing signs of the man he would never become.

Bobby switched channels. Joe pretended not to notice.

'Not hungry,' Bobby grunted.

'Mustard mayo.'

Bobby snatched a roll and tore a bite from it.

'Bad about Matt.' Joe looked at his brother from over the rim of his coffee cup.

'Yeah.'

'You okay?'

'M'fine.'

'Mate, if I'd seen what you saw today, I wouldn't be fine. I'd be pretty far from being fine.'

'Leave it, Joe.'

'I remember when Matt used to come round here. Little blonde kid, right? Freckles, nose always running like a tap? Yeah, he was round here all the time when you were in your nerd phase. Nice lad.'

'I said leave it.'

'I'm just trying to . . .'

'I know what you're trying to do. Don't put that shit on me.'

'What "shit"?'

Bobby threw the remains of the roll onto the tray.

'You know what *shit. This shit.* The shit you always do. Do you get off on it or something? Bad things happen and you prod and prod until it all comes tumbling out. I think I prefer the way dad handles stuff. Not giving a crap – at least it lets people deal with things in their own way.'

'Jesus Christ, Bob, I'm only trying to help.'

'How? How is this helping? I've told the police everything I know. Matt was a whiney little dweeb, always hanging round me until he finally got the message. I haven't spoken to him for ages. I don't know why he killed himself. He was just weird, I guess. Just because I found him doesn't mean I . . .'

'Hey. Chill, okay?'

'I'll chill if you leave me the fuck alone.'

'Look, it's just that, if you feel as though it was your fault . . .'

'How the hell could it be *my* fault?'

'I'm just saying – if you thought it was, you're wrong. No-one knows why Matt did it, but ultimately it was *his* decision. You know, a lot of people who experience death close-up feel they're to blame in some way. That it must be someone's responsibility. Like the hugeness of it can't be an accident, or just the way of things, or down to the person that died. But, you know, most of the time it *is* just like that.'

'That what your therapist said?'

'What?'

Bobby switched off the TV. In the darkened glass, Joe watched the spite twist his brother's features.

'That woman you saw after Mum died. Did she tell you that? Accidents happen; it's not your fault.'

Joe stood up, hesitated.

'What's the matter, Joe? Don't you like it when you're the one being prodded?'

A hairline fracture cracked along the wall that Joe had built up around his guilt. This wall had been strengthened by the belief that Bobby and the Old Man did not hold him responsible for the accident. Not really. Now he found that there were weak points in the structure. Joe shored it up as best he could.

'Fuck you,' he whispered.

He put down his cup and headed for the front door. Once outside his heart slowed a little.

Joe stood in the drive for a long time. His gaze moved beyond the gate and followed the road that wound out into the woodland. In his mind's eye, he swept through the forest until he came to the carriageway. Then he backtracked to linger on the spot where his old life had ended.

None of the Nightingales' neighbours had heard the sound of the impact. The scream of metal had been deadened by the trees. By the time the emergency services had got to work, however, a small crowd had assembled. Picked out by flashing blue lights, Joe had seen the Smiths and the Friedmans, the Goyles and the Brandts as, limb-by-limb, he was cut from the wreckage. Through the pain and panic that rattled his senses, Joe had read their faces. In their hard stares, in their pursed lips, he saw the first outward signs of condemnation. Later, when the therapists had got to work on his bruised psyche, part of him had longed to see those expressions again. He did not want to be told that it was an accident; that he was not to blame. He wanted wrath and justice. Now, as Bobby's words hit their mark, he almost felt relieved. He really was elbow-deep in his mother's blood.

Joe reached into his pocket and took out his phone. He wasn't at all sure that he was ready to face her but, at that moment, he needed Samantha Jones. For the last seven months, fear and misunderstanding had kept them apart. He could not rationalise his rejection of the girl and, for her part, Sam had been confused by his coldness. Now Joe felt that he must make contact with someone outside his family. He brought up her name on the phone's contact list. About to connect, he paused.

A flicker of colour – a smear of red among the dark shapes of the trees – had flashed in his peripheral vision. He turned to the woods.

There was no movement in the undergrowth, no bird flight between the branches. It might have been a fox, he supposed, yet the colour had seemed deeper than the russet of fox fur. He had also had the impression that the shape between the trees had not been crouched, like an animal, but standing on two legs. A human form, in fact, child-sized, watching him from the shadows. Except that wasn't quite right either. No, not watching *from* the shadows but made up *of* shadows. How could he be sure of such a fanciful idea? After all, there was at least twenty metres of road between him and the forest edge, and he had only glimpsed the form. Yet the impression remained and could not be shaken. He *had* seen a small figure, and now his mind embellished the image. It became a little girl in a Red Riding Hood cape, her feet bare, her face hidden. For all the detail with which his imagination textured her, however, she remained indistinct.

A child composed of shadows.

– *Interlude* –

The First Guest of Daecher's Mill: Augustus Pye Made Absent on 14th October 1988

Augustus gave up. He pulled over, wound down the car window and threw the road map of Lincolnshire into a dyke. Now, if only the county itself would likewise disappear into an abyss he might begin to feel a little better. He had never driven through such brain-numbing monotony in all his life. There seemed to be nothing but hedgerows and bramble bushes, stumpy churches and fallow fields. Couple this with the fact that there were signs pointing towards villages – Scarsby, Crow Haven – which, according to the map, did not exist, and it was little wonder he was lost.

The salesman reached into the glove compartment and withdrew a tin box and a sleeve of cigarette papers. He rolled, tamped and lit. One hungry breath consumed half the fag but the shot of nicotine did little to improve his humour.

The whole thing wasn't right. He had been with the firm for eighteen years, for Christ's sake. He had thought his repping days to be behind him. After all, he'd paid his dues. Crisscrossing the midlands, he'd sold thousands of these second-rate encyclopedias ('Thirty volumes in all, madam. Everything covered, Aardvark to Zygote.'). There wasn't a pensioner within his designated area he hadn't tried to convince that, by purchasing volume one of Attabers' Young Persons Encyclopedia, they might transform their turd-brained grandchildren into regular little eggheads. Yes, Augustus Pye had been a good salesman. For the last six months, however, he'd been manning the phones at HQ. A desk job: the reward for a road-weary shyster whose reserves of snake oil were, perhaps, running a little low.

So why was he now door-to-dooring again, working a patch as unfamiliar to him as the definition of 'aardvark' was to the compilers at Attabers'? It was simple really. The firm wanted shot of Augustus Pye. On the road he had interacted with people in short, impersonal bursts. It had been possible then to maintain 'The Act'. When he left those cash-strapped grannies, he knew very well what they thought of him: a nice man, well-spoken, very considerate of our circumstances. In truth, however, Augustus was *not* a very nice man, and he knew that The Act could never hold up under close scrutiny. Say, for example, in an office environment.

Disaster struck when Siobhan Pringle, secretary and part-time whore, had returned from compassionate leave. How they had all clucked around her, those willowy cunts. It made him sick to the stomach. Still, for appearances sake, he had joined the huddle. Handing Siobhan a Kleenex, he had asked how the hospital had disposed of her miscarried child: the incinerator perhaps? Or had it been plopped into a jar of formaldehyde, ready for dissection? Gasps. Silence. Then Siobhan had, to put it politely, upbraided him. Augustus, in his turn, had said some . . . unfortunate things. Unfortunate in the sense that he had been given a formal warning and put back on the trail.

Augustus stubbed out the dog-end. It was no good; he would have to find someone to ask directions. He restarted the Mini Mayfair. Checking the mirror, he caught sight of something in the field behind him – a house set in a wide expanse of open ground. He reached onto the back seat and retrieved his briefcase. Might as well try for a sale while asking the way out of this shithole.

The property was separated from the road by clumps of hawthorn. Cramped between these bushes stood a kissing gate that led to a dirt track. Augustus backed around the gate, holding his briefcase aloft. He picked his way along the path, careful that as little mud as possible adhered to his shoes. A breeze, cool and briny, snuffled the grass on either side of the track. Gannets and gulls wheeled in the distance.

Sixty feet or so away from the building, Augustus began to make out its purpose. It was, or had been, a watermill. Against the north-facing wall of the swaybacked structure clung a wheel of wood and iron. It was somewhat lopsided, its axle popped like a dislocated arm. Augustus felt that, at any moment, the wheel might topple and break against the dried-up riverbed below. Of course, it must have hung there many a long year but, to the mind of Augustus Pye, the prospect of it falling seemed imminent. The idea caught hold of him and he stopped in his tracks, his attention focused on the wheel . . .

When at last he roused himself, the moon was riding high. Odd, he had not noticed the sunset. He glanced at his watch. Impossible. He had been staring at the wheel for a full hour! Even more disquieting, he was sure that, in the last few moments, it had started to *move*. Slowly, o so slowly, the wheel had turned, dark water churning through its paddles.

'I said, who are you? What do you want?'

The question came from a woman standing on the porch steps. She was lit by a single bare bulb that shone from the corridor behind her. Her black hair was flecked with grey and her eyes were sharp.

'I'm sorry,' Augustus said. 'I seem to have lost my way. I need to get back to the A1.'

'I don't know the roads,' the woman called. 'Drive on. There are villages everywhere. Find one. Ask. I can't help you.'

'I'm very thirsty. Perhaps I could trouble you for a glass of water?'

The woman looked back into the darkness of the house. She shook her head. Augustus thought he heard her whisper the word 'No'. Was it the answer to his request or was she speaking to someone in the corridor? He perched on his tiptoes to get a better look.

The wind picked up. It swept into the doorway and made the house groan, like an old bear troubled in its sleep.

'Come here,' the woman said. She looked down at Augustus and something in her face made the salesman shudder. 'Wait on the porch.'

She stepped inside, leaving the door open a crack.

Augustus climbed the steps. From this vantage, he could see tracks of Fenland stretching out on all sides of the mill. There was a small cottage near the roadside but no other building for miles. Not even a cowshed interrupted the flat, vacant terrain. Doubtless it would be a paradise to a more plebian mind, but Augustus could never live in such a place. His heart was in the city, in the heat and the bustle, the sweat and the dirt.

'Yes, that was my promise. To bring them to you.'

Words whispered from inside the house.

Augustus pushed against the door. Listened.

'I know what I did' – the woman again, her voice discordant – 'what I denied you. But don't ask me to do this. Not yet. I'm not ready.'

A sigh. It might have been the wind, but to Augustus it sounded something like a voice.

The woman again: 'Yes, I took her from you. Her *and* the child. How could you expect me to let you keep them . . . ? No, you know *I* have nothing left to give you. All those years in Gannet's Rest, you drained me, Alice. Just allow me a little more time, I can't bear it. No, please don't . . . Don't *whisper.* I'll . . . All right.' Augustus could hear the defeat in her voice. 'All right, but then please let me be.'

Footsteps on bare boards. A shape moved in the gloom of the hallway. Something was wrong, Augustus felt it in his gut. Still, he wasn't one to obey such instincts. So called 'primal feelings' were just inherited, superstitious notions, they did nothing but hold one back. Allow them to rule you and you miss out on so much. He had learned that lesson in Morocco many years ago. The kid had begged for him to stop and Augustus had felt the tug of humanity stay his hand. It had been a momentary hesitation. No, instincts were for the weak. In any case, he needed to make up his monthly sales target.

He stepped into the hall.

'Miss? I wonder, do you have a child in the family?'

The passageway was cold and the smell of abandonment was heavy on the air. If he had walked into this place, without knowing that the woman lived here, he would have sworn that it had sat empty for decades.

'Perhaps a niece or a nephew?'

Augustus opened the door to his right. His eyes strained.

What he saw in the dimness made him cry out.

A semi-circle of pale figures – eight, ten, a dozen perhaps – sat around the walls, their forms turned towards him. Deep shadows lined their crumpled and unmoving faces. He stood before this convocation, like a condemned man about to be judged. For a long time, neither Augustus nor his judges moved. Then a breeze swept through the room. In the same instant, the figure nearest the door reached out, its white hand fluttering towards the little man. He shrieked and staggered back from its grasp.

Then, with a slight adjustment of perception, he laughed.

He made out the shapes of the chairs and the dustsheets that covered them.

'Miss? Are you there? I'm sorry. Silly of me, but I thought I saw . . .'

The words caught in his throat.

A small figure, standing behind one of the chairs, giggled.

Augustus could see bare feet, caked in dirt. Nails, horny and yellow, curled over the child's toes and scraped the floorboards. A rat's nest of black hair sprouted from just above the chair back. Augustus had almost regained his composure when the thing giggled again and darted from its hiding place. A flash of red clothing – the click of those birdlike talons on the floor – and it had disappeared behind another armchair. There was something wrong with the way it moved, a rolling, stumbling gait, that suggested the child must be at least partially crippled.

The salesman slipped back into the corridor.

'Hello? I think the little girl needs you. It's very dark in that room. Accidents can so easily . . .'

Again, the giggle. A hungry laugh that ran out from a throat thick with saliva.

Augustus looked back into the room. The feet were gone. He thanked God, though he knew not why. All he wanted to do now was to get out of this house.

He turned to the front door . . . and screamed.

There was no door.

The little man ran down the corridor. He pushed and hammered against the wall. It was solid. He span around, convinced he must have lost his bearings. But no, the door *had* been here – could *be* nowhere else.

Footsteps shuffled along the hallway. Augustus' mind filled with bloodstained feet. He smelled the phantom scent of incense and screamed again, for it brought back memories in stark detail: Marrakesh, a stone room far below the city streets. On the raised marble slab in the centre of the room (the 'Operating Table', as it was known by the establishment's clientele) blood had been allowed to dry into almost black patches. Antique chains and manacles, the use of which was forbidden by the Management, hung from the dripping walls. Torches burned in sconces. All rather clichéd touches, Augustus had thought, there really was no need to be quite so medieval.

Ready for his punishment, the boy lay upon the slab. He didn't complain as the straps cut into his wrists and ankles, didn't murmur when the candle wax burned his flesh. The semblance of ecstasy – not the real thing of course – tightened those beautiful, chocolate features. Only when the House Attendant left the room did disquiet creep into the boy's eyes. As Augustus opened the Samsonite holdall he had brought with him, and took out his toys, the boy began to struggle. Approved torture implements were provided by the Management, and it was the House Rules that no other apparatus could be used. It was also a rule that an Attendant must always be present, in case things got out of hand. A bribe had allowed Augustus Pye to move beyond rules.

'*Non*' the boy whispered.

He strained but the bonds only tightened. Augustus pulled out a surgical steel table from the corner of the room and set it up beside the slab. His toys clanged as he dropped them onto the table's upper shelf. The boy's gaze skipped across the hammers and pliers, pincers and fishhooks. Blunt, brown-stained scissors snipped at the air, an inch from his nose.

'*Non*.'

'*Je suis desólé*,' murmured the salesman, 'but Mr Pye is hungry and he must be fed . . .'

Yes, the boy had been maimed – terribly so – but he had not

died and could not be ghostly. Now, however, in the corridor of this strange house, a hand gripped Augustus' shoulder. He looked down as mangled fingers brushed his face.

'I'm sorry. I'm so sorry.'

'Shhhh, *mon maitre*. You made me. You are my creator.'

Fingers moved into Augustus' mouth. He tasted blood. The house began to tremble and he heard the rush of water and the turning of a great wheel.

'Look at your creation. Look at your shadows.'

The salesman resisted, but there was no choice now. He turned and saw the devastation that his lust and fury had wrought. Broken, sexless, the thing grasped Augustus' hand and brought it down to the warmth and wetness between its legs.

As his cries rang out, Augustus Pye and his shadow was consumed.

Five

Joe Nightingale looked around the regenerated Brayford Pool. Out on the marina, pleasure crafts were docking for the night while the mute swans that patrolled the waterway glided towards their nests. The great glass edifice of the university glinted from its position on the far bank. Seated outside one of the new chrome and steel bars which fronted the Pool, Joe closed his eyes, remembered . . .

'Penny for them.'

Samantha Jones reached across the table. Her eyes flickered as, involuntarily, Joe brushed her hand away.

'I was just thinking about this place,' he said. 'I used to come down here with my mum when I was little. We came to feed the swans. It was pretty different here then, before the uni opened up and the regeneration projects started. Then it was all just sheds and derelict buildings. A wasteland, really, filled with old railway engines, dumped and rusting to pieces. It was weird, though. Kinda magical. Over there, I remember big bits of iron poking out of the ground like the half-buried ribs of a dinosaur . . . It got me thinking: do you think they felt bad when they tore it all down? Cleared all those ancient warehouses and scrapped those engines. The council or whoever it was.'

'I don't know, Joe. It was a bit of a dump.'

'I know. And things have to move on, I get that. But it *was* history, in its way. Dirty, like all real history is. To take a wrecking ball to the old place, to change the fabric of it . . . There was a spirit here. I just wonder what happened to it.'

'Joe?'

'Hmm?'

'You're really weird.'

Joe held up his hands.

He hadn't really looked at her since they'd ordered their drinks. Now, as she leaned across the table and gave him a playful poke, he thrilled at her closeness. Even when goading him – sticking her tongue beneath her bottom lip and crossing her eyes – she was beautiful. He took in those sea-green eyes, rimmed with mascara, her pale skin and tiny hands with their black-painted nails chewed to the quick. He wanted to reach over and kiss her, to taste the juice on her lips.

'Thanks for picking me up,' he said.

'Thanks for calling. Why did you? Call, I mean.'

'I needed to get out of the house. To see someone. Anyone.'

'Well, I guess I count as "anyone". Glad to oblige.'

'I didn't mean it like that.'

Joe crunched on a pork scratching. He could almost feel the gristle clogging his arteries. Sam, who practically lived on this sort of junk, finished the bag.

'Can't believe what happened to that Linton kid,' she garbled.

'Yeah. Nasty.'

'Your brother found him, didn't he? Poor Bobby. Is he okay?'

'You know, Sam, I . . . If I hurt you, I didn't mean it.'

'Okaaay. Strange answer.'

'It was just, when my mum . . . When what happened happened, I couldn't deal with being in a relationship and . . .'

'Is that what it was? A relationship? We went on, like, four dates, Joe.'

'I know. I just wanted to say that it wasn't you. It was me. When you came to visit me in the hospital afterwards, and I said those things, I didn't mean any of it. I wasn't thinking straight.'

'You don't have to explain.'

'It's just, I feel bad. I was screwed up.'

'And what about now?'

'I don't know. There're things I've got to work out.'

'Look, I think we both need a bit of cheering up. I know it'll be corny, but what say you take me to the upper-sixth prom?'

'You think it'll still be on? With what happened today, don't you think they'll cancel?'

'Come on, Joe, you've worn the uniform for seven years. Red, purple and beige? One thing our school excels at is the unbelievably tasteless. The prom'll be on and you better be there. Unless you're scared to let me see your dance moves.'

'Hey, I've got moves.'

Sam shook her head. She finished her juice and hooked the car keys around her little finger.

'You're a freak, Nightingale,' she said. 'Shame you're a cute freak. Come on, I'll take you home.'

Bobby stumbled back into the woods. Kelvin Hope followed, keeping the knife pressed against the kid's throat. A tree trunk hit Bobby square between the shoulders and he came to an abrupt stop. He bit down on his tongue but had no time to think about the pain. The belly of Kelvin's blade rode the waves of his Adam's apple. One slash and he'd be just like Matthew Linton: a dual-mouthed horror, spilling his lifeblood onto the forest floor. But surely that wouldn't happen. Logic dictated that this was all just bluff, a bit of strong-arming to keep him in line. The only problem with this happy notion was that logic and Kelvin Hope were barely on nodding terms. One mistake on Bobby's part and this lunatic might really cut him.

'What did you tell them?' Kelvin demanded. 'Tell me straight or I'll fuck you up.'

'Nothing. I swear, I didn't tell them anything.'

Bobby asked himself, not for the first time during this nice little chat, why the hell he had agreed to meet Kelvin. The psycho had called an hour ago: they needed to talk about what had happened. Bobby suggested meeting at the junction between the forest road and the carriageway. From the moment Kelvin parked his scooter in the lay-by, Bobby knew he had made a big mistake. It was the walk that gave it away – a restless stalk of agitated ticks. Everyone knew that Kelvin was well on the way to full-blown heroin addiction. Problem was, whereas smack sent your average dopehead to a fluffy Shangri-La, it transported Kelvin someplace very different. Bobby didn't want to catch the slightest glimpse of that world if he could help it. Yet, as he looked into the dealer's pinprick pupils, he was forced to confront a small part of Kelvin-land. It was a realm of pure Self, of one God. A place in which the aspirations and miseries of others had no currency, except in so far as they aided or hindered the pleasures of Kelvin Hope. Pain could be inflicted here, and justified upon the smallest provocation. And if there was no provocation? Well that didn't matter much either.

'You fucking swear it? You told the cops nothing?'

'What could I tell them? I didn't know anything about it.'

'Don't bullshit me.' The knife grazed the downy stubble at Bobby's throat. 'You were pals with Linton, right? I seen him hanging about you like a lost fucking poodle. He didn't have no other friends to tell, and he knew you and me had done business. He must've asked you.'

'He didn't ask me anything.' The knife inched away. Bobby swallowed. 'You didn't do it, did you?'

'What the fuck?' The blade was back, biting deeper now. 'You think I killed that little pussy? I was home sleeping the whole time. He topped hisself.'

'Then why're you so freaked?'

Shut up, Bobby. Why in God's name was he provoking this shit-for-brains?

Kelvin flicked his pocketknife shut and took Bobby's face in his hands. He squeezed until skin stretched taut around cheekbones.

'Why am I so freaked, you dumb cunt? I'm freaked because I tortured that little cocksucker for a whole year. Day after fucking day. He was terrified of me. Do you think I want the cops finding out about that? What with my business at the school and everything? So I wanted to know whether Mattie told you about how I was shitting with him, and whether *you* told the cops. But you've promised me he said nothing, so we're okay, right?'

'Right.'

'Right we're right, 'cos I hear any different? You're dead, Bobby boy.'

Kelvin punched Bobby low and hard. The dealer stepped back and watched the boy cough up his guts. Then he went to his scooter and took something from the seat pocket.

'Here. A present. Don't say I never give you anything.'

The bag of marijuana smacked the earth between Bobby's feet. A moment later, Bobby heard the kick of an engine and the scooter's headlight flashed across his face.

Bobby picked up the weed and shoved it into his jacket.

To avoid the scrutiny of passing traffic, he shunned the road and stumbled into the forest. Once or twice he stopped to hawk a gob of coppery spit. The pain dulled to a throb as his insides reordered themselves. But that was no good. He jammed his fingers into the place where Kelvin's fist had connected. He did not want to lose the pain, not yet. The presence of it, cleaving deep, made him feel a little better . . .

'Please, Bobby. Please help me. You don't know what it's like. He won't leave me alone.'

'I just don't get it, Matt. You say Kelvin's been beating you up, what for? Have you bought gear off him and not paid up?'

'Don't be stupid. I wouldn't touch that stuff.'

'Then why's he . . . ?'

'He just likes *doing it, Bobby. He gets off on it. I think that's why he deals. Not just for the cash, but because he wants to hurt people. Wants to make them like him. All I know is this is killing me.'*

'Oh, come on.'

'It's all right for you. You've got in with the cool set. I'm just left behind.'

'Jesus Christ. Look, it's not that I don't like you, Matt. We were good friends. But people grow apart and . . .'

'I know why we're not friends, Bobby. S'nothing to do with growing apart. It's because of what happened that day in the woods, isn't it?'

'Shut your fucking mouth.'

'Fine. Okay. You don't want to be my mate, that's fine. But please *help me. Remember how I was there for you when your mum died? I was there every day. I helped you get on with stuff. Maybe I didn't do a great job . . .'*

'What the hell's that supposed to mean?'

'Nothing. It's jus', I don't think much of your friends these days. And that crap you're putting into yourself.'

'It's just a little weed.'

'My mum says that's how it starts.'

'Bollocks.'

'Well, whatever. All I want you to do is talk to Kelvin. Look, Bobby, I can't do this anymore. I can't sleep, I can't eat. The guy's a one hundred percent nutter. He phones me all the time. In the middle of the night sometimes. He says crazy things. He's everywhere I go. He's already cut me once and . . . Look, I'm just scared that one day it'll go too far. Please, Bobby, talk to him. I'm so scared . . . so fucking scared . . .'

'Matt, hey, calm down. Fuck, you're shaking. Look, I'll talk to him, but I think you're blowing this all out of proportion. Why don't you just tell a teacher or your parents?'

'Don't be stupid. You don't tell teachers about people like Kelvin Hope.'

'Well, why not just try and stick it out? This time next year you'll be finished with school. You can go to sixth-form college and . . .'

'Forget it. You don't understand, do you? This guy is killing me.'

'Matt.'

'He's killing *me.* Please.'

'Okay. I said, I'll talk to him.'

'Thanks. I mean it. Really, thank you.'

Bobby held onto the pain until he reached home. Only when he was undressing for bed, examining the fist-shaped bruise, did he understand why he had goaded the smackhead. He wanted to be hurt. Not killed, but hurt enough so that it meant something. The image of Matt Linton, blood-dappled and razor-handed, filled Bobby's mind. His inner eye lingered on the glistening cleft cut into the boy's neck. In that instant,

Bobby Nightingale wanted to feel the sting of the razor at his own throat, to see his own redness clot across the tiles. To feel the wrath of Kelvin Hope.

Taking the bag of weed from his coat, Bobby rolled himself a spliff.

Six

'Who are you?'

Richard's question echoed along the Nave. It reached the junction of the Crossing and was lost in the space of the great transept. The figure standing at the cathedral altar did not stir.

'I knew you once. I loved you. Who are you?'

No answer.

Daylight burned against the windows but, inside the church, only shivers of light penetrated. It was as if the stained glass conspired with the darkness. Outside, Richard could hear the clamour of sightseers pressing to get in. There were throwaway cameras to be used up and postcards to be bought. But the souvenir shop was closed, its plaster effigies of the Lincoln Imp safe from sticky-fingered schoolchildren. The great west door was, likewise, tight shut. Save for Richard's footsteps upon the flags nothing disturbed the ancient stillness. He walked between the pillars that straddled the cathedral like the legs of petrified giants. From their shadows, he watched the figure.

Janet Nightingale's arms hung at her sides. Her head remained bowed, as if in prayer. She stayed perfectly still. Her mane of dark hair, that once he had held to his lips and kissed, fell forward across the altar. Unable to bear her silence, her *Absence*, Richard started forward.

'Janet, please just tell me, where did you go?'

Perhaps detecting his proximity, the figure turned. Richard hesitated. He peered into the gloom, but could see nothing of the face beneath the veil of hair. He crept further into the heart of the church.

Janet's head twitched, her jaw dropped: sudden, spasmodic movements. Like the carved image of a supplicating Christ, she held out her arms, as if inviting her husband to share an embrace. Richard stopped in his tracks. His hand covered his mouth. He stepped back, eyes rooted to the figure of his late wife. Blood had begun to weep from the sleeves of her dress and drip from her fingers. Her ankles and feet ran red. As the flow reached the altar steps, the colour and consistency changed, thinning and darkening into inky water. What had started as a trickle soon became a flood, pouring out into the transept. The sound of water filled the stone belly of the church.

Richard glanced down, saw the flow lap at his feet, saw his face, livid in the pool.

'What happened to you? For God's sake, tell me.'

The woman's body convulsed. Her knuckles rapped upon the altar table, beating out a hollow tattoo that made Richard's blood run cold. Her arms flailed and her head snapped back and forth, each limb moving as if tugged by invisible strings. An exhalation of breath tickled the curtain of hair. This little sigh, more than anything else, tore at Richard's nerves.

'Stop it!' he shouted. 'Don't. Please, don't. Just let me help you.'

He sloshed through the water. Reaching the figure, he held out a trembling hand. Her body ceased to rattle and Janet's head inclined towards him.

'I'm sorry,' he whispered. 'Jesus God, I'm so, *so* sorry.'

Her coffin-breath billowed against his face. The hair parted.

Features, redolent of the earth and of putrefaction, were

revealed in snatches. Bone and cartilage, striated muscle and warm, corrosive juices shimmered in the rainbow light from the stained windows. A rictus grin animated an otherwise expressionless face. Richard whimpered. He had wanted to find something written on those decaying features: hatred, pity, blame, anything that resembled human emotion. Instead the eyes that met his were blank. He saw no trace of humanity there.

Nothing but *The Absence.*

'JANET!'

Richard woke with the bed sheets knotted around his body. He stared up at the bedroom ceiling, thinking for a time that it was ribbed, like the vaulted roof of a church. At the top of one of the columns, from which the boughs of the roof were planted, a face loomed. Milk-white eyes examined his naked form. It was a gargoyle, he guessed – a creature like the mischievous Lincoln Imp that had been turned to stone by angelic intervention – except that this face possessed no mischief. Instead, it was utterly vacant. He closed his eyes against it. When he opened them again, the face was gone, replaced by the swirl of the Artex.

Richard heaved himself into a sitting position. Something dropped off the mattress with a *chink* and rolled under the bed. The room felt hot, the air stale. The smell of the half-eaten pizza congealing on the dresser made his head thud. He blinked the room into focus and groaned. This was the refuge of a student, not the bedroom of a forty-year-old businessman.

His bladder griped and Richard obeyed. He went to the bathroom, dropped onto the pedestal and directed his penis between his legs. One bottle, he thought, and I don't have the energy to stand to take a piss. Without getting up, he stretched towards the basin, ran the cold tap and scooped handfuls of water to his lips. His headache eased. His vision cleared. Fractured memories of the night before stitched themselves together. He had ordered a pizza, and then . . .

Chink chink

The bottle, of course. Glenfiddich. One of the multitude hidden behind the skirting in the spare bedroom. He wondered just how many he had secreted there over the years: let's say five hundred as a good round figure. Five hundred bottles over the course of, what, five years? Yes, it was about five years ago when the last traces of Janet had been lost to him. Five years since *The Absence* became complete. He took a breath through his nose and held it. So, five years: that works out at roughly one sozzle session every three-point-five days. Conservative, perhaps, but not too wide of the mark. And all that time Joe, Bobby and his late wife had remained ignorant of his hidden stash.

Ignorant.

The selfishness of the phrase struck him. Hot on its heels, the shame of the hiding and the closeted drinking hit home. As was often the case during these morning-after reflections, the moment of crisis was a brief one. Each man must cope with misery in his own way, Richard told himself, and, after all, he had hidden his 'weakness' – if you wanted to call it that – pretty well. He'd never been a mean drunk; never so much as raised a finger to his children. No, they didn't know a thing about it. They were 'ignorant'. And even if they *did* suspect, well, what then? He *needed* it. They wouldn't begrudge him this one solace. Not if they knew what, for their sake, he'd had to live with all those years.

You see, Janet had never shown the children her *true* face.

The ringtone of Richard's mobile set his teeth on edge. He wiped a palm across his brow and shuffled back into the bedroom.

'Ye . . .' He summoned saliva. 'Yeah?'

'Mr Richard Nightingale?'

'Uh-huh.'

'Mr Nightingale. A pleasure. An absolute pleasure, sir. What good fortune that I could convince the estimable Miss Marchant to give me your private number. A find you have there, Mr Nightingale, a real treasure. If I were a man given to purloining, I might whisk her away to my little office in Potter's Drake. Now, I did try to make contact with you yesterday afternoon but I believe we suffered some kind of telephonic breakdown. I'm not at all sure you could make me out.' A dainty voice, marked on the 's's with a sibilant hiss.

'I'm sorry, who is this?'

'To the point, Mr Nightingale. Admirable, sir, admirable. So often these days, in the discharge of my duties, I converse with people to whom needless verbiage is de rigueur. Verbal diarrhoea, I call it, to mask inadequacies of intellect. Young people are particularly culpable. We are turning out a generation of village idiots, Mr Nightingale. I often say . . .'

Richard was beginning to see why his manager had buckled and handed out his private number.

'Please. Who are you?'

'Ah. I have not said? Mea culpa. I am Cuttle. Mr Cuttle of Cuttle and Runerby, Solicitors-at-Law.'

'What do you want with me?'

'Why, business, sir. I have been charged, in my professional capacity, to convey to you a happy honour. We each of us strive, do we not, Mr Nightingale, to make our way upon this inhospitable globe. We earn our crust and hope for rewards, in this world or the next but, if we *can* be remembered in this physical plane, then we may say that we are fortunate of such kind indications as to our merit . . .'

'I'm going to put the phone down now.'

'My apologies,' Cuttle piped. 'It's just that this is the most pleasant of my duties. And I do so enjoy the "big reveal". Now then: in the county of Lincolnshire, in the great expanse of the Fenlands, there lies a house. It is, I may say, the most beautiful domicile in the area. A millhouse, no less. Once a leviathan of industry, now a picturesque retreat. The Daecher Mill. It's yours, Mr Nightingale, and is waiting to receive you.'

Seven

It was too hot to visit the dead today, and so no-one moved among the headstones. Flies gathered in swarms above dog-shit-pebbled pathways. Birds squabbled beneath a leaky water pipe. In his hut, the caretaker dozed as peacefully as any of his charges, a racing paper draped across his face. All of these things were within the boundaries of the graveyard.

Beyond it, Joe Nightingale held fast to the gate. The bars, blasted by the sun, burned his palms. Sweat trickled from his fists and spotted the bouquet at his feet. He looked down at the bluebells. The heat was making short work of them. He should have bought artificial flowers. Among the silk and wire approximations of the florists, however, there had been no bluebells. It had to be bluebells or nothing.

Joe heard a crunch of gravel. A finger poked him in the ribs.

'You okay?'

'Yeah. Sure,' Joe said, blinking against the surprise of her being there. 'How'd you know where to find me?'

Samantha Jones slung the suit bag she carried over the back of a commemorative bench.

'It was easy,' she said. 'You weren't at home, you weren't at the library, you have no friends . . .'

'Ouch.'

Her smile faded. 'Only one other place I could think of.

Sure you're all right?'

'Nope,' Joe admitted, 'not really. Hopeless, eh?'

'People who say they're fine, when they've got a bloody good reason not to be, creep me out. Anyway, I like self-confessed screw-ups.'

'Are you screwed up?'

'Totally. Which you'd have found out if you'd stuck around for date five. I was planning to hire a dwarf chauffeur for the evening and wear a low-cut gorilla suit.'

'Grrr.'

'Was that for the monkey outfit or the midget?'

'A little of column A, a little of column B. So what about date six?'

'You like foot rubs?'

'Yeah.'

'I don't. They hold up the sex.'

It was thirty-two degrees in the shade. To Joe, it seemed suddenly much warmer.

'Cute, you're blushing.'

'It's gout, I swear. Manly gout.'

'What are you, an Eighteenth Century squire?' She poked him again. 'But seriously, I want to know something. Why were there only four dates?'

'I don't know.'

'I think you do, and I've been waiting seven months for you to tell me. I didn't want to go into it after your mum's passing. Jesus, "*passing*"? Joe, I'm sorry . . . Look, I just don't understand why you pulled away from me.'

'I was fucked up, Sam,' Joe said, running his fingers through the railings. 'I'd just lost my mum. I was in counselling. What do you want me to say?'

'Just that. That would've been fine. But you didn't say anything. You just blanked me, and I wasn't sure if it was something

I'd done or not done.'

'It wasn't about you. I was . . . grieving.'

Sam took hold of his hands. She opened his palms, exposing the blisters made by the hot iron bars. 'It was something more than just grieving, wasn't it?'

They stood in silence, Joe unable to express the hateful truth. Why had he rejected Samantha Jones? The answer glinted inside his mind, an irrational resentment focused and reflected in the smooth surface of a glass ball.

From a nearby street came the jangle-chimes of an ice cream van. The tune stole into Joe's thoughts. Banishing the image of glass it extracted another memory, vivid but incomplete. He was a kid, no more than five years old, torpedoing plastic boats in six inches of bathwater. His mother sat on the edge of the tub, her back to him, fingertips caressing the suds. Her beautiful ebony hair hung past her shoulders so that, even when he leaned forward, her face remained hidden. She sang:

Row, row, row your boat

gently down the stream.

Merrily, merrily, merrily, merrily,

life is but a dream . . .

About to execute a lethal manoeuvre on a submarine, Joe called out to her.

Look at this, mummy. Mummy? Please look at me.

He caught a hint of pale flesh behind the hair. His mother's head half-turned towards him.

Not now, Joe.

He could still taste the fear, brackish in his mouth. The harrier jet slipped from his hand and span in soapy circles. That was not mummy's voice. There was no mummy in that voice at all. It was toneless. Empty . . . Little Joe started to cry.

Don't cry. Mummy needs a little rest, that's all. Quiet now. Merrily,

merrily, merrily, merrily; life is but a dream.

The memory lost its power. It crept back into that stockpile of things best forgotten.

'Those flowers have had it,' said Sam, bringing him back.

'Bluebells,' Joe said. 'Mum's favourite. She knew all about flowers; their names and superstitions. In the Middle Ages, bowmen used bluebell sap to glue feathers to their arrows. That's why the bluebell keeps her head bowed. She's ashamed of her association with death.'

'So are we going in? I mean, I can wait here if you'd prefer to be alone with your mum.'

Joe looked into the cemetery. His gaze passed over the confusion of old tombs and mausoleums, reaching into that area of the graveyard where the newer plots had been laid out.

'I don't ever go in,' he said.

'Joe.'

She kissed his forehead and put her arms around him. A cold wave rolled through the boy, bristled the hairs on his arms and salted tears into his eyes. Sam's hold tightened. She absorbed some of the shivers into her own body. Her lips moved to his ear.

'It's okay. You're gonna be okay, you know that, don't you?'

There was hesitation, but he nodded. Close up, he breathed in her scent. There was the faintest tang of perspiration layering a perfume of citrus and jasmine. Some other aroma, too, contributed to the whole: an unmanufactured fragrance, natural to the woman that held him, that put Joe in mind of the refreshed air of a forest after heavy rain. He longed to hold her, but his arms remained at his sides. Sam must have noticed his reluctance. She let go and he saw the colour run high in her face.

He said, 'So, what's with the bag?'

Sam picked up the dry cleaning from the bench and threw it to him.

'Knew you'd forget.' She managed a smile. 'You know, you're like some kind of idiot savant but without the savant bit. Anyway, I got Bobby to get it for me from the furthest, foulest reaches of your bedroom.'

Joe blanched: 'You saw my room?'

'Yes. And I think there's something living under your bed. Some creature conceived of hair and underpants and used tissues. I thought about reporting you to the government for illegal genetic experimentation, you Frankenstein of Filth. Anyway, you owe me twenty quid.'

Joe peeked under the plastic to find his dress shirt and dinner jacket, starched and pressed.

'Is this date five?' he asked. 'I thought *you* were the one supposed to be wearing the monkey suit.'

'Don't even try to be funny. I'll be wearing a homely little dress.'

His face a picture of scepticism, Joe stepped back and gave her an appraising glance. From pierced eyebrow, down to the hem of her flower-patterned vest dress and pink-and-black twickers tights, Sam was the sartorial antithesis of 'homely'. Though she incorporated elements of the subculture's fashions into her look, Joe knew that she balked at the term 'goth'. Her taste in music, stuck in a Nineties confection of Take That and East 17, backed up her position. She preferred her own term: 'kooky-chic'. It summed her up nicely, Joe thought.

'Okay, maybe it won't be a gingham gown,' Sam admitted, 'but it'll be more Marilyn Munster than vampire-mummy-Munster.'

'Lilly Munster,' Joe said, 'husband to Herman, mother to Eddie.'

'You're such a nerd.' Sam poked him one last time. 'Have

you even had sex yet?'

'I've had my share, honest.'

'Then you'll know what to do tomorrow night.'

'But – but it's only date five.'

'You're talking yourself out of action, sweet cheeks.'

Sam left him gulping at the gate.

Joe picked up the bluebells. Beyond resuscitation, they teetered on the verge of the great horticultural hereafter. If he pulled back the gate, ran through the marble forest all the way to the new plots, it would be only to leave a bunch of dead flowers at her grave. What was the point of that? Better to come back tomorrow with a fresh bouquet. Tomorrow he would stand before her at last. He would lay flowers and pull weeds. He would take a rag and wipe the bird shit from the headstone, so that her name and the span of her life could be read. Then he would whisper to the stone, say the things that needed to be said.

Joe set his face against the sun. No. Not tomorrow. He would do it now. He reached for the gate . . . His hands stopped short and closed around invisible bars. What if the stone spoke? What if *she* answered him? He saw himself again in the bathtub, tiny fingers reaching out to the figure that sat on the rim.

Please look at me, Mummy.

The head of the figure turned to face him. Little Joe looked down into the water, seeing garlands of hair reflected there. Child-eyes widened. He felt warmth at his groin as urine streaked the bathwater. Behind the ebony cascade, a waxy unmoving face was watching him – a face from which his doting mother had been drained. Nothing was left of her. She was . . . hollow . . .

Please forgive me, Mummy.

Eight

Two days had passed since Matt Linton's death, and Bobby hadn't slept a wink. Dawn of the second day found him lying on his bed fully clothed, memories burning behind his eyes. He remembered: his first day of school, playing Pogs with his new best friend; breathless on the drive home, as he told his mum about how great Mattie was, and of their plans for a gigantic fort; summer holidays, making bows and arrows with bamboo nicked from the Linton's herb garden; sleep-overs, during which Matt told the creepiest ghost stories Bobby had ever heard; painting the mythical figures that made up their Warhammer battalions; their first tentative discussions about sex and girls. These, and many other once treasured memories, paraded in the darkness.

At six am, Bobby gave up on sleep and sat at his drawing board. Instead of going to his brushes, he chose pencils and a few sticks of charcoal. He laid a pair of sepia and grey brush-tip pens within easy reach. For him to work from the basis of a sketch was unusual. Ordinarily, he would begin a new piece straight from paints. This difference of approach did not register until he had delineated the background and central figures of the piece. Nor did he think too much about the fact that, instead of using plain illustration paper, he had started working on the much thicker and more expensive Bristol board.

As the basics of the drawing started to take shape, Bobby

reflected on the process and upon the scene. The subject was certainly striking, rendered in the mute tones of pen and charcoal. Perhaps, subconsciously, that was why he had decided to use those materials. But why the Bristol paper? Even now he wasn't sure that the picture would be anything special. Putting his face close up to the sheet, Bobby breathed in the charcoal dust and the crisp smell of the Indian ink. The bird in the foreground, wheeling into the arms of a distant shadow, filled his vision. Its beak gaped, as if screaming into the unfinished sky.

It called to him . . .

The doorbell buzzed from downstairs. Bobby checked his watch. Ten-thirty. Time flies when you're drawing weird birds, he thought. He yawned and toed a pair of slippers onto his feet.

It was quiet downstairs. Joe might be asleep; the Old Man was probably at the gallery. Bobby opened the front door.

Harold and Diane Linton looked ragged. Sleep appeared to have been a stranger to them these last few days. Bobby sympathised. He remembered them as caring, if very proper parents, strict about meals and bedtimes. Now the vaguely authoritarian manner they exuded was gone.

'Bobby. It's good to see you,' said Harold Linton, his voice husky. 'May we come in?'

'Yeah. Sure. Course.'

He led the way into the sitting room and offered them something to drink.

'No, thank you,' said Mr Linton. 'Well, let's get straight to it, shall we? We've come to ask you something, Bobby. We'd like you to answer honestly, can you do that?'

Bobby felt a sharp sensation in his stomach. He looked down, almost expecting to find that Mr Linton had stuck him with a knife. *This is for our boy,* Mrs Linton would say, animated by the revenge her husband had taken. *You evil little bastard, you should've protected him. Our son's dead and it's all your fault. You abandoned him – I hope you fucking burn in hell.* They would stand over him as he fell to his knees, perhaps kicking him to the floor. In his mind's eye, he saw Mrs Linton retrieve the blade from his belly and thrust it into his chest, saw her face flecked with blood and round with rage.

But there was no knife. The sensation had been an internal twist; his own body toying with him.

'What can I do for you, Mr Linton?'

'We know that you and Matthew were not as friendly as you once were,' said Diane Linton, 'so we don't like to put pressure on you.'

What was this? The police must have told the Lintons what Bobby had said. Didn't they believe him? Something like hope shimmered in Diane Linton's eyes. Maybe she suspected that Matt had come to Bobby for help. Maybe she and her husband thought that, if they spoke to him, face-to-face, Bobby would tell them what had been troubling their son. How could he respond to such a question from these people? These grieving parents who had taken him into their home, who had trusted in the friendship he had enjoyed with their delicate child. If they asked, he would tell them. He must tell someone or he would never sleep again.

As this determination seized him, he remembered the feel of the blade at his throat.

I hear any different? You're dead, Bobby boy.

Mrs Linton was speaking: 'You don't have to answer right now. There'll be the post mortem, of course, and the coroner might not release Matthew to us until . . . Well, there are lots of things that could cause a delay. But if you could let us know by the end of the week? The vicar might want a full order of service by then, you see?'

'M'sorry?'

'Oh, Bobby, you're exhausted, aren't you?'

Mrs Linton crossed the room and held Bobby's face in her hands. He looked into sleep-starved eyes that mirrored his own.

'You *were* his friend, weren't you, Bobby? You loved him. He thought the world of you.'

Bobby gasped despite himself. From across the room, he heard Mr Linton sobbing. Christ, what did they want from him?

'You'll do it for us, won't you?' she asked. 'You'll read a prayer or something at the funeral. Harold and I were hoping you'd compose a little piece yourself. I think it'll be good for you to do that. Then you'll feel like you've said goodbye properly.' She glanced over at her husband and her face crumpled. 'We all need to say goodbye.'

From their conversation the previous day, Richard had conjured a mental picture of the Cuttle half of Cuttle & Runerby, Solicitors-at-Law. The man he envisioned was small and neat with a marked touch of femininity about him. He would have a pinched face that, through a lifetime's experience of human nature, never betrayed a hint of surprise. His eyes would glisten with a certain liveliness of character. All in all, Richard imagined a dapper version of Mr Pickwick. It was somewhat shocking, then, to see the man that Miss Marchant ushered into the gallery's back office.

There was nothing neat or dapper about Cuttle. His suit, twenty years or more out of date, strained to accommodate his massive frame. The lawyer's pocked and lumpy face reminded Richard of those unflattering portraits of Oliver Cromwell painted after the Restoration. Waddling into the office, Cuttle held out the slab of his hand. As Richard shook it, he noticed the gold watch stretched around the man's wrist. An expensive, jewel-encrusted timepiece, its face was scratched and the hour hand appeared to be missing.

Richard retrieved his hand. It came back damp. The lawyer sat and, for the first time in his life, Richard felt sympathy for a chair.

'An honour, Mr Nightingale. And an unparalleled delight to meet you, Miss Marchant.'

The wattles of flesh around Cuttle's neck trembled as he spoke.

At least I was right in one respect, Richard thought: there *is* something effete about the way in which he lisps his words. Richard shuddered despite himself.

'Would you like tea or coffee, Mr Cuttle?' asked Miss Marchant.

She looked at him with the kind of expression she might have used had the lawyer's squid-like namesake just sprayed her with ink. Oblivious to her distaste, Cuttle said,

'No thank you, my dear. Though I daresay refreshment from the pot of Miss Marchant would be as ambrosia to the gods.'

Miss Marchant sniffed and left. Cuttle watched her go and then turned back to Richard. A smile widened the already over-wide face. He opened his briefcase and took out a manila envelope, which he held up with a flourish. If this guy was trying out for the Magic Circle, Richard figured that he needed a lot more practice.

'The deeds, Mr Nightingale. The deeds to a rather special property. With a few scribbles in the places indicated, it shall be yours. But I envy you, sir. What tranquil repose might be enjoyed in the rustic environs of this bucolic estate? Indeed, I should say that, were the poet Wordsworth alive today, he could find no better setting for one of his excellent pastorals.'

'Mr Cuttle, you said on the phone that a Mrs Sutton left me this property?'

'Yes, sir. Mrs Muriel Elizabeth Sutton. A lady of . . .'

'The name rings a bell. I seem to have heard it recently.'

'She was a relative of your sadly deceased wife. A cousin, I believe, some way removed. Perhaps Mrs Nightingale spoke of her?'

'No. We don't have much to do with my wife's family.'

'So sad. So very . . .'

Thinking that Cuttle would expound upon the difficulties he often encountered between relatives, Richard opened his mouth to stem the flow. He was surprised to find the solicitor momentarily lost for words. Cuttle had taken what looked like a rabbit's foot from his pocket and was busy stroking it. The totem, attached to a keychain, was practically hairless from years of pawing. Half a minute passed before Cuttle stirred.

'Mr Nightingale. Ah, I'm sorry. Talk of family disputes sometimes upsets me. A silly weakness.' He replaced the charm in his pocket. 'Let us resume. Mrs Sutton, then. An old and very much valued client of the firm. She had lived alone at Daecher's Mill ever since the death of her younger sister thirty or more years ago. Your wife was her nearest relative. Mrs Sutton was unaware of Mrs Nightingale's death and so, as next of kin, you are the beneficiary of the estate. There is a little money but the real asset is the house.'

'You say it's a mill?'

'A watermill. Or was. The machinery is still in place, but it's all been made safe. It hasn't been an active mill for many years. Instead, it is a good-sized and rather beautiful house.'

'What's it worth?'

'I'm not an estate agent, but I should say somewhere in the region of three hundred thousand. It has been somewhat neglected of late. Mrs Sutton hadn't been in the best of health for some time and repairs were beyond her.'

'I may want to sell it. Is labour readily available in the area?'

'We are getting somewhat ahead of ourselves.'

Cuttle's voice rose an octave. The layers of his distended neck trembled with the violence of his irritation. Puzzled, Richard could see the effort it took for the lawyer to master himself.

'Let us sign the documents first. Then I can advise you on anything you might wish to know.'

They went through the deeds, clause by clause. There was something odd about the whole thing, but Richard could see no disadvantage in accepting the bequest. Aside from the customary obligations of a house owner there appeared to be nothing onerous hidden in the small print. Still, he declined to sign until he had given the paperwork to his own solicitor. Again, Richard detected irritation in Mr Cuttle's hooded eyes, but the lawyer did not press him.

'Very wise, Mr Nightingale,' he said. 'But you will let me know by the end of the week?'

'Sure. Now, about this labour question. I really don't need a country retreat. I'd like to sell it and put the money in trust for my sons. So could you tell me . . . ?'

'May I make a suggestion, sir? In my experience money unearned is the ruin of many young men. I have seen it time and again.'

'My boys are not . . .'

'No, I'm sure. But why give one gift when you might bestow two? Let them have the money at twenty-one, but allow them the satisfaction of knowing that, in some small way, they earned it. Hard graft will teach them the value of your beneficence. The work that needs to be done to the mill is all fairly superficial. DIY jobs mostly. Why not spend the summer there, away from distractions and diversions? Father and sons toiling towards a just reward.'

'My gallery.'

'But the excellent Miss Marchant is more than capable. And I'm sure you are successful enough to take a little holiday whenever you please. En route down the hill, I noticed that the other galleries look rather less prosperous than this fine establishment.'

'I'm doing better than most,' Richard admitted, pleased by the compliment.

'Schadenfreude, Mr Nightingale. Nothing wrong with that, Sir. Nothing at all.'

Richard's smile died. The great pink creature opposite slapped his hands upon the desk and drew back the deeds.

'A summer labouring in heaven,' said Cuttle. 'A time for building character and for quiet reflection. They grow up so quickly, Mr Nightingale. Soon they will have flown the coop. Nightingales finding their wings. This may be the last chance you have to be a father to them. A father in the truest sense.'

Cuttle heaved himself from the chair. He stood by the door, looking down at Richard, who remained lost in thought.

'Mrs Sutton loved children,' he said, his lisp pronounced as he spoke the dead woman's name. 'She would be happy to know that a new family was about to make a home of her beloved millhouse. Yes, indeed she would.'

- *Interlude* -

The Second and Third Guest: Elsie Cuttle and Brother Samuel Made Absent on 22nd December 1993

The wind whipped off the sea and shivered the scrubland. It rattled the winter birds in their nests and sugared the tips of dead reeds. On the porch of Daecher's Mill, two figures huddled against the blast.

Elsie Cuttle tugged the shawl around her shoulders. She had never known cold like this. Even without the carriage of the wind, the chill pierced her clothes. No-one would believe it back at the Hall, but even Brother Samuel, a field service veteran well used to the savagery of the elements, shuddered. He shifted the reading matter – copies of *The Watchtower* and *Awake!* – under his arm and rapped the door. They waited and, though Elsie longed for a warm parlour and, perhaps, a cup of tea, she abided with the gale. God's will be done.

The sky in the west darkened, though eastward, out across the flat white carpet of the Fens, it was tinged pink with the promise of more snow to come.

'Nobody home,' grunted Brother Samuel.

'Perhaps we might have more luck in town?' Elsie suggested.

'It is indeed a wretched spot.' Samuel took off his Gore-Tex raincoat and draped it around Elsie's shoulders. 'But we must sometimes go into the wild places, to give light to those that move in the darkness. To guide their feet to the way of peace.'

'Amen.'

'Come on, I'll buy you a hot chocolate.'

They were about to descend the porch steps when the door opened. A tongue of light stretched into the night.

'Bless you,' Brother Samuel smiled.

It was difficult to make out the face of the woman silhouetted in the doorway. She looked to be in her late forties, possibly early fifties. A little hunched over, the long arms that hung at her sides gave her the appearance of an aged chimpanzee.

'What do you want?' the woman asked.

'Sister Elsie and I have come to spread the word of Jehovah's plan, Mrs?'

'Sutton. And I don't go in for . . . all that.'

'May I ask why not?'

Unlike many ministers with whom Elsie had undertaken fieldwork, Brother Samuel's smile was never fixed nor combative. He was genuinely interested in the spiritual health of those to whom he preached. Without a hint of condescension, he would try to convince doubters of what he believed to be the one inconvertible fact of life: that God loved. Everything extraneous to that message – intricacies of dogma and doctrine, rites and rituals – was just so much detail. It was a joyous message, and yet Elsie found the old man's faith disturbing. In quiet moments of reflection and prayer, she often sensed him watching her, the strength of his faith probing her own. He knew her history, had judged her contrition. She owed him her place in the Hall, but she feared him, too.

'I believed once,' Mrs Sutton muttered. 'This place drove the God out of me.'

'In hard times we often feel He has deserted us,' Samuel nodded.

The woman gave a bitter laugh. 'Whatever gods there are have never left me.'

This curious response hardly registered with Elsie. She had seen something in the shadows of the hall. A movement – a figure – glancing behind Mrs Sutton's legs. Surreptitiously, Elsie edged sideways and peered into the corridor. It was empty. Whatever had moved there must have slipped into one of the rooms off the hall. Brother Samuel, fussing with his pamphlets and magazines, had noticed nothing. At first, Elsie thought it might have been a cat but, re-running the image in her mind, she became convinced that the thing had been much larger. And surely it had scampered on *two* legs. Yes, 'scampered' was the word.

Elsie looked up to find Mrs Sutton following her gaze. The lady's lips thinned.

'Please wait there,' she said, and disappeared into the house.

The door flapped on its hinges, inviting and forbidding. Elsie and Samuel stepped nearer to the body of the house. Their breath billowed and their eyes teared. The winter sun on the horizon flared before it died, silhouetting a flock of gulls and the spire of a distant church. Snow drifted onto the porch and spotted the windows. Brother Samuel shivered. Elsie was about to return his coat when she heard Mrs Sutton's voice. The words were interrupted by the sway of the door and the bray of the wind, but this is what the young evangelist made out:

'Please, must it be now?'

There came no reply. No human voice at any rate.

'You *have* been good. A good, quiet little girl, all this time . . . Yes, I know you are . . . I know you're hungry.' And now Mrs Sutton's tone grew weary. 'All right, dry your tears. I will do as I promised.'

Elsie leaned forward to catch the words.

'I will bring them to you.'

'Did you hear that?' Elsie asked.

'Hear what, my dear?' said the preacher.

Mrs Sutton reappeared. She steadied the door and beckoned them into the house.

The hallway felt as cold as the porch. A naked bulb, strung from the ceiling, illuminated the low corridor. To Elsie's left stood a flight of stairs, to the right, two doors that led, presumably, into sitting rooms or studies. There was no carpet underfoot. Green felt wallpaper, exhausted by decades of brushing shoulders and warping woodwork, hung in tongues above the wainscot.

Mrs Sutton led them to the end of the hall and into a sizeable kitchen. Elsie felt a swell of gratitude. The temperature here was at least bearable.

'Please sit down.' Mrs Sutton indicated the chairs that surrounded an oak dining table.

'A lovely kitchen,' Samuel observed. 'You don't see Agas like that anymore. An original feature?'

The woman nodded absently. Arms folded, she remained inside the kitchen doorway.

'And this used to be a watermill? I thought I saw the wheel when we arrived.'

'It *is* a watermill.'

'But the riverbed looked dry.'

'The water comes,' the lady said, as if reciting a lament, 'and the wheel turns. The wheel of the mill grinds slowly, yet grinds exceeding small.'

'Amen,' said Brother Samuel. Yet, to Elsie's mind, Mrs Sutton had not intended her quotation to reference God.

'Where is your daughter?'

Mrs Sutton's head snapped in Elsie's direction. 'What do you mean?'

'I heard you talking to someone in the hall. I thought it was a child.'

'There are no children at Daecher's Mill. Haven't been for many a long year.' Her tone was hard, but shot through with something akin to regret.

'I'm sorry.'

'No need to be sorry. Children were a blessing denied me. Such precious things, don't you think?' Elsie felt the woman's eyes upon her. 'So cruel to bring them into worlds not meant for them.'

'You live here alone, Mrs Sutton?'

The interjection had been a kindness on Samuel's part. Nevertheless, Elsie felt stirrings all too familiar. She clenched her fingers into her palm, digging the nails deep. By degrees, the voices of Brother Samuel and Mrs Sutton grew more distant.

'So what are you, Jehovah's Witnesses?'

'No, madam. Many of us did once belong to that movement, but we broke away some years ago. We call ourselves the Twenty-First Century Bible Students, and we hold true to much of the eschatology of the Jehovah's Witnesses: that Christ has returned as King, that the great tribulation is imminent.'

'Then why'd you split away?'

'We believe the Witnesses to be a little severe in their practice of reproof and disfellowship. In our view, Christians must always be generous and indulgent forgivers.'

Elsie pictured her shame as some dark creature curled up at the back of her mind. Never truly sleeping, it twitched at Brother Samuel's words. It unfurled long limbs and began, once again, to dissect what had gone before: fieldwork with Brother Stephen. Coy glances that had led to invitations and unsupervised meetings. Meetings during which, after only a short time, flesh had been unveiled and yearnings satisfied. There, in

Stephen's bedroom, where monk-like order had for so long kept wanton thoughts in check, sin had taken root and grown as surely as the seed. Months passed. A chemist-bought kit revealed the truth and a doctor confirmed it. Congratulations had withered in her ear.

It was strange, considering her years of worship, but the murder had been accomplished with little fuss. The clinical nature of the thing did not feel like an act of slaughter. Instead, it had been nothing more than unwanted tissue, a potential disease even, being sucked out of her. The need to confess came later.

The shame-creature plucked a nerve and the faces of the three elders rose up before her. There was kindness in their eyes as they pronounced judgment. It was this tolerance that had undone Elsie's mind. Had they looked upon her with condemnation, with contempt even, she could have borne her crime; might even have come to live with it. After all, though her offence had been great, her repentance was deemed genuine. But the spiritual correction, spoken in measured tones, gave birth to the thing that played now inside her soul. If only they had told her how bad she really was.

'You may think God has abandoned you, Mrs Sutton,' Samuel said, 'but you are wrong. He moves in even the darkest of lives.'

'No.' Mrs Sutton closed the *Watchtower* magazine. 'It is you who are wrong.'

The woman's eyes strayed to a portrait Elsie had not noticed before. A thickset man in his early forties stood before the millhouse, sheaves of corn at his feet. A sense of strong, bucolic health radiated from the miller. Behind him, in the shadows of the porch, lurked the indistinct form of a child.

A cry rang through the house. Mrs Sutton turned and shuffled into the hallway.

'My dog,' she said, and closed the door behind her.

'Didn't sound like a dog,' Elsie said.

'No.'

'It sounded like a child.'

'Something like a child, yes.'

'Like an impatient child.'

Elsie watched the passage of five minutes on the face of the clock above the sink. Then her gaze wandered to the window. She saw herself framed against the textureless night. In this flat rendering of reality, Brother Samuel was also represented, but it struck Elsie that she was set apart, as if someone had picked her out with a spotlight.

'Wait here,' Samuel said.

'Where are you going?'

He patted her shoulder. The gesture was avuncular, but Elsie shrank from his touch. Samuel seemed not to notice. He stepped into the hall, leaving the kitchen door open a crack. The gloom of the corridor soon absorbed him.

'Mrs Sutton?' he called. 'Sister Elsie and I are needed back at the Hall.' A little lie dissolving into the darkness. 'We'll leave you with some literature.'

There came the hollow report of a closed door, then the yowl of another opening.

'Perhaps we could call again at a more convenient . . .'

The door slammed: a shattering tremolo that jarred through the house. Elsie felt her heart shudder in time to the vibrations. As they died away, her ears strained at the silence, desperate for some acoustic clue that Brother Samuel was all right. None came. Instead, there was only the ticking of the clock and the patter of snow upon the windowpane.

Cleck – cleck – cleck. Seconds regimented into minutes.

Elsie felt in her pocket for the rabbit's foot George had given her. 'If you're determined to go off with these religious lunatics, take this' – her brother had said, pressing the token into her hand – 'It'll bring you luck. And you come back to me, Elsie darling, whenever you want. You hear me, you come back . . .' She hadn't, of course. Not even when she left the Witnesses. To do so would be to admit that George was right, that only nutters believed in God. She held on tight to the charm and recited a favourite nursery rhyme.

'Georgie Porgie, puddin' and pie.'

Maybe she would go and see him soon. Just for a visit. They spoke often on the telephone but she hadn't seen her brother for six years. Blood bound them together, but God kept them apart.

'Kiss the girls . . .' Air caught in her throat. 'And made them . . .'

The kitchen door opened.

'Samuel?'

Then she heard it: a soft mewling. She gripped the rabbit's foot.

'Mrs Sutton? Please, who's there?'

The resonance of the sound increased and, at the end of each intonation, a cry gargled. It had a synaesthetic effect on Elsie. It rattled in her ear and she saw the world around her quilted in a red gauze. Disinfectant, and the smell of sterile medical equipment, burned her nostrils. Her legs parted and she seemed to feel fingers delving deep inside. She looked down, half expecting to see a face, covered with a surgical mask, smiling up at her:

Nearly done, Miss Cuttle. Nearly out.

But that was not what she saw.

It crawled across the kitchen tiles: a baby . . . of sorts. Reaching the centre of the room, it stopped, turned its head one hundred and eighty degrees and blinked up at its mother.

Elsie did not scream.

Spewed into the world half-made, the foetus displayed all the motor-functions it might have possessed had it been born the year before. There was even an air of curiosity, as it slapped the ground with a plump palm. With this movement, flecks of amniotic tissue fell from its shoulders and from the caul clinging to its head. Much of the sac membrane, however, remained fixed to the child, like strands of swaddling. Between its legs trailed a stunted umbilical cord. Snot bubbled from the slits that served as the infant's nose and threaded to the floor. Again, the mouth opened and mewling erupted over toothless gums. It called to her, this thing of her making, this creature that she had failed to destroy. It wanted its mother. It wanted to suckle.

'Shhh, shhh,' Elsie implored.

But her child would not be hushed.

'Are you hungry?'

'Ma . . . ma'

A remnant of sanity made itself felt. Elsie shot out of the chair and pressed her back against the sink. She watched as the child screamed and toppled onto its back. With a horrible snap its arms and legs inverted and it skittered, spider-like, towards its mother. Only now did Elsie see that the thing was sexless, like a doll.

'I'm sorry,' she shrieked. 'Please, I'm sorry.'

Little hands grasped her legs. With surprising force they dragged her to the ground. There was no fight in Elsie Cuttle, for this was God's judgment upon her. She allowed her skirt to be hitched above her waist and her knickers to be pulled down. Allowed her legs to be bent and parted.

'Our Father, that art in heaven. Hallowed be . . .'

Little toes spread the lips of her vagina. It was then that she heard a low, heavy rumble. She thought of stones moving against each other: yes, the mill of God had set to work at last, grinding slowly, but exceeding small.

Elsie looked down when the real pain began. Inch by laboured inch, the baby dragged itself back inside her. It wriggled and squirmed until its head filled the dilated cavity. Elsie screamed. Her stomach inflated and blood flowed between her legs. Choking on the stream, the child made one final effort. Its eyes rolled white as the unstitched plates of its cranium folded together. Then it was gone.

Elsie Cuttle held fast to George's rabbit's foot. Her dead baby kicked inside her and she was taken into the family of the millhouse.

A year later, George Cuttle came in search of his sister. In finding her, he lost himself.

Nine

Richard leafed through the deeds. The text swam and he had to blink to bring it back into focus. He stifled a yawn and pinched the corners of his eyes. Even after two days, he imagined that he could smell Susan Keele on his fingers: vanilla and sandalwood.

Away from distractions and diversions . . .

His head throbbed. He clapped a dirt-dry mouth. Sweat sprang out upon his brow and then it hit him: the thirst, pitching square into his gut. *Chink chink.* He reached into the bottom drawer of his desk and his hand closed around a bottleneck.

Away from her.

Richard sat the scotch on the desk. He had just broken the seal, when he caught sight of his reflection in the framed print of William Blake's *The Lazar House* that hung on the opposite wall. Captured inside that gothic nightmare, he hovered above the bodies of recumbent lepers, his face superimposed over that of the god-figure. He was monstrous, a blind creator indifferent to the suffering of his children, *ignorant* of their pain . . .

Richard flipped to the back of the deeds and signed his name.

At the office door, he felt something slip beneath his shoe. Cuttle's rabbit's foot. Richard picked it up and turned the talisman over in his hand. A few stray hairs adhered to the grey flesh of the charm. Richard thought of the ill-fitting clothes, the battered briefcase, the broken wristwatch. Weren't these totems supposed to be lucky? He shoved it into his pocket, called a goodbye to Miss Marchant and set off after Cuttle.

Plenty of large, middle-aged men puffed along the street, but none were in suits. Cuttle said that he had come *down* the hill. There were a limited number of car parks around the castle and cathedral. Richard set off at a jog, dodging back-packers and historical tour parties. He took the path to the castle parking lot. Arriving there breathless, he scanned the faces of the people picnicking in their cars. He was about to head off again when he saw the solicitor in the driver's seat of a G registration BMW. The car's shabby appearance reflected that of its owner – a mud-splattered licence plate, dints in the bodywork and a windscreen that served primarily as an insect graveyard.

Richard approached the window. He had half raised his hand to tap on the glass when Cuttle turned to face him.

Richard Nightingale cried out.

He saw something impossible in the lawyer's face. Something that he had buried seven months ago in the cold, hard earth of the local cemetery.

The Absence.

Two years after their marriage, when Bobby had been no more than a month old, Richard had witnessed the first signs of *The Absence* in his wife. Brief periods in which her face lost its vitality and character. Janet had been able to talk about it then, in those years before it took her completely.

'It's nothingness,' she told him. 'Absence. I don't see you or Joseph or the baby, or anything around me. I don't hear anything. But I know that I go somewhere. Somewhere I've been before, though I can't remember where it is. I go to the Shadow House.'

That was how Richard heard it, capitalized. Was that where Cuttle had gone now: to the Shadow House? Beads of saliva hung from the man's blubbery, blue-tinged lips. His face remained frozen, his eyes immobile. Richard was reminded of a great aunt who had once suffered a debilitating stroke. He had been forced to sit by her bed, his little-boy hand placed in her palm. The memory of that old woman, trapped inside her fleshy cell, still held a certain horror, undimmed by the passage of years. Mostly, he remembered her eyes – how they implored from the confines of the husk. *End it*, they had pleaded, *please God, let me be free . . .*

A cloud passed across the sun. Richard blinked. When his vision returned, he saw that Cuttle had wound down the window. The man grinned, features animated and ruddy.

'Mr Nightingale? You just caught me, I was about to head off.'

Dazed, Richard held out the deeds. The rabbit's foot sat on top of the envelope.

'Ah, my charm. Thank you. Most precious to me. And what's this? The deeds? Excellent, sir. There really was no need for your solicitor to see them. A needless expense for nothing more than a rubber-stamp. Just don't let on that I told you so, or I'll be drummed out of the Law Society. I look forward to seeing you soon, Mr Nightingale. And your boys, of course.'

Cuttle shoved the gear stick into reverse and backed out of the car park. Richard watched until the BMW passed out of sight.

Bobby's finger hovered over the mouse. He was within a click of deleting the email when the title caught his attention. It sat among a host of spam, most of it offering ways to increase both fiscal and fleshy endowments. The cursor ran over the subject and sender: Cutthroat Carnage from slasher@lincsmail.com.

It was just a coincidence. Bobby had heard how these outfits operated. Thousands of emails were sent out, some addresses bought from online companies that specialised in information trading, others generated by a random assortment of words and phrases. For every few thousand emails delivered, only one needed to spike a potential client. Then it was wine and gravy for the pimps, pirates, pornographers, pill-peddlers and plastic surgeons. This email was probably from some pseudo-snuff site claiming to have real pictures of genocide and torture victims. Just because the title touched upon something in Bobby's life didn't mean squat . . .

But what the hell.

He opened the mail. There was no text in the body of the message, just a winking smiley. Again, Bobby was about to delete when he noticed the attachment. He scanned the file and, finding it virus free, started the download. Within seconds another page opened, this time displaying a picture of a door. Bobby recognised it as the entrance to the boys' changing room at school. The file must have been programmed in a graphics interchange format because, a second later, the picture became animated. The doors swung back in stilted frame jumps. Meanwhile a funeral march, picked out on a keyboard synthesiser, buzzed through the computer speakers. The scene opened onto the familiar locker room. The music faded and Bobby felt his heart steady.

Screams shrieked through the speakers.

Bobby toppled over the back of his chair. Picking himself up, he saw that Matthew Linton had appeared onscreen. Matt stood in the foreground, a two dimensional image plastered onto the Photoshopped backdrop. He was smiling his sheepish smile, hair falling over his eyes. The photograph used - a school portrait - must have been taken at least two years ago: the bone structure of the face was not as developed as it had been when Matt died. Also, he was wearing the Warhammer lapel badge that Bobby had made him: the imperial aquila emblem – an eagle with two heads – attached to a square of card. Matt hadn't worn the badge since Bobby had called time on their friendship.

Matt's mouth fell open like one of those illustrations from an old Monty Python episode. Bobby was about to mute the screams when the animation kicked in again. A cut-throat razor appeared out of frame and flicked open. It slashed a path across the screen before entering the mock-up of the locker room. Matt, grin fixed, eyes downcast, watched the progress of the cartoon blade as it sliced across his throat. Rills of stiff, pixilated blood spilled down the screen. They hit the base of the picture and formed into words.

SUICIDE IS PAINLESS!!!

These, in turn, reformed into:

WHY DIDN'T YOU SAVE ME, BOBBY???

The question flashed, growing larger and larger as the scream pitched ever higher.

Bobby wrenched the plug out of the PC tower. The screen blipped to black. In the dark mirror-image of the room, Bobby saw himself, white and trembling.

Ten

Sam had been right: the death of one of its pupils had not deterred the school from holding its Upper Sixth Prom. Indeed, the tragedy seemed to have added a frisson of excitement to the evening. Even among those teachers supervising the event, the chatter was all about the late Matthew Linton.

'Told you,' Sam sighed, 'our school: a taste free zone. So, you ready to show me those moves?'

She dragged Joe onto the dance floor. Slung from a rig high in the roof of the gymnasium, a mirrorball dusted light across the dancers. Most of them moved in self-conscious patterns, while a select few demonstrated some natural rhythm.

Joe held her close. She had received a few bitchy comments from traditionally pretty contemporaries, but such remarks only went to show how stunning she looked. Further evidence of her allure, and the surprise it generated, was not hard to find. As Joe guided Sam around the floor, boys, who in the course of a normal school day wouldn't have given her a second glance, stopped and stared. Chat-up lines were left hanging, jokes robbed of their punchlines. Joe smiled and took in the scent of her hair. Their fingers interlaced. He had loosened his tie and her breath tingled against the exposed skin of his collarbone. She stretched to meet him and their lips brushed against each other. It was a stimulating, teasing gesture, both a promise and a prelude. Her toes on pointe, she leaned in and whispered,

'Nice moves.'

The boy toked deep. The infusion of pot did little to relieve his nerves. His fingers hovered over the keys, as if he hoped that, by their proximity to the potential letters and digits of the password, they would be guided to input the correct combination. The cursor flashed inside the box:

ADDRESS [slasher@lincsmail.com]
PASSWORD [_]

It was useless.

He returned to his own inbox, reopened the email and downloaded the file again. This time he ticked the mute option on the volume display. Taking deep breaths through his nose, Bobby clicked the mouse. The gif played. Matt Linton's suicide sprang into animated action.

Bobby had spent the last few hours scouring the internet in an attempt to hack the sender's emails. Although it was possible that the account had been set up for the sole purpose of sending the gif, it may be that other messages were stored there. If so, they might contain a clue as to the identity of the hoaxer. His efforts at circumnavigating the security passwords of the system had been fumbling at best. Bobby knew only one person with the nous to achieve what he was attempting. The picture of that person haunted the screen in front of him.

Bobby thought over what he knew. Whoever had sent the email *had* to be from school. He had checked the 2004 Year Book and found the photo that corresponded with the one used in the gif. There were about a dozen people who would be both technically adept and sick enough to perpetrate the prank. Of those, ten were in Bobby's immediate circle: that group which he had courted after dumping Matt. He thought of them now – a bunch of dopeheads and skanks, not one among them would have been fit to lick the dirt off Matt Linton's boot.

Stubbing out the joint, Bobby watched the gif repeat. In any other circumstances, he figured, Kelvin Hope would be suspect number one. If he hadn't mentally tortured Matt for all those months then, sure, Kelvin would find it hilarious to put together this sort of twisted amusement. But his contribution to the death, and his fear of police involvement, made that unlikely. Kelvin wanted Bobby to keep his mouth shut. Baiting him like this could only put that silence in jeopardy. So who else could have sent it?

Footsteps sounded in the corridor. Bobby threw the Coke-can-cum-ashtray out of the window and switched off the computer. He spent the next few seconds wafting the curtains and flapping his arms.

A tap at the door.

'Just a sec. Okay, yeah?'

Richard Nightingale stepped inside. His gaze swept the room.

'You been smoking?' he asked.

'You been drinking?'

'What?'

'Come off it, Dad,' Bobby said, letting the words spill out. 'Do you think me and Joe are complete 'tards? Just because we don't *care* doesn't mean we don't *know*.'

Richard's eyes glimmered in the light from the hall. His body stiffened, as if the blood pumping through his limbs had cooled like tempered steel. If Bobby didn't know better he could have sworn he had hurt his dad's feelings. But that was impossible – the Old Man didn't have feelings.

'I've got some news,' Richard said at last. 'Someone's left us a bit of property. A relative of your mother's. Distant aunt or something. It's a house, down by the Wash.'

Bobby shrugged. He turned back to the monitor and rebooted the computer. The boy could feel his dad moving into the room, could see his shadow grow large across the wall. It passed over a few pieces of Bobby's recent artwork: paintings, abstracts and collages, nudes and landscapes, which his gallery-owner father had never thought worthy of comment. Only his late mother had encouraged Bobby with his art.

Bobby twisted round in his chair. He found his father standing directly behind him. Some expression, halfway between shock and guilt, lengthened Richard's face. It took a moment for the man to master himself.

'I thought . . . Well, maybe we could go down there for a few weeks. Me, you and Joe. It – it could be fun.'

'Fun? Right, because it's usually a laugh a minute when us three get together.'

'Bobby . . .'

'I know. You're trying. I just don't know *what* you're trying.'

'I thought you might want a break. You know, from what's happened. Space to get your head together. It was a big shock, finding that kid the way you did.'

'So this is for me, is it?'

'We all need some time.'

'What was his name?'

'I'm sorry?'

'The kid. My friend that died. Your getaway idea is for my benefit, so you must have thought it through. Yeah, you must've thought long and hard about what I'm thinking and feeling right now. So go on, what was his name?'

'I don't . . . Look, Bobby, I just thought a change of scene . . .'

'Matt. Matt Linton. His folks came round today and asked me to read something at his funeral.'

'That's a nice idea.'

'Is it?'

Father and son contemplated the floor space between them. Bobby took the time to weigh up the suggestion. A few weeks in the countryside, away from those familiar places that dredged up memories. Away from this room, in which he and Matt had played and fumbled their way towards adulthood. A little distance from the spectre of Kelvin Hope.

'Okay,' Bobby muttered, 'why not?'

'You're sure?'

'Weeks stuck alone together. I wonder who'll go crazy first. Yep, could be interesting.'

'Good. There'll be work to do,' Richard said, his voice artificially light. 'The place needs a bit of renovation. I thought we could work on it as a team. Like a project.'

'A "team"? Sounds "fun".'

Again, Bobby felt a strange twist of emotions: the urge to punish his dad and the guilt that knotted his stomach when he did so. He watched his father move over to the square of Bristol paper taped to the drawing board. Richard's eyes played across the sketch: tatters of mist caught between the fingers of trees; a sea of dark waves breaking through the shore and flooding the land; a trio of birds frozen against the bulk of a reaching shadow.

'What is it?'

'I don't know yet,' Bobby said. There was a trace of hope in the kid's voice. He joined his father at the board.

'Get a clear idea before you go on,' Richard said. 'It might be okay, but you're just groping in the dark at the moment. And the birds are out of perspective with the house.'

The door closed behind Richard Nightingale.

Bobby stared at the drawing, seeking out imperfections that were not there. Convinced of them, he did not hesitate. He took a craft knife and slashed the vellum surface of the board. A moment later, the work was reduced to tongues of grey pencil strokes; strips of something strange and beautiful, terminated in its infancy.

Bobby held the knife up to the light. The fresh blade glinted, reflecting the capillaries of his eye. The eye grew large in the lethal mirror until all that was represented there was the black of pupil. Bobby's hand shook. His lashes brushed the thin, surgical edge of the knife. A movement was all it would take. One twitch of his wrist and the tip would puncture jelly. Then, with syrupy ease, it would slide home into the warmth of the socket.

An eye for an eye.

All he had to do was push . . .

Eleven

Teeth colliding, they parted, and laughed at a moment of shared clumsiness. Then the hunger took hold and they came together again. This time Joe did not close his eyes. She was so close he could make out the beauty in her flaws. In the little pits that peppered her cheeks, in the scars left by pimples, he saw perfection. Of course, he would never tell her this. It would be impossible to make her believe that he loved her scatty, wire-brush hair and crooked teeth. That – honest to God – he cherished every so-called blemish and inadequacy as much as he loved that creamy-white complexion and those full curves.

Sam laid a hand on his collar and gave him a playful shove. Through jewelled lips, she told him to slide back his seat. Joe watched the undulations of her body as she hitched up the hem of her skirt. His dick grew hard.

'This isn't date six,' he croaked.

'Shut up.'

'Yes, ma'am.'

Sam wriggled across the gear stick and straddled Joe's lap. He held her above the hips, steadying her. She guided his hands to the straps at her neck and they laughed again as he fumbled with the ties. The dress fell away.

'You're beautiful. God, you're so beautiful.'

In the silence afforded by the glade, Joe sat, neither touching nor breathing. His eyes roamed across her nakedness and luxuriated in every detail.

They had parked off the main road, in a spot shielded behind a wall of trees. Moonlight, caught in the teeth of aspens, swayed across Sam's body. Joe laid his head against her breasts. He listened to her heart, feeling the beat of his own fall into step. With the tips of his fingers, he caressed her nipples. They grew hard and tight. He pulled her to him and suckled. She gasped. Shuddered. His hands slid down the small of her back and slipped inside the band of her knickers.

'Jesus God, you're so beautiful.'

He felt her dampness. She arched back, head resting against the windscreen. Rain brattled the roof of the car. It ran behind her, the moonlight turning the droplets into a hail of stars. Her mouth parted. A ribbon of saliva stretched between her teeth. Joe's dick ached against his trousers, but right now he wanted pleasure only for her. His middle finger reached inside her while the ball of his thumb pressed down on her clit. That little pebble swelled under his touch. She took a few short, hard breaths through the nose.

Joe smiled . . . glanced down . . .

Froze.

Her phone. It must have dropped out of her bag. Asserting its connection, the Nokia glowed, lighting up the cavern of the footwell. Without thinking, Joe reached for it. His movement jarred Sam into the glove compartment. Startled, she asked what he was doing, but her voice was lost to him. That simple prompt – a mobile lying discarded – acted like a spark in a forest of dead wood. Flames skipped across his mind, igniting images, sounds and smells, until he was drawn back into the full horror of the memory.

He saw himself, body twisted, slouched semi-conscious in the Spitfire's driver seat. The car was a wreck but, all things considered, the boy behind the wheel had come off worse. The impact had snapped his seatbelt and thrust him forward. Poleaxed by the steering wheel, he looked around groggily. One eye, fat with blood, rolled up into his head. Nose broken, lips torn, drool and mucus dribbled down his chin. His left hand flailed at his feet. He was reaching for something.

The mobile. Imprisoned behind the brake and accelerator, it glimmered in his sights. He strained to reach it. Even now, lost in the memory, Joe felt exhaustion and desperation fight for supremacy. Red-flecked saliva burst from his lips and he tasted an iron tang. Maybe he was bleeding internally. Visions of impacted organs, lodged in foreign parts, filled his mind. He saw his heart skewered upon a spear of bone and his lungs, crushed and sagging through his ribs like deflated beach balls. These images cried out for his attention while the air caught in his throat. He felt cold. Tired.

All at once, the darkness took him.

A surge of panic – and the smell of petrol – brought him round. Had to stay awake. Must call for help.

The trees muffled everything on this stretch of road. No-one would have heard the crash and, at this hour, few cars used the lane. He must reach the phone or he would lie here until someone happened to pass by. He pitched forward.

Pain ratcheted through his shoulder and gripped his stomach. Spasms convulsed his arm. Managing to turn his head, Joe saw the source of his agony and screamed. A metal grapnel, sheared from some part of the car, had imbedded itself at the joint between arm and shoulder. Rusty barbs flowered out of the wound. Joe pinched the shrapnel between forefinger and thumb. If he could remove it then he might move a little freer. Sweat lathered his face and stung his eyes. Here goes. He tugged.

Flesh and cartilage tore away from bone. Screams exploded from the boy's mouth. Through the fractured windscreen, he saw birds spiral out of the trees and climb in tight, panicked circles. They passed across the sky like smoke signals warning of danger.

'Joe? Joe are – are you there?'

'Mum?'

He had forgotten all about her. The wound gaped as he tried to turn.

'Don't look, darling.'

'Mum, you'll be okay. We're going to be okay.'

'Silly boy.'

He strained to see her. Through a mist of tears, he could make out the hazy outline of his mother. She . . .

Terror raked along Joe's spine.

She *glinted*.

At first, he couldn't understand what he saw. Then, slowly, he started to put together what must have happened: after missing the felled tree, they had careered across the road and toppled down the siding. Strange, but he had not realised until then that the car, though upright, was pitched onto its side. The nearside of the vehicle was lifted, as if the wheels rested on a bank, while the offside had slid into the undergrowth.

Glinted . . .

Caught by the moonlight, a strange carnival of light danced around his mother's head. It must have happened when the car left the road. The crystal ball, bought for his sweetheart and nursed, at his insistence, in his mother's lap, had been pitched directly into her face. It had shattered there, puncturing her with a hundred razor-sharp slivers.

'Mum? Mum, oh, God. *Oh, Jesus Chriiiist.*'

'Shhh, Joe.'

Some of the splinters worked deeper as she spoke. Others fell away, leaving thin, pouting wounds.

'Move on,' she murmured. 'Move on from this. Don't ever st-stay still, Joe. Promise.'

Shudders wracked her body. Her long, beautiful hair fell across her face. Needles of glass poked through the curtain, but her eyes had been veiled. Crying against the pain, Joe jolted forward.

The grapnel's metal spikes ground into his shoulder. His head felt light and a fit of giggles smothered his airway. Laughter roared through him. It was all so fucking stupid. She was dying and he was pissing about like some little cry baby. He had to help her. Had to reach the phone. He stretched . . . Blood made his hands slippery but, at the third attempt, he snatched the Nokia from behind the pedals. He brought up the first number he could think of and pressed dial.

'We're gonna be okay, Mum,' Joe laughed.

The interior of the car began to fall away again. He slumped back into the seat. Desperate to see her before the darkness took him, he turned.

'I love you,' he whispered.

Her head canted in an odd mechanical jerk. The hair fell back from her face. Later, he would remember what he saw as a dream: a hallucination brought on by the pain. The woman before him was still alive, but his mother was gone. Nothing moved behind the eyes that fixed upon him. No emotion stirred her features. It was as though something alien, without possessing the finesse with which to articulate her form, had taken control. She looked at him as if he were a stranger.

Joe's vision blurred. He heard someone pick up the phone.

'Hello?'

'Dad.'

'Joe? Where are you? What's the matter? Talk to me.'

'The woods. Dad, it's Mum. She's . . .'

The creature opposite smiled, her mouth thick with blood and glass.

'Dad . . . Please . . . *Who is she*?'

The thing put its fingers to its face – a scarlet, dripping face that *glinted* in the moonlight. It toyed with each splinter, working them ever deeper, through skin and muscle, straight down to bone. Its mouth fell open and a stream of dark sputum poured over its teeth and dribbled down its chin.

Joe cried out and the strength left him. His head cracked against the driver window. He could hear his dad shouting questions down the phone, but the mobile in his hand was so very heavy. He dropped it into his lap.

'Who are you?' he asked.

'I am . . . *rebegot* . . .' As if spoken from the depths of a well, the voice echoed, its locutions dripping and toneless. 'I am absence, darkness, death: things which are not.'

Joe's vision tunnelled. In the pinpoint focus of his perception he kept the stranger in view. Even as the shadows threatened to swallow her, he watched the thing that occupied his mother's shape.

'Her body's broken, Joe. Her heart is slowing. She's coming home. Soon enough you will join her. Soon you'll play with us in the shadows for ever and ever.'

The thing that was not his mother held a finger to his mouth. It probed his lips and forced his teeth apart. Joe tasted mother-blood, warm upon his tongue.

'Taste the shadows, Joseph Nightingale.'

'What is it? What's the matter?' Sam reached out and Joe pushed her away. 'Joe?'

'I don't want this. I can't. Please.'

He waited until she slid over into the driver's seat. Then he opened the passenger door.

'My house isn't far,' he said, 'I can walk from here.'

'Okay.' Sam sounded panicked. 'It's my fault, I know. I was pushing you and . . .'

Joe looked up at the moon, hanging like a glass ball in the sky.

'I don't deserve this.'

He slammed the door. The sound echoed like a gunshot in the darkness.

Twelve

Chink chink

Richard swilled the Tennessee malt around his mouth. He tried to savour the blend of maple and liquorice, but it drained through him like ice water. In an attempt to divert his mind from the chills, he tried to read the Will through the bottom of his glass. Words trembled, at once magnified and distorted:

'I, Muriel Elizabeth Sutton, being of sound mind and body, hereby leave the property known as Daecher's Mill, Yallery Lower Field, Potter's Drake, to Mrs Janet Nightingale, in consideration of the family bonds that tie me to her and her children, Joseph and Robert. Mrs Nightingale may dispose of the mill as she sees fit, but I should like the family to visit the property at least once. It has been a home to their forebears, and so it seems only right that Joseph and Robert should see the old place. It would give me great . . .' Here the writing became practically indecipherable. Richard squinted. Surely the word was 'pleasure'. '*. . . to think of the Nightingales housed within these walls.'*

During their telephone conversation, Cuttle had confessed that the Will was somewhat curious. Clearly, Muriel Sutton had possessed no knowledge of how to draw up a legal document, and had allowed sentiment to run away with her. Despite this, Cuttle confirmed that the legacy was enforceable, especially as there were no other living relatives to contest it. Something about those names, 'Sutton' and 'Potter's Drake', seemed familiar to him, but Richard could not pinpoint why.

In one long swill, Richard finished the glass. His hand went to the bottle, but found only dregs remaining. There was more upstairs, of course, hidden in that place he had believed secret and safe. Why not just toddle up there and get it? Why not bring down every last bottle? He could sit here and drink the sound of Bobby's words away.

You been drinking? The smirk. That knowing, fucking smirk. *Just because we don't* care *doesn't mean we don't* know.

Richard saw himself back in Bobby's room. The boy had turned away, his body language contemptuous. Shame stoking his anger, Richard had approached his son, fists clenched. He reached the boy and stopped short, wondering at the violence that pulsed through him. He'd never once laid a hand on the kids, but now he wanted to inflict some real pain. The pain *he* felt every day of his life. He imagined striking Bobby, drawing blood, but it did not stop there. He would beat the kid to the ground, and go on beating. Only the satisfying crack of bone would stop him. While these images raced through his mind, one thought continued to scream at Richard Nightingale: *They know. They've known for a long time. And they've been laughing at you, Richard. Both of them. They're their mother's children all right. They have no emotion in them, no understanding, no pity. They're monsters, just like her . . .*

And then he had seen the drawing. An elegant, soulful sketch, it was the most accomplished thing Bobby had ever produced. The purveyor of art had been moved by it, the father, reassured. Only an artist with a finely tuned and textured emotional intelligence could have executed it. Even now, after some reflection, Richard could not say why the piece had so affected him. Pride perhaps? Yet surely it was something more than that. He had sensed empathy in the drawing, a natural harmony between artist and subject. Those had not been mere sketches of birds, but considered studies. The fluidity of their movements, even that strange avian telepathy had been captured. Justice had been done to the trees, too, for in the flow of their lines and the shading of their torsos, immense age and authority had been communicated. Only the house looked incongruous. Sitting in the foreground, it was made up of shadows and ill-defined proportions. Compared to the accuracy of vision displayed elsewhere, it struck Richard as a blur of artificiality. That aside, the piece was breathtaking; easily better than any of the local art displayed in the Nightingale gallery. Richard wondered why he hadn't told Bobby so.

'Dad? What are you doing?'

Richard looked up to find Joe standing at the end of the table.

'Hello, son,' Richard slurred. 'You have a good time?'

'It was okay. What's the matter with you? Are you cold?'

Joe cared. *His son cared.*

'No. I'm just . . .' Richard dropped his glass. 'Fuck it . . . Listen, Joe, come here a minute, will you?' He pulled out the chair next to his. Joe didn't move. 'I just want to talk to you.'

'What about?'

'Anything. Whatever you like. This new girlfriend of yours. She came round the other day. Picked up your suit.'

'Look, I don't want to talk about . . .'

'She seems nice. What's her name?'

'Sam. Samantha.'

'Really? I used to go out with a girl called Samantha. Before I met your mum, of course.'

'Course.'

'What the fuck do you mean by that?' Richard saw how

his son shrank from him. 'I'm sorry. I just meant . . .'

'I'm going to bed.'

'Wait. I've got something to tell you. Bobby and me, we've talked it through.'

Richard told Joe about his meeting with Mr Cuttle and of Muriel Sutton's bequest. The only part he omitted was his later encounter with Cuttle in the Castle car park. He had, in any case, convinced himself that his mind had been playing tricks: the lawyer's blank expression had been nothing like *The Absence*. Perhaps the heat had affected him, or maybe it was the shadows of recent dreams breaking into the waking world. Anyway, describing such a thing to Joe could only lead to awkward questions.

'We were thinking of going down there. Maybe next week or the week after. Whenever that poor kid's been buried,' Richard concluded.

'And Bobby agreed?'

'Yes. So what do you think?'

'Why are you doing this?'

His real motive made Richard waspish. 'Do I have to get the third degree every time I suggest something? S'jus' an idea.'

'But that's what's odd. Jesus, dad, we're not the Brady Bunch. We're not even the Manson family, at least they did stuff together.'

'Jus' an idea,' Richard repeated.

'Why? Why now?'

'For Christ's sake.'

Richard's voice dipped to a mumble. The thirst prickled his tongue. He wanted to go upstairs and lose himself in a bottle. He wanted to be far away from this boy and his questions.

'I want to understand,' Joe said. 'Is this something to do with what's happened to Bobby? Is it just a jolly getaway, because that's what normal families do and, for once, it'd be nice to be normal? Or is it about me?' Joe took the seat beside his father. 'Is it about what I did? About Mum?'

'Fucking hell, Joe, it's a holiday. We're going on fucking holiday. Does there have to be a reason? I'm fucked up, you're fucked up, Bobby's fucked up, and all us fucked up people are going away. That's it. Okay?'

'Okay.'

'And now, as it's what's expected of me, I'm going upstairs to get pissed. That all right with you?'

Richard did not wait for an answer.

Joe tapped on Bobby's door and entered. The room was its usual contrast to Joe's: neat and ordered, though there was, as ever, an atmosphere redolent of unwashed socks.

'Hey. So what do you think about this trip idea of dad's . . .' Joe caught sight of his brother. 'Christ, Bobby, what happened?'

Bobby held a wad of cotton wool, saturated with blood, to his eye. Spots of red blemished his T-shirt and his fingers were stained pink.

'It's nothing,' said Bobby, 'just nicked my eyelid. I was doing some close-up work with the craft knife and it slipped.'

'Bloody hell, you could've blinded yourself. Here, let me take a look.'

Joe stood over his brother and reached for the cotton wool.

'Leave it, Florence Nightingale,' Bobby said. Then, when Joe persisted in trying to see the damage, his tone hardened. 'I said leave it. Can't you just mind your own business for once?'

'Fine. I'll leave you to bleed to death.'

'Yeah, you're good at that.'

For a split second, Joe thought that he would hit his

brother.

'You twisted little bastard,' he muttered.

'I didn't mean that. I'm sorry.'

Joe shrugged off the hand that tugged at his shirtsleeve.

'I just don't know why you say those things, Bobby. What have I ever done to you?'

The question remained unanswered and Joe was glad of it. He tried to look Bobby in the eye and found that he couldn't. Exhaustion rippled through him though he knew, when he laid his head on the pillow, sleep would not come. For a while the anti-depressants and sleeping tablets had numbed the pain of fevered thoughts, but when, at his father's insistence, the counselling had been brought to an end, the drugs had stopped. Now he lay awake through the long nights, aching for sleep. Tonight would be no different. Instead of dreams, new concerns would torment him: why had he pulled away from Sam? Why had his dad started drinking openly? What was with this family holiday idea, and why had Bobby agreed to it? And, finally, was Bobby okay? The kid hadn't been right since the death of the Linton boy. Although, in truth, no-one in this house had been 'right' for a long time.

'What's this?' Joe asked. He picked up the remains of Bobby's sketch.

'Just a piece I was working on. Started out well, but I fucked it up.'

Joe nodded and went to the door.

'Hey, you know I'm sorry, don't you?'

'Sure, Bobby.'

Bobby removed the cotton wool from his eye. A scarlet tear trickled down his cheek.

'You don't sound convinced.'

'I'm tired.'

'Okay. Oh, hey, how'd it go with Sam by the way?'

'Like your picture,' Joe said, managing a tight smile. 'Started out well, but I fucked it up.'

Thirteen

It had been over a fortnight since Matt Linton's death, and now the crows had gathered. That was how Joe saw them, with their heads bent and their black coats flapping in the breeze. He imagined harsh caws rising out of their throats, pictured them jostling for space in which to peck and tear. He wasn't sure why this image should occur to him, it seemed a heartless simile in the face of such grief. Even from the cemetery gate, he could hear some of the mourners sobbing.

It was a large assembly. Tragic death always brings out the crowds, Joe thought, but the death of a child by its own hand? That really packed 'em in. They came to satisfy curiosity, to express their grief, to find answers. But Joe knew that there were no answers here, just a wound that wept long after the grave had been filled in. All the wailing in the world could do nothing to stem the flow of that lesion. Instead, it ulcerated, the pain of it a constant reminder: you did not see, you did not listen. Each person who knew Matthew Linton would take a share of that wound, some overburdening themselves, others shirking their true portion. Joe wondered what share would be borne by his brother.

Bobby and Richard were standing among the first line of mourners. Joe watched them from just inside the gate. It had taken all his nerve to step over the threshold. Thank God the day was stifling; no-one noticed how much he perspired. What they might have *felt,* had he gone down to the graveside and stood shoulder-to-shoulder with them, was the trembling. Nothing would have been said, of course, but afterwards, at the wake, questions may have been asked:

Did you notice the Nightingale boy? The older one? Is he ill, do you think?

Not physically, no. I did hear that he was 'cared for' after that dreadful accident.

'Cared for'?

Mentally. Pills and evaluations and the like. His father put a stop to it. Heaven knows why, the child is obviously still unwell.

Does he ever visit the grave? Yes, it's that untidy little stone in the south-east corner. The letters are fading already, you know, and the weeds! *It's heartbreaking. Still, I suppose he can't bring himself to face it.*

Even at this distance, Joe could pick out his mother's stone. It blinked in the afternoon sun, like a beacon warning of treacherous waters. Joe slipped back through the gate and headed for his father's car. He got into the passenger seat and turned on the radio. On one of the local stations a discussion was just beginning about the problems of housing being built on the Lincolnshire flood plains. Joe found himself half-listening to the argument between a farmer and a representative from the Environment Agency ('the water's gotta go somewhere, Mister, and you mark my words as a Fenman: t'will end up where you least except it. Water finds its path and won't be denied forever. Those wi' no respect for it end up sacrificing more'n most'). His gaze passed across the shrubs that fringed the brow of the hill and moved down into the cemetery below. He could see movement among the congregation.

Bobby had taken his place at the head of the grave.

Most of the faces remained downcast, but a few looked straight in his direction. There was sympathy in their eyes and twists of encouragement in their sad smiles. From behind his sun-glasses, Bobby stole a glance at Mrs Linton. Christ, was the woman ever going to shut up? She'd asked him to speak, the least she could do was give the caterwauling a rest for a minute. As if the bitterness of his thoughts had produced some tele-pathic connection, Diane Linton choked back her sobs. Her husband, perhaps grateful for the respite, hugged her to his chest. He nodded at Bobby.

The bullet points on the scrap of paper had seemed feeble before. Now that he had to compose a eulogy from them they stood out as nakedly insincere. Two weeks had passed since the Lintons' invitation. Two weeks in which he had done every-thing to avoid addressing what Matt truly meant to him. Weed had blurred the hours and facilitated snatches of sleep. When a spliff was not to hand he pushed pen and paper aside and tried to hack the emails of his mystery tormentor. Two further gifs had arrived since the original, both variations on the same theme. The first had been set in a crowded classroom; the second, received this morning, was located here, in the cem-etery. Indeed, the photograph of Matt had been layered onto the spot where Bobby now stood.

And this time Matt Linton had spoken:

You killed me, Bobby. You killed me, Bobby. You killed me, Bobby.

A haltering, computer-generated voice.

Bobby screwed up his notes.

'Matt was my friend. We'd been friends since primary school and he . . .'

Light flashed across Bobby's face. In the relative darkness below, the coffin's silver nameplate dazzled. *Matthew Linton. Born 12th August 1991. Died . . .* Dirt obscured the date. A polite, priestly cough signalled for Bobby to continue. He did not heed it.

Something in the pit had caught his attention. He looked down into the open grave and listened to the sound of knuckles upon wood. *Thump-thump-thump*. Bobby's hands trembled and he dropped his notes. The sheet of paper fluttered into the darkness, like a white bird consumed by the night. And then that same darkness moved. Strands of shadow reached out from the trench and drew his eye. It was cool down there, in the embrace of the earth. Away from the glare, the heat and the staring eyes, Bobby might rest easy. All it would take was a flick of the craft knife. Just a touch more courage and it would be over. Had it hurt, he wondered, the tearing of the razor? No, the knocking insisted, it was just a bright stab of pain followed by . . . oblivion.

'Matt was my friend.'

Disturbed by the knocking – louder now, as the sides of fists pounded against the coffintop – soil crumbled from the walls of the hollow. The earth fell upon the lid and danced.

Coughs. Murmurs. Shuffling feet. Bobby heard nothing, only that *clunk-clunk, clunk-clunk, clunk-clunk*.

'Matt was my friend.'

His words drowned in the pit. The long screws around the edges of the casket began to turn.

'We played together.'

The screws span, dropped and rolled across the lid. Wood splintered. The coffin burst open.

'My best friend.'

A dead face, bolstered with chemical preservatives, glowed waxy in the gloom. The arrangement of the features into a natural expression had been approximated from photographs. It was crudely done, skin pulled and prodded until the mortician had called it a day. Matt had never smiled like that. He looked grotesque, the slouch of his lips suggesting brain damage. A new suit hid the Y-cut of the post mortem and a high-collar shirt disguised the fatal wound.

'Matt loved life.'

Matt's eyes snapped open. He stared up at his betrayer, his Judas. Bobby, in his turn, glanced at the faces around him. None of them seemed to have noticed that the boy they had come to mourn had reawakened beneath their feet. Mr Linton's eyes were closed as he dreamed his dreams of pain and solace. Mrs Linton sobbed on while her baby boy writhed in his casket. And now Matt's hands were reaching for his throat, tearing the collar aside. His fingers trembled as he traced the pout of the wound. Pain – or the memory of pain – made him grimace. His spine arched and the heels of his highly-polished shoes rattled against the coffin bottom. Frantic now, his fingernails slipped beneath those ragged lips of flesh and tore the stitches apart.

'It's not my fault,' Bobby hollered. 'None of it. It's not my fault, you stupid little . . .'

Matt chuckled, his tones thickened by the preservative fluid that pumped through his body. His voice whistled out of the gash in his throat.

'I'll find you, Bobby. I promise.' His words echoed into the living world. The cemetery birds cawed against them and took flight. 'When the shadows come, when the wheel turns, I'll find you. In the dark, I'll take your hand and we'll be together. I'll find you in the Shadow House . . .'

Fourteen

A hand shook the boy. Bobby focused on his father. Then his gaze swept around the circle of startled faces. Looking back into the grave, he saw the coffin, its lid closed and the soil undisturbed.

'Bobby, what the hell?' Richard whispered.

Bobby broke away from the group. He sped through a sea of black and didn't stop until he had crested the hill. Short of breath, he rested against the iron bars of the gate. Back at the graveside, order had been restored and the vicar had resumed reading the last rites. Meanwhile, Richard Nightingale was cutting a path through the crowd. Bobby wanted to run but his legs wouldn't carry him.

Richard reached his son and took hold of him by the shoulders. 'Look at me. What was that about?'

What did he mean? Bobby wondered. And why were all those people staring at him? He had read his eulogy and then walked away. So he needed some air, what was the big deal?

'Don't understand.'

'You don't understand? You don't understand that you just garbled a load of nonsense? That you insulted those poor people? Christ, son, are you on drugs or something?'

'The fuck do you care?' Confusion and fear sparked Bobby's resentment. 'Just go do what you do best. Turn up to the wake, drink the free booze and pass out. You didn't even let me come here for mum's funeral. Don't pretend you care now.'

Richard caught hold of Bobby and slammed him against the gate.

'Watch your filthy little mouth. You push and push – one day someone'll push back.'

Faces turned towards them. Under their scrutiny, Richard released his son. He wiped his mouth with a shaking hand and turned back down the hill.

Bobby burned. He lifted his eyes and watched his father stride away. They called him 'the Old Man' but, to his children, Richard Nightingale had never seemed old. Indeed, compared to Harold Linton, grey and freshly weathered by his grief, Richard appeared positively youthful. But now Bobby noticed a marked weariness in the way his father walked. The sight roused something like pity in the boy's heart but it didn't last long. A thought occurred to him that renewed his contempt. Whereas Mr Linton was breaking under the weight of his loss there had been no such effect on Richard after the accident. His wife had died – been mangled to a pulp – and he hadn't given a toss. That was the truth behind the bastard. All these plans for family bonding, all this pretence at caring, was common or garden bullshit. It was nothing more than a show to make the Old Man feel like a normal human being.

'A normal human being.' Could Bobby claim that he belonged to that category? He didn't think so. He was just a self-centered little arsehole, whose eulogy to a lifelong friend had passed by in a blur of weed-induced incoherence. Someone who couldn't remember how, just five minutes ago, he seemed to have offended the entire funeral party.

Beyond where his father commiserated with the Lintons, Bobby saw the white stone of his mother's grave. He visited every so often, sponging away the bird crap and pulling the odd weed. He couldn't say why he did these things. To his mind, all that lay six feet below was a casket filled with rotting meat. Yet still he visited. Duty, he supposed. Maybe it was a similar sense of duty that brought the little girl here. She picked her way between the graves, a tiny figure, surely no older than ten. Despite the heat, she wore a red rubber raincoat with the hood pulled up. The kid's affectation made Bobby smile.

What happened next wiped the smile from his face.

The girl stopped beside his mother's plot and dropped to her knees. The action, so sudden and unexpected, drew a cry from Bobby's lips. It was a puling sound and he looked around to see if anyone had heard. None of the mourners filing through the gate paid him the least attention. His eyes wandered back down the hill.

The child was still there, motionless on the ground, back to Bobby, legs tucked beneath her. A heat haze trembled around her little body, as if the summer sun was cooking her alive. She remained very still, perhaps reading the inscription. Then her arms shot into the air. The pointed tip of her hood dropped back as she stared up into the sky. Her face remained hidden and, though he could not say why, Bobby felt glad.

Her hands began to claw at the air. It was a strange, scrabbling motion, as if the child was attempting to scale an invisible cliff face. Her arms pumped and her head thrashed to and fro. From the way her limbs jarred, Bobby got the impression that, at one time, her arms had been broken and improperly reset.

The flailing ceased. The girl's head turned to the east.

Bobby hadn't noticed the rain clouds. They swept in and blotted out the sun. A veil of darkness drew across the graveyard. The change was so sudden that decorum was forgotten. The crowds quickened their stately pace and bustled out of the cemetery. Harold and Diane Linton hurried past without giving Bobby a second glance. The snub went unnoticed. Bobby could not drag his eyes away from the child. She sat in the gathering gloom, inanimate once more, her shadow draped across the tombstone. Bobby wanted to go down there; to tell her that this was his mother's grave and to ask what she was doing. He yearned to go, and yet the very thought of descending the hill terrified him. He saw his hands reaching out for the hood and snatching it away from the child's head. What lay beneath was *not* a child. Instead, he had revealed something fluidic and black, running in the bowl of the hood. Something that chuckled like a stream.

No, he would not go down into the cemetery.

Rain spat into Bobby's eyes. Engines started and cars roared away. He was being left alone with . . .

'Tid . . . Tid . . .' The word formed in his mouth but the last syllable would not pass his lips.

Bobby's attention remained fixed on the nameless figure in the red coat. And, as he watched, its head began to turn towards him . . .

Kelvin Hope slapped Bobby's face.

'Heard you gave one shitty speech, Bobby-boy.'

Bobby looked back down the hill. The little girl was gone.

'What – what do you want?'

'Just checking in. Hoping you've remembered our deal.'

'I haven't said anything, have I?'

'You don't want to take that tone with me, kiddo. I know you haven't said anything, otherwise you wouldn't be so pretty about now.'

'You been sending me emails?'

'What the fuck?'

'Shit over the internet. Stupid little cartoons. If you're trying to scare me . . .'

'Yeah, that's what I've been doing with my free time: thinking of ways to shit you up. I want to scare you, buddy, I don't need a computer to do it. Anyway, why would I want to? Not in my interests. The only thing I want is for you to forget that little queer they just buried. And, in appreciation for you doing that, I've brought you a present.'

Kelvin took a clear bag from his pocket and thrust it into Bobby's hands.

'Put it inside your jacket, shit-for-brains,' Kelvin spat.

'What is it?'

'You know what it is.'

'No. I don't want to get into that.'

'Like I said, it's a gift. Look, Bobby, I know you think I'm a nasty wanker, but I'm your mate, okay? All that stuff with the blade the other day, I was just scared. I didn't mean for the stupid kid to go and do that to himself. It was just a laugh, right?'

Kelvin wiped the rain from the hollows of his eyes. He looked genuinely frightened. Doubtless his nerves were raw. A death on your conscience can do that, Bobby thought.

'Anyway, I know how you're feeling right now,' said Kelvin. 'I've been there. A lot of shit's happened in my life. A few years back my big sister OD'd. I was fucking distraught, man. The stuff in that bag helped me loads. It makes you forget. Makes you feel like none of it's your fault. No obligation, Bobby. Take it, don't take it; s'up to you. You know how though, yeah?'

'Yeah, I know,' Bobby said.

'Adios then, fuckwit.'

The rain eased. Clouds fractured. The sun broke through and spilled hard shadows upon the ground. Bobby thought about going down to tidy his mum's grave but the ghost of a memory kept him by the gate. He had seen something down there just moments ago – a silhouette cast over her stone

– something small, smothered in shadow. It was no good. The memory would not be coaxed.

Joe felt a familiar poke in his ribs.

'Penny for them.'

'Hey. I wasn't sure you'd be here. Hi,' he fluffed.

'Want to share my umbrella?' Sam offered

'You're okay. I think it's stopping.'

The sounds of departure – car doors slamming, gravel cracking under foot and tyre, plans being exchanged and considered – weighed heavy in the silence between them.

'You look great,' Joe said.

'My mum's old funeral weeds. They're falling apart. I think she last wore them to the crucifixion or something . . . How did you find the English resit?'

'Not too bad. Better than first time around. You?'

She shrugged. 'Pretty lousy.'

'Sam, I'm sorry about what happened. If I thought you were distracted because of me . . . I should've called. Set things straight before the exam.'

'Give the martyr act a rest, will you?' she said, pushing him playfully in the shoulder. 'Oh Christ, sorry, Joe. Did that hurt?'

'Nah, anyway it's the other arm.'

'Look, I had lots of reasons to screw up that exam. On a psychological level, I can blame my parents. Being a latchkey child must have freaked with my brain. Even if the key *was* to a three-quarter of a million pound house, complete with pool, extensive grounds and a nanny from the Maria von Trapp cloning program. On a personal level, my identity is stuck in a fashion limbo between undead rock chick and Girl Guide. On an academic level, I did bugger-all work. As far as I'm concerned, "Hamlet's Oedipal Complex" could be the name of the latest celebrity baby. So chill, okay?'

Joe spluttered on his laughter.

'Just friends is cool with me,' Sam said. 'But I'm sorry *I* didn't call.'

'It's me who should be sorry.'

'Do you ever let anyone apologise? I *know* it was my fault. I pushed things too quickly. You've still got issues, and that's cool. I just hope you'll let me help you, as a friend. Maybe we can get together for a coffee or something later. No groping, I swear.'

'I'd like that, but I'm going away for a few weeks. Bobby, my dad and me: the whole Nightingale freak show. We're rebuilding a watermill or something'

'Really? Wow.'

'I know. But it might be good for us. Therapy through toil, all that rubbish.'

'Where is it?'

'Somewhere down by the Wash, I think. But when we get back . . .'

'Yeah. Well, you take care.'

She brushed her lips against his cheek.

'Gotta go,' he said. 'We're all packed up. Heading straight off.'

Sam gave him a nod and walked away.

Joe crossed the car park to where his dad and Bobby waited in the Mercedes.

'And so the happy holidays begin,' Bobby said, as Joe got into the passenger seat.

Without a word, Richard turned out of the cemetery and took the A15 south. His eyes stayed on the road while Joe took out a dog-eared AA road map and plotted the fifty or so miles to Potter's Drake. Bobby scrunched down in the back seat and opened a Terry Pratchett novel.

Had any of them looked back at the cemetery gate, they

might have seen the figure that watched their passing. A small, delicate frame huddled in a red rubber raincoat. Its face was obscured by a hood, its head unmoving until the Nightingale's car disappeared from view. Then it nodded, turned back to the graveyard and rejoined the dead.

II

- JULY 2006 -

Into the Shadow House

. . . early will I seek thee:
my soul thirsteth for thee,
my flesh longeth for thee
in a dry and thirsty land,
where no water is

Psalm 63:1

- *Interlude* -

The Fourth Guest: Fiona Harringdon
Made Absent on 17th May 1998

THE FENLAND COURIER
VANISHING CREAM 'MONSTER' VANISHES

As the stock market value of her company crashes, Mrs Fiona Harringdon – the well-known manufacturer of luxury beauty products – has disappeared more convincingly than any overnight pimple. Yesterday, Harringdon found herself on the brink of professional and financial ruin. A class action lawsuit, brought against Harringdon Health and Beauty Ltd by over one hundred parents, had succeeded in the High Court with damages totalling £130 million. The main allegation, accepted by Judge Maddox, was that, as senior partner of the cosmetic giant, Mrs Harringdon knowingly put on the market products likely to cause serious defects in unborn children. These beauty treatments, including anti-aging creams and nail polish, contained dangerous compounds called dibutyl phthalates. As far back as 1995, Harringdon Health and Beauty boffins were warning Mrs Harringdon of the risks posed by phthalates. Employee, Dr Carl Birch, testified that he had attended several meetings with Harringdon in which the dangers, including defects to the genitalia of male lab rats, were discussed. Further, Dr Birch said that he had participated in a human study that confirmed that those abnormalities were probable in the babies of mothers that habitually used Harringdon products. Mrs

Harringdon ignored all evidence and advice, saying the science was spurious.

Outside the High Court, Mrs Harringdon's solicitor read the following statement: 'I must now accept the findings of the court and offer my sympathies to the mothers concerned. I have been branded a monster in the popular press, but please believe me when I say that I feel your pain. I, too, am a mother. Through my actions, children have suffered. I can do nothing to put that right. I must now try to come to terms with what I have allowed to happen.'

Mrs Harringdon may yet have to work out her 'demons' in rather less luxurious surroundings than her palatial estate on the Lincolnshire Fens. It emerged yesterday that the CPS are considering bringing criminal charges against the entrepreneur.

As this news reached her, Mrs Harringdon was, according to her fashion-designer husband, 'plunged into despair'. 'She went out for a drive to clear her head,' Eddie Harringdon reported to the police. 'She said she'd take the Range Rover and drive along the coast, as far as the Wash, and maybe do a little shooting to let off steam. She took her shotgun with her. I'm really afraid Fiona may have done something stupid. No-one believes her, but she was so sorry about those wee babies.'

At the time of going to press, no sign of Fiona Harringdon has been discovered. Meanwhile, Margaret Lloyd, one of the mothers involved in the class action, had this to say: 'Fiona Harringdon can run but she can't hide. She knew about the effects of the chemicals in her filthy treatments and still allowed them to be sold on the open market. I want her to stand trial and go to prison. But, wherever she is, I hope that she is haunted by the faces of our poor children. Haunted until her dying breath.'

Fifteen

They left the main road and passed through a tapestry of managed countryside. Patches of fields, worked and fallow, ran out on all sides. Hay bales rose in cubic towers like the columns of ruined temples. Occasionally they saw a meadow with the odd Friesian grazing on the banks of a raised river, but in the main this was agricultural land. As such, the handprint of Man was pressed deep into the soil. His mastery here, hard fought, was centuries old. In the marshes, now drained and divided, he alone was god.

Inside the car the atmosphere had grown piano wire-taut. What passed for conversation was exchanged in one word questions and answers.

Joe rolled down the window. A blast of air stung his cheeks.

'Wind that up,' Richard barked. 'It'll mess with the air con.'

'But it's boiling in here.'

'Just put it up.'

'Could you send some of that fabled air conditioning back this way?' Bobby asked.

Richard fiddled with the temperature controls to no noticeable effect.

'You do know that this is a form of abuse?' Bobby muttered. 'I oughta call ChildLine.'

'We've got about five miles left to go,' Richard said. 'I'll give you a tenner if you can keep your mouth shut until . . .'

'A whole tenner? Mister, you've got yourself a deal.'

Five miles seemed like fifty in the unchanging vista of the Fens. It had a certain spartan beauty, Joe figured, but there was no variation to engage the eye. After a while, searching the landscape for a hill or valley became an exercise in futility. The only break in the monotony was the occasional sign that tallied up the number of road deaths for that year. With the heat misting the horizon, Joe suffered a kind of snow-blindness. Traces swam before his eyes. His corneas burned. He longed to open the window, but his father's drumming fingers signalled that it would be a bad idea. Instead, he rested his face against the glass.

One of those declarations of death whipped past – then another – and another. Road safety was all well and good, Joe thought, but this was just ghoulish. He focused on the verge ahead and his eyes widened. A parade of those grim little notices blinked in the near distance; a dozen at least. The first whooshed by.

Its proclamation slammed into Joe's brain. He watched it repeated on five successive plates before he truly registered what he was seeing. He read with wonder and horror:

On 11th November 2005

On the palimpsest of his history it was a date that would never be overwritten. An epoch seared into his soul. With the following signs, the message changed. He watched their passing and felt both the relief and dread of a secret stripped bare.

In Molseley Woods

–

Janet Nightingale

–

Was Brutally Murdered

–

By Joseph

–

Her Beloved Son

Blood dripped from the last plate. It spotted the grass and formed into a dark, glinting pool.

Glinting

The motes retreated and Joe's vision cleared. He looked back along the road and saw nothing to interrupt the strip of the verge. He clasped his hands between his legs and took a long breath. It was the heat. Just the heat.

They drove now along a raised country lane, shaded by clumps of alder trees. In the dykes that bordered the road, water glistened like the guiding lights of a landing strip. They passed a car that had toppled into a ditch, its passenger side crumpled in. A 'Police Aware' notice had been plastered across the windscreen. Joe looked away.

'Potter's Drake,' Richard said. 'Thank Christ.'

They entered the outskirts of a community gone to seed.

The sign proclaimed it 'Best Kept Village 1985', but the two decades since that accolade had been bestowed had not been kind to Potter's Drake. The pub, the primary school, the post office: everything looked as if a layer of dust had settled over it. Museum dust, Joe thought – although, in this case, the museum's exhibits were being left to rot. Small efforts had been made to brighten up the aspect of the place: bedding plants struggled at the heart of a mini-roundabout; a banner, wrapped around the clock tower, announced that the timepiece had just been refurbished 'for the enjoyment of the villagers'. What enjoyment could be derived from the structure was not made explicit; perhaps telling the time was an entertainment only recently discovered here. The town hall might have been painted in the last year and the union flag, drooping listlessly against its pole, looked new. For all these 'improvements', a sense of decline, common to many Fen villages, could not be disguised. Lack of jobs meant that those born here moved away. The only newcomers consisted of commuters buying up holiday homes. That kind of root never bedded down and was easily pulled up. And so it was left to the old to see out the death of Potter's Drake. As the Nightingales crawled through the village, seeking the offices of Cuttle & Runerby, Joe saw these guardians of the flame. They waited at the bus stop or shambled in and out of the post office. Proud, feeble people, looking out at the storm of the modern world as the ground crumbled beneath them.

'This really is the arse end of nowhere,' Bobby grumbled.

'No tenner for you, big mouth,' Richard said.

Bobby snorted lemonade from his nostrils and dropped the can on the floor. It span and fizzed in the footwell. Following its example, the pressure in the car jetted free. For the first time in years, Richard and his sons shared their laughter. Joe struggled to breathe. He beat a fist against his leg.

'Come on,' Richard said at last, 'we've got to pick – up – the – keys.'

The Old Man gave way to another fit of giggles. For the life of him, Joe couldn't understand why the hell they were laughing. All he knew was that it felt good.

The solicitors' office was housed in a Victorian villa on the High Street. Its steps were crusted with bird shit and crumbs of masonry, coming loose from the cornices and the architrave, gritted the entrance. Some of the letters stenciled upon the glass of the door had peeled away, so that a passerby might guess that the practice was owned by Messrs Cutt & Run. In these things, Joe was struck again by that atmosphere of decay that permeated the village.

The Nightingales filed into the waiting room. A secretary, who looked so desiccated Tutankhamun might have advised her to moisturise more often, glanced up from her typewriter.

'We're here to see Mr Cuttle,' said Richard.

The old lady sniffed. It was the kind of sound she might have made had she arrived home and found the cat coughing hairballs into her purse. Her gaze slipped from Richard to Joe to Bobby. She sniffed again. The cat was now squatting over the purse and pinching one out.

'Please take a seat.'

Bobby dropped into an armchair. Richard leafed through a copy of Reader's Digest that had probably kept Noah entertained during the Flood. Joe wandered around the room, examining artistic prints of the local Fenland prior to its drainage. In one, he found a depiction of the Marshman. The sketch showed a stalk-like figure lost among the reeds, his form supported by a pair of stilts. He had a sack slung over his back and a scarlet hood rested on his shoulders. He stared out across the swamp, his weatherbeaten features unreadable in the gloaming.

The secretary reappeared at the waiting room door.

'Mr *Runerby* will see you. This way.'

They followed her upstairs. Reaching a door off the landing, she knocked and waited.

'Come.'

The Nightingales were left to the senior partner's care.

Runerby indicated for them to sit.

Joe had not met Mr Cuttle but, if he had, he might have reflected on the differences between that man and his business associate. Runerby was prim and pinched, the sharpness of his features echoed in his spiky style of speech. Everything about the little man was pointed, from the tips of his shoes to the crown of his hairless head. The handkerchief, standing to attention in his breast pocket, acted as a signpost, commanding that attention be focused on the solicitor's face. He smelled of old documents and the damp places in which they were stored.

'Hello,' Richard began. 'I'm sorry, but I thought we were meeting Mr Cuttle today.'

Runerby coughed and looked at Richard over the rim of his glasses. 'Mr Cuttle is dead.'

'God,' Richard said. 'My – my condolences. I only saw him a few days ago. Was it very sudden? Unexpected, I mean.'

Runerby sucked his teeth. He clacked his tongue. A lifetime of keeping secrets made divulging even common knowledge difficult.

'Sudden . . . yes,' he conceded.

'Had he been ill?'

'Not that I'm aware, although his weight, of course. I believe he suffered a coronary.'

'It must be a sad loss for you, Mr Runerby. I guess you were partners here a long time.'

'Not so long. Cuttle joined the firm twelve years ago. Moved up from Colchester, I think. Said he wanted to live near to some sister or other, though I believe she's now dead. Tragic, of course, though I always told him to take better care of himself.'

Something in Mr Runerby's words, so clipped they gave the impression of languid boredom, told Joe that he considered his partner's death little more than an inconvenience. All in all, he seemed to be the kind of man that would consider Mr Tulkinghorn the misunderstood hero of *Bleak House*.

'Still, tragedy must not interrupt the flow of business,' Runerby said, taking an envelope from his desk and passing it to Richard. 'There are the keys to the house and a printout of directions. And unless I can help you any further?'

'I'm not very familiar with the area.'

'Directions, sir. Inside the envelope.'

'What I mean is, my boys and I plan to do some renovation work while we're here. We might need to find lumber yards, DIY stores.'

'Holbeach is best for that sort of thing. Nothing around here.'

'I see.'

Runerby exhaled between his teeth: 'You can always call my secretary, if you must. Doubtless she will help you find what you need. Now, sir, I must get on.'

Runerby flicked through the letters awaiting his attention. Sensing that the Nightingales had not heeded his dismissal, he looked up.

'One more question,' said Richard.

'Of course.'

'Did you ever meet Mrs Sutton?'

'Beg pardon?'

'Muriel Sutton. The woman who left us the house. I believe she was a cousin of my late wife, but I'd like to know more about her.'

'Cuttle dealt with Mrs Sutton.'

'Did she live here all her life?'

'I believe so. Her family bought the mill in the thirties or forties, I think.'

'But you said Mr Cuttle only came here twelve years ago. Who dealt with her legal affairs before that?'

'Not me, Mr Nightingale. I believe my father had something to do with her defence during the trial. Said she was a very uncommon sort of woman. Very . . . odd. Still she had *suffered*, I suppose.'

'What trial, Mr Runerby?'

'The murder trial.'

Runerby sighed and threw his spectacles onto the table.

'You don't remember? "The Fenland Horror" the papers called it, in their typically lurid fashion. Still, it was rather *unpleasant*, I suppose. 1972, sir. Mrs Sutton murdered her little sister – Alice Daecher – in the millhouse that bore the girl's name. Murdered the child by burning her to death. I heard it all from my father who saw the post mortem photographs. He had been in the war, gentlemen, had witnessed at first hand a Junker bomber cut his platoon to ribbons. Remembered how it *strafed* his comrades until there was nothing left, just tattered uniforms and helmets filled with gore. He said he sometimes still felt the blood and brains in his hands. He learned to live with such memories. But I don't think he ever came to terms with what happened to that little girl. That her own sister could . . .'

Mr Runerby dried up. There had been something like sentiment in his voice and he seemed embarrassed by it.

'It was a bad business,' he muttered, 'but it's in the past. I hope you will enjoy your new home, Mr Nightingale.'

Sixteen

'Jesus *fucking* Christ!'

There was no bracken bordering the road, no trees. The woman had stepped out of nowhere. A form hardly glimpsed before she struck the wing of the Mercedes. Richard slammed the brakes. The wheels locked and the car bunny-hopped to a standstill. Boxes, stuffed with tinned food, spilled their contents across the back seat.

Richard freed himself from the seatbelt and jumped out of the car. Burnt tyre rubber salted the air. The road, freshly scorched, glistened in the sun. On either side, fields of barley, harvested to stalks, stretched into a dusty haze. There was no sign of the woman.

He ducked back into the car and demanded: 'Did you see her?'

Dumbstruck, Joe nodded.

'Wha'appened?' Bobby, stunned from sleep by a falling can of sweet corn, half-muttered, half-shrieked the question.

Richard's heart hammered. Saliva dried against the leather strap of his tongue. He turned back to the road, called out. There was no reply. Had he really seen the woman? Wasn't it possible that the stress and heat of the day had got to him? First, there had been his poor handling of Bobby's behaviour at the funeral, and afterwards the long journey and the surprise that awaited them at the solicitor's office: the double whammy of Cuttle's death and the knowledge that their inheritance had come from a convicted child-killer. Maybe all these factors had conspired in the hallucination.

But Joe had seen her too.

Richard jogged along the road. He tried coming up with comforting scenarios. The woman had dusted herself down and continued on her way. Unlikely. There wasn't a chance he could miss seeing her out on the road or walking in the crew-cut fields either side. Someone had picked her up, then. No, not enough time, and they hadn't passed another car for a good mile or so. A large hay bale stood in the field to his right with a tractor sitting idle nearby. Dazed, she might have stumbled in that direction. That was at least possible.

At the edge of the road, Richard stopped dead. What if she was really hurt? Or worse . . . He saw himself reaching the tractor cab – empty – circling the bale – nothing. And then, the tiniest of movements, the merest twitch of a stalk. Grabbing handfuls of straw, he would expose her hiding place: a blood-dappled nest that she had thrown over herself. Not a lot of blood, just enough to know that she was beyond help. Caught up in this vision, Richard stood amazed. On the shattered stilts of her legs, this slow-dying woman had dragged herself from the road. He tried to say something but the sight of bone testing the elasticity of skin, in some places shearing through, made speech impossible. Instead, he stared into her clouded eyes and saw himself exposed.

She *knew*. She saw what he had done to the *other woman* . . .

'Are you looking for me?'

The vision fell away.

Richard blinked at the woman standing before him. She raised an eyebrow, as if waiting for a response from a simple child.

'I thought . . . Are you all right? I don't understand.'

'Yes, you hit me. No, it wasn't your fault. And, yes, I'm fine.'

'I see. I think. Do I see?'

'Is that a rhetorical question?' the woman smiled. 'Because I'm not very good at answering those.'

'You're not hurt.'

'My bag's hurt. Look down there and you'll see its remains.'

Only now, as Richard took a step closer to the field, did he see the channel running alongside. It was a concrete-lined levee used for irrigation. Scattered along its bottom were the contents of one of those old-fashioned handbags; the kind that could be used to carry around the annual produce of a small country.

'Don't worry,' the woman said, 'you didn't knock me down there. Your wing mirror caught the strap and, hey-presto.'

'Christ. If I'd hit you. I just didn't see you on the road. How didn't I see you?'

'Maybe you're tired. Long day?'

'You could say that. Look, can I help? Give you a lift somewhere?'

'You can do both,' she said.

Richard nodded and scooted down the side of the levee. Now and then, he glanced up at the woman who supervised the collection of her belongings. She looked to be about thirty or so. Her eyes were grey-green and her salt-and-pepper hair was tied up at the back in a rather dated style. She wore a thin, sequined scarf around her neck. The woman regarded him with amused concentration, sometimes pointing out objects he had missed. Hardly beautiful, she had, nonetheless, an interesting face, the features delicate and evenly spaced.

A strong hand clasped his forearm as he climbed out of the levee.

'You've got quite a grip there,' Richard panted.

'Runs in the family,' the woman said.

'You're my tenant then?' asked Richard.

'I suppose so, though I expect a rebate on the rent this month. You owe me that for the bag.'

Richard recalled the plans that Cuttle had given him. He had a vague recollection of a hatched square occupying the southwestern corner of the property, a good hundred yards from the millhouse. It had looked such a small building that he had imagined it to be nothing more than a shed or outhouse. Certainly he had not thought it large enough to be a cottage.

The woman, who had introduced herself as Gail Bedeker, looked back at the boys crushed into the back seat.

'Sorry about this,' she said. 'We're nearly home.'

She received tight smiles in response.

'Bit of a coincidence, me nearly running you down,' said Richard, 'seeing as we're neighbours.'

'Not when you think about it. There *is* no-one else around here *to* run down.'

'Mystifies me why a young woman like yourself would want to live out here at all.'

'I don't. My grandmother used to live here. She and grandad worked up at the millhouse for years. He was the steward for old Mr Daecher. Grandad died in '71 – and that was when the mill closed for good. Mrs Sutton let my grandmother stay on as housekeeper. I used to come up and visit during the summer holidays. When Gran died a few years ago, Mrs Sutton rented me the cottage through July and August. I always come back. It's like a pilgrimage to youth, I suppose.'

'Were you here when Mrs Sutton died?'

'No.' Gail wound down the window and breathed deeply. 'Mr Cuttle found her. He told me she'd been lying there on the study floor for days. Said the smell was unbearable. Oh, I'm sorry. I forgot. She was your relative.'

'We never met.'

'She was a strange old thing. Hard, I think. Life had made her hard.'

Bobby leaned forward. 'Was she a psycho?'

'Bobby,' Richard warned.

'What? I think it's cool we've got a nutter in the family. Do you know how she killed her sister?'

'All that was a bit before my time,' Gail said, her eyes surfing the rows of corn. 'Gran never spoke much about it. I certainly don't think Mrs Sutton was an angel, but I suppose looking after that kid can't have been easy.'

'Why? What was wrong with her?'

'Alice?' Gail shrugged. 'I never really found out. She died a good five or six years before I was born. From the few things my Gran *did* say, I guessed that she was crippled somehow. I was aware of Alice in a vague sort of way – the memory of her, I mean. If I came into the cottage unexpected, I might overhear her name spoken between Mrs Sutton and my Gran. They'd always change the subject when they saw me. I *did* see a picture of her once. It was an old instamatic print. You know, those terrible pictures that flared all the strong colours and bleached people's skin. I found it in my Grandad's tea chest. It must be twenty years ago now, I've probably distorted the image in my mind. Still, I remember her as a funny looking little thing, skinny arms and legs, yellowy complexion. She was twelve years old when she died, but she looked much younger . . . No, not younger. *Smaller.* Elfin. Hunched over, shying away from the camera. You couldn't see her face properly. Anyway, my Gran always said Mrs Sutton would never have harmed Alice, even though the jury convicted her. I don't know, though. Muriel Sutton was . . . hard.

'Here. Stop here.'

Richard pulled the car onto a grass verge. Through a clump of overgrown brambles, the whitewashed walls of a small cottage could be glimpsed. Cradling her bag, Gail got out of the car.

'We should talk about rent for the summer,' she said.

'Forget about it,' Richard smiled. 'My way of saying sorry for the near-death thing.'

Gail nodded. 'Carry on along the lane for a bit and you'll see a kissing gate. There's a side alley right next to it. Turn down there and you'll find a larger gate leading up to the mill. It was nice to meet you.'

With that, Gail Bedeker disappeared between the hedgerows.

Joe held the gate open as the car trundled through. He waved his father on and re-hooked the securing string over the gatepost. Then he followed the car's jaunty progress up to the house. He walked through a wide savannah of tussocks and sun-splintered earth. To the west, the sun flared. It tingled the nape of his neck and threw his gangly shadow across the hardpan. Soon the silhouette of his head bobbed against a set of porch steps. Joe stopped short of the house and surveyed the area.

On three sides – north, west and south – the property was bordered by fields of corn. The trees that punctuated the landscape were limited to a few clumps beside the road and a grove that gathered about the northern wall of the millhouse. Otherwise the land was barren. Turning on the spot, Joe followed the uninterrupted circle of the horizon. Then he glanced upwards into the bowl of the sky. At school, he had studied the history of the Native Americans and their kinship with the Earth. Standing here, in this Albion version of the Great Plains, it was easy to see how the Indians had derived their belief in Nature's cyclical character. He wondered whether those long-dead marshmen, depicted in the drawings that adorned the waiting room of Cuttle & Runerby, had developed similar beliefs. How could they not, living as they had upon this disc? A people, much like the Indians, now made extinct by the devices of man.

Joe took the air through his nose. It smelled lifeless. Maybe the summer heat had parched all living things from the Fen. As if to correct him, he heard the chatter of crickets in the grass and the hum of a dragonfly darting through the reeds. In the dried-up belly of the river, that had once galvanised the mill, he saw a regiment of red ants march into their hole. Life persisted in this place, you just had to look hard to find it.

He turned back to the house.

Facing the road, its doorway hidden beneath the shadow of the lintel, stood the Nightingale's inheritance. Daecher's Mill. The red clay of its skin blazed, as if the entire structure had emerged fresh from some gigantic kiln. Recessed deep into its walls, three windows overlooked the scrubland. Their glass sparkled, reflecting the sun while allowing no light to penetrate. In places, the roof had fallen in and the ribs of the ceiling poked through. This, coupled with the broken waterwheel which overhung the riverbed, gave the impression of something crippled by the toll of long years. Even at a distance, Joe could see the crumbling of its shell and smell the dust of its slow decay.

Sadness sat heavy in the air around the millhouse.

The boy switched his attention to the living quarters attached to the mill. This grey brick building, girdled around on three sides by a covered porch, looked to be no more than eighty years old. Like the mill, it was made up of three storeys.

Joe reached the car and began to help with the unpacking.

Typically, Bobby had unloaded his own gear and was now recumbent on the ground, pulling fistfuls of grass and staring up at the sky. Handing Joe a box of food, Richard slid the keys from the Cuttle & Runerby envelope into his son's palm. Joe clasped the key ring between his teeth and mounted the steps. He jiggled the box until it sat more comfortably under his arm and inserted the key into the lock. The barrels resisted, but eventually the mechanism snapped and the door loosened in its frame. Stale air reached out to greet him.

About to step over the threshold, Joe hesitated. A bird, its stomach bloated, lay dead at his feet. It was an ordinary looking little thing, no bigger than a sparrow. A pool of dark water glinted around it, dirtying the white flecks of its tail and collar. Its beak, slightly agape, gave the impression that death had come as something of a surprise.

'Come on, Joe,' Bobby snickered from the grass, 'get going. I want this wagon unloaded by sundown.'

Richard gave Bobby a kick as he passed. He joined Joe on the porch.

'Been in yet? What's it like? Joe?'

Joe looked down. The bird was gone. All that remained was a set of forked footprints dissolving in the pool.

'All right, son?' Richard asked. He placed a hand on Joe's shoulder.

'Sure,' said Joe. 'I just thought . . . Doesn't matter.'

Joe Nightingale kicked a path through the pool and entered Daecher's Mill.

Seventeen

Over a meal of corned beef and pickle sandwiches, Richard tried to recapture the moment when the barriers had broken down. A joke had done it, an off-the-cuff remark that tripped, without premeditation, from his lips. In the few seconds that followed, years of reserve and resentment had been washed away, but the moment had been short-lived. Stepping out of the car and entering the offices of Cuttle & Runerby, Richard had felt its passing. It was as if someone had turned on the light in a neglected room and then, just as suddenly, switched it off again. He looked now at his sons, eating in silence. It was not a large kitchen table, but acres of oak seemed to separate him from them.

'You boys ready for a bit of hard graft tomorrow?'

'Yeah, okay.'

'Whatever.'

'I thought we could start with the flooring. Check out the boards, see what needs replacing. What d'you think?'

'Fine.'

'Uh-huh.'

Pipes clanked and the sink gurgled. At least the plumbing seemed to be able to hold a civil conversation.

'Been exploring yet, Bobby?'

'*Exploring*? I'm fifteen years old.'

Richard put down his sandwich. He twisted the wedding

ring on his finger and glanced out of the window. Behind the house, a pair of meadow pipits tried to outdo each other in a display of aeronautical prowess. At last they tired and glided off across the scrubland, flying low against the bruised sky.

'S'getting dark,' Richard said. 'What time is it?'

'Ten-ish, I think.'

'So what do you reckon about this murder thing, Bobby? Bit creepy, huh?'

'I thought that wasn't an appropriate topic for conversation.'

'When I said that, Miss Bedeker was in the car and . . .'

'Yeah, yeah.'

'Look, we're all dead beat,' Joe said. 'Let's call it a night.'

Richard watched his sons rinse their plates and stack them in the rack.

Long after Joe and Bobby had left, he remained seated at the kitchen table, tracing the knots and whorls in the oak. The house flexed and groaned around him. Richard imagined the cavities behind these walls. His mind lingered there, calculating how many bottles it would take to insulate the entire house.

'Can't win,' he muttered.

He took the mobile from his pocket. Bringing up *Susan*, his finger hovered over *dial*. He had the strange idea that he could smell her: a phantom scent layering the dank odour of Daecher's Mill. Somehow, she was still clinging to him. He pushed the button. While he waited for the call to connect, Richard justified this action. He'd only broken it off with her for the sake of the boys. He wanted to get close to them again, and introducing a prospective stepmother, seven months after the accident, wasn't the best way to achieve that. And so he'd given her up; dumped the woman to whom he owed his fragile grasp on sanity. He had done this for Joe and Bobby – his sons – who didn't give a toss about him. Richard told himself this tale of self-sacrifice and the lie made him sick to the stomach. He knew very well why he had ended it with Susan. It had nothing to do with the boys.

Connection Failed flashed on the mobile's display.

Bobby set out his Warhammer figures on the dressing table. Reflected in the mirror behind the troops, the attic bedroom gathered shadows. The skylight set into the pitched roof, now a square of black, also mirrored the room. These artificial extensions did little to increase the sense of space. In this cramped portion of the attic, stroking a cat, let alone swinging one, would prove a tricky manoeuvre. The bed, upon which he had chucked his sleeping bag, felt like a slab of granite. The only storage space was the drawers of the dresser and a squat wardrobe. All in all, hardly the Ritz. So why the hell had he chosen it?

'Bobby? You still up, son?' Richard poked his head round the door. 'You know, there's a broom cupboard down the hall if this is too spacious for you?'

'Funny.'

'What're you doing?'

Richard went to the dresser and removed a warrior orc from its platoon.

'Getting into this stuff again? Thought you'd finished with all that fantasy rubbish.'

'Just sorting out my old gear.'

'You brought it *here* to sort it out? You know, Bobby, you ought to concentrate on your art. You're not bad, but talent isn't everything. You gotta work at it. These things'll just distract you.'

'Thanks for the pep talk.'

'Bobby, I'm trying. This isn't easy for me either, you know. Honestly, I'd rather go downstairs and . . .'

'Have a drink?'

Richard replaced the model soldier. Bobby concentrated hard on the army arrayed before him.

'I thought we made a bit of progress today.'

'We had a laugh. Doesn't mean shit. You think a laugh makes up for anything?'

'Look, I'm sorry for what I said to you after the funeral. It's obvious you were very upset. That's why you behaved the way you did.'

Bobby flinched. He could still remember nothing of the words he had spoken at the graveside.

'And I shouldn't have come at you like that. If you want to talk about it, about how you feel and stuff, I'm here. Okay?' The boy didn't look up. 'All right then, that's fine.'

In closing the door behind him, Richard created a draught that cut a swathe through the miniatures on the dresser. Bobby sighed and dropped to his knees. As he replaced the fallen soldiers back into their regiments, he caught sight of the satchel he had thrown under the bed. An impulse took hold of him. He made a grab for the satchel and searched the inner pockets. His hand closed around the cool steel of the craft knife and he withdrew it from the bag.

Reflected by the blade, the light from the bedroom's bare bulb shimmered across the wallpaper. It danced over the faces of fairies and elves, sprites and goblins. Faded, curled back at its edges, the wallpaper was the only clue that this had once been a child's bedroom. The impish figures that adorned it, however, did not strike Bobby as appropriate night-time companions for a child. Their smiles were grim and somehow hungry. Bobby could imagine himself as a little boy, waking up and seeing their eyes shining from out of the darkness. The snickering laughter of those little people would run like water in his ear. And then, one by one, they would drop from the wall and scamper towards him on their paper legs. Climbing the bed and reaching his ear, they might whisper to him. In the dark, in the shadows, he could understand their fairy-talk.

'He is coming, Bobby. The dead boy has woken. He reaches now across the miles. He calls out from his second mouth and his cries cut through the earth. His soul longs for you, his flesh thirsts for you. And, in the end, he *will* find you, as surely as the others have been found . . . in the Shadow House.'

Bobby's eyes remained glazed as the papery voices rustled in his ear. He rolled up his sleeve. The knife felt right in his hand. He grasped it firmly, forefinger pressed hard against the head. Veins pulsed, arteries throbbed. The haunted boy made a single, smooth incision. Blood tickled down his arm and spotted the figurines at his feet. Bobby felt the warm flow of release.

'I didn't know, I didn't know.'

He repeated the mantra. The words filled his head, drowned his senses. It was only as a vague background noise that he heard the scratching of fingernails. Had he listened, he might have concluded that the sounds came from behind the wardrobe. Further investigation would have revealed that they actually originated from behind the walls – from behind the faces of elves and goblins.

But Bobby Nightingale was busy with his knife.

Joe wandered through the house.

He started in the attic corridor, where he had to tilt his head to clear the ceiling. He counted two blank spaces. Then he went through the first floor bedrooms. Seven spaces. The bathroom, with its network of exposed pipes, roll-top bathtub and mottled mirror had a hook but no corresponding discolouration upon the wall. He discounted it. Downstairs he noted four faded rectangles in the hallway, two in the kitchen, six in the lounge and three in the study at the back of the house. Twenty-four in total. Twenty-four places where, until recently, pictures had hung.

The inspiration for his quest had come from the shadow above his bed. Joe had taken the large bedroom above the lounge, the logic being that it was west-facing so there was less chance of the sun waking him in the morning. A lifelong arachnophobe, he had been lying on the bed, testing the strength of his character. A spider, directly above his head, abseiled from the ceiling. The nearer it came, the more monstrous it appeared. Something that, three feet away, had been a fragile black body soon focused into a lustrous exoskeleton, strung with powerful legs and dripping mandibles. He managed to remain still long enough for a leg to brush his nose. Then the panic set in and, giggling like a schoolboy, he darted across the room. Glancing back, he had watched as the spider skittered into a pale square of wall. His curiosity shifted. Something about that block of wallpaper, undimmed by the sun and faintly luminous in the gloom, drew his eye. He examined the rest of the room and found two similar patches.

Now, in the study, he looked at the only pictures that had been left untouched. They were a series of illuminated sketches, depicting fourteenth century millers and threshers at work. He wiped the dust from the glass of the first print. The scene showed a crookbacked old woman and a man on horseback delivering grain to a windmill. Typically with medieval art, the sense of perspective was a little comical to the modern eye, the miller being almost as tall as his place of work. Two further scenes depicted men straining against the harvest wagon, and women on all fours, reaping corn with sickles. The print that occupied pride of place was that of a watermill.

The flatness of the image belied its energy. Water surged

downriver, passing the sluice gate and crashing against the wheel. A fish and an eel had been caught upstream in a woven net, saving them from the lethal mechanism. The millhouse itself was white-brick, thatched and fronted with a heavy door. Beneath this last copy, printed in a neat hand, was the legend *Scenes from the Luttrell Psalter* and a few lines of verse. Joe recognised it as from *The Miller's Daughter* by Tennyson:

> The sleepy pool above the dam,
> The pool beneath it never still,
> The meal-sacks on the whiten'd floor,
> The dark round of the dripping wheel . . .

The selection, plucked from halfway through the verse, struck Joe as odd. It was as if it had been chosen to deliberately invert the tone of the poem. Gone was the melancholy romance of the Laureate's lines; instead a sense of menace had been imposed. He reread the fragment.

In his mind's eye, he saw the millpond, languid before the rush of the sluice. It was deep and dark, full of lurking power. Next, he imagined the room with the meal-sacks – a place made kinetic by the rush of water beyond its walls. Flour billowed, obscuring the working of men and of gears. In the centre of the room, stone wheels grumbled against each other, dribbling kernels of grain from between their lips. The noise of their appetite rocked Joe to the pit of his stomach. He clasped his hands over his ears and stared through the flour-clouds.

A little figure, sitting upon her rocking chair, watched him closely. Through the shouts of the miller and his steward, Joe could hear her. She was singing:

'Row, row, row your boat
Gently down the stream'

She rose and hobbled through the mist, a child with the gait of an old woman.

'Merrily, merrily, merrily, merrily'

Her face took shape. In the hallway, Joe staggered back against the stairs. Inside the millhouse in his mind, he had nowhere to retreat. She came at him, lumbering and rolling. She wore a costume of red which appeared to flicker about her. Like flames, Joe thought.

Her face . . .

'Life is but a dream.

'*We will meet very soon, Joseph,*' she said, the white clouds enveloping her. '*Then you shall* see *me. Then you shall* know *me, as once you did. Remember me, my child, for I am as once you were: rebegot, of absence, darkness, death; things which are not.*'

Joe shook himself. He felt cold and tired. He looked at the pictures on the wall and wondered why he had come downstairs.

Eighteen

In the boot of the Mercedes, squirrelled away in the spare tyre compartment, sat a bottle of scotch. An ordinary, over-the-counter, fourteen quid bottle of Famous Grouse. Nothing special. Yet the vision of it haunted Richard Nightingale. Every detail of that bottle, of its confinement, blazed in his mind. He saw the tissue paper taped around it – protection lest the glass shattered against the jack; the label beneath, half-rubbed away by a pawing thumb; the amber liquid pressed against the cap. He even thought he could smell it. Taste it. Richard wrapped sweaty sheets around his body. A second later, he sprang from the bed, clattered downstairs and out the front door. Before he knew it, the boot was open, he had broken the seal and the bottle was at his lips.

Don't pretend you care.

The whisky greased his gums.

You think a laugh makes up for anything?

Richard doubled over. Scotch dribbled from his mouth onto the back of his hand.

This may be the last chance you have to be a father to them.

Straightening up, he hurled the bottle into the scrub. The report of breaking glass came out of the distant darkness. He closed the boot and pulled himself up the porch steps. The rail provided support and so he rested there, gulping down lungfuls of night air.

Laughter trickled into Richard's ear. Someone was laughing at him, mocking his pain. The sound came from the far end of the porch, where the decking turned with the corner of the house.

'Who's there?'

No answer. Just that musical, tinkling laughter. He advanced.

Leaves scurried along the walkway and crackled around his feet. Autumn leaves, aged before their time. He felt his stomach pinch and the sweats return. His mouth ran salty for the scotch. Maybe if he searched the scrubland he might find the bottle. It would take hours, of course, but surely there was a chance. Then he would hold the shards of glass to his lips, desperate to taste that which he had so recklessly abandoned. Fuck the boys. Fuck them. They didn't want him anyway. He could just sit in the Fenland, sucking whisky from the earth.

The laughter again. The lightness of those tones made the Old Man angry. Fists clenched, he pounded across the porch.

Richard came to a halt. He smiled and slapped the wind chime. Its peal – its laughter – shivered once more in his ear. Like the outdoor lamps, electric lights housed in old storm lanterns that ran all around the outside of the building, the chime was fastened, via a chain, to the porch roof. It was a strange sort of decoration. Clearly homemade, the lid of a metal teapot had been used for the umbrella section from which the chimes hung. Odd sorts of chimes they were, too: bolts and nails, tiny cogs and bits of coloured glass, the broken minute hand of a large clock. This last hung lower than the other chimes and pointed, like a finger, towards the ground.

The artificial voice grew softer. Richard thought again how human it sounded – how like the contented laughter of a child. At that moment, light from the study window cut through the coloured glass and danced across Richard's face. Blood-red light that set blades behind his eyes. He recoiled, as if burned.

'My love. My *love*. My world,' he said, his voice trembling. 'Tell me you're still there.'

No. He would not remember.

He went back into the house, sat at Muriel Sutton's old bureau and started work.

Despite his precautions in room selection, streams of sunlight roused Joe early. He groaned and scooted further into the bedroll. The footage of an erotic dream, its cast amalgams of people he knew and Hollywood starlets, began to spill out of the projector inside his mind. His erection twitched. The dream had been a keeper. Eyes screwed tight shut, his brain worked hard to recapture the orgy of moments before.

He barely heard the knock at the door.

'Good, you're awake,' Richard said. 'Breakfast downstairs. 'fraid there's no hot water yet.'

'No problem,' Joe muttered. 'I need a cold shower.'

He zombie-walked to the bathroom and ran a bowlful of icy water.

Downstairs, he dropped into a chair at the kitchen table and sipped a mug of black coffee. Richard popped toast under the grill. Then he passed Joe the list that he had spent much of the night compiling.

'What's this?' Joe asked.

'For the next couple of weeks, *that* is thy God.' Richard looked around the kitchen, a boyish grin plastered across his face. 'S'a bigger job than I thought. Leaking pipes, rotten floor-boards, paint build-up on the doors, replacement sash-cords for the windows, cracked radiator fins, loose grouting in the bathroom, broken banisters, and a fuse box so ancient Thomas Edison would turn his nose up at the sight of it.'

'You know we're not Buddhists, right, dad? We've only got *one* lifetime to finish this stuff.'

'Don't worry, we won't finish it all this trip.'

'You're thinking of coming back?' Joe asked. 'I thought this was a one-off thing. You know, Dad, I can't hang around here all summer. I've got my results and then uni to sort out.'

'I just wanted to make a complete list,' Richard said, eyes fixed on his mug. 'For my benefit. You don't have to do anything if you don't want to.'

'No, I want to. Really.'

Pulling off 'convincing' at nine-o-five was difficult, Joe thought. He needed to sidetrack the conversation, and quick.

'Hey, you know these pictures?'

'What pictures?'

'Well, exactly. There're no pictures in the house at all. I've searched every scrap of wall. Nothing, except those old prints in the study. It's like someone went through the place before we got here and took them all down.'

'Mrs Sutton could've done that ages ago. If they were paintings she could've taken them to Oxfam or something. Or they might be stored somewhere. Maybe in the millhouse'

'Yeah, but it can't have been that long ago that they were removed: the impressions are still fresh on the walls.'

Richard frowned. He went to the windowsill where he had left the envelope given to him by Mr Runerby.

'"Inventory of Daecher's Mill,"' he read, '"drawn up by Mr George Cuttle following the death of Mrs Muriel Sutton. Furniture . . . Hangings . . . Cutlery . . . Crockery . . . Ornaments . . . Pictures. Three framed prints of the Luttrell Psalter . . . All other pictures, consisting entirely of family portraits, left as per the Last Will and Testament of Muriel Sutton."' Richard reached for the wodge of documents that Cuttle had handed over. He leafed through until he found the Will. '"Minor bequests. Five hundred to . . . Clothes to the Salvation Army" . . . Ah, here it is: family portraits. "In consideration of her kind friendship, and in acknowledgement of the service of her grandmother, I leave all family portraits and photograph albums to Miss Gail Anne Bedeker."'

Nineteen

Bobby felt weak. Heat buzzed at his temples. He would not open the window until he was finished, and so the little bedroom baked like the inside of one of those iron sweat-boxes he'd seen in Japanese POW movies. Again, he dipped his finger into the palette of his arm and used the hot paint to execute one last swirl of cloud. Then he stepped back from the wall and appraised his work.

It was remarkable. Despite the difference in materials, and the fact that the composition was no longer rendered in blacks and greys, but tones of red, the picture taking shape was a natural progression of the one he had destroyed. The few trees and the hedgerows had been replicated exactly. In the background, the sea broke across the dunes and flooded the land. It refilled the extinct river and dotted pools across the landscape. Captured in the foreground, the birds craned towards the house. Pink smudges feathered their wings; a fingernail had cut the shape of their beaks. Saliva, diluting the blood, had achieved the different textures between land and sky, stillness and motion. It was all coming together.

Bobby pulled the wardrobe across the mural. Satisfied that his work was concealed, he went to the bathroom. Bruises were already forming around the agitated cuts across his left arm. He rinsed the wounds and reached for the first aid box on top of the cabinet. Due to the kind of work that the Old

Man had anticipated the house might need, he had foreseen the possibility of accidents and put together a comprehensive kit. Bobby took out a couple of plasters and a roll of bandages. He did not use the sterile wipes. The prospect of the cuts festering struck him as an eventuality he had no right to guard against. He stretched a bandage tight around his arm. Almost immediately, specks of blood formed on the gauze. Bobby rolled down his sleeve and repacked the kit, trying his best to make it look like nothing had been disturbed.

At the head of the stairs, he paused. There was no movement below, no voices. The house appeared to be empty. He went downstairs and into the kitchen. Two mugs sat soaking in the sink. A note was sellotaped to the Aga.

Bobby – gone to get DIY stuff and supplies. Be back by lunchtime – some bread + jam etc in fridge. Dad & Joe.

An electronic shriek shattered the stillness of the house. Bobby felt his bladder almost give way.

'Jeeze.'

He fumbled in his pocket for the mobile.

'Yeah, hello.'

'Bobby? This is Diane Linton.'

Bobby's guts started performing acrobatics.

'Mr Linton would like a word with you.'

Now his insides felt like the main attraction at the Cirque du Soleil.

'Bobby, Harold Linton here. Diane and I have been thinking about what happened yesterday. It was unforgivable. Really, it was absolutely unforgivable.'

The crowds were agog. The knots into which Bobby's stomach had tied itself made the contortions of Houdini look like the work of a stiff-jointed amateur.

'Unforgivable,' Mr Linton repeated. 'And we, Diane and I, are so very sorry. We realise now that it was selfish to put you under such pressure. And then to blank you the way we did, I just hope you'll forgive us.'

Diane Linton's voice rustled next to that of her husband's. 'We're so, so sorry, Bobby.'

'Of course it was too much to ask. Please know that we don't blame you for the obvious difficulties you had with your speech. How could you have spoken about Matt? You loved him. You . . . Just know that we underst . . .'

Bobby cancelled the call.

'Stupid FUCKS.' He dug fingers into his forearm.

The phone rang again. Bobby switched it off. He released his grip and gasped. Blood seeped through the material of his shirt. He would have to change before Joe and the Old Man got back, but right now he needed some air.

The front door opened onto the scrubland. Birds hovered listlessly a few metres above the ground, their eyes searching for movement in the yellow grass. Through the heat haze, Bobby picked out a church steeple wavering in the distance. The effect, an example of the science of light and optics producing something artistic, captivated the boy's imagination. So enthralled was he that the sound of the millhouse door slamming against the side of the house hit him like a bullet in the back.

Bobby crossed the porch and grabbed hold of the door. There was not a breath of wind and yet it strained in his grasp. A Yale padlock hung loose from a loop on the jamb. He had given the mill only a cursory glance yesterday, but he could have sworn that the place had been locked up.

'Hello?' His voice did not echo, but sank into the gloom. 'Anyone here?'

A lick of sunlight stretched beyond the doorway. Forms, both slender and hulking, smooth and jagged, loomed out of the darkness. Already, Bobby could feel the coolness of the mill lying against his skin. It raised the hairs on his arms and neck. The smell of brick dust and the blood-like tang of rusty metal reached out to him. Crouching to clear the door, Bobby stepped inside.

The house had been silent, but here, in the millhouse, there was true stillness. The stillness after chaos. Hard earned and brittle, Bobby felt that it might fracture at any moment. It was as if something waited here, some memory of industry that threatened to devour the silence. Even his footsteps upon the stone floor sounded like a precursor to thunder. The place was eerie, he guessed, but eerie in the manner of a vacant elevator or an empty seat. The absence, the vacuum: that was what made Daecher's Mill unnerving.

Bobby's eyes adjusted to the darkness. Scattered across tables, and on raised brick platforms, he saw cogs with missing teeth and levers twisted or snapped in two. Broken belts and leather straps coiled across the floor like sloughed snake skin. And everywhere there were bolts and nails, chains and pulleys, chutes and gears. There didn't appear to be a single piece of machinery still intact. For some reason, the sight of these innards, torn from a once vibrant mechanical body, made Bobby feel sad.

The ceiling was held up by iron joists meeting timber cross-beams. How on earth those struts, very nearly the circumference of ship masts, had been hoisted into place, Bobby could not guess. He ran a hand along one of the spars. An atavistic sense, bedded deep within, gave him a feel for the immense age of the wood.

The light inside the millhouse changed. Bobby felt the skin pucker along his spine. He did not need the shadow on the floor to tell him – he knew that someone was standing in the doorway.

Twenty

Joe slid a pencil point down the list. He got to 'install vapour barrier on subfloor' and grimaced.

'Dad, seriously, do you know what the hell you're doing?'

'O ye of little faith,' said Richard. 'I wasn't always a picture dealer, you know.'

They drove off the dual carriageway and headed towards the town of Holbeach, following the directions given by Mr Runerby's secretary. If that desiccated tapper of the typewriter knew what she was talking about then the reclamation yard couldn't be far off.

'Really?' Joe said. 'Hard to imagine you as anything else.'

'Don't let the cultured façade fool you,' Richard grinned. 'Years ago, I was an honest-to-God labouring man. The old hands have softened up a bit but, once upon a time, I could hammer masonry nails in with these fists.'

'Right.'

'I'm serious. Summer I met your mother, this is what I did. Working for a firm renovating old houses. Good times.'

'Then why'd you go into the art business?'

'There's not much difference really. Remember when the gallery used to restore pictures? Not much coin in it for a small operation, but I used to love doing that. Bringing art back to life. Well, that's what a good house renovator does, too. It's like an act of worship, restoring beautiful things. It fills you up, makes you feel like you've done something worthy. You might never be remembered, like some great cabinet maker or architect, but you leave a little part of yourself in the buildings you touch. Houses have memories, Joe, and if you really *touch* them, then they will remember you.'

Joe had never heard his father speak like this before. He turned to face him. For once, Richard Nightingale was as far away from the 'Old Man' of his sons' characterisation as could possibly be imagined. His eyes shimmered with nostalgia and his voice lost that hard edge. He seemed *young* – not much older than Joe himself.

'Sounds cool,' Joe said. 'And you met mum that summer?'

'Yeah.'

'Well? Tell me about it.'

'Not much to tell.'

'What was she like?'

'She was beautiful. Janet Tregennis . . . Her dad – your grandad – he'd bought an old house on the Wolds: Georgian, with some ugly Victorian additions. Needed a good job of work doing to it. My firm got the contract. She came round one day delivering lunch. We laughed about it later; she was like the daughter of an oilman in one of those old Westerns, handling out victuals to the rousties. One of the arseholes I worked with knew I liked her. He said something. Something bad. She didn't blush or kick up a stink; she was so innocent I don't think she understood what he meant. It was that innocence in the face of his coarseness that made me angry.'

Joe could tell that his dad wasn't really talking to him. It was possible that he hadn't been all morning. From the moment that he had shown Joe the list of jobs there had been a marked difference in the man. Now his face was open and warm, the expression one of rapt remembrance.

'Before I knew what I was doing,' Richard continued, 'I'd

decked the guy. She didn't look too pleased about it. In fact, she drove the bastard to hospital. Broken nose. I thought she'd tell her father, get me the sack. I *did* get a dressing down, but somehow I knew she hadn't been the one to grass me up. Anyway, she started hanging around the house, asking me questions about what I was doing. Pretended to be interested, bless her. Wasn't long before I asked her out for a drink, and that was that really. Her dad didn't like it. Thought she could do better, and he was right. Summer of '87. Christ, that's nearly twenty years ago.'

'What happened next?'

'What do you mean?'

'You started dating, and?'

'We liked the same sort of things: books and art and stuff. Musically, we were light years apart. She took me to a T'Pau concert once, but I didn't hold it against her. Yeah, we really liked each other.'

'And you got serious pretty quickly. The next summer, I was born and you got married.'

'It wasn't that easy. We had our problems before then. Your mother didn't tell me about . . .'

Richard blinked. He glanced at Joe and then turned his attention to the road. His features hardened and, in his eyes, the shutters went up.

'It was a long time ago.'

'Did you argue? What did you argue about?'

Joe felt a cold realisation begin to dawn. Things had been going well between his parents throughout the summer of 1987. Then something had come between them. Something new and unexpected that rocked their relationship: the news of a child, perhaps?

'We're here,' Richard grunted.

'This is the Meal Floor,' said Gail Bedeker. 'The ground floor where the power of the water was harnessed.'

She joined Bobby overlooking a narrow trench beside the far wall. Poking through the brickwork above the trench, the axle of the waterwheel reached inside the building. Like the crossbeams that held up the ceiling, this huge, squared-off wooden limb gave the impression of great age.

'How did it work?' Bobby asked. It was not politeness that provoked the question, but a genuine desire to understand the science that had shaped this primitive engine.

'The whole mill?' Gail asked. 'It was based on the principle of gravity. Centuries before Newton discovered it, millers were employing gravitational forces every day. Firstly, sacks of grain from the harvest were brought in here and attached to a hoist. You see that little trapdoor in the ceiling? The grain sacks were drawn up through there to the top floor. That was where the process started. And everything, the hoist, the millstones, each working part, was powered from here.' She slapped the axle. 'Outside, the sluice gate was raised and the river diverted. Water hit the millwheel, causing the axle to turn. The axle then connected with a cast iron shaft that sat in this pit.' Gail pointed to the trench. 'This "pit wheel" turned the main shaft.'

She laid her hand against a thick bar of wood that reached through the ceiling.

'This goes right through the building and into the roof. Come on, I'll show you.'

She led Bobby to a rickety ladder. Throwing back a trapdoor, she guided him up onto the millhouse's first floor. This level, like that below, was a chaos of dismantled machinery. Immediately, Bobby's eye was caught by an iron wheel, a good ten feet in diameter and set around with inlaid teeth. Torn from its original fitting, it rested upon two pitted millstones.

'This is the Stone Floor,' Gail said, 'so named because it was where the millstones ground the grain. Okay, so the main shaft reached up here and turned this thing.' She tapped her foot against the iron disc. 'The spur wheel. Through a series of mechanisms, the spur rotated the millstones. You see that chute in the ceiling? Well, the grain came through there and siphoned between the stones. Then it was ground into flour and drained back to the Meal Floor below. Simply put, the whole thing is like a chain of cogs working from that first water-propelled wheel outside. And the grain, which started downstairs, journeyed through these components until it ended up as flour back at ground level. Gravity, like I said.'

'Genius.'

'It was. Genius in the smallest detail. Stuff like never having metal parts working against other metal parts. The axle of the waterwheel – wood – connects with the pit wheel – iron – which connected with the main shaft – wood – which connects with the spur wheel – iron.'

'Why was that?'

'Risk of fire.'

Gail picked up a sliver of sheared-off metal. For a time, she said nothing.

'Many watermills burned down,' she murmured. 'Flour is highly combustible. If you had metal turning against metal, you got sparks and then . . .'

Her hands swept over the walls.

'Can we go upstairs?' Bobby asked.

'There's not much up there. Just the sack hoist mechanism and the grain chute.'

'Still, I'd like to take a look.'

'You go. I'll wait here.'

Bobby ascended. The second trapdoor proved resistant, but he put his shoulder to the wood and, after a little shoving, it gave way.

The smell here was different. The air, no longer laced with brick dust, smelled bitter and acrid, like burnt charcoal and singed hair. The window, corresponding with the small openings on the Meal and Stone floors below, was so caked in filth that sunlight could not penetrate. What little light there was came from holes in the roof tiles. Nevertheless, Bobby's eyes soon adjusted.

'The Bin Floor,' Gail's voice echoed up into the rafters. 'Although *we* called it "the Garner".'

Bobby was not listening. His gaze wandered over the walls where scorch marks – shadows of flame – showed the fire's passage. The floorboards, too, were blackened, though none of the wood appeared to have been consumed. Charred rope hung in strands from the crossbeams, and again the image of burned hair filled Bobby's mind. He went to the window and ran his finger across the pane. It came back black, not with dirt but with soot. Looking closer, he saw that the glass had warped in its frame. Its bubbled surface reflected his face like a funhouse mirror. He turned away from the window, and was about to descend the ladder, when he saw something that stopped him in his tracks. In the darkness of the Garner Floor, Bobby Nightingale remembered the bedtime stories told to him by his mother. Tales of children lost in the woods, of inviting cottages and the monsters that lived within them. Cottages with little doorways, just like the one set into the attic's back wall.

'The sacks were emptied into the grain chute . . .'

Beside the door was a child's rocking chair. Bobby moved towards it.

'. . . there the grain began its journey.'

He prodded the headrest and the chair see-sawed. Twigs and leaves, resting on the seat, scattered across the floor. As the rumble of the rockers settled, Bobby's attention switched back to the door. He moved the chair aside and tugged at the handle. It wouldn't budge. He laid his hands flat against the wood. It was moist to the touch. The dampness tingled and a charge burned through Bobby's skin. With the shock came a sudden, instinctive certainty. The boy flinched and stepped back, his eyes rooted on the door. He didn't need to make a mental picture, setting out the rooms of the house, stacking them against the floors of the mill. He *knew* that *his* attic bedroom – the room with goblins and sprites dancing across its walls – connected directly with the mill's Garner Floor. Just as he knew that, upon the plywood wall blocking off the other side of this fairytale door, a masterpiece was taking shape. A painting of birds and shadows, scratched into existence with his own hot blood.

'Often the steward kept a tally of sacks. He scored it into the brickwork.'

A breeze whistled through the roof. It took up the twigs and leaves and danced them in the square of light above the trapdoor.

'You can see examples on the walls up there.'

Bobby stumbled backwards. He wondered now whether he had been drawn to that spot on the bedroom wall. Had it been predestined that his artwork should occupy that particular space?

'You know, Bobby, there's something I've been meaning to tell you.'

Bobby's hands slipped against the bricks. He felt the indentations. Just tallies, he thought, like Gail had said. Then his eyes picked out the letters. A word or name carved into the stone. He mouthed the word and then repeated it out loud. It rolled off his tongue, like a playground chant:

'Did you hear me, Bobby?'

'What? I'm sorry, what did you say?'

Bobby stood over the trapdoor. Gail Bedeker smiled up at him.

'I lost my mother at an early age, too.'

'How do you know about my mum?'

'Mrs Sutton told me about her,' Gail said. 'She knew Janet Nightingale, you see? Or Janet Tregennis, as she was then. Yes, old Mrs Sutton knew your mother very well indeed.'

Twenty-one

- JULY 1988: Tregennis House -

'Where is she?'

'I don't know.'

'There are men outside who'll make short work of you, son. Now, I'll ask just one more time: where is my daughter?'

Richard Nightingale folded his arms. 'I don't like you, Mr Tregennis. Not one little bit. But if I knew where Janet was, I'd tell you.'

He stood his ground as the older man circled. Sitting on the green leather sofa, illuminated by rows of track lighting, Stella Tregennis wept. Richard could see nothing of her face, just a mask of fingers that ended in scarlet talons. Her hair, a gigantic arrangement held in place by half a tonne of mousse, bobbed as she cried.

'For Christ's sake, Stella,' Tregennis growled.

'He's done something to her,' Stella spat from behind her hands. 'Make him tell you, David. You make that little cunt tell you what he's done to my precious girl.'

'Mrs Tregennis, I haven't spoken to Janet since February. We had a row and . . .'

'You broke her heart, you cunt. You no-good cunt. Cunt-cunt-cunt.'

The hands fell. Mascara ran from her eyes as Stella came at

Richard like a maternally outraged panda. David Tregennis blocked her path and returned his wife to the sofa. He took a moment to adjust his Rolex. Even with his daughter missing, the old man couldn't help but rub Richard's nose in the Tregennis wealth.

'You tell me where she is,' he said, his finger pointing back at Stella, 'or she'll be the least of your worries.'

'I'm gonna say this again,' Richard said, 'and I'll speak very slowly, so that you can hear me above the rattle of fake jewellery. *I – haven't – seen – Janet – for – five – months*. It wasn't my decision to break up with her.'

'I bet it wasn't,' Stella muttered. 'Knew you were on to a good thing here.'

Those red claws swept the Tregennis lounge: shag pile carpets, wicker high-backed chairs, seashell wall adornments, felt portraits of whiteface clowns.

Richard nodded: 'Sure. I'm curious though: when *did* you shoot your last porno here?'

'You smart aleck bastard.'

Tregennis punched his guest in the gut. If it hadn't been for the cadre of goons waiting outside, Richard would have kicked the old man's arse. Instead, he tried his best to hide the pain.

'Least you think I'm smart,' he wheezed. 'Okay, look, this is what I know. After we went on holiday to your Spanish villa – very nice, by the way, guess you had a different decorator for this place – we got back and everything seemed fine. Then, out of the blue, we have this row and she won't see me anymore. I tried calling her, she didn't want to know. You guys seemed pretty happy about it at the time, I remember. Anyway, I couldn't find a way to speak to her. She wouldn't answer my letters or calls, so I gave up. My firm moved down to Birmingham and I went with them. Then your monkey-boys turn up and suddenly it's like I'm living in an Al Pacino movie. You know you make sweets, right, Mr Tregennis? You're really more Willy Wonka than Scarface.'

'Janet's pregnant.' Tregennis' smirk was almost victorious.

'What?'

'Now you're going to tell me you didn't know.'

Richard dropped back onto the sofa. He was within clawing range, but didn't care. Janet was pregnant. And now that seemingly hypothetical argument made a lot more sense. He remembered what he'd said and cringed: *Kids screw up lives, honey. I've seen it. You're getting on with being young and carefree and* – bam – *some snot-nosed little bastard throws a spanner in the works. Anyone our age getting pregnant should fall down on bended knee and pray to the god that helped legalise abortion.* Richard drew a hand across his mouth, as if wiping the words from his lips.

'I didn't know, Mr Tregennis, I swear.'

Perhaps in the suffocated, seldom-visited part of David Tregennis that served as his soul a spark of sympathy flared. Stranger things must happen, Richard thought. Not often, but sometimes. In any event, the confectioner's tone softened.

'And you've not seen or heard from her? You promise me that?'

'I promise. You're sure . . . you're certain it's mine?'

'My Janet's not a whore,' Stella screeched. 'She hasn't seen anyone since you left her.'

'When did she go?'

'Three days ago,' said Tregennis.

'Just three days?' Richard couldn't help laughing. 'She's probably just pissed off to see friends or something.'

'The baby was due yesterday. Whatever you think of us, Richard, she wouldn't run away from her family, the people who love her, with the birth so close.'

'You don't think she's done something stupid?'

'Too late for that.'

Richard didn't believe Tregennis' self-assured confidence in his daughter's love. Many times, during their eight months together, Janet had confided what she felt about her parents. Stella's affection was wildly schizophrenic, alternating between overbearing motherliness and complete indifference. David Tregennis was a man of forbidding reserve, demonstrative only in the violence of his protectiveness. Richard could quite easily imagine a situation in which Janet, lost in this gaudy prison, had yearned to escape. But escape to where? He pictured her alone in some dingy bedsit, the advent of their child drawing ever nearer.

'Let me help you,' he said.

'You? Help?' Stella laughed. 'You've said you don't know where she is, what good are you?'

'It's my child. I have a right.'

'Right? You lousy little shit . . .'

'Stella, shut up.' Tregennis turned to Richard. 'You love her?'

'Yes. And I'll find her.'

'All right. You'll find her and you'll marry her, understand? No grandchild of mine is gonna be a bastard. Here's what we know.'

Tregennis detailed what he had established thus far. All it amounted to was that Janet had packed a bag, withdrawn a few hundred pounds from her savings, and taken a train to Peterborough. Tregennis and his lackeys had interviewed everyone at the station, from the stationmaster to the tramps that congregated in the car park. A few remembered a pale young woman, heavily pregnant, taking one of the Village Link buses. None of the drivers could recall such a passenger. From there the trail went cold.

'Do you know anyone in those parts?' Richard asked.

Tregennis shook his head. 'Okay, I'll go down there.'

'I've told you, no-one remembers . . .'

'People don't like being intimidated, sir. Maybe a friendly face'll do better than your gorillas.'

Richard went to the door.

'You find her, Nightingale,' said Tregennis, 'and you bring her back to me.'

I'll find her, Richard thought, and I'll do right by her. I'll keep her and my baby safe. And you, and that wailing bitch of a wife, will never hurt her again.

A fortnight passed. Two weeks of pounding pavements and repeating the same questions until they chanted in his dreams. Two weeks of cold shoulders and dead ends. And then, quite suddenly, Richard found her. One question had done it: a connection made in the first days and long forgotten. Visiting a Salvation Army soup kitchen, Richard had handed out one of the passport-size photographs he'd had printed up, the number of his hotel scrawled on the back. At the end of another frustrating day, his feet hot and aching, Richard made his way back to the Earl of Walmshire Guest House. Halfway up the stairs, and already dreaming of a good long soak, the landlady called after him. An officer of the Salvation Army Family Tracing Service had left a message: '*My dear Richard, Miss Janet Tregennis is staying at the Peterborough Temple. She would like to see you very much. Your brother in Christ, Henry Foulds, Captain.*'

On reaching the Temple, Richard listened with ill-disguised impatience to Captain Foulds' story. Janet had wandered into the Temple that morning and asked for milk for her baby. She was gaunter than the woman in the photograph, but Foulds recognised her immediately. Told about her family's search, she insisted that Richard, and Richard alone, should be contacted.

'Where's she been all this time?' he asked.

Foulds shrugged. 'She doesn't appear to know.'

At last, Richard was shown to a comfortable room at the back of the building. There he found her, sitting on a cot and cradling their child. Fear shivered across her face as she held the baby out to him, her arms trembling.

'His name's Joseph,' she said. 'Joseph Richard.'

Richard lifted the child to his chest. Miniature fingers clenched his own. A snub nose wrinkled. He took his time, absorbing every detail of the life he had helped to create. Then he kissed his son's forehead.

'Joe. His name is Joe,' Richard said. He reached for Janet's hand. 'Joe Nightingale.'

Richard looked at his son. It was hard to believe that eighteen years had passed since that night in the Salvation Army Temple. Two of those had been the happiest in Richard's life. In that space of time, between Joe's arrival and Bobby's birth, he had thought that he, Janet and their perfect child were the luckiest people alive. Husband and wife shared everything: the love for their boy, for each other, and for the beauty they found in art and buildings and books. They revelled in the hours of each other's lives and found something worthy of celebration in each passing minute. Those had been precious days, before the birth of the second child. Richard looked back on them now, across sixteen dark years of *The Absence*.

Only one thing had remained unshared: the secret of those missing days. He asked her, time and again, if she could recall where she had spent the final weeks before Joe's birth. No hospital record could be found, and so it was assumed that Janet had endured her labour alone. When she reached the Salvation Army, a midwife had checked mother and baby over, pronouncing both healthy. A little tidying up had been required.

Stitches, that would indicate medical aid with the birth, were not found; otherwise there was no sign of infection

And so the mystery remained: where had the child been born? Therapists asked the same question, but no answer was given. (The seeds of Richard's distrust of psychotherapy were sown during these sessions. Two years later, when *The Absence* began to show itself, other therapists would ask why Richard thought that his wife was, in his words, 'becoming empty'. Others did not notice this 'soullessness', why did he? To Richard's mind, the science that such people professed to understand was still in its infancy. Expecting a twentieth century psychologist to comprehend the human brain was like plonking a particle accelerator in front of Isaac Newton, and asking him how such a device generates high-energy gamma rays. Give these nut doctors a few hundred years, Richard thought, and they might know what they're talking about.) Nevertheless, the closest to an answer for the disappearance came from the report of Janet's psychiatrist:

'During the final days of her pregnancy, Janet suffered a period of dissociative amnesia, or fugue. This is not unheard of in cases where the patient is experiencing life stressors, such as expecting a first child. During these episodes, a patient may go missing for hours, even days, and have little or no recollection of where they have been and to whom they have spoken. Fugues, as in Janet's case, often disappear on their own account. Hypnotherapy has been used in this case, but with no significant results, and drug-facilitated interviews would likely prove no more successful. During hypnosis, a few phrases were often repeated by the patient:

– Stones.

– Wheels – perhaps the wheels of the train that took Janet away from home.

– Fairy children or fairy child.

– Allusion to shadows (the weaving of shadows, like lace).

– A sense of drowning in peat or clay. The sense of hands shaping clay.

– Birds: perhaps referring to 'nightingale', the name of her estranged partner.

– Black water. Black spit/sputum.

– Fire and the smell of burnt hair.

I feel unable to say with any certainty what these themes might indicate, although the reference to children seems fairly self-evident.

There is some indication that, wherever Janet ended up, something traumatic happened to her there. This may be no more than the stress inherent in imminent childbirth, especially in an alien environment. In conclusion, I do not believe that Janet is in danger of lapsing into further fugue states. No follow-up treatment is required.'

Richard remembered these things with crystal clarity. It was a mystery that he had pondered often in the early days of *The Absence*, wondering if the clue to his wife's vanishing soul might be buried in the physical disappearance she had once affected. It seemed unlikely, however, for they had lived together, contented for two whole years, before *The Absence* began to eat away at her.

'All right there, mate?' The owner of the reclamation yard slapped Richard on the back. 'You busy dreamin' while your boy does all the hard graft?'

'You tell him,' Joe said, heaving the last of the floorboards onto the trailer they had hired.

Richard pinched the corners of his eyes. He felt exhausted. 'What's the damage?'

'Boards and radiators? Call it a grand.'

Richard counted out the money. Then he shook hands with the dealer and got into the car.

'A grand?' Joe said. 'For that load of old crap.'

'Trust me, those floorboards'll look cracking when we get them sanded down.'

'I hope that's the Royal "we", cos I'm knackered.'

Richard started the motor. He headed out of the yard and onto the dual carriageway.

They hadn't gone a quarter of a mile when he slammed on the brakes. A chorus of horns blared from the traffic banking up behind.

'Dad? What is it?'

Richard pulled the Mercedes into a lay-by. He got out of the car and stood in front of a large road sign.

'Stupid,' he murmured. 'Jesus Christ, so stupid.'

The sign:

Spalding 8m
Kings Lynn 20m
Peterborough 25m

Ever since George Cuttle had slapped the deeds on his desk, Richard's thoughts had been elsewhere – on drink, Susan Keele, the boys. On recapturing those days of his youth, in which he had worked with his hands, bringing beauty back to a tarnished past. He hadn't stopped to think about the *location* of Daecher's Mill. Now he considered: Mrs Muriel Sutton, a relation of Janet, had lived only twenty or so miles from the Salvation Army Temple. The mill: a retreat far away from David and Stella Tregennis – somewhere that a young girl, facing the birth of her first child, might find space in which to think. It made sense. But, if she *had* fled there, why did Janet then leave the sanctuary of the millhouse? And why had she suppressed her memories of the place? Of course, it may be a coincidence. Just because the mill was within a fairly close proximity to Peterborough, didn't mean . . .

Richard remembered the therapist's report. *Clay. Wheels. Birds.* Those phrases, repeated so often during his wife's hypnosis, gelled with that strange feeling of familiarity he had experienced upon hearing the name of the village. Subconsciously, he must have made the connection.

Clay and wheel= Potter. Birds= Drake. Potter's Drake.

Wheel and stones and water= The Millhouse.

Daecher's Mill. The place where the fugue had taken her. The place where his son, Joseph Richard Nightingale, had been born.

Twenty-two

Back at the millhouse, they started unloading the trailer. Richard helped with the heavier floorboards but left Joe to shift the smaller pieces unaided. As he worked, the boy thought back to their conversation en route to the reclamation yard.

So much about his father had been revealed in those few exchanges. He wondered why the Old Man, usually so reticent, had decided to open up. Whatever the motivation, Joe had finally got a sense that his father possessed some inner-life, some spark of emotional vitality. Richard Nightingale had loved beautiful things, and it was this passion which had drawn Janet Tregennis to him. But something had changed. A development that altered their affections and reconfigured the parts they played. Joe had often wondered what strange occurrence had brought his parents together, and what miracle kept them bound to one another. Now, having heard part of his father's story, he believed he knew. Their passion, although intense, had not been built to last. It was a fire taking flame over one summer, the kind that consumes ferociously and soon burns itself out, never to be rekindled. Afterwards, each would have gone their separate way, thankful to the other for the experience they had shared. That was how it should have played out, but such romantic notions were not to be. Events got in the way. A child was born. And then, two years later, Richard's fate had been doubly sealed when another baby came along.

In these events, Joe began to understand the character of his father; a man trapped by circumstance, trying to make the best of the situation in which he found himself. A man of honest passions, who could not remain buttoned-down, year upon year, without a little of the resentment he felt seeping out. He had been unable to relate to his children because, in reality, *they* were his gaolers. Was it any wonder he seemed forever distant? Had anyone – his wife, his kids – ever talked to him about *his* feelings? No, they had been too ready to brand him a bastard. And even now, after the accident, Richard Nightingale was not free. Perhaps the strain of eighteen years in a loveless marriage had broken him. It had certainly spurred him to drink, and now that dependency was fracturing his reason. What other explanation could there be for the way he had stood before that road sign, murmuring:

She was here. Here all the time.

As Joe dropped the last board onto the porch, his phone rang. The display flashed: *Sam Jones Mob*. He marched through the scrub until he stood far away from the house. She barely had chance to say 'hello' before Joe started telling her the events of the last few days. He kept back his thoughts about his parents, but everything else came gushing out: the journey down, the meeting at the solicitors and the death of George Cuttle, the missing pictures, the murder of Alice Daecher, anything and everything. It acted like a purgative. Afterwards, he began to feel a little better.

'Interesting relatives you have,' said Sam. 'What did you say her name was?'

'The little girl was called Alice, the sister was Muriel Sutton. Why'd you ask?'

'I'm bored silly sitting around watching reruns of *Murder, She Wrote*. I might do a little sleuthing myself.'

'Hey, Jessica Fletcher, leave my family skeletons be.'

'Oh, you're no fun. I'd poke around in the Jones' family closet, except I already know what messed up things I'd find in there.'

As was often the case when Sam referred to her family, Joe didn't know how to respond. He knew that she resented her parents, but wasn't sure to what extent. Of course, she had every right to be angry at their treatment of her. She hadn't seen her mother for a long time, and Mr Jones made Michael Jackson look like Father of the Year.

'You don't mind, do you?' she asked, 'if I do a bit of research? It just sounds so cool and creepy: a deranged woman living in a remote millhouse murders her younger sister.'

'Okay,' Joe sighed. 'S'pose it doesn't matter much. It's not like we knew them or anything.'

'Cool.'

'I better get going, my dad's probably arranged for me to row a slave ship or mine quarry rocks this afternoon.'

'Poor baby.' Then her voice took on a serious tone. 'You're doing okay, aren't you, Joe?'

Joe filled up. He tried to speak, but feared that his voice would crack.

'Please, talk to me.'

'I'm fine,' he said, covering the emotion with a cough.

'Good . . . I love you.'

Maybe she was frightened of what he might say back or, worse still, of hearing only the crackle of static. Whatever the case, she cancelled the call before he could answer.

In his assessment, Joe was wrong. He did not know then about *The Absence*. Nor did he realise that Richard had loved his wife with a bone-deep, consuming love for two years after Joe's birth. In fact, he had gone on loving her long after Bobby had been born and well into the period when *The Absence* asserted itself. And, in the bleak years to come, when he could no longer feel for the physical presence that shared their bed, he went on loving a memory. It was only in the last days that he had been forced to extinguish his love once and for all.

Richard leafed through the address book. He found the number and began dialling on the old Bakelite in the hall. Four digits in, he stopped and replaced the receiver. Why was he doing this? Even if Janet had come here all those years ago, what did it matter now? He had no answer, except the simple need to know whether his suspicions were true: that his son had been born in the home of a convicted child-killer.

He dialled again. Six rings later, he heard the click.

'David?'

'This is the Tregennis household. No-one is here to take your call. Leave a message.'

'David, it's Richard. Call me when you get this. It concerns Janet. I think I might have found the place she disappeared to in '88. It's possible you knew the woman she stayed with, and . . . I . . . I hope Stella's no worse. Bye.'

Richard put down the phone.

He had not spoken to the confection magnate for sixteen years. Even at Janet's funeral the two men had avoided one another. The boys had been encouraged to get to know their grandparents, but Richard was proud that both Joe and Bobby had never succumbed to the showering of expensive gifts which, at Tregennis House, passed for affection. The last he had heard David had sold the business and retired. A little time later, Stella had been diagnosed with Alzheimer's and was now in the advanced stages of the disease. Richard recalled those scarlet talons pointing at him and the machine-gun rattle of obscenity: *cunt-cunt-cunt*. It was hard to imagine such a woman confused and powerless.

He stepped onto the porch just as Joe returned from the scrub.

'Nice work, son,' Richard said, admiring the neat stack of boards. 'Tomorrow we can start laying those in the study.'

'Great. So that's it for the day?'

'Fraid not. After lunch, we need to take up the old floorboards and do a bit of groundwork. Go rouse Bobby. I'm off to stretch my legs.'

'What did your last slave die of?'

'Scurvy? Rickets? Running with scissors? That's the thing with slaves, you forget.'

Richard felt a rush of pleasure as his son laughed. He reached out and patted Joe's arm.

'Shoulder holding up?'

Joe stepped back. His hand went to the scar and he nodded. 'Yeah. S'fine.'

Bobby watched them from the Stone Floor window.

He saw his father and Joe unload the trailer and, later, share a joke on the porch. Then Richard walked off in the direction of the road, and Joe went into the house. Through the wall of the mill, Bobby could hear his brother calling his name. He would not answer. He would stay here and remain very still. Even if Joe went to the attic bedroom and uncovered the painting, Bobby would not budge. Pushing his back against the wall he felt that, if he wished, he could press himself into the stone of the millhouse. Behind him, the brick was cool and pliant, and the atmosphere of the place welcomed him. 'Stay here' – it said – 'out of the hard, cruel sun. Away from those whose actions speak of hard, cruel thoughts.'

Sunlight flashed against the window. It swayed across the millstones and the disc of the spur wheel. All at once, the room came alive with shadow. Regular blocks of darkness stretched from the joists and timbers. Stranger shapes were thrown by broken bottles and the amputated innards of the great machine. The dance of the darkness soothed the boy. He felt at home here, far away from the father that did not care, from the brother that, by sharing a simple joke, had betrayed him. Far away from Kelvin Hope and the police, who must now know that he *had* killed the Linton kid. Far away from Matt Linton himself, whose ghost could not penetrate the millhouse.

Bobby luxuriated in his newfound security. He would not go upstairs, of course. That upper room – 'the Garner', she had called it – troubled him. But here, on the Stone Floor, he found peace and absolution. And why should he not? Gail Bedeker had told him: this place had once been home to his mother. He could almost feel her presence here, sunk into the fabric of the building. It called to him and told him that he was right to feel safe. As long as he remained here, nothing outside could touch him.

All the same, there *were* dangers in the millhouse. Nails, full of the rusty promise of lockjaw, poked through the floor. Scythes and axes, saws and blades, sat ready to punish a simple trip. And then there was the water.

The black water that dripped from the Garner Floor. Bobby wasn't sure why he saw this as a fracture in the mill's security, but he did not like the seeping invasion from the room above. Just as he didn't like the rocking chair, the little door, or that curious word etched into the stone.

He looked at the underside of the trapdoor and saw the water dribble through. Soon he would take a piece of sacking and block up the gap. The prospect of this victory against the water made him smile. He felt a rush of exhilaration. One last toke, and then he'd cut the sack.

Bobby waved his lighter beneath the bowl and sucked on the end of the tube. Crystals bubbled and spat, releasing a white vapour into his lungs. He couldn't remember why he had gone back to his room and retrieved the bag of crack. Maybe guilt and lack of sleep had finally broken him. Or perhaps he had wanted to come back here, but had needed a little Dutch courage to sit beneath the weeping trapdoor. Whatever the reason, he was glad he had done it – with the drug firing his senses, Joe's betrayal did not cut so deep. He had thought they were brothers. Brothers standing against a common enemy.

'Do you want to hear a story, Bobby?'

She sat on the millstone. Gail Bedeker. Was she really here? Didn't matter. Nothing mattered except blocking off the black water.

'Sure,' Bobby grinned. 'Stories are cool.'

'If you hear this story, you must promise to think long and hard about it,' said Gail. Her fingers twisted in her lap as she glanced up at the trapdoor. 'Think about what you should do. Think about *who* you *must* tell.' The water, no longer dripping, rained down in thin columns. 'Think about your family and what they mean to you.' The pools upon the floor thrashed, and Bobby felt the spray against his face. 'The water will come, and *she* will come with it. The wheel shall turn and the shadows will be woven.' The ceiling, stained black, appeared to buckle. 'The story of the marshes,' Gail said, her voice almost lost against the roar. 'The story of the mill. Of the Shadow House.'

Above the water, Bobby heard thin, fluidic laughter.

It came from beyond the trapdoor.

Twenty-three

The afternoon passed in heavy hours. Unable to find Bobby, Joe set about prising up the old floorboards in the study. There was no cellar to the house, but the crawl space under the floor was surprisingly deep. Hidden in the cavity, Joe found a junk-yard's worth of bric-a-brac – fragments of broken china, Victorian and Edwardian coins, the bowl of a snapped teaspoon, the glass casing from a fob watch. Beneath one rotten board he discovered a doll's leg wrapped up in a hammock of webs. It reminded him of images from Vietnam War movies: blasted limbs snagged in the tendrils of trees.

While Joe worked, he shut out the disquieting thoughts of the morning. Instead, he concentrated on Sam Jones and her declaration. *I love you*. The words made him feel warm and nervous, hopeful and undeserving.

By three o'clock, he had taken up all the boards in the centre of the room and was ready to start on those running along the study's porch-facing wall. Reaching the place where the old writing bureau had once stood, Joe paused. In the rush to get started, he had moved the furniture into the hall without taking much notice of the spaces it had occupied. Now he saw, in the dark wood rectangle, that the writing desk had been concealing a secret. A hatchway, roughly the size of an A4 sheet of paper, sat flush against the wall. Joe looped his finger through the hatch's iron ring and pulled. It wouldn't budge. He pressed the crowbar into the fitting and strained. There was no give. A child-like excitement took hold of the boy as he imagined what might lay hidden beneath . . .

He flipped the crowbar in his hand and brought the head down hard. Pieces of wood flew in all directions and glanced off his safety-goggles. As he withdrew the bar, he heard the scrape of metal against stone. He dropped to his knees and peered into the freshly made hole.

It appeared that the hook of the crowbar had smashed through the outer wall of the house. Joe was puzzled: surely the wall was too thick to come away like that. He lay down flat upon the floor and wriggled, shouldering his way between the joists to get a better look. He saw that he had hit a ventilation brick between the study's subfloor and the raised porch outside. As he stared into the cavity, something glinted in the darkness. He put out a hand and reached into the hatch. His fingers scrabbled around in the dust but found nothing.

Outside, the wind chime tinkled.

Joe got to his feet and followed the sound out onto the porch. He tapped the porch boards with the heel of his boot and leaned over the rail. The space below the walkway was boarded up on all sides. The crowbar would make short work of it, but it seemed senseless to go digging for imagined treasure. What had glinted at him from inside the hatch was probably just a bit of old junk, like everything else he had found at the roots of the house.

The chime jangled. Joe caught hold it, muffling its voice. Clasped in his fist, the long minute hand, snapped from the face of a grandfather clock, pointed to that dark space beneath his feet.

The cottage stood behind a wall of hawthorn. Richard broke off a branch and tried to hack out a spyhole. It was no good, the thicket was nigh on impenetrable. He completed a circuit of the property, and had come to the conclusion that Gail Bedeker must pole vault her way to and from the cottage, when he saw a break in the barrier. It was such a narrow opening that he had to shuffle through sideways. Branches prodded the small of his back and bramble scratched his skin. Spitting out leaf membrane, Richard emerged into the cottage garden.

'Garden' was perhaps the wrong term for such a wilderness. The grass, verdant at its roots, straw-yellow at the tips, reached almost waist-high. Inside this blanket, things that Richard hoped would remain hidden chattered away. He strode up to the front door and knocked. While he waited, his eye passed over a sign, glazed beneath layers of old and new webs: *Bedeker Cottage* and, written beneath: *SHAMUS'S PATCH*. A rusted chain with a rotten leather collar had been bolted to the wall beside the sign.

Richard flipped the letterbox.

'Miss Bedeker? Gail? It's Richard Nightingale.'

He peeked inside, but could see nothing beyond a coat rack sporting a green Gore-Tex jacket.

Curiosity got the better of Richard. He walked around the house, spying through windows. Most of the furniture had been corralled into the kitchen: tables, chairs, a bedstead, a sofa. The bedroom contained a spring-ruptured mattress with a pillow and sleeping bag and a few tins of food lined up on the windowsill. A dozen or so oblong shapes, shrouded beneath a white sheet, stood in the fireplace. Probably the portraits Gail had inherited from Muriel Sutton, Richard thought. Grime and dust covered every surface while rotting cocoons and rat droppings littered the floor.

The sight of that filthy room ignited a sudden itching all over Richard's body. As he scratched his arm and grazed his scalp, he heard the insects chirrup in the grass. The sound inspired visions of legs crawling beneath his clothes, clicking and scuttling across his skin. Sweat sprang out upon his brow and back and his tongue felt big and dry. Doubled over, Richard coughed up a throatful of sputum.

Chink chink

He needed a drink. Desperately. There was a bottle hidden in the boot of the car. With Joe and Bobby working in the house, he could . . .

A cry escaped Richard's lips. He had thrown the scotch away. There was no more. He grasped the car keys in his pocket. Potter's Drake wasn't far. He'd find an offie and strip the shelves. Richard ran through the grass, heedless now of its hidden monsters. He hardly noticed the barbs of the hawthorn cutting his cheeks.

Beyond the stink of the Bedeker garden, he breathed easy. The attack had been a brief one and rationality was returning.

'You're all right,' he told himself.

He rubbed the heel of his hands against his eyes. A distraction – that was what he needed – something to orient his thoughts before he returned to the house. The kids would know otherwise. They would see the hunger.

Richard climbed up the bank and onto the road. There were no cars, no cyclists, no ramblers. His nerves sang as he thought: this is an empty (*Absent*) place . . . Turning south, he saw a patch of woodland. The spire of a church jutted from between the trees. It was probably medieval, he thought, built here when agricultural industry demanded close-knit communities. Doubtless the building had been desacralised and abandoned long ago. Richard decided to investigate.

The spire was deceptive. Being unusually short, it had given the impression that the church was farther away than it was.

A ten-minute ramble through the glade brought Richard to the brownstone chapel and its modest graveyard. He stopped some way short of the lich gate and, suddenly conscious of his intrusion, slipped behind an oak tree.

Gail Bedeker was kneeling beside a weathered stone. Her hands worked, dipping a rag into a pail of water and smoothing away moss and lichen from the headstone. Her bare feet pointed towards him, and Richard found something shocking in the sight of those black soles.

Still, it was very peaceful here. Birds twittered in the ramparts and the breeze sighed inside the empty shell of the church. The spire broke through the branches like a quill through a canopy of green skin. What sunlight penetrated, came in bursts of quick-dying fire, giving the little glade the olive tones of a Hobbema landscape.

At last, Gail shuffled back and assessed her work. Then she bent over and kissed the stone.

'I'm sorry.'

Richard had to lean forward to catch the words.

'But, please, I had no choice. Don't you see? I had to give them a chance.'

She threw the pail of water across the ground and headed for the gate. Before reaching it, she turned and faced a smaller headstone. This slab of white marble stood out as the newest monument in the graveyard. Indeed, it seemed to be the only recent addition.

Gail Bedeker spat upon the stone. She tore up handfuls of earth and smeared them across the inscription. The violence broke the quiet spell of the place and Richard found himself gaping at the spectacle. His breath quickened and he hunkered down in the undergrowth. When he looked up again, Gail was gone.

He stayed hidden for a while, his mind going over what he

had witnessed. There were no answers to be got from staring at tree roots, and so he broke cover. Gail was nowhere to be seen. He stepped over the wall that girdled the church and entered the graveyard. The first stone he came to was the one that Gail had been tending so assiduously. The letters were faded but the marble gleamed:

Alice Daecher
Born 23rd September 1960. Died 17th October 1972
Daughter of Mariah and Guido
Cruelly taken from
her loving sister, Muriel Sutton
'Absent in the flesh, yet I am with you in the spirit'
Colossians 2:5

'Cruelly taken from her loving sister.' The same sister that had been imprisoned for her murder? Was the dedication some kind of joke?

Richard rose and walked towards the lich gate. Reaching the newer grave, he used his shirtsleeve to wipe away the dirt and saliva Gail had deposited there. He recalled what she had said in the car: Muriel Sutton was no angel – she was hard. Strong sentiments that barely hinted at the hatred which Gail clearly bore for the dead woman.

A bird trilled overhead.

Richard stared at the stone:

Muriel Sutton
Born 18th April 1945
Died 13th May 2006
'Thou art weighed in the balances, and art found wanting.'
Daniel 5:27

Twenty-four

Sunlight slanted through a chink in the curtains. The beam hit Joe square in the face and he groaned and rolled over. Tired, but content, the boy looked back on his day's work. He had taken up most of the study floor and started the groundwork for the new boards. As he tore out rot and smoothed away decay, the passion of which his father had spoken had stirred, both in his soul and in his blistered hands. In the short hours of the afternoon a revelation had begun to dawn upon Joe Nightingale.

He was not cut out to be an academic. Of course, he had always been indifferent to the idea of studying economics. The only reason he applied for the course was because the Old Man had insisted upon him choosing something with a clear career path. English, which he loved, was not good enough. Joe had not argued because he had had no strong ideas of his own about his future. Today all that had changed. It was the experience of a single afternoon, but he now knew what he wanted to do with his life. He wanted to work with his hands, to restore beautiful things. To end every day with that same honest sense that he had earned his rest.

Joe yawned. His mind skimmed the surface of consciousness, slipping occasionally into an ocean of sleep. As he pivoted on the brink of reality and dream, his thoughts seesawed between clear, logical snatches and images tinged with the surreal.

Sam loved him. Did he love her? Could anyone truly love another person? What if the other 'person' was, in fact, a cavity of nothingness? A hole in the floor, a hatchway, its lips smattered with mother-blood. A dripping hole, like a dripping cunt. *Her* cunt, warm, pressed down upon his dick. He needed to get out of these trousers – needed to get her out of the car and fuck her senseless on the bonnet. Her mouth crushed against his and he tasted her tongue, moist and bark-like. Their lips parted and she whispered in his ear:

Row, row, row your boat

Joe sprang from the dream-ocean. Perched on the edge of the bed, he tried to sidestep his dream by taking in the hard reality around him. He went to the window and drew the curtains.

It was night. A thin rind of moon sat directly above the mill-house. By its light, Joe looked across the scrubland towards the roof of Gail Bedeker's cottage. There had been no sign of the woman since their meeting yesterday. He thought his dad might have paid her a visit during his afternoon walk but, if so, the Old Man hadn't mentioned it. His gaze moved on, out across the road and along the dykes and cuts. A yellow nimbus hovered on the horizon: the glaring brow of some distant town.

Joe's head snapped towards the bedroom door.

The sound coming from the corridor made his balls shrink and his throat run dry. As he listened, his hand sought out the scar that puckered his left shoulder.

The crystal ball – for what else could it be? – rolled along the corridor. Joe felt its rumbling passage reverberate in the chambers of his heart. He pictured it, black at its centre, its surface rainbow-textured in the light from the landing. But what was it doing here, in this lonely old house? And who was following it, their wet soles slapping against the floorboards?

Reaching Joe's bedroom, ball and stranger came to a stop.

A shadow wavered in the gap beneath the door.

Silence, but for the beat of Joe's heart.

He asked, 'Who's there?'

A giggle rippled in his ears. It was a youthful, malicious laugh.

Trails of water slipped under the door. The threads joined and gathered into a pool. Joe watched and felt his own insides turn to water. He glanced back at the bed, half-expecting to see himself tangled in the sleeping bag, caught up in a dream of broken glass and tiny feet. But the bed was empty.

'*Merrily, merrily, merrily, merrily.*' The words tripped through the door.

This was ridiculous. Some stupid game of Bobby's, no doubt. Joe crossed the room and gripped the door handle.

'*Life is but a dream.*'

With a swell of courage, he threw open the door.

The light on the landing fizzed.

There was no-one there.

A draught locked cold manacles around Joe's ankles. He looked down to find footprints drying on the boards. Apart from two complete prints, the other footmarks along the corridor were mainly toes, confirming what he had heard: the flight of a child.

The house, dark and unmoving, awaited his decision. Urine pressed against his pubis. The slightest relaxation and it would flood down his legs. His brain stumbled as it tried to frame explanations for what he saw: there was a little stranger inside the house; a kid with the voice of a guttering drain. A child that sang to him through a closed door, stirring memories he preferred to remain buried.

Contrary to every resisting instinct, Joe followed the footprints.

At the head of the stairs, he tried the landing light. The

switch crackled. The filament burned low and died. Joe tapped the bulb. Flecks of water sprang from it and, fearing electrocution, he tottered backwards. His heels slipped against the floor. He tried to grab hold of something, but found only a pull cord, which whipped through his fingers. He fell. A door slammed to. Its whipcrack report coincided with Joe landing on his tailbone. Pain bowled through him and, for one terrifying moment, he thought that the crack of the door had been the sound of shattered vertebrae. He rolled onto his side and concentrated on not choking to death.

Piece by piece, Joe's senses came out of the green mist of nausea. He saw that he had fallen into the bathroom and that the door had closed behind him. By some inadvertent dexterity, he had managed to switch on the light while entering the room horizontally. He staggered to the toilet and sat down. As his head cleared, the reason for his being there came back to him. He looked across the tiled floor and saw the footprints leading right up to the claw-foot bathtub. The shower curtain had been drawn around the bath.

Joe swallowed hard and put out his hand.

Giggles shivered from behind the screen.

'Who's there?' His voice was small. 'How did you get into this house? You're trespassing here and . . .'

Two needle-points of light pierced the curtain. They moved across the screen, slipped in and out of the folds of material, like the headlights of a car glancing between trees. Joe put a hand across his mouth. Desperate to leave, he couldn't tear himself from the shadow play. The lights approached the edge of the curtain. Tyres screeched, beams glared, and Joe heard the squeal of metal. He smelled burnt rubber and spilled petrol. Then, for a time, everything was still. The heating pipes rattled, that was all. Joe began to feel as if the dream was fading. Any time now, he'd wake up.

'Silly boy.'

His mother's voice.

'Such a silly, silly boy.'

Joe thrust his palms against his ears. He wouldn't listen. This wasn't real. But the voice persisted.

'Don't you understand, Joe? *Here* - inside your head – is where I scream the loudest. Now, stop being such a cry-baby and let me look at you.'

Joe took hold of the shower curtain. The rubber squeaked between his fingers. He didn't want to draw it back, but the old adage compelled him: Mother Knows Best.

'Yes, that's right, darling. Good boy. Mummy's waited so long to see her handsome Joe again. I've dreamed of you, my sweet, in the endless night. I've reached for you through the dry, dry earth. And even when the worms took my eye, I knew that one day I would see you again. Let me see you, Joseph.'

He pulled back the curtain.

Pond-scummy water rippled in the tub. Waves lapped against the brim and splashed over the side. There was a scent to the stuff reminiscent of forest pools and underground caverns. Joe leaned forward. He saw his face, ashen in the dark mirror. He dropped to his knees and ran his hands around the edges of the bath. A suicidal instinct willed him to dip his head beneath the surface. He could not resist. Captivated, the boy lowered himself, inch by inch, until his nose brushed the waters. He could lose himself here, in the darkness . . . in the depths . . .

A splinter of glass broke the water. It speared within slicing distance of Joe's eye. The boy fell backwards and scuttled towards the door. Heart bursting in his chest, he glanced back in time to see a dozen shards, greasy with blood, cut the surface. They rose slowly out of the slime. He knew what must come next and wanted to look away. He could not.

A shattered mirrorball of a face, wax-white and *glinting*, emerged from the water. Every inch of skin had been forested with glass. Desperate to breathe, Janet Nightingale opened her mouth and snatched at the air. As she gulped it down, tiny shards fell from her lips and tinkled into the water. Her hands grasped the edges of the bathtub. In one sudden movement, the dead thing jackknifed out of the water. Blood hit the wall with a soft splatter while an arterial spray hissed from the wound at her throat. Joe felt the blood splash against his toes. His face long with terror, he drew up his feet.

Meanwhile, the figure rose to her full height.

Here was a woman in the process of sloughing her skin. All across her body it hung from her in tattered strips. Her breasts, now empty sacks, lay flat against her stomach. Water dripped from her boney fingers and the skeletal shelf of her jaw. Her private parts had rotted away and, beyond a few scraps of gore, Joe could see the snap of his mother's pelvis and the fused vertebrae at the base of her spine. Her left eye remained intact but the right was gone. Like a worm emerging from its hole, a stalk of optic nerve drooped from the socket. The reek of decomposition filled the air.

Joe's screams could not break through the horror of what he saw. All he could do was to mewl quietly.

The thing must have heard his whimpers.

Its head snapped in his direction. Arms shot out, as if the late Janet Nightingale wished to embrace her son. As they moved against each other, the bones and sockets crackled through long disuse.

Her mouth fell open.

'Mummy's always here, Joe,' she said, lips slavering over crumbs of glass. 'Always here, inside your head. Always singing, always bleeding. Always *dying*.'

Joe found his screams.

Fear and grief threatened to take him, there and then, into the millhouse. His shadows were ripe, but the time was not. His mother turned and lowered herself back beneath the water.

Joe, once more in his bed, whimpered in the throes of a bad dream.

The little girl that weaved his nightmare stood beside him. She smiled and stroked his hair. Before returning to her chair in the attic of the millhouse, she whispered in his ear.

'*She came home to the shadows, Joe. And now you've come home, too. It's been such a long, long time, I'm sure you won't remember me. But no matter. Soon we shall play, my child. Soon I shall cast myself in the darkness of your mind.*'

Twenty-five

Bobby reopened his wounds and refreshed the vibrancy of the painting. Completing the work with quick retouches to the wings of the birds, he pulled the wardrobe back across the plasterboard wall. Then he tugged on a long-sleeved shirt, shoved a few bits and pieces into his rucksack, and eased open the bedroom door. He tiptoed to the bathroom and redressed the cuts.

At the top of the stairs, he stopped and listened. The radio was playing in the study: Bob Dylan's *Like A Rolling Stone* just audible above the hammering. When Joe had popped his head around the door first thing that morning, Bobby had tried to speak to him.

'I saw that woman yesterday – Gail Bedeker,' he said. 'In the millhouse. She told me things about this place. Weird things.'

'What d'you mean?'

'I can't – can't remember. I think she wanted me to tell someone. I think it was important.'

'Look, Bob, I really need to get to work. You gonna help us today or not?'

Joe wasn't interested in the vague dreams that troubled him. Bobby had snuggled down into his sleeping bag and mumbled something about a headache. Joe hadn't pressed the point. Of course he hadn't, he and the Old Man were best buds now. They were only asking for Bobby's help out of politeness.

As if to reinforce this conclusion, the sound of their laughter sailed out of the study.

'Fuck you,' Bobby whispered. He reached the hall and the front door. 'Fuck you both.'

The world outside was less like a blast furnace today. It was still very warm, but the sting had gone out of the sunshine. Bobby went straight to the millhouse. He didn't notice the padlock until the door refused to give. Someone had sealed the place back up. The who and why seemed obvious: Richard had noticed his son spending time here and must have concluded that Bobby was faking his 'illness'. This petty act of discipline was the Old Man to a T. Well, fine, let the fucker have his little victory.

Bobby looked up at the Stone Floor window. He longed to sit with his back against the bricks, to smell the comforting scent of aged wood and iron. To listen to Gail Bedeker relate the tales of the millhouse and the marshes. Surely it *had* been her: that figure seated upon the stone circles, the truth of this place falling from her lips. A truth that he could no longer recall. The memory was fragmented, blasted by the short-lived euphoria of the crack.

Bobby crossed the bridge that spanned the dried-up spillway. From this vantage, he could make out the crater-like belly of the millpond behind the house. It was quiet here. Once there would have been the burble of the pond, or the rush as the sluice was lifted. Now there was only the call of mating insects. Bobby followed the dead river east.

The sun dazzled, and so instead of seeing the gradual segue of Fen into coast, he noticed the changing landscape in snatches. The earth became less solid. Sand slipped underfoot. At the edge of the dunes, the air sharpened and seagulls squalled overhead. Marram grass cut Bobby's shins. Standing upon an outcrop, he shielded his eyes and took in the view.

As far as he could see, from north to south, the coastline was deserted. The North Sea ran out in a ribbon of gunmetal grey, flecked here and there by the occasional whitecap. Bobby pulled off his trainers, dropped down from the rock and strode to the water's edge. He skimmed a few flat stones. In the shallows, a shoal of silver fish fluttered like a white hand beneath the waves. It reminded him of something: a fist, bloodless, clutching the haft of a razor . . . Bobby watched until the semblance was lost. Then he turned back to the dunes.

His toes squelched. He looked down and saw markings in the sand.

Footprints. Bare feet emerging from the sea.

'Good work,' Richard's words came muffled from behind the dust mask. 'That's the subfloor down.'

Father and son stood in the doorway of the study. They had spent the morning stapling resin paper and roofing felt into place. Now it was time to lay the new floorboards.

'Okay, ready for the hard bit.'

'You're joking?' Joe grinned. 'You're not joking.'

'First we've got to establish a baseline, then saw off the bottom of the door jambs.'

They had already felted over that space once hidden by the hatchway.

For the third time that morning, Joe asked, 'So it's definitely not worth investigating that cavity?'

'I've told you, son,' Richard said, snapping the protective goggles from his head, 'if there's anything there, it'll just be a load of old junk. The hatch was probably used to lay rat traps under the floor, that's all.'

'S'just, I thought I saw something under the porch.'

'Joe, let's not get distracted, okay?'

Joe nodded, peeled off his riggers gloves and headed upstairs for a quick wash. He knocked on Bobby's door as he passed but received no response. In the kitchen, Richard had cut a few rounds of turkey sandwiches. They took their lunch out onto the back porch and ate, like mad Englishmen, in the midday sun.

'Do you like it here, dad?' Joe asked, tossing his crust to a pack of starlings.

'I suppose. Bit out of the way. Why'd you ask?'

'No reason.'

With questions, instructions and the easy banter of the working day suspended, they fell back into familiar trenches of silence. Joe did not want this. He struggled to find an avenue of conversation. The only one that occurred to him was a subject he was nervous to pursue. In the end, Richard relieved him of the burden.

'So, that girl. Sam wasn't it? How's it going with her?'

'Early days,' Joe felt the heat suffuse his face. 'She . . . she said she loved me.'

'Jesus.'

'I know.'

'How long you been seeing each other?'

'Not long. A few weeks before mum . . . We've picked things up again.'

'And she said she loves you? Go easy, son. You'll be away at uni soon.'

'Yeah. Dad?'

'Humph?' Richard answered, his mouth full of processed fowl.

'You remember what you were saying in the car yesterday? About how you used to love this work? Well, I was thinking . . .'

Richard's mobile rang. He looked down at the caller ID and flipped the phone.

'Hello? No, I can't hear you . . . Hello?'

Joe could hear a voice stutter through the static: 'This is David . . . avid Tregen . . . got your. . . . chard . . . any sooner . . . where are you?'

Richard reeled off the address of the mill a couple of times before the line went dead.

'Was that grandad?' Joe asked.

'Yes.'

'Why'd you tell him where we are? We haven't seen him since . . .'

'It's nothing,' Richard said. 'Your grandmother's not well. I thought I'd let him know we were here. Just in case.'

The lie hung between them and brought to a close any notion of further conversation.

'C'mon,' Richard muttered, 'let's get back to work.'

Bobby followed the footprints to the door of a pillbox, half-submerged in the sand. A dank, earthy smell sat at the entrance to the wartime outpost. It reminded Bobby of the scent of the woods that surrounded their house on Ellison Gardens. The woods in which he and Matt Linton had built their forts. Deep in that undergrowth, the worlds of Tolkein and Lewis had come to life, as the boys competed for the roles of Bilbo and Boromir, Frodo and Gandalf, Aslan and Prince Caspian. Once glorious memories, made sharp by his betrayal.

'S'not my fault,' Bobby shouted into the doorway. 'You baby. You fucking *child*. It's not my fault.'

His voice came back to him from the mouth of the pillbox and rang ugly in his ears. He swung his rucksack against the wall. The bag impacted and he heard the chink of the crack pipe. He plucked at the drawstring and withdrew the glass tube. Full of the promise of escape, it shone in the fire of the sun.

Bobby's throat constricted. His breathing came in short bursts.

Someone was watching him.

His eyes flickered across the sandbanks and the distant chalk cliffs. No-one on the beach; no-one in the shallows. And yet he could *feel* eyes upon him. Glancing down, he saw footprints in the loose sand of the dune. He ducked into the pillbox.

Inside, the air was moist. Cold. The remnants of a fire scorched the earth and broken bottles poked through the sand. A scree of litter: sweet wrappers, toilet paper, empty tins of corned beef and cocktail sausages, the broken clasp of a belt, the wrinkled skin of a used johnnie, lay heaped in one corner.

Bobby settled down to prepare a fix. It was the work of moments. The lighter danced under the bowl. The crystals crackled. Grey smoke filled his lungs.

It was safe here. Just like the Stone Floor of the millhouse, this concrete womb cradled him. Joy fizzed through his body, broke into his fingers and coated his senses. Honeyed light glazed the walls of the pillbox. He stretched out his feet towards the reborn fire, taking warmth from what he knew to be phantom flames. The lighter and the crack pipe fell from his hands. Bobby hummed a happy tune. He would stay here, hidden from the traitors that shared his blood; safe from the *drip-drip-drip* of the black water. No-one would find him in his fort between Fen and sea, between the cawing gulls and the deep, dark peat.

Not the child from the Garner Floor.

Not even Tiddy Mun of the stone.

No, he was safe. He was . . .

Mr Linton's razor gleamed in the light from the doorway.

Bobby bellowed something between a scream and laughter. Bringing his knees up to his chin, he stared at the razor, its blade burnished with golden blood, and knew that he was *not* safe. Not here, not in the millhouse, not anywhere.

The sand at his feet ruffled. An unseen finger traced the words:

PICK IT UP

Tears formed in his eyes and Bobby shook his head. The invisible finger underlined the message.

PICK IT UP

The boy pinned his hands beneath his arms. His bottom lip trembled. There was nothing Matt Linton could do if he did not move.

The razor flinched. Its handle rose slowly into the air. The tip of the blade sliced through the sand and came to rest against Bobby's naked toes. It hovered there, an enchanted object awaiting the injunction of a sorcerer. At the sound of footsteps outside, it twitched against the knuckle of Bobby's big toe.

A shadow fell across the entrance.

'Why are you hiding from me?'

Matt's voice. Bobby dug fingernails into his wounds.

'It's such a nice day, why don't you come outside? We could play. Play anything you like. Kissing games, maybe. We both liked kissing games, don't you remember?'

The razor nicked Bobby's skin. He ground his fingers into his arms so that the blood flowed freely.

'Remember that day in the woods behind your house? In the heart of the woods where no-one could see, we held each other. I could feel your heart, Bobby, hammering against my chest. Could taste you on my tongue for hours afterwards. Remember how we tried not to notice how hard we were?'

Cold, blunt steel sank into Bobby's foot. It found bone and the boy screamed.

'We didn't scream then, did we, Bobby? Oh, no. We were very quiet afterwards. Could hardly look at each other. Couldn't even speak, though our tongues were still salty with the thrill of it.'

The last shred of nerve was torn away. Bobby's eyes burned as he saw the razor jerk, flicking the amputated stub into the fire. There was something absurd about the sight of it: the trimmed nail, the hairs adhering to the knuckle, the white needle of bone. It looked like a novelty horror from a joke shop. But there was nothing to laugh about. The razor rose to Bobby's throat and pressed against windpipe and artery.

'And that's why you abandoned me, isn't it? The thrill turned sour. Turned to shame. Made you feel bad.'

Matt Linton's lower half filled the doorway. He was naked – erect – the way he had been that day in the woods. Precum, flecked with blood, dripped from the eye of his dick.

As his friend spoke, Bobby felt the blade worry itself into his throat.

'I'll forgive you, Bobby. I'll make it so that you never have to feel bad again. But first you have to *pay*.'

The razor cleaved deep.

Bobby's eyes rolled into the back of his head. He could almost see the hunger of the steel as it bit, exposing new and secret flesh. He tried to speak – to plead – to beg forgiveness – but all he heard was the susurration of wasted breath. His lung fluttered. His chest grew warm under the spill of blood. The crack pipe shattered beneath his legs.

His final thought: *I love you.*

And then the ringing of his mobile brought him back.

Automatically, he reached into his pocket. Meanwhile, his eyes ate up the surroundings. There was no figure in the doorway, no blade at his throat. His toes were intact. The only real part of the vision had been the breaking of the pipe. Amongst the glass, blackened crystals lay scattered in the sand.

Bobby glanced down at his phone. It was a picture message. He opened it to a familiar face.

'You killed me, Bobby. I was a little queer and you killed me. I hope you fucking *BURN!*'

This was no drug-hallucination, no guilt-induced spectre. The tormentor had tried to disguise his voice, but it was a poor attempt.

Bobby now knew his identity.

Twenty-six

The remainder of the day and the rest of the night passed peacefully for the Nightingales. For once, Daecher's Mill slept. At the breakfast table the following morning there were no disturbing dreams to mull over, no half-remembered visions. Joe crunched his toast and sipped his coffee. There *had* been one incident, a small thing really. En route to the shower, he had hesitated at the bathroom door. It was crazy, but for a moment he'd been convinced that something lay in wait for him. Some figure behind the shower curtain, its mouth glinting, full of glass . . .

Joe got up and rinsed his cup and plate. He looked through the kitchen window, out across the scrub, taking in nothing. At home he hardly ever dreamed, but here dreams lingered and focused the mind on unwholesome thoughts and the obsessions of the day. Like the hatchway and the space beneath the porch. He couldn't get that square of darkness out of his mind.

Richard slapped his son on the back. 'Ready to get started?'

They worked through the morning, talking little but growing closer in the performance of simple tasks: steadying wood while the other sawed, passing nails and hammering them home. Bobby's absence was not remarked upon.

Joe fitted the final tongue into its groove. Then both men

stood back and admired the fruit of their labour: a neat wooden carpet, beautifully joined and laid.

'Not bad,' Richard grinned. 'Yep, a pretty spot-on piece of flooring. See what I told you about the first two courses being put groove-to-groove, with a bit of moulding taking the place of the tongue? Now the boards can expand and contract from the centre out. It all allows movement and . . .'

'Dad. Please. I enjoyed this, don't make it sound boring.'

'Hey. Just for that you can rub down the edges while I go and hire a drum-sander.'

Joe groaned. He attached the paper to the hand-held sander and prepared to scrub a circuit of the room.

'You know, dad,' he said, 'I meant what I said. I really loved putting this together.'

'Good, 'cos we've only just started. There're the radiators to plumb in, sash cords to replace. A hundred-and-one jobs to get through.'

'It's just, I could really see myself doing this sort of thing.' Joe kept a careful eye on his father. 'You know, work-wise.'

Richard stopped at the door. For a long time nothing was said. The house groaned, as if anxious to break the silence.

'Don't be stupid.'

'I don't think I'm being stupid.'

'You've done, what, three days graft?' Joe could not see his father's face but he could hear the sneer in the Old Man's voice. 'You don't know what you're talking about.'

'But *you* do,' Joe countered. 'You loved this work. You could show me what it's really like. I'm not academic, dad, and I reckon I could really make a go of something like this. I don't want to study economics, that's all.'

'This work . . . it'll get you nowhere, son. Pursue it as a hobby if you want, but it's not where your future lies.'

'But I'm happy doing it. Please, just listen.'

Richard's shoulders tensed. 'No. We're going to finish off here and then leave it. It's too big a job. I shouldn't have started this. It was a mistake.'

With that, the Old Man left the house.

Joe crossed the room and switched off the radio. He collapsed into a sitting position, his back to the sawhorse. Picking up a stray piece of off-cut, his fingers played in the notches and kerfs worked out of the wood. As timber motes whirled about his head, so Joe's thoughts stirred and settled. In the flurry, he was angry, asking himself over and over why the Old Man would object to his plan. Was it because he had a practical reason? Maybe the restoration business was dead on its arse. Or was it because seeing his son in this role would remind Richard Nightingale of his past? Of that perfect summer when, for a brief spell, he had been happy with the young Janet Tregennis. In the calm, when his mind settled, Joe found no answers to these questions. All the same, he acknowledged that he had always known that this would be his father's response.

'Penny for them.'

It took a moment for Joe to realise that the girl in the doorway was not a ghost.

'Sam,' he sighed. 'I've missed you.'

The acne-scarred shop assistant was keeping a close eye on him. Richard knew it and didn't care. He had been standing in front of the drinks display for a good fifteen minutes, his gaze passing between the bottles. (*Chink chink*) Good friends these – old pals that he had shamelessly abandoned. Here was Gordon and Jack, Jim and Johnnie.

'Hello, boys,' Richard whispered. His tongue slipped across his lips. 'No more hiding for you, eh? What say I take you home right now? That'll show the little bastards.'

He reached out and clenched a random neck. No need to taste, touch told him all he needed to know. A cheap draught of piss, his experienced fingers signalled, not worth the £8.99 mark up. Never mind, it was all grist to the mill. In the trolley it went. And now they were calling to him: Gordon, Jack and the rest. 'Long time no taste, Richie old son. Where've ya been, ya shiftless old soak?'

They chattered in their *chinking*, glassy voices all the way to the checkout. Sat upon the conveyor belt, they set about insulting Acne Kid as he scanned their tattoos and fed them into bags. The two dozen kept up their conversation in the boot of the Merc. It was bollocks, of course, but it was not the first time that the drink had spoken to Richard, especially when he was upset.

He turned in at the millhouse gate, rage burning beneath his skin.

'Don't want to study economics,' he spat. 'Can see yourself doing this. Stupid kid.'

The anger was irrational. Richard wasn't even sure where it came from or why he should be feeling it. What was wrong with the boy wanting to work in restoration? Hadn't *he* encouraged Joe to look upon such work as fulfilling and worthy? These thoughts, excuses, did nothing to quell the rage. He ground the car to a halt.

There was no air. The sun baked his face and arms, parched his throat. Although they had ceased to chink, the bottles sang to him. Soon, he promised them, mounting the porch steps. First there's a little business to take care of.

The house breathed silence. From every corner, it hit him. No hammering, no sawing, no grit of sandpaper against wood. It was absence, he decided; cold, hard absence and he didn't like it.

'Joe! Where the hell are you?'

Now the silence taunted him. He threw open the study door. Tools lay abandoned, strewn across the floor. That perfect floor that his son had constructed; work of which any father would be proud.

'Joe? JOE!' He went through the house. Thundered upstairs. Kicked open doors. 'Are you sulking? Answer me. I won't be made a fool of, son. You answer me right now!'

Returning to the study, he saw the note tacked to the sawhorse. It was written on the back of the invoice for the radiators. Richard read it twice and then pulped it in his fist. He closed his eyes and found the words etched on the backs of his lids.

Gone out with Sam. Bobby coming too. Be back early evening – Joe.

Richard sank to his knee. He smirked and ran his fingers across the new floor.

'Okay, son. That's fine, you go off with your little girlfriend.'

He went to the hall and retrieved the pickaxe. Lifting it above his head, he thrilled at the weight and threat of the tool.

'I'll just finish up here.'

Twenty-seven

It was high season at Scarsby Point. Like Skegness and Mablethorpe – those other institutions of the British seaside further up the Lincolnshire coast – Scarsby's population increased tenfold during the summer months. On this baking July afternoon, most of those extra bodies seemed to be squeezed along the town's Coronation Parade. The crowd bustled and barged, bottlenecked and surged. The slightest hesitance was punished by a pushchair rammed into the shins or a 99 ice cream jabbed between the shoulder blades. With the temperature hitting around thirty five-degrees, Joe wondered what pleasure these campers and caravaners could possibly take from streaming up and down the Scarsby Mile.

'Remind me,' Joe muttered, 'why've we come here?'

'Don't you like it?' Sam smirked.

'No. It's lurid and tacky, and that's the opinion of a man who likes Dario Argento movies.'

'You're such a snob. Come on, I'll buy you a stick of rock.'

Bobby stopped at the entrance to the rock shop. 'If you two are gonna do the couple thing, I'm bailing,' he said. 'Call me when you're ready to head back.'

Joe watched his brother shuffle off in the direction of the Edwardian bandstand. Bobby hadn't said a word during the thirty-minute drive from the millhouse. Something about the way he moved through the crowd, his limbs loose and awkward, concerned Joe. He should call out, ask if the kid was okay.

'Everything all right?' Sam asked.

'Yeah. Course.'

They entered the shop. The first thing to confront them was a basket of enormous phallic confections with the invitation to 'Suck a Rock, Cock.'

Joe turned to Sam. 'Where in God's name have you brought me?'

He sat in the fire of the afternoon, cross-legged as if in meditation. Sunlight came through the Venetian blinds and lay in white-hot zebra-stripes against his back. Sweat sodden, Richard dared not move. To do so would be to invite the siren song of the bottles, and so he endured the heat, his hands flat on the boards. The floorboards that his son had laid and that, in his rage, he had intended to destroy. They stretched out around him, unscathed.

Richard felt the weight of the pickaxe resting against his thigh and shuddered.

'Mr Nightingale? Are you all right?'

Richard blinked. A woman stood in the doorway. At first, he thought that it was Janet. Pretty Janet Tregennis, who had brought him lunch and laughed at his lame jokes. Janet, full of questions and passion; a girl who appreciated beauty restored. His girlfriend, his lover, his wife, before the dark days following Bobby's birth; before *The Absence* erased her from the world. But Janet was dead. He felt no guilt about that fact, because what the glass had punctured was a husk, a shell. He was certain of that, wasn't he?

No, not Janet standing on the threshold. Who then? Susan Keele perhaps: the woman who had saved him and whom he had never loved.

'Miss Bedeker,' Richard said, shaking his head. 'Gail. I'm sorry, I was away with the fairies.'

Something twisted her features – not quite a smile.

'I think it's time we talked, Mr Nightingale,' she said. 'About this house. About Muriel Sutton and Alice Daecher. About how your late wife came here.'

'You look nice,' Joe said, aware that this was his fifth such observation since Sam had surprised him at the millhouse.

'I look like I usually do,' she said. 'A cross between Dorothy Gale and Marilyn Manson.'

'Pretty though.' Joe was glad to see her mouth crease into a smile.

They walked along the main beach in the direction of the pier. A storm in the late seventies had swept away much of the structure, leaving only a few hundred yards of boardwalk jutting into the shallows. About a quarter of a mile out, six iron stanchions rose from the sea like the legs of some colossal drowned spider.

'Bobby okay?'

'Yeah, I think. Why'd you ask?'

'No reason, I guess. Just, he doesn't look well. And he didn't say much in the car.'

'None of us did.'

I love you. That was the stumbling block to conversation. The big, pink polka dot elephant in the room. To skirt the issue, Joe thought up another subject of neutral conversation.

'I'm surprised you found us,' he said. 'We had a bitch of a time trying to locate Potter's Drake, let alone the millhouse.'

'Three men in a car without a map,' Sam mused. 'Let me guess, the drive down was no picnic?'

'There have been a *few* more tense situations in world

history, I guess. I think the Nightingales, cooped up together in a car on a hot summer day, comes somewhere between the Bay of Pigs and Hitler realising that maybe the Eastern Front campaign wasn't such a great idea. Seriously, though, how'd you find us?'

'You forget,' Sam said, 'I've been playing sleuth.'

'Ah, yes. And what did you find out? Am I really related to Norman Bates' mother?'

'Nothing quite so mundane. In fact, I've got a little surprise in store but, like all good detectives, I'll save the best bit 'til last.'

They sat down beneath the wreckage of the pier. It was cooler here, the sand pleasantly moist. Joe felt the warmth of the girl beside him. It was all he could do not to put his arm around her. He stared out to sea. Reddening bodies bobbed on cheap inflatables, heedless of the notices that warned of tidal shifts.

Sam took a file stuffed with papers from her bag. Joe raised an eyebrow.

'Jesus. You have been busy.'

'Yep. Amazing what you can learn by spending a day and a half in the county library. Court transcripts, newspaper reports, even a piece from a psychology journal: "Isolation and Superstition: Triggers for Psychosis. The Alice Daecher Case and other instances of violence resulting from confinement disorder."'

'Catchy title.'

'Right, are you sitting comfortably?' Sam asked. 'Then I'll begin. Guido Daecher came to England in 1938 . . .'

'My grandmother said that old man Daecher came over because he knew the way the Nazis were heading,' Gail Bedeker said. 'Mr Bedeker, my grandad, had some German blood from a few generations back – lowland German, like Daecher. Mr Daecher told my grandfather that there were signs as early as '33 of what Hitler was planning. The confiscations and concentration camps, of course. Not that Daecher was Jewish, but he foresaw the kind of hell that was just around the corner. He couldn't bear the stain of a holocaust, the shadow it would lay across the future of Germany. And so he sold his textile business and came over. He bought this place in October '38, one month before the first pogrom: Kristallnact, the Night of Broken Glass. They say he wept for days afterwards. He was a good man, Guido Daecher.'

'Can I get you a drink?' Richard asked. His throat felt like a dustbowl.

'Shall we have some tea?'

'Tea. Yes.'

Richard left his guest on the back porch and busied himself in the kitchen. While the kettle boiled he rinsed the teapot and cups. This done, he made an inventory of the food in the fridge and compiled a mental list of fresh supplies. If he occupied each testing second until the kettle sang, his mind would not wander to the cargo in the boot of the car.

Chink chink

'Fuck it!' He had burned his hand as he poured the water into the pot. The sweats were upon him. Never mind, he would concentrate on Gail Bedeker's story until they passed. Back on the porch, he slopped out the tea. Gail seemed not to notice how his hands trembled.

Now that he came to look at her, he saw that she was quite pretty: a clear complexion and a cute snub of a nose. He would focus upon these qualities and ignore the picture that kept returning to his mind: filthy feet, curling lips, and those mud-splattered hands smearing dirt across Muriel Sutton's grave.

'You're going quite far back,' he said, 'starting with the father.

What does this have to do with Alice Daecher and how my wife came here?'

Gail shrugged. 'History's always instructive. But, if you prefer, I'll cut to the chase.'

'No. I'm sorry. Please go on.'

The more she talks the longer she will stay, he figured. *And the longer she stays the more chance I have of the fit passing.*

'Well then, Guido. He bought the mill from Michael Ryans and set about re-establishing it. It had been in the Ryans family for generations, but with the move to mass flour production in the eighteen-sixties, when the steam-powered mill came into being, the old place went to rack and ruin. By 1910, it was no longer a working mill. I don't know why Guido was so passionate about restoring it. He was a wealthy man when he came here, and there certainly wasn't any financial incentive to get the mill back up on its feet.'

'Maybe he did it for the work's own sake,' Richard said. He laid a hand against the porch post. 'Drawing out the beauty of a mechanical home, the desire to see it in its prime. I can understand that.'

'Well, whatever the reason, his hard work bore fruit. Within six months, he had rebuilt the Garner Floor and restored the machinery. He'd even managed to salvage the original wheel. Daecher's Mill was in business and, due to rationing in the early forties, it began to make a tidy profit. Just before the war, Guido met and fell in love with Mariah Kelly. It was a love match, so they said, though he was twenty-seven years her senior. She was a contradiction, old Mariah.'

'How'd you mean?'

'Hard and yet loving. Generous in large gestures, she gave away nearly-new dresses for jumble sales and talked Guido into parting with big sums for charitable causes. But in small ways she was mean. She'd buy my grandmother new bits of furniture on a whim, but would balk at the loan of a cup of sugar. I think it was the Irish in her. She used to say her forefathers had suffered hard during the potato famine. Experiences like that can ingrain generosity into a family, but also make them careful when it comes to the day-to-day practicalities of living.

'Religion was another example of her contradictory nature. Mariah was staunchly Protestant, a rare thing in the heart of the Irish republic. She was of that old school of Puritanism that despised the hocus-pocus of the Catholics. Yet, for all her rejection of one form of grandstanding spirituality, she indulged another. Mariah was deeply superstitious. She came from County Westmeath, somewhere near the Scragh Bog, off the Sligo Road. Such a place breeds nonsense: the leprechauns and the cluricauns, the banshees and the far darrig, pookas and dullahans. And, of course, the fairies. When her family moved here, to this extinct marsh, I think Mariah saw the echoes of her homeland. Maybe she thought that the sprites had followed her. Or perhaps she found new ones waiting to be discovered. Whatever the truth, she kept up her old practices, scattering salt before the door, hanging witch balls in the windows.'

'Sorry, Miss Bedeker.' In his mind's eye, Richard saw the plastic shopping bags and the bitter ambrosia they contained. 'I don't see what any of this has to do with . . .'

'Mariah was just twenty when Muriel was born. It was 1945 and, though the war was over, it was the beginning of troubled times for the Daecher family.'

Seaside towns in high summer are stalking grounds. The façade of the traditional British family resort – jaunts along the pier, toffee apples and kiss-me-quick hats – is a paper-thin veneer. Behind it lurk dark industries. Fake merchandise, illegally imported cigarettes and pirated DVDs were sold off pasting tables up and down the Scarsby Mile, but these were mere criminal sidelines. Drugs was the meat and potatoes operation, and drugs were everywhere in Scarsby Point.

Bobby Nightingale was not hooked. Not yet. He'd only inhaled the crack twice, hardly enough to generate dependency. In any case, he hadn't enjoyed either experience very much. He remembered a burst of euphoria, of feeling invincible, but the come down had been troubling. Why? He couldn't say. Try as he might, the memories of what followed those spells of elation would not be coaxed, even though the last had been mere hours ago. All he knew was that the high made him feel safe. With Joe and his father secure in their new relationship, and with the ghost of Matt Linton ever at his shoulder, Bobby needed to feel safe.

After an hour of scouring the town, he found a stretch of stalking ground. It lay in an alley between the rear of an amusement arcade and the front of a Victorian boarding house. The house itself was now a block of squalid bedsits, paid for by the DSS or the pitiful wages of illegal immigrants. Curtains flapped from its open windows like dirty bannerettes.

On the steps sat a boy younger than Bobby. The kid recognised a customer and sidled over. They formed a human windbreak, in which the kid displayed his wares.

'What sorta shit you after?' the boy asked, leafing through bags of brown pellets, white powder and pastel pills.

'Crack,' Bobby muttered. 'Couple'a rocks.'

The kid selected two twists of cling-film and held out his hand. 'Thirty quid.'

'Some hash, too.'

'Forty total.'

Bobby handed over the money. The kid resumed his seat.

Bobby watched him for a time, taking in the similarities and differences between this dealer and Kelvin Hope. Although younger, the boy was clearly more experienced. He exuded a kind of cool professionalism, far removed from the skittish mixture of threats and inducements that characterised Kelvin's sales pitch. There was also a sense of control here which Hope, stoked on his own product, did not possess. For all this, a similar hunger could be observed, burning dully in his eyes.

'You wanna suck my cock?' the dealer asked.

'What? That's not what . . .'

'Cos if you do, you better have tits and a pussy. Fuck off, will ya?'

Bobby hurried back to the promenade. He was burning up, but it had nothing to do with the still-soaring temperature. He bought a Dr Pepper from a newsagent and stood in the shade of the shop, rolling the bottle against his neck. The fever eased and he stepped back into the street. From the greasy spoon behind him, a woman emerged, all biceps and burst blood vessels, and threw a bucket of water into the gutter at his feet.

Bobby watched the dark water flow into the drain.

Memories stirred.

He still couldn't recall clearly what he had seen in the millhouse after his first fix. What he started to remember, however, was the story he had been told. The tale of the millhouse and of what could happen there; the shadows it could throw and the punishments it could dole out. Surely it was madness, and yet, sitting below the Garner Floor, hadn't he felt the threat lurking behind the trapdoor? If the story was true, then it was a fitting place to bring his tormentor. Somewhere in which the bastard could taste a little of his own medicine. And even if it was all in his head, it was about time he faced the monster.

Taking out his phone, Bobby called Kelvin Hope.

Twenty-eight

'Muriel was born in 1945,' Sam continued, checking the date scribbled in her 'Hello Kitty' notepad. 'The mill was still doing okay, though its glory days were behind it. Guido had plenty of money anyway, so the family lived quite comfortably.'

'You've been thorough,' said Joe. To occupy his hands, he aimed stones at the nearest pier support. They ricocheted off the metal post and buried themselves in the sand.

'Okay, boring bit done,' Sam said. 'Let's get to the crux of the story. The birth of Alice Daecher . . .'

'Why the pause?'

'Dramatic effect. You see, little Alice came into the world in a rather strange way . . .'

'Stop it.'

'Okay,' Sam laughed. '1960, Mariah was pregnant again. First daughter Muriel was fifteen by this time.'

Gail Bedeker sipped her tea.

'This was how I heard it,' she said. 'It was late September, the night of the Harvest Moon, and Mariah's time was drawing near. Guido had agreed to help a neighbouring farmer with the last of the threshing. My grandfather had gone too, and my grandmother was away on some errand. Only Mariah and Muriel remained at the house. I've already told you how irresponsible Muriel was, so it came as no surprise to her mother that, when called, the girl did not answer. It was later discovered that the stupid creature had gone off 'picking wildflowers' with a local farmhand.

'At about seven o'clock, Mariah felt her first contraction. There was no telephone installed at the mill, and so she had to weigh her choices: find Guido or deliver the baby herself. The pain decided her. A grinding pain, she said later, deep and unnatural.

'Now, of course, what comes next is nonsense but, in her last moments, this is what Mariah told my grandmother.'

Standing in the doorway of the house, Mariah Daecher felt the breeze on her face. A wind of transition, she could smell upon it both the ghost of summer and the promise of frost. The seasons were turning.

Her legs trembled, but the miller's wife crossed the porch without too much trouble. She reached the rail and looked out across the full spread of Hyam's south field. This was where the menfolk had been working during the day. Stripped fallow, the field sat empty. Guido and the rest would now be settled by the hearth of the Hyam farmhouse, a property some two miles distant. Mariah took the porch steps one at a time. She shambled past the millhouse and rested for a moment on the sluice bridge. That strange, sickening pain ebbed. Perhaps she had imagined it. In any case, she would catch her breath before setting out.

The sluice was up. Only a trickle ran out from the millpond. Though the mechanism was out of gear, its brake in place, the millwheel groaned. It was a low, age-weary cry, as if the old place knew that its fate hung in the balance. There was talk of the river being diverted. Guido was fighting the decision through various forums and authorities and, knowing her husband, Mariah was sure he would carry the day. It was impossible to think of the river extinct, of the mill impotent and crumbling. Mariah knew her history. Water – the lifeblood of this place – had been drained too much already. What remained of the marshland could not be allowed to fall into an arid desert. The harmony of things, between Man and Nature, between the mechanical and the spiritual, epitomised perhaps by the mill itself, would be out of joint.

The pain hit again. Mariah gasped and cupped her stomach. Something was very wrong. She must reach Guido. The quickest route was over the fields, but the damp furrows would slow her progress. Better to head across the scrub between the farmland and the dunes. She ignored the pain as best she could and set off.

As she shuffled onward, Mariah stared up at the moon. It was nearing the autumnal equinox, the first point of Libra. Time was in flux, the world of Nature and Spirit turning against that of Man. As if to reinforce this idea, the rain of the last week had returned to the Fens something of their old mercurial vitality. Water had re-cut many of the ancient avenues across the land. Pools ruckled among the reed beds and stagnated in hollows. It was a weak reminder of the great marsh, but the encroachment of water into the scrub seemed to reawaken a forgotten landscape.

Staggering through this domain, her feet sloshing, Mariah felt at once comforted and afraid. The scenery reminded her of her childhood home by Scragh Bog, but that was a place of both safety and danger. There were pools in the bog, drowning places that her father had made sure she memorised. Although she knew that such quicksands were long extinct here, still she caught her breath every time her foot snagged in the mud. Drowning was not the only terror of such places, however. A waterland was the playground of spirits. It teemed with creatures of strange, capricious temperaments. Stories of old advised that encounters with such beings were best avoided.

Mariah ploughed on, though the pain went down to the bone. In the west, the sky darkened while, to the east, a fret swept in from the sea, rolled across the dunes and layered the Fen. Mariah soon found that she could see no more than ten paces ahead. Mud caught at her heels and made the going hard. In places, the rain had softened the peat into curled snags. Seeing this, she thought of the stories her mother had told her: of crones moulding snakes out of the peat and riding them across the waters. Even now, a grown woman with her second child on the way, Mariah half-believed these tales.

The contractions increased, and with them, the agony. Mariah's legs quaked and sweat lathered her body. She looked around, hoping for some sign that she was nearing the Hyam farm. All she could see was the grey mist. Away to the east, the waves ground against the shore. They sounded very distant. She should not be so far from the sea. Somehow, she had lost her way.

A fresh access of pain brought her to her knees. Another pitched her forward, so that she rocked on all fours. The water was cold. So cold that it numbed her limbs instantly, and it was only by the splash that she realised she had fallen into a shoal. The chill juddered into her bones and tears stung her eyes.

A dark stain grew against the fabric of her dress. From the hem, spots of blood dripped into the pool.

'I'm sorry, I'm sorry, I'm sorry. Please, God.'

The blood quickened into a steady run. Her legs eased themselves apart. Pain, above and beyond that of childbirth, tore through Mariah Daecher.

'Muriel!' she screamed the name. 'Muriel! God, please, let her hear me.'

Her cry sank into the mist and was lost.

Mariah rolled onto her side. With her lower half below the waterline, she tried to raise herself up onto drier ground. The effort was exhausting. Iron ran in her mouth as her muscles flexed and tugged. It was no good. Her feet could find no purchase in the shifting, sucking earth. Her head lolled back and, for a moment, she lost consciousness.

She woke again with a cry.

'Muriel! Help me! Please! Anyone, anyone who can hear, please help me. I'm dying. My child's dying. Anyone.'

Blood bloomed into the pond. Mariah saw it flare like a red sun before losing its shape among the reeds. Her fingers plucked at her knickers and she tore them free. As she did so, the baby crowned. She knew now that she would never make it to the bank. The pain, signalling some terrible defect with the child, no longer mattered. Whatever she was birthing, it would drown in the dark Fen water.

A monochrome world swam before her eyes: the pale grass, the silver mist, the black water. The reeds bowed their heads, as if in pity. Mariah ploughed her hands into the dirt, stifled her screams. Such sounds had no place in this nothingness – in this absence. Water lapped against the twin islands of her knees, against the surface of her emptying stomach. Down in the shallows, where her eyes refused to stray, the child's head emerged.

'In God's name,' she whispered. '*Anyone . . .*'

And that was when The Forgotten answered her.

The sough of the wind weakened. The sound of the waves, echoing across the dunes, faded. Marram grass fell silent. Only the water kept up its steady ripple.

He was coming.

Mariah heard his tread – quick and light – passing through the grass. With it she heard the flap of wings as frightened marsh birds escaped their nests. They blinked between the folds of the mist and shot out into the night sky. As they ascended, the lapwings screeched, and she remembered that the call of the peewit was his herald.

She could not help it. The pain was too much. Mariah screamed.

The Forgotten slowed its pace as it approached.

'*Hush-a-by, sweet maid. Here I come through the thick, thick mist.*'

The voice ran like water in her ear; like the swelling of lodes and the draining of dykes.

'*Bid me closer,*' it said. '*Flip the stone. Turn over the Stranger's Table.*'

Mariah kept silent.

'*Come now, I can help you. Save your life. Save your baby. Just whisper my name.*'

She was hallucinating. The voice was the work of an addled brain, conjuring fireside stories. If she waited here long enough, doubtless a whole horde of creatures would come to her: will-o-the-wisps and the fair folk, merrows and silkies emerging from the pools, puckish phantoms with mischief on their minds. No, there was no voice in the darkness. No little man waiting behind the reed.

Bubbles erupted between her legs. At last, she glanced down.

Blood-bathed, christened in the black water, the child's face looked up at her. The baby was dead.

'No. No, please! Help me!'

'*Whisper my name,*' came the voice, '*and all will be well.*'

The mist parted.

He stepped onto the bank.

'Who are you?' Mariah sobbed.

The Forgotten ran a black, slug-like tongue across its teeth. '*You know who I am.*'

Mariah closed her eyes and found it. A name for a being

without a name.

'*That's right. Now say the words and that which has passed shall return. Black water shall be as air in her lungs.*'

'No. I know what you are, *Old One*.'

'*Very well. If you think better of it, I am but a call away*.'

Eyes burned beneath the tangles of hair that matted his face. The creature turned its back and melted into the mist.

The pool lapped, green and red. Between Mariah's legs, the face of her drowned child shone like a reflection of the moon. She could not bear it. Madness and grief brought forth the name. Spoken once, there was no reason not to scream it into the fog. This time her cry was not swallowed.

As good as his word, The Forgotten reappeared from behind the reed.

He came to the pool's edge and sank down. Wading forward, his long hair spread out, eel-like in the water. He was within a few feet of her when she changed her mind.

'Keep away,' she said. 'You musn't. You can't have her.'

'*Too late. Bargains are bargains. But do not be sad, my dear. She shall be yours as much as mine. She shall play, just like the village children. Only in the source of her amusements will she be different.*'

He drew closer. Long, webbed fingers reached for the child. Mariah shuddered. She could not resist him.

'*Tokens they gave me*,' he said, his voice bitter. '*Mere pails of what once was mine, poured into dry, dry waterholes when the moon was fat. But even that was soon forgotten, until all that remained were their shadows. Sad and terrible shades. Oh, my child . . .*'

Hands encircled the dead baby's head.

'*. . . what shadows we shall weave*.'

Twenty-nine

'When they found Mariah both she and the baby were half-dead.'

Joe helped Sam to her feet and they set off back towards the promenade.

'They took mother and child to the Hyam farmhouse, but Mariah was too far gone,' Sam continued. 'Hypothermia took hold and she was dead within hours. Miraculously, Alice survived. The garbled story Mariah told, of little men and stolen children, was put down to deathbed delusions.'

They reached the prom and sat on a wall overlooking the botanical gardens. Children played between the sunken beds while grandparents dozed in seafront shelters.

'Okay, I'm hooked,' Joe said. 'Come on, what happened next?'

'Life went on, I suppose. The period between Alice's birth and her death twelve years later is pretty much skimmed over in the trial reports.'

'Someone told me Alice was deformed.'

'Really? There's no mention of deformity in anything I've read. She *was* mute, of course.'

'Mute?'

Sam nodded. 'She had tests, brain scans and stuff. They all came back normal. I suppose the circumstances of her birth, the hypothermia, the exposure, might've been the cause. It was an issue at trial. Psychiatrists, brought in by the defence, suggested that the sister's muteness might have psychologically affected Muriel. Long nights in that isolated millhouse without the company of a human voice. Cabin fever. Maybe it got to her, especially after the husband's death.'

'Husband? You mean Guido?'

'No. Guido Daecher died five years after Alice's birth. He'd never really recovered from Mariah's passing and blamed himself. Witnesses at the trial said he changed greatly; withdrew from the community, took no interest in his children. He suffered a stroke one day while working in the mill. In his Will, the old man gave custody of Alice to the elder daughter. And so Muriel brought the kid up on her own. She was only twenty. The husband I mentioned was Silas Sutton, a local farmer.'

'Muriel Sutton. Strange, it didn't occur to me that the name wasn't Daecher.'

'Like Guido and Mariah, Silas was much older than Muriel. There was some suggestion that it was a marriage of convenience. Silas got himself a fit young wife and Muriel had the company she yearned for. However it started, they ended up deeply in love. Witness after witness testified to that. Silas comes across in the testimonies as a good man, and certainly no slouch. He kept up his farm while, at the same time, attempting to reinvigorate the mill business. Tried to reinvent it as a cottage industry; you know, middle-class types buying authentic, mill-ground flour and making their own bread. The next year – this was '71 I think – the steward, Patrick Bedeker, died. This hit the business hard, as Bedeker more or less ran the place. Then, after years of wrangling, the water authority succeeded in getting permission to divert the river. Muriel and Silas finally agreed to a large payout and the mill was closed for good.

'The following year, Silas killed himself.

'No-one could work it out; there were no signs of depression or mental illness. According to Muriel, just before it happened, her husband had been in the millhouse with Alice.'

Short of breath, Silas Sutton struggled up the ladder onto the Garner Floor. His calls had gone unanswered. Of course they had, the little bitch couldn't talk, but she could hear well enough. She knew that, when called, she must ring her bell. There was no excuse. Still, what could you expect from such a child?

'Alice,' he muttered, standing in the light of the trapdoor. 'What're you doing here?'

The pale figure did not answer, just sat in its rocking chair, grinning at him. She must have dragged the chair through the door that connected the Garner Floor to her attic bedroom in the main house. The door had once been an escape hatch, used by the miller if a spark ignited the flour. Alice had been told, time and again, not to use it. Though the mill was now defunct, there were dangers aplenty in the old place.

Silas brooded. Such wilful disobedience ought to be punished. If only Muriel would allow him to discipline the brat. It was the one subject on which his otherwise cowed wife stood firm. On no account was Alice to be touched.

'It's very dangerous inside the mill,' Silas said. 'And you know not to use that door. It was naughty of you, Alice. And not ringing your bell, that was bad too. We might have thought something terrible had happened to you.'

Her fixed smile unnerved him. Tingling sensations tickled inside his stomach. As a boy, he had called them 'Fear Worms'. They had wriggled without fail whenever he had heard his father singing in the lane. Those barked verses of 'My Darling Clementine' meant daddy was home from the trawlers. Home to play. Little Silas had shivered, knowing that soon enough he would break beneath sea-salted knuckles.

Silas Sutton hadn't felt the Fear Worms in such a long time. To experience them as a full-grown man made him angry.

'You might have drowned in a lode like your mother,' Silas smirked, 'and then what would we do?'

The viciousness of his words did not regain him one ounce of authority. Alice's smile never wavered.

'Muriel would have been very sad.'

Alice shook her head. She bent over. A thread of dark saliva wound down from her lips and dropped onto the boards between her feet.

'Dirty, filthy girl!' Silas shouted. 'Of course your sister would be sad. She loves you . . . I love you.'

Again, that slow sway of the head.

Heat rushed into Silas' face. It felt as if, in the child's dissent, some hideous truth had been exposed. A truth that Silas had kept hidden from his wife: he wanted rid of the subnormal creature that shared her blood. If they were to have children of their own, then the freak had to go. There were special schools, weren't there? Places with incontinence sheets, restraining harnesses and bars on the windows. Somewhere Alice could be put away and forgotten.

It was then, as his anger peaked, that Silas saw the scratches on Alice's hands. Fear Worms nibbled at his nerves. He crossed the room and spread the girl's palms. The tip of her index finger was torn open to the bone.

'What've you done to yourself?' he asked. His concern was real: would Muriel think him responsible for the injury?

The only answer he received was a broadening of that idiot-grin.

'Come now,' he said, 'tell me. Then we'll take you straight to Dr Williams. No-one is angry.'

Alice turned in the rocking chair. Face to the wall, she drew a bloody line across the brick beside her head.

'Hhmmff.' She seemed pleased.

Indented in the stone, Silas saw eight crudely carved letters. They could not have been made with fingers alone, but there was no tool lying around that could account for them. His eyes ran over the word. It seemed at once familiar and strange.

TIDDY MUN

'What is this? What have you done?'

Alice's mouth gaped. For a moment, Silas thought she was going to speak. The prospect of this dumb animal emitting any kind of noise, other than bird-like shrieks and nonsensical burbling, horrified him. What would be the first word of a child that had remained silent for twelve years? A child that, if Muriel was to be believed, spoke only in dreams? It was the one fault that Silas had found with his bride: that superstitious dread of her little sister. It was bunkum, he told her, but he could not dissuade Muriel from her beliefs. Silas blamed the girls' late mother. Word had it that old Mrs Daecher had been a real loon in the spirits department. No doubt she had passed on some crazy notions to her first-born. Whatever the truth behind it, Muriel persisted in her assertion that Alice haunted her. Yes, actually *haunted* her.

Now, as Silas stood before Alice Daecher, he started to wonder about those stories of hunger and shadows.

'No matter,' he said, 'it's only an old brick.'

Alice's mouth snapped shut. She hunched over in her chair.

'What are you doing? Alice? Are you ill?'

Trails of saliva issued from between her lips and pooled on the dusty boards.

'Stop it. Mind me, Alice, or I'll fetch your sister.'

Fear Worms bit. Silas reached for the girl. The sound of her laughter stopped him in his tracks. It was clear, full-bodied and articulate. In the two years that he had lived at the millhouse, he had never heard Alice laugh.

'You *will* mind me,' he demanded. 'You *will* stop. Stop or you'll regret it. I'll take my belt to you, Alice. I'll beat you. Hurt you. Make you bleed.'

It was more than sputum now. Alice's mouth stretched wide and a stream of bile spewed from her throat – pints of it gushing onto the floor.

'Christ. Oh, dear Lord Christ. What *are* you?'

The laughter changed. Now it resembled the patter of rain from the eaves. Or the tinkle of the wind chime that he had pieced together from old cogs and bits of glass. As Silas watched, the hue of the bile darkened.

The farmer retreated to the trapdoor. His right foot dropped onto the first step. Then, from below, he heard something that made his blood turn to ice. The grind of gears. The meeting and turning of metallic teeth. The rumble of the great wheel. Lost in a corner of the impossible, Silas Sutton tried to reason his way into the light.

'But – but the water's gone,' he stammered. 'The river's dry. There is nothing to power the wheel. Nothing to . . .'

'*Ruby lips above the water*
Blowing bubbles, soft and fine
But, alas, I was no swimmer
So I lost my Clementine.'

His father's voice. He turned, expecting to find the long-dead monster looming behind him. Instead, he saw the tiny figure of his sister-in-law, her mouth thick with darkness.

'*She is gone and lost forever*
Awful sorry, Clementine.'

The Fear Worms devoured.

Silas closed the trapdoor, shutting out the daylight. Before his eyes adjusted properly to the Garner Floor, he heard the rush of black water peter out. Gradually, he began to make out the shadow of the girl, ever more elfin in the gloom. She crouched on the chair, her feet drawn up, chin resting between her knees. Her hair reached down to her toes like a long, bedraggled beard.

'Alice . . .'

'*I am here, Silas Sutton.*' The voice was not that of a little girl. '*Will you know yourself? Will you look into my shadows?*'

Silas shook his head. Whatever sliver of sanity remained told him to resist.

'*But why not?*' the figure asked. '*They are of* your *making.*'

The black pool lapped at the farmer's feet. Surely one little glance couldn't hurt . . .

What Silas saw in the water – the horror, the salty brutality that he tasted often on his lips – remained his secret. For precious seconds, he indulged in the fantasy of being his father's son. And then, as the vision faded, shame took hold. He clattered out of the mill and headed for the kitchen, and the block where the knives were housed.

Thirty

'The day Silas was buried, Muriel set fire to the millhouse.'

Joe tuned out the laughter of the children from the sunken garden.

'Set *fire* to it? But that was, what, thirty-three, thirty-four years ago? Don't tell me she then rebuilt the house from scratch.'

'You're not listening,' said Sam. 'I said she set fire to the *mill* house. And then not the entire structure. Just the top floor. The "Garner Floor" the papers said. The fire service got there before it spread too far. Muriel had barricaded the room and thrown a lighted bottle of petrol through a connecting door.'

'But why?'

'Because it was where her sister was playing at the time.'

'She blamed Alice for her husband's suicide?'

Sam nodded. 'Said the child drove him to it. She told the police a lot of crazy things, most of which were probably never made public. In interviews, she went so far as to accuse her sister of causing the deaths of Guido Daecher and the steward, Bedeker, the year before. It was so much jabbering, of course. The steward's death might've been a bit odd, but it *was* an accident.'

'Odd how?'

'The Bedekers had a collie. It was Patrick Bedeker's faithful companion, he was never seen without it. The year before Silas

Sutton died, the dog attacked little Alice. It caught her outside the millhouse and very nearly tore her throat out. Bedeker had been away shooting all afternoon. He was on his way home when he saw the attack. He set off running, shotgun in hand. At the sight of his master, the dog retreated. Bedeker must have stumbled on the uneven ground. Somehow, the gun went off. It blew half the man's face away. Like I said, a tragic accident.'

'What happened to the dog?'

'Destroyed. The odd thing was it had never so much as nipped an ankle before that day. But still, hard to see how it was Alice's fault. Anyway, after a day or two's cooperation with the police, Muriel took her lawyer's advice and kept her trap shut. At the trial, the defence pleaded insanity and the prosecution didn't object. The transcripts of the police interviews convinced the jury that her mind was unbalanced. She spent the next sixteen years inside the walls of Gannet's Rest Psychiatric Hospital. In 1988, at the age of forty-three, she was released. She returned home and lived there until her death last month.

'The only other strange thing is that, the week before her death, she was interviewed by the police again. A schoolboy – Thomas Ray Jennings – had gone missing from the local area. That's just a side note, though; Muriel was too frail to be considered a proper suspect.'

'Sad story,' said Joe. 'I guess Muriel must've hated herself when she finally realised what she'd done. To burn an innocent child . . .'

'Oh, Alice didn't burn to death. It was much worse than that. A friend of the steward's wife saw what happened. Here.'

Sam reached into her file and pulled out a sheaf of printed reports. She selected one and handed it to Joe.

'FENLAND HORROR' LATEST
HORRIFIC MURDER OF MUTE CHILD
– Eyewitness Report

At four-seventeen pm on Friday 17th October, Mrs Muriel Sutton, nee Daecher, attended the funeral of her husband, Silas. Fellow mourners have since testified that Mrs Sutton was very quiet throughout the ceremony, afterwards taking time to thank the vicar and congregation. Upon returning home, the widow went in search of her younger sister, Alice. Finding the child in the adjacent millhouse (which had served as the family business for many years), Mrs Sutton threw a lighted flame into the room and barricaded the door. The fire caught quickly. It consumed the dust-dry timbers, hemp sacks, tar barrels and, tragically, the twelve-year-old Alice Daecher.

Alerted by the child's screams, Mrs Hilda Stanhope, who had been taking tea with Mrs Wilma Bedeker, a neighbour of the Suttons, ran out to see what was happening.

'When I reached the house, Mrs Sutton was standing outside, staring up at the Garner [upper floor of the millhouse] window. It's a wee little window, hardly big enough for a cat to pass through. I could see the flames filling the glass and then, bless me, I saw *her* . . . Little Alice, beating her fists against the pane.'

Mrs Stanhope went on to describe how the child, wreathed in fire, managed to open the window and squeeze through it. By this time, Alice was barely alive. Recent rains had swollen the millpond and, although the river had been diverted the year before, the spillway of the mill was running.

'Someone must have left the mechanism in gear,' Mrs Stanhope continues, 'because the old wheel was spinning

> away like the devil. Anyway, poor Alice, she clambered out onto the sill. She was still aflame, you see, and she must have seen the water . . . The poor child threw herself into the wheel. We saw her dragged around in the buckets, churned to pulp and bone. It was horrible, just horrible. The spillway ran red . . . I was still there when the ambulance men dragged her out. Like a torn rag doll, she was, dashed to pieces. And that sister of hers, looking on. If ever I saw the Mark of Cain, it was on that face.'

'Jesus,' Joe murmured, handing back the article. 'How could anyone do something like that?'

'Muriel had a hard life,' Sam said. 'Mother dying like that when she was fifteen years old. Father withdrawing into himself. Having to bring up a disabled sister when she was only twenty herself. And that was 1965, remember, she didn't get much help. For five years, she'd looked after Alice, all alone in that remote millhouse, only the steward and his wife for company. Then, when she finally got a bit of happiness, a bit of companionship, her husband kills himself. No wonder she lost it.'

'I suppose. Still . . .'

'Bizarre as all this is,' said Sam, 'it isn't the strangest bit of the story.'

'Don't tell me, you've discovered that long lost Aunt Muriel was really Jack the Ripper.'

'You told me that a solicitor came to see your dad, right? And that this solicitor said you'd inherited the mill from a distant relative? Well, that's the thing that doesn't make any sense at all.'

'What'd you mean?'

'Inquiring minds aren't a Nightingale family trait, are they?

Have any of you stopped to ask just *who* your benefactress was?'

'I don't get it.'

'Well, remember, Guido Daecher came over from Germany before the war. He was alone. No relatives. Mariah emigrated from Ireland, and I guess you have no Irish blood in you?'

'Not that I know of.'

'Well then. We know Muriel and Alice were the only Daecher children, and neither of them had kids. So *how* exactly are you related to Muriel Sutton? Answer: you're not.'

In the distance, darting between the bodies that crowded the promenade, Joe could make out the waxy face of his brother. Sam was right. The kid didn't look well.

'Joe, are you listening? The woman who left you this house, she didn't know your family at all. She was a complete stranger.'

Thirty-one

Richard studied Gail Bedeker as the young woman finished her tea. He saw tiredness around her eyes, bitterness at the corners of her mouth. Yes, Gail's story had been shot through with bitterness. As he listened to the description of Alice Daecher's emotionally deprived upbringing, and of her callous murder, Richard could not rid himself of the image of Gail in the churchyard. Once again, he saw her bent over Muriel's grave, hands defiling the inscription. He wondered why this girl felt such hatred for a reclusive old woman that she had, by her own admission, barely known. He wondered too why she exuded such sympathy towards Alice Daecher, a child that had died years before Gail had been born.

'You didn't like Muriel Sutton.' His statement seemed blindingly obvious, but Gail flinched as though the observation surprised her.

'No,' she said. 'I did not.'

'Why? It seems to me that she didn't have an easy life. As for the murder, don't you believe the jury's verdict? Isn't it reasonable to suppose the poor woman lost her mind after her husband's suicide?'

'You don't know anything about it.' The venom in her voice was unmistakable.

'No, I don't. But I wonder what makes you think *you* do,' Richard shifted in the wicker chair. Turning to face her, he said, 'I saw you, Gail. Yesterday. I saw you tending Alice's grave. And I saw what you did afterwards.'

Later, he would wonder why he had confessed to what was, on his part, no better than spying. Usually he was keen to avoid confrontations.

'It goes beyond dislike, doesn't it?' Richard said. 'You hated the woman.'

Gail's lips thinned. Cool grey eyes remained fixed on the slowly incinerating scrubland. When at last she spoke, her tone sounded weary, aged.

'Why did you come here, Mr Nightingale?'

The question caught Richard off-guard. He felt that he had been wrong-footed, put on the defensive, but could not help answering her.

'Why? Because Mrs Sutton left it to me. To us.'

'You could have sold it via an estate agent. Why come here?'

'I was curious. I'd never been inside a millhouse before.'

'You've still not been *inside* the millhouse.'

'No. I – I wanted to bring Joe and Bobby. I wanted . . .'

What had he wanted? He struggled to both answer and deflect her questions. He thought of Susan Keele, pulling on her clothes in Room 14 of the Castle Lodge Hotel. Then a less arousing image filled his mind: the gigantic form of Mr Cuttle. Cuttle who had promised an idyll. Cuttle who now lay rotting in some local cemetery.

'I wanted to escape,' he confessed. 'I lied. Said it was for the boys. For us as a family to get together. To bond. The truth was I just wanted to escape.'

The woman sitting next to him said nothing. She waited, spider-like, as he wrapped himself in the gossamer of her silence.

'I needed to get away. There was a woman I was involved

with. Had been involved with for a few years. I started seeing her when the grief became too much. You see, my wife died last year, but I lost her a long, long time ago. I can't explain it to you, what happened to Janet. Not really. She drifted. Lost her anchor and slipped away; that's the only way I can describe it. I don't know why or how it happened, but it wasn't my imagination. No-one else saw it, but her . . . *Absence*. . . It was as real as if she'd walked out of the house one day and never come back. The only difference was that she was still there. In body, she never left. I think there might've been a small part of her that stayed, but it wasn't meant for me. She reserved it for the children. Only I was left with *The Absence*.'

Tears ran down Richard's face. He hadn't cried in such a long time.

'I was with Susan Keele for five years, but I never loved her. Not like I loved Janet Tregennis. My wife. And, though she was gone, I loved the memory of her, even when I was making love . . . no, *fucking*. *Fucking* other women. I came here to get away from Susan, because *fucking* her reminded me of *loving* Janet, and I couldn't bear that memory any more. I think that's it. I think that's why I came here. Not for the boys, but for me,' Richard smiled through the tears. 'I never realised before how cowardly I am. But the lie has become true: these last few days, working with my son . . . He's a good lad, they both are.'

Gail Bedeker appeared to have stopped listening. She stood up and walked to the edge of the porch, her back turned to Richard.

'You did something bad, didn't you?'

'What?'

'Tell me.'

'I don't understand.'

'Tell me what happened to your wife.'

'I told you, I don't know. She faded, she drifted.'

'Not then. Later. What did you do?'

'Nothing. I didn't . . .'

'Your wife came here. She took a bus from Peterborough to Potter's Drake and walked through the rain. Miles she walked, through country lanes, across fields, until she reached the sea. She planned to wade out into the surf until the current took her. She saw no point in living. Her father was an abusive bully, her mother, a self-centred grotesque. She had no friends, and the man she loved had abandoned her. She was exhausted and the baby was stirring inside her. She got to the water's edge. And that was when Muriel Sutton found her.'

'But I thought Janet made her own way here. She was looking for her cousin and . . .'

'Muriel Sutton was *not* your wife's cousin. She was no relation at all.'

'I don't understand. Mr Cuttle said . . .'

'Never trust a lawyer, Richard. Cuttle had his reasons for saying what he did.'

'Then why did Mrs Sutton take Janet in?'

'Common human decency, I suppose.' Gail's lip curled. 'Or guilt. Perhaps it stirred memories of her mother's death, seeing the girl in the water like that.'

Gail's meaning struck Richard like a hammer stroke.

'You mean Janet was in labour.'

Gail nodded. 'Muriel brought her to the house. I was there, with my grandmother. A ten-year-old is pretty useful in these situations, good at carrying hot water and fetching towels. There was no telephone and so no hope of getting help before the child came . . . I remember thinking that this frightened young girl, soon to give birth, was the most beautiful woman I had ever seen . . . That room behind us, the kitchen, that was where your son was born, Mr Nightingale.'

'Joe.'

'Your wife stayed with us a couple of days, though her mind wandered. We couldn't get her to tell us who she was or where she'd come from. Eventually, my grandmother suggested to Mrs Sutton that she be taken to the Salvation Army in Peterborough.'

'But why didn't Mrs Sutton tell the people there where Janet had been?'

'Very private woman, Mrs Sutton. Probably didn't want any fuss.'

Richard shook his head. 'Makes no sense. How did Muriel find out who Janet was? And why'd she leave us this place?'

'She found out through the papers. Disappearance of a wealthy young woman, and pregnant to boot, that gets reported. As to why she left you Daecher's Mill?' Gail shrugged. 'Maybe she thought you deserved it. Do you deserve it, Richard?'

Gail turned. Shadowed by the porch roof, and with the blazing sun behind her, it was difficult to make out her expression. Only her eyes, darting across the back of the house, could be separated from the gloom.

'If you tell me, then maybe it won't be so bad.' Her voice had softened. At the high end, it quivered. 'Tell me what you did to your wife.'

'I don't know what you mean.'

'It'll save you. It might even save your children. But only if you confess it, if not to me then at least to yourself.'

Richard got to his feet. He took hold of Gail by the arm and steered her down the porch steps. She felt light, almost insubstantial.

'You're insane,' he muttered. 'What are you, some sort of religious nut? Get out. Don't come near me or my boys.'

'These shadows are of your making,' she said. They skirted round to the front of the house and he pushed her away. 'You can only escape them by facing what you've done. Please, Richard, believe me, I know. There is something inside this house. A presence that will . . .'

Gail Bedeker's words died on her lips. Thunderstruck, she stared up at the millhouse. Richard followed her gaze to a tiny window set high into the face of the structure. He stepped back and shaded his eyes. Was someone standing at the glass?

'I'm sorry. I'm sorry.' Gail shook her head and twisted her fingers. She didn't seem to be talking to Richard. 'I'll go now. Forget what I've said. I'm sorry.'

And then she took off across the scrub, back towards her grandmother's cottage.

Richard stood for a long time, watching the Garner window. The window through which little Alice Daecher had climbed, screaming and burning. Alice, who had been murdered by her big sister.

The same sister that would later deliver Richard's firstborn son into the world.

Thirty-two

The first thing Joe saw when Sam turned in at the gate was the figure of his father. At this distance, Richard looked tiny against the hulk of the millhouse. The Old Man had his back to them, his head craned upwards, as if he was looking into the eaves or the topmost window. He stayed that way, even as Sam pulled the Beetle up beside him.

Getting out of the car, Joe asked, 'Dad? What's going on?'

Richard flinched. He looked from Joe to Bobby, sniffed and drew his shirtsleeve across his mouth. His eyes were red and it looked as if he had been crying. But the Old Man never cried.

'Where've you been?'

'I left a note,' said Joe. 'Sam came for a visit. We went to Scarsby Point.'

'So you had a little day out?'

Richard's eyes fixed on Samantha Jones. There was something in those dilated pupils, mean and accusatory, that Joe did not like. Sam must have picked up on it. Her face flushed and she lowered her gaze.

'Is there a problem here, dad?'

Richard managed a smile. 'No problem. Why should there be a problem? You go off on a seaside jolly and leave me with all the work. What possible problem could I have with that?'

The heat intensified the silence that followed. There was

no breeze to rustle the grasses and the sun-drunk birds stayed songless in their nests. Even the timbers of the old house, expanded now to their limits, made no sound.

'You told me you wanted to do this work,' said Richard at last. 'Then you just – *pffft* – disappear.'

'Wait a minute, *you* said we were finished here,' Joe seethed. '*You* said it was a mistake.'

'And you've proved my point. A few days work and already you want a break? Christ, son, you've got some growing up to do.'

'Me? Look at yourself, you hypocritical . . .'

'Joe, don't.'

Sam touched his shoulder, her fingers light on the scar beneath the shirt. He closed his mouth, allowing home truths to go unsaid.

Richard broke the standoff and lurched back into the house.

'Freak,' Bobby muttered. He drained his Dr Pepper and headed off across the sluice bridge.

Left alone with Sam, Joe found himself prey to that strange vein of embarrassment suffered when close relatives behave badly in public. The kind that insists on explanations and excuses being made, just in case anyone believes that acting like an arsehole is DNA coded.

'I'm sorry,' he said. 'I just don't . . . Christ.'

She put her arms around him and rested his head against her breast. The beat of her heart resonated in his ear. Beyond that sound he could hear nothing.

'Sam, what you said on the phone the other day . . .'

'Don't. Not now. Later, when you've got your head sorted. We'll talk then.'

Sam stepped back, held his face and thumbed away his tears. Then she gave him a playful slap across the cheek.

'Hey, what was that for?'

'Just felt like it.'

She got back into the Beetle and shoved the gear stick into reverse. Winding down the window, she blew him a kiss.

'I'll see you back at home, then,' he said.

'Will you?'

'Well, if you want. I mean . . .'

'I'll see you *tomorrow*, Joe. Can't miss the big day, can I?'

'What?'

'Come on, you think I forgot? I'll be here bright and early.'

'But where're you gonna stay? You – you could sleep here, if you wanted.'

'Hmm, a night with the Nightingales. Maybe not. Paternal guilt provides me with an outrageous amount of pocket money, so I might as well spend it on a gloomy B & B. See you later, sweet cheeks.'

The car whined down the track, grunted as Sam found first gear, and vanished behind the hedgerows. Eventually it reappeared, trundling along the road that ran through the fields like a vein of iron embedded in sandstone. Joe watched until it blinked and disappeared over the horizon. Then he went in search of Bobby.

Joe's voice approached, passed, doubled back, and finally drifted behind the dunes. Huddled inside the pillbox, his heart in his mouth, Bobby waited. He had reached a soft point; a place in his journey through guilt and grief in which he might break down and tell all. There was no reason for it to happen now, and he knew that the experience would last only moments. Soon the antagonistic defences would be shouldered back into place. He would become Bobby Nightingale, astringent and insular once more. But if Joe had poked his head through the pillbox door, and started asking his Joe-questions, Bobby would not have been able to withstand it. Guilt would flood out of him.

As he had foreseen, the moment passed. Now he took out the twist of crack from his pocket. Placing the rock into the empty Dr Pepper bottle, he fitted the broken crack pipe into a hole he had cut out of the side. His lighter scorched the plastic and made the crystal fizz. He inhaled deeply.

A second or two later, Matt Linton sat cross-legged beside him.

'Hi, Matt,' Bobby said, 'how you doing?'

Matt spoke from his second mouth, the one torn out of his neck. 'I'm tired, Bobby. I want to go home, but she keeps me here.'

'Who?'

'You know who.'

'Don't worry, I've got a plan.' Bobby whispered, just in case *she* should overhear. 'I'm gonna bring someone else here. She can have him instead. Then you can go home. He deserves it anyway.'

Matt shook his head. 'Sorry, doesn't work like that. Bringing him here won't change what's going to happen. In fact, it might make it worse. For you, I mean.'

'I don't care. It doesn't matter anymore.'

As his synapses fired, Bobby sensed the razor in his fist.

'Bobby?'

'Yeah.'

'Do you want to play a game?'

A cold, dead weight pressed into his lap. He saw the red mouth and the grey, tattered lips before his eyes.

'A kissing game . . .'

Thirty-three

Kelvin Hope checked the time – 01.53 am – and listened again to the message –

This is Bobby Nightingale. I'm at Daecher's Mill, Saltsby Fen, near a village called Potter's Drake. You get this message, you come down to see me. Wait until two am and I'll meet you out front. I think I'm gonna tell my dad about what you did to Matt; how you tortured him all those months. I think I'm gonna tell the police. About that. About the drugs. It all depends on what you do for me. You better be here.

That little fucker. That little, shit-for-brains, turd-munching fucker.

Parked up behind a clump of bushes, Kelvin waited and plotted. Images paraded inside his head, as he imagined what he was going to do to his blackmailer. The violence started out straightforwardly brutal: punches to the face, kicks to the body, a crushed nose and, perhaps, a dislocated jaw. Repeated plays of the message, however, inflamed Kelvin's anger and stimulated his imagination. What was left of Bobby Nightingale after an hour of psychic pummelling wasn't worth scraping from the pitch-black gutter of Kelvin's mind.

At precisely two o'clock, Kelvin left his Lambretta SX range and headed up to the house. Every step jarred his travel-weary body. Much as he loved his scooter, the forty-odd mile trek from Lincoln had been no pleasure ride. His hands ached and his bones throbbed right down to the marrow. Whether this was due to the drive, or his needing a fix, he couldn't say. The different textures between everyday twinges and those cramps and shivers, sweats and agonies that preceded a wrap had become blurred. Natural pain, and that which was the price of the dragon, was now one and the same. As much as blood and air, heroin had become a working part of his body – he could not do without it.

Kelvin knew that drugs were rife in Young Offender Institutions, but their inside-cost reflected the difficulties inherent in smuggling them in. Visitors, having to pass bags of gear on through a kiss, had to be well paid. Outside contractors – electricians, builders, plumbers – risking jail themselves, demanded more than basic minimum wage to carry contraband in their toolboxes. Cocaine-stuffed tennis balls lobbed over the prison wall, and acid-lined birthday cards, don't come cheap. And how, when his operation had been exposed and shut down, was Kelvin supposed to pay for such things? For it would be jail when Bobby Nightingale told his story, of that he was certain. Previous convictions for selling weed would go against him. Couple this with testimony of violent bullying, leading to the death of that fat little queer, and there was no doubt at all. Kelvin pictured himself in his cell, aching for a wrap. Without coin, there were only a few things a young lad could do to get a fix.

Well, that wasn't going to happen. Not to him. Not ever. Even if it required extreme measures, Bobby Nightingale was going to stay quiet.

Kelvin reached the house. With no sign of Bobby, he took out his phone. No signal. He glanced over the place: a Shitsville dump and no mistake. Probably reeked of damp. It was not damp that he smelled, however, but a more complex mix of aromas. Piss-soaked, shit-stained sheets, the burning coil of the electric fire, mealy vomit, five-parts vodka, one-part carrots.

The smell worked as a catalyst on his senses, spurring the sounds and sights of the sickroom. Yeah, that was what it had been: a room where sick things took place . . .

A whitewashed door swung open.

'In here.'

Kelvin followed Bobby's voice. He ducked low and entered.

'The fuck is this place?'

'A millhouse. They called this the Meal Floor. It was where the grain sacks were brought.'

'What? You some kind of fucking tour guide?'

A flash of white. Did the little bastard smile at him? It was difficult to tell in the darkness.

'Come upstairs.'

'Talk here and talk now. Think you can frighten me with that message?'

'I'll explain everything upstairs.'

Kelvin buried his anger. Let the cunt feel like he's in charge. Then, when he can be seen properly, he'll get what's coming to him. Kelvin groped for the ladder and followed Bobby through the trapdoor. Sweat was pouring out of him by the time he reached the second level.

'The Stone Floor,' Bobby announced. 'So called because here was where the millstones were housed.'

'Fucking Christ, Bobby, I'm not interested in . . .'

'You should be. This is where it all happens. This is where the grain is powdered. Where the kernels are ground down. Where the hard parts are made into flour. Most of it is siphoned into sacks below, but a little is dusted into the air. It sinks into the bricks and becomes part of the building.'

'I've about had it with this bullshit.'

'But you're not ready for that, Kelvin. First you must be garnered.'

Kelvin tried to grab hold of the boy, but Bobby's heel slipped through his fingers.

'That's it,' Kelvin roared. 'I've had enough.'

He scrambled up the ladder onto the third floor. The dealer's head impacted on the low ceiling and he cried out. The sound masked the clunk of the trapdoor and the snap of the catch beneath, which Bobby had rigged with a length of twine pulled through the floorboards.

For a few seconds, Kelvin couldn't think of what to say. What was the kid up to? The situation was just too weird. Desert-yellow moonlight flickered through the window at the end of the room. By its light, Kelvin started to make out rude forms: the beams that ribbed the roof, hessian sacks, discarded cogs and metal discs, a child's rocking chair . . . And Bobby, white-faced, grinning.

'You won't be laughing much longer,' Kelvin promised.

The smile didn't waver. 'You killed him.'

'What?'

'You killed Matt Linton.'

'You outta your fucking box? *I* killed him? He killed himself.'

Bobby shook his head. 'Your hand was on the razor. Yours and mine.'

'Bobby, you keep your mouth shut about what you know – what you *think* you know – and I'll see you right. You liked the stuff I gave you? There's more where that came from. Or other gear. Whatever you want.'

'Are you sweating, Kelvin? Don't you like being tormented? Bullied?'

'You're pushing me.' Kelvin whipped the blade from his pocket. 'When I'm pushed, I push back.'

'Not here you don't. You can't push against shadows.'

One minute the kid was there, the next he was gone. The

movement was so sudden that, at first, Kelvin didn't realise what had happened. When it hit him, he crossed the room and hammered on the little door set into the wall. Threats met with silence. He went to the trapdoor and, finding no handle on the upper side, dug his knife into the fitting. The blade snapped.

Lost without a weapon, Kelvin smashed an old beer bottle against the wall and returned to the door. He laid his face against the panel.

'Let me the fuck outta here! Bobby, I'm gonna fucking cut you, I swear to God. I'M – GONNA – FUCKING – *KILL* – YOU.'

No answer. Dropping the bottle, Kelvin went back to work at the trapdoor, this time worrying at it with his fingers.

Dampness coated his hands. Thinking that it was sweat, he continued to prise at the wood. It was only when the knees of his trousers were soaked that he noticed the black water. It flooded across the floorboards in fine lines, cutting together and pooling. Rills ran down the posts supporting the roof and across the brick walls. Kelvin traced the path of the stream back to its source.

The impossibility of what he saw – what he thought he saw, because it could not be true – made his heart spasm in his chest.

'*Hello, Kelvin Hope*,' said the little girl.

Her voice trickled. Dressed in a thin, russet-red frock, she sat in the rocking chair, watching him from under her hair. Hair woven with leaves and vines. Beneath it, Kelvin could make out a dark, twisted face, the features melting into one another. As she swayed, water ran down her arms and legs, dripped from her fingers and toes. This was the source from which the black water streaked.

'*Hope. That's a funny name for someone like you*,' the girl chuckled. '*I don't think you have much hope do you, Kelvin?*'

'The fuck away from me.'

'*Tut-tut. Such language in front of a child. Did your sister teach you no manners?*'

'Who are you?'

A hand shot out from the folds of the frock. Although he stood a good ten feet away, Kelvin staggered back, as if he expected the child to grab hold of him. Her thin, brown-mottled arm was long, but not that long. She caressed the stone beside her head. Her fingers traced the word carved there.

'This is my name,' she said. '*A funny name, like yours. And, like yours, it means nothing. Hope? For you, such a word is meaningless. No hope for Kelvin Hope. Not since . . .*'

The girl pointed. Unable to resist, Kelvin turned and confronted his shadows.

The Sick Room. His sister, what was left of her, lay upon the bed. Her breathing came in febrile snatches. As she inhaled, her skin pulled so taut that the skeleton beneath loomed through the flesh. More or less naked, strips of bedding covered her frame.

He stood nearby, a boy of thirteen, waiting for the command. In their hollows, ravenous eyes shifted. Blinked. The signal.

Kelvin Hope felt the needle in his hand. The reek of decomposition filled his senses. He wouldn't do it any more: clean up the days-old vomit, wash her stinking parts, mop the shit from her arse. He wouldn't. Couldn't. Sick of the Sick Room, nauseated by this thing that would not die, he delivered the poison. Once. Twice. A half-dozen times for luck, stabbing it into her abscessed vein.

He saw himself lean over and take the St Christopher from her neck. In the millhouse, he felt it now beneath his shirt. She'd kicked a little, that was all. In the end, it had been so simple he wondered why he hadn't killed her months ago. She had died so very easily.

But that was in the world of memories. In the world of shadows things were different. Guilt manufactured a thousand variations on reality, augmented and twisted what had been. Many that had come to the millhouse had found this to be true. Kelvin Hope was just the latest.

Candice Hope plucked the needle from her arm. Shit and urine streamed down her matchstick legs and vomit spilled from her mouth. She rose from the Sick Bed and, with the forgiveness only a sister can bestow, she embraced her little brother.

In his bedroom, Bobby crouched behind the wardrobe. He had removed the plasterboard wall earlier, cutting around it so that his picture remained intact. He pressed his ear to the door and listened. The voices had long since ceased: Kelvin's and the other. Still, he dared not open the door. What if it had all been his imagination? What if Kelvin and his blade lay in wait?

And then he heard it. The sound that he both longed for and dreaded.

As Bobby listened to the rumble of the wheel, the grind of the stones, he remembered some of what Gail Bedeker had told him.

The wheel shall turn and the shadows will be woven . . .

Not all of the story was clear in his mind, but he remembered its message. The millhouse was a dangerous place, a trap of one's own devising. Somewhere that, once entered, could not easily be escaped. Had he believed such nonsense? It was only a story after all . . . He decided that he must have believed it on some level, why else would he have brought Kelvin Hope here? Risking a beating, or worse, his threats had led the tormentor to the millhouse door. In order to achieve what? To punish Kelvin for sending the emails and text messages? Perhaps, although that would seem a harsh judgment. Whatever his reason, Bobby was now responsible for the loss of another life. A tainted, brutish sort of existence, but a life nonetheless. For there was no point in opening the door. The working of the crippled machinery told him everything he needed to know. Gail's story was true. Kelvin Hope had faced whatever haunted him and was gone.

Bobby tried to comfort himself. Kelvin was a leech, a bully, a parasite. He fed drugs to kids barely out of kindergarten. He took joy in the physical and mental torture of others. When his 'empire' expanded, when he had found his feet in the wider world of crime, how many deaths, directly or indirectly, would he have been responsible for? Surely Bobby should be commended for lancing this weeping tumour. Surely . . .

He curled up on the bed and didn't flinch when the covers rustled and a cold body pressed against his back.

'You did it for me, is that what you tell yourself?'

Bobby trembled.

'But you've made it much worse. So much worse now. You've made her stronger and the shadows denser. It's going to end badly for you, Bobby. So very, very badly . . .'

Thirty-four

'Happy birthday, sweet cheeks.'

Joe yawned and stretched across the bed. Suddenly conscious that he was not alone, he raised his knees to disguise a solid case of morning glory. Sam appeared not to notice. She passed him a cup of coffee and two rounds of toast.

'Hello,' he said, his greeting groggy. 'What time is it?'

'Six-thirty in the morning.'

'There's a six-thirty in the morning now?'

'Yeah, sorry. Couldn't wait to give you your present.' An oblong – wrapped in green shiny paper and tied with a pink bow – landed in Joe's lap. He grimaced as it impacted on his deflating penis. 'By the way, I think I've broken your toaster. Jammed a fork in it and – *kapowee*. And do you know you left your front door open? Anyone could just wander in.'

'Like some crazy bint who goes around stabbing innocent toasters?'

Sam flicked his forehead, jumped off the bed and threw back the curtains.

'What are you, some kind of sadist?' he groaned.

'What's the matter? You seemed pretty alert when I came in,' Sam winked. 'Oh, you're blushing. Cute. Anyway, open your present while I eat your toast.'

Joe wrestled with the wrapping. Eventually he triumphed over yards of sellotape. He uncovered a book, *The Complete*

Guide To House Restoration.

'When we spoke on the phone the other day, it sounded like you'd found your niche. Hope you like it. I've got the receipt if you don't. You could get something else: economics textbooks, Dating For Dummies . . .'

'It's great,' Joe said. 'It's perfect. Thank you.'

'No biggie.'

'So, do I get a birthday kiss?'

Sam strolled over from the window. She bent down and placed her lips inches from Joe's. He leaned in towards her and she executed another flick to the forehead.

'Maybe later,' she laughed, 'if you're good.'

They spent the morning under the shelter of the back porch. With the humidity at eighty percent the only relief came from ice cubes deposited at intervals down the fronts of T-shirts. Cotton shirts that clung to their bodies. Joe tried not to notice the points of Sam's nipples.

'Weather gave storms for later,' he said.

'It needs it. You can feel the static in the air.'

The sound of a boiling kettle and a hacking cough shattered the relaxed atmosphere. Sam sat up a little straighter in her chair.

'Good morning, Mr Nightingale,' she said, when Richard poked his head through the door.

'Morning.' He turned to Joe. 'You're up early. No need to be. I told you, we're finished here. If you can't be trusted to do the work, then we'll leave it.'

'Fine. Whatever.'

'What's this?' Richard picked up the restoration book. 'You bought this?'

'It's a present from me,' said Sam hurriedly. 'Joe told me how much he enjoyed working with you on this place and . . .'

'Nice thought,' Richard sniffed.

'Do you know why she bought it, dad?'

Richard put down the book. He looked lost.

'Because it's my birthday. My eighteenth.'

'Christ, Joe. Of course it is. I'm sorry.' Richard fished out his wallet. 'Here, let me . . .'

'Doesn't matter.'

'Yes it does. You'll need a bit of extra money soon. What'll we say, two hundred? That'll buy a few beers in freshers' week, eh?'

'I told you, I don't want to go to uni.'

'Just take the money.' Richard thrust the twenties into his son's hand. 'We'll talk about it later. When we're alone. In fact, let's go out for a meal this evening, you me and Bobby.'

'And Sam, of course,' Joe said, his voice full of cynical cheer.

Richard did not reply. He disappeared into the kitchen where the kettle sang and his coughing resumed.

David Tregennis completed his examination of the vintage Silver Wraith II. This performance – checking everything from oil and water levels to counting the dints and scratches on the bodywork – was ritualistically observed prior to a journey of significant distance. 'Significant distance' these days amounted to anything over the twelve-point-six mile round trip to the shops. Very occasionally, his wife's check-ups and hospital visits required a longer drive, but nine times out of ten he got someone else to take her.

It was not just the hollow presence sitting in the passenger seat that made David a reluctant chauffeur. Rather, it was what that presence represented: chaos, loss of self. In the past, during his reign as the self-appointed Confection King, he had thrived in the helter-skelter, ever-changing world of business. These days such unpredictability terrified him. He strived for order in all things, for without order anarchy soon took root. Then, in the natural order of disintegration, there came babbled conversation, empty stares and the messing of one's self in public. The very thought of such decay made David sick to his stomach. What had happened to Stella must not be allowed to happen to *him*.

The auto inspection complete, David checked his own appearance. Hair neatly parted, moustache trimmed, Round Table tie straight-and-centre. Now pockets: wallet, left trouser; cardholder, right trouser; comb, left jacket; phone, right jacket. Car keys . . . His hand fluttered. Where were the sodding car keys? He was certain that he had picked them up off the hall table. Panic plucked at his nerves, like a tone-deaf child snatching at the strings of a harp . . . Wait – ah, yes – left trouser pocket, hidden behind his wallet. David took a long breath and got into the Rolls Royce.

He adjusted the rear view mirror before pulling out of the drive. Eyes, scored with crow's-feet, stared back at him. He looked tired. Scared. The Confection King of fifteen years ago would have laughed at this feeble old man. Would have wondered what an old boy of seventy-eight, with three million plus in the bank, could be so worried about. But the King had not known then that money had its limitations. Despite the claims of cosmetic companies and charlatan surgeons, it could not resist the grind of years. Death and disease continued to hold out against it. One disease in particular had proven resistant to all the pills and potions private medicine could throw at it. For six years he had watched, helpless as his wife's mind fell apart. Now there was nothing left of the once quick-witted, foul-mouthed Stella Tregennis.

David left the undulations of the Wolds behind and hit the A16 and the uniform flatness of the Fens.

'Daecher Mill. Saltsby Fen. Near Potter's Drake.'

David repeated the address, though he knew it by heart. He remembered Richard Nightingale's message too:

It concerns Janet. I think I might have found the place she disappeared to in '88 . . . I hope Stella's no worse.

Oh, no, Stella was no worse. To be honest, she could get no worse. There was only 'better' now, and that meant slipping away as painlessly as possible.

Hitting ninety on the arrow-straight roads, David wondered why he was doing this - driving fifty miles to meet the husband of his dead daughter. Natural curiosity, he supposed. Somehow, the once loathed, now barely thought of Richard Nightingale had discovered the secret of Janet's disappearance. Yet, to be honest, the mystery, almost two decades old, did not register much with David these days. Janet had left them, been found by the wastrel who later married her, and then cut her parents out of her life. Six-monthly visits – Joe and Bobby in tow – was the most David and Stella ever saw of their daughter.

After her death in the motor accident last winter, David had found himself standing alone beside an open grave. He had shaken the hands of strangers; all friends of Richard, for it seemed his daughter had had few of her own. A stiff nod from his son-in-law was all the acknowledgement he received from that quarter. The boys had stayed with friends. Knowing that he was not welcome back at the family home, David lingered. He read the cards attached to the floral tributes. They seemed stilted, as if the writers had no knowledge of the dead woman. Only one really stood out.

I miss you Janet. I've missed you for such a long time. All my love, Richard.

David had stood over his little girl's casket and tried to summon tears. He'd cried at last, but the grief was only in part for the stranger that lay beneath him.

So why was he now en route to this millhouse by the Wash? The answer was obvious, though he did not care to admit it, even to himself. It was an excuse to get away.

A year ago, he had arranged for a granny flat to be built on the side of the house. No expense was spared and all his wife's garish tastes had been replicated in the décor. Comforted by every luxury, she lived there in cooing bewilderment, while round-the-clock nurses doled out pills and wiped her arse. There was only one thing Stella Tregennis lacked: her husband's company. In the beginning, the nurses had asked him to help out with Stella's cognitive therapy. A familiar face would aid the process of remembering, they said. He had found excuses, until the lies became so transparent that continuing to ask was an embarrassment for all concerned.

Richard's call had come at an opportune time. Separated by a few feet of wall from the empty shell he had married, David's guilt had begun to overwhelm him. Months of that tiny voice telling him – 'you must visit her, she's your wife' – had taken their toll. He needed to get away, but where would he go? A message from his son-in-law, asking for help, provided a legitimate excuse to be away. It might even show those quietly judgmental nurses that he wasn't all bad.

He wasn't, was he? All bad . . .

A series of wrong turns started to panic David. He had plotted the journey with care, but the labyrinthine country lanes defied his map-reading skills. Some of the roads had no signs and the names of others were not to be found in the map's index. His hands felt wet inside the driving gloves. Was this really the fault of confusing topography and nameless roads, or was it his own failing mind that was amiss?

He pulled the car onto the side of the road.

'Don't.' He gasped and put a gloved finger into his mouth.

'Just don't.'

Clouds – the first he had seen in a week or more – rolled over the fields. Their bellies crackled with the oncoming storm. In the spaces between them, the sky loomed in wine-red snatches.

Against the windscreen reflection of these swelling elements, a figure moved. A woman strode up the lane towards the car. David wiped his face and got himself together. She waved and indicated that he should wind down his window.

'Mr Tregennis?'

Grey-green eyes contemplated David. He felt uncomfortable under their scrutiny.

'Yes, I'm David Tregennis. And you are?'

'A friend of Richard's. He asked me to look out for you.'

'But he didn't know I was coming.'

'Not to worry, I'm sure Richard'll explain everything when they get back from the birthday dinner. Meanwhile, why don't you come up to the house?'

'Shall we drive?'

'No need.'

David got out of the car and followed the young woman a little way up the road. She pointed through a break in the hedgerow and he saw the corner of a tiled roof.

'You mean I've been parked outside the bloody place all this time?'

'The countryside round here can be deceptive,' the woman said, leading him through a kissing gate. 'It always has been. The sea frets, for example. A mist can roll in suddenly, blanketing the Fen, turning day to night. A man caught out alone, eel fishing or cutting reed, had to be careful. Had to remember the byways of the marsh. You see, the story of the marshland is the story of water: how man lived with it, profited by it, was sacrificed to its whims. How, in the end, he turned against it.'

'Yes, I see. Tell me, will Richard and the boys be gone long?'

They reached the millhouse. The woman climbed the porch steps and opened the door as if she owned the place. She laid a hand on David's breast as he tried to enter.

'Water was a way of life,' she said. 'A religion almost. These people – the Fen folk – were only ever Christian in a nominal sense. Through invasion and occupation, the pagan ways persisted and the old spirits clung jealously to their lands.'

'Miss, I'm very tired . . .'

'Impish, ancient beings who lived in the callow pits. Yallery Brown, the trickster imprisoned beneath the Stranger's Table. The Green Children who passed into the Fen from another world. Black Shuck, the Dane-hound that portended death. And, of course, there was the face behind the reeds, the soul of the Drowned Lands . . . There was *Tiddy Mun* . . .'

David, who had been staring at the woman as if she were mad, stopped thinking of polite ways in which to dismiss her. He latched onto the name she had spoken and repeated it.

'Tiddy Mun.'

The word felt strange in his mouth. It started at the tip of his tongue and rolled back down his throat, like a glass of water, swirled and swallowed.

The woman nodded. 'A name given to something nameless.'

'Who was he?'

She shrugged and smirked. 'They're just stories, Mr Tregennis.'

That smirk. He had been toyed with, made to look a fool. In the days of the Confection King it would not have been tolerated. Now such disrespect made David feel the impotence of age.

'Thank you for your folk tales,' he grunted. 'Now you can

run along home.'

His attempt to patronise didn't register with the woman. She took hold of his arm and guided him into the house.

'Nonsense,' she said, 'if I'm not here, who will introduce you?'

'Introduce me?'

'To those who knew your daughter.'

'There are people here who knew Janet?'

'Not just knew her, but helped her. She had her baby here, you see. Little Joseph.'

'Who are these people?' David snapped.

'Muriel Sutton. Old Mrs Bedeker and her granddaughter, Gail, to name but three,' the woman laughed. 'Don't worry, you'll meet them all in good time. But first, there is someone else here who wishes to see you . . . Alice! Alice, are you coming down?'

They stood in the empty corridor at the foot of the stairs. David followed the woman's gaze to the landing.

'Alice, please. I said I was sorry. See, I've brought Janet's father to say hello.'

There was something wrong here, David could feel it.

'Come now, Alice . . . I know you're hungry.'

'I'm sorry,' said David. 'It's getting late. I'll see Richard another time. My wife is very sick and I must get back to . . .'

A movement on the landing. The swish and rustle of a red dress. Between the banisters she moved, a child with lank dark hair. His senses screaming 'flee', David turned to the front door.

The effort was in vain. He was already lost.

From behind, he heard the slap of tiny, wet feet descending.

III

- JULY 2006 -

Through the Mist

Here lies one whose name was writ in water

John Keats' Epitaph.

- *Interlude* -

The Fifth and Sixth Guest: 'Slim' Jim Cafferty and Suzie Mars Made Absent on 8th March 2001

Missing Person Report Form – Frampton Station

Report Date: 26/3/01 **Date/Time Missing:** 5/3/01
Risk Status: Medium/High
Surname: Cafferty **Forename:** James
Aliases: Slim Jim
Gender: M **Sexuality:** Heterosexual
Marital Status: Single
Nationality: British **DOB**: 1/6/81
Place of birth: Ipswich
Home Address: 14 Dolan St, Frampton.
Accent: Lincolnshire
Distinguishing features: Chinese letter tattooed on inside left wrist.
Build: Slender/small. **Height**: 175cm **Eye Colour**: Blue
Hair: Brown. **Facial Hair**: Goatee
Complexion: Pale
Circumstances: (From PC Mitchell's notebook)

Jim and his 'live-in' girlfriend, Suzie Mars (see MPRF- MARS, S attached), left his parents' house, where they had been residing for the last two years, on 5th March. Both long-term heroin addicts, Jim and Suzie have been living off the Caffertys for some time. Jim's parents have been very supportive throughout the three years of their son's addiction, but attempts to help with private counselling and drug-therapy were rejected. For a considerable period, the young couple had been stealing from Mr Cafferty's bank account to pay for drugs. Cafferty Snr was aware of the situation, but felt unable to report his son to the police. Items of furniture, jewellery (Mrs Cafferty's wedding ring included), and even the family car, were sold to fund Jim and Suzie's habit. Mr Cafferty had been driven to the brink of bankruptcy and both parents were on medication for depression. Indeed, Jim's mother has made an attempt on her own life.

On 5th, Mr Cafferty had a heated argument with his son. He insisted Jim leave Suzie (whom he considered the 'rotten apple') and attend a rehabilitation retreat that the Caffertys had paid for out of their remaining funds. Jim refused. Later that day, Mrs Cafferty found that the couple's room had been stripped bare and their clothes were gone. Such disappearances were not uncommon but, after three weeks with no word, Mr Cafferty thought it proper to contact the police.

Several items removed from the family home tend to indicate that the pair intended to live rough or, more likely, take a short holiday: a two-man tent, a camping stove, sleeping bags, a few tins of food and a pair of nearly new mountain bikes. Also, Jim had taken his grandfather's solid silver antique compass, worth about £500.

A note (see photocopy) was stuck to the back door: 'Sorry, but I have to go. It hurts my heart to stay here and see how you look at me. I love you both. Jim.'

After leaving the house, a friend – Paul Adams – drove the couple as far as Scarsby Point. Paul has since reported that Jim and Suzie had been in low spirits and were talking of hiking north along the coast. Jim wanted to call his mother to check that she was okay but Suzie dissuaded him.

UPDATE: 2/4/01- A Mr Jonas McVickery, manager of the Pottery Motel, Potter's Drake, Lincs (see full statement attached) reported seeing two individuals answering to Jim and Suzie's descriptions on 8th March, three days after their disappearance from the Cafferty residence. Jim had tried to get a room for the night with Mr Cafferty's expired credit card. There was an altercation and McVickery threatened to call the police. Jim and Suzie left, grumbling about having to spend another night on the beach. A sweep of the shorefront has been completed but, aside from the remains of a fire in an old pillbox south of Potter's Drake, no trace of the young couple can be found.

Thirty-five

Thunderheads, shot through with ribbons of purple cloud, hung low over Potter's Drake. Not a breath of wind moved through the empty streets and, in the square, the union flag drooped against its pole. Everything was silent and still, waiting for the heat to be dispelled, for the storm to break.

'Christ, what a backwater,' Richard muttered, running an eye over boarded-up shop fronts.

Just out of the village, they turned in at the gate of the Pottery Motel. Aside from the odd B&B, this was the only hotel in the area, catering for agricultural reps and fishing parties. Richard slipped his Mercedes between a rusting Citroën Sedan and a flyspecked Fiat Panda.

Glancing up at the sky, Joe shivered. Ever since childhood, he had hated the gathering of elements. The lightning crack always came as a relief.

Sam hurried out of the motel and approached Joe's window.

'We've done a circuit of the village,' Joe reported. 'Doesn't look like there's anywhere much to eat.'

'We could get a bite here, I suppose,' Sam said, brushing storm flies from her face. 'They've got a bit of a restaurant.'

'Either that or we could drive further out,' Joe suggested. 'Maybe Peterborough.'

'I'm tired,' said Richard. '"Bit of a restaurant" sounds fine.'

They got out of the car. Sam slipped her hand into Joe's and squeezed. The gesture was comforting, but he only had to glance at his father and brother to feel that reassurance slip away. Richard was sporting the kind of expression that would make Genghis Khan appear jolly and approachable, while Bobby had been switching from sullen to jittery and back throughout the journey.

The restaurant was decorated in a mid-seventies vision of the continental dining experience. Red crepe tablecloths and scarlet candles, housed in half-coconut shells, adorned the tables. Over the sound system Renee implored Renata to 'save her love'. Nets and lobster traps hung from the ceiling. Around the walls, someone had painted a series of maps that could have depicted regions of Italy, cantons of Switzerland or the Merry Old Land of Oz; it was difficult to tell.

A waiter appeared from behind the restaurant bar with five laminated menus under his arm. Except for the fact that no fish-faced demons followed in his wake, his sharp, delicate features suggested he had just stepped out of a painting by Hieronymus Bosch.

'Table for five?'

'No,' Richard sighed, 'there're four of us.'

The boy rose onto tiptoes and glanced over Richard's shoulder. He looked at the empty space in front of Bobby and shrugged.

'Sorry, thought there was someone with you. Over here, please.'

Squeezed around a circular table by the window, their drinks order was taken and they were left alone. Utterly alone, for there were no other diners. The silence that followed was filled by Julio Iglesias, singing about a horse with no name, and fitful rumbles of thunder. In the glass opposite, Joe saw the reflection of the party. It was a grim tableau. Sam stared fixedly at the menu, her little finger twisted in her hair. Bobby, lost in thought, gnawed at a hangnail. Richard examined the wine list and coughed his dirt-dry cough. When his mineral water arrived, the glass trembled in the Old Man's fist. The chink of the ice made Joe feel nauseous.

They ordered their starters and mains. This time Sam made a determined effort to resist the lull.

'So, Bobby,' she said, 'how's your art going?'

Bobby flinched. He looked up, as if confused by his surroundings.

'Yeah,' he mumbled. 'Sure. I'm doing fine with it.'

'I liked your pieces in the castle prison building. Really interesting stuff. That sculpture of found objects was brilliant.'

'What's this?' Richard asked. He glared at Bobby. 'You had pieces on display in the castle?'

Bobby shrugged. 'A few of us did. It was part of the GCSE art course.'

'But Bobby got selected to have his sculpture as the centerpiece,' Sam smiled. 'Made up of bricks and masonry from old buildings, wasn't it? Buildings torn down after the development of the marina, with glass and steel interwoven to represent the new development. What did you call it, Bobby?'

'Metamorphosis,' Bobby said.

'That's right. It was really . . .'

'It was bullshit,' Bobby said, necking his coke. 'Arty-farty bullshit.'

'Why didn't you tell me about this?' said Richard. 'I would've liked to have seen it.'

'Would you?'

'Of course I would. What sort of question is that?'

'Have you been working on anything new while you've been here?' Sam interjected. 'I'd imagine that somewhere like this would be an artist's dream. All those brooding skies and barren landscapes. Don't they call this area the Land of the Three-Quarter Sky? Be a good title for . . .'

'Yeah, I've been doing a bit of painting.' Bobby's voice became shrill. His face cracked into a grin. 'It's not ready yet. Not quite. I can't show it to anyone until it's ready. I think you'll like it, though. Especially you, dad. I think you'll love it.'

The starters arrived and the tetchy silence started to reassert itself. Joe admired Sam's persistence but, as she tried a new tack, he hoped that she would soon accept defeat.

'But you're a pretty artistic family,' she said, between mouthfuls of grilled mushroom. 'Tell me, Mr Nightingale, how did you get into housing restoration?'

'It was just business. Work.'

'But I'd imagine it takes a lot of heart to do that sort of thing well. You'd have to love the idea behind it to get it right.'

Under the table, Joe tapped Sam's leg. He knew what she was doing, and the thought of it made his insides curdle. Sam did not know his father.

'Restoring a place to its original glory,' she continued. 'There seems just as much artistic merit in that as creating something from scratch. Joe was telling me how much he enjoyed working with you on the house.'

'He told you that, did he?'

'Yes, and I thought . . .'

Richard laid down his fork and stared at the girl opposite. 'Don't you think that this is a private matter between me and my son?'

'Of course, but I just think that . . .'

'Sam's been doing some research,' Joe interrupted. He grabbed hold of a napkin and wiped his lips. 'Into the house.'

'S'that right?'

'The history of the place,' Joe nodded. 'I meant to tell you yesterday, but . . . Well, it's fascinating. The old miller, Mrs Sutton's father, he came over from Germany before the war. He married this Irish girl. They had Muriel and, later, Alice. Muriel had to bring up the kid on her own and she, well, we think she couldn't take the pressure of it and . . . But, you see, the really interesting thing is, it turns out that Muriel Sutton isn't related to us at all. Sam's checked it online and through the official records and stuff. So it's funny, isn't it? That she left us the place, I mean. A complete stranger and . . .'

'I know all this,' Richard grunted. 'She was a family friend, that's all.'

'On which side, Mr Nightingale?' Sam asked.

'What?'

'I just wondered whose family friend Mrs Sutton was. I know that your family originally came from Somerset, so I suppose the connection must be on Mrs Nightingale's side. Guido and Mariah never left Lincolnshire after their arrival and, of course, Muriel was a near recluse, so I wonder how the Daechers and the Tregennises met. That was your wife's maiden name, wasn't it? Tregennis? Maybe she . . .'

'Who the hell do you think you are?'

A little sound escaped Sam's lips. It wasn't a cry exactly, more like a startled sigh.

Rain pattered on the window. The droplets held for a few seconds before coursing into streaks. For a moment, Joe thought that his father's question would be the end of the matter; that they would continue the meal without another word being spoken. He glanced up and something in Richard's face told him that he was mistaken. Sweat glistened on the Old Man's lip. His jaw worked as he tore his serviette to pieces.

'Samantha Jones,' he said. 'I know your father, don't I?'

Scars of colour whipped into Sam's cheeks. 'I don't know.'

'Yes, I think I do. Steven Jones, the architect. Well, you come from wealthy stock, Miss Jones. Peculiar, but wealthy. See much of your old man, do you?'

'Dad, just leave it,' Joe said. 'Sam didn't mean anything . . .'

'What's the problem? I'm only making observations.' Richard laid the tattered rags of his napkin on the placemat in front of him. With the back of his hand, he swiped the perspiration from his brow. 'True, I haven't done my research like Miss Jones, but I've heard a thing or two about her dear old dad.'

'Please, Mr Nightingale,' Sam murmured, 'I didn't mean any offence.'

'Offence? Why should I take offence? Some girl – some *child* – I don't know thinks it's okay for her to rummage about in my family history. No, I don't take any offence at that. Just as long as *she* doesn't mind if I have *my* say. See, I know Steven Jones. Most people in the Lincoln business community do. It happened a few years back, but I remember the gossip very well. How his wife found out about him dipping his wick with most of the trollops in his company. How she left him, only to fuck herself royally on tranquillisers and booze. How he got lumbered with a little girl he didn't know how to raise. How he just plain gave up on *that* little endeavour. Much too hard for a man like Jonesy. I know he pays for her upkeep, sends the odd card or birthday present when he remembers. Nice daddy you've got there. Doing a bang up job . . .'

Bobby shot to his feet. Plates spilled off the table and shattered.

'You've got a fucking nerve,' the boy roared. 'A *fucking nerve*.'

Richard started to pick up the breakages. When he spoke, his voice was level.

'Sit down, Bobby.'

'You dare to talk about *her* father?' Bobby spat. 'You hypocrite bastard. *You're* the worst father on this shit-hole planet. Do you know anything about us? Joe and me? Do you care? I can't remember a single day since I was born when you gave a flying fuck about me. And now, all this stuff here, little attempts to get to know us. It's just too late, dad. Joe might be taken in by it, but I'm not. Why're you doing it, eh? Why now? You've had fifteen years to get to know me, to help me. Whatever I am now, it's too late for you to take an interest. Too late for you to try and change. Just admit it, you don't care about us and you never have.'

'I won't tell you again, Bobby. Sit down or I'll sit you down.'

'Ah, yes. I've been waiting for this – going to start hitting me, are you?'

Sam laid a hand on Bobby's arm. 'Please, don't.'

'Don't what? Say something I'll regret? Something like I blame *him* for every fucked up piece of my life. I blame *you*, dad. I'm miserable. Scared. Alone. And you're the one who's responsible.'

'Bullshit.' Richard almost shrieked the word. Then, in a lower register, he said, 'You're not alone. I – I care about you, Bobby.'

'I don't believe you. I'm sorry, I just don't. Because you've never loved anything. Not me. Not Joe. And certainly not mum . . .'

Joe knew what was coming. He felt the white-hot sting of anticipation. This was the night of home truths and there was no escaping them. The thing that he had dreaded these last seven months was about to happen. Bobby in his honest, spiteful way was apportioning blame, and Joe would not be overlooked. When the diatribe against his father had dried up, his turn must come. Tonight, in front of this girl he truly cared for, those three words would at last be spoken.

You killed her.

Bobby's denunciation came with cruel inevitability.

'You killed her.'

Relief and confusion rang inside Joe's mind. Without looking up, he knew that the accusation had not been directed at him.

Richard rose to his feet. He stood, arms sagging, back hunched. He looked defeated. Spent. Then, in one sudden movement, he struck Bobby hard across the face. The handprint blazed like a brand on the boy's cheek. Richard's eyes widened and he reached for his son.

'Point proved,' Bobby murmured. 'You're just an animal after all.'

'I'm sorry, Bobby,' Richard gasped, 'it was an accident. You were going on and on and I . . . I didn't. Son, listen, I didn't hurt your mum. I could never . . .'

'*You* hurt her,' Bobby said. 'Every day *you* hurt her. And don't think for one minute she didn't know about the affairs. Leaving all those little clues around the place; it was almost like you wanted her to find out. You hurt her and you *killed* her.'

'It was an accident,' Richard said. His eyes flitted to where Joe sat, dumbstruck. 'It was no-one's fault. These things . . .'

'Just happen? No they don't. People injured like that . . . they hang on. If they've got something worth living for, they hang on. But you didn't give her that chance, did you? Your silences, your affairs, they left her with nothing. So when the darkness came she just gave herself to it. She didn't fight because you'd abandoned her. In that way, in that very real way, you killed my mum. And all the bad things that have happened since, they're your fault, dad. It's all your fault.'

Bobby broke down. Huge, braying sobs tore out of him. Without tears, the cries sounded somehow inhuman. Joe watched as Sam wrapped her arms around his brother.

'I'm going to take him to my room,' Sam said. 'Get him cleaned up.'

Joe nodded. The pair of them left, their feet crunching across the remnants of cups and saucers.

The storm had still not broken. Rain drilled against the window and the thunderheads scudded towards the horizon, but lightning had not yet cracked the sky. The window reflected the table darkly, making the faces of the two remaining Nightingales appear like death masks. Surrounded by the debris of shattered china, father and son tried to find words. Words to comfort. Words to challenge.

'It wasn't my fault your mother died,' Richard said. 'It wasn't. I tried to save her when I could, but there was nothing I could do . . . She wasn't there. After Bobby was born, she wasn't there.'

Unable to make sense of these ramblings, Joe stared at his father. Then, very quietly, he said, 'No, it wasn't your fault. It was mine. But you didn't make it better, dad. And that's what fathers do.'

Joe got to his feet. He laid a hand on Richard's shoulder.

'They make things better.'

Richard watched his son leave the restaurant. He looked old, shambling towards the exit like a man of seventy rather than a kid of seventeen. Eighteen. That was why they had come here, to celebrate a forgotten birthday.

'I didn't kill her. I loved her.'

'Jesus Christ. What the hell happened here?' The Bosch boy, steaming plates in his hands, stared at the devastation.

'Tot up the damage and put it on the bill,' Richard said. 'And take that stuff back. The party's over.'

The kid could do nothing but nod and gape, like a particularly amenable halibut.

'And one more thing.'

'Sir?'

'Get me a double scotch. Two doubles. Or, unless you've got any objection, you can bring me the bottle.'

Thirty-six

'Bobby, look at me,' Joe said. 'I want to see you're okay.'

Bobby did not answer. He curled up on the back seat of Sam's Beetle, arms wrapped around his face.

'Leave him be,' Sam whispered. She took a hand from the steering wheel and reached for Joe.

They left Potter's Drake behind.

With a clear sky overhead, the Fens had once struck Joe as a rolling landscape encased in a giant dome. Now that sense of space was gone. The storm clouds, tapering into the mist that slunk across the fields, narrowed the gap between earth and sky. In this shrunken world, swarms of bittern came together and parted as they tried to escape the oncoming fury.

The car rolled up to the millhouse just as the first vein of lightning split the sky.

Bobby threw open the back door and ran across the scrub. Reaching the porch, he grabbed the key from its hiding place and disappeared into the house.

'Wait!' Joe shouted. 'Bobby, we have to talk.'

His pleas were lost against a fresh report of thunder. The front door swung in the wind, slapped the side of the house and slammed home.

Wind clawed the long grass and whistled into the car. Rain chattered across the bonnet. From somewhere in the bulrushes, birds cried out against the elements. Joe felt Sam's grip tighten around his fingers. From the corner of his eye, he saw how her chest rose and fell, how her breath steamed the window.

'I killed my mother,' he said.

Thunder boomed. Lightning sawed at the sky.

Sam shook her head as tears scalded her cheeks.

'It wasn't an accident.' Joe pressed his palms against the windscreen. 'How can something so . . . so *huge* be an accident? It can't. There has to be blame. Someone *must* be responsible.'

'No.'

He swallowed hard. 'The car. Mum and dad, they both said about the car. I wanted a classic, you see, after I passed my test. Something with a bit of character. Dad said the Spitfire was too hard to drive, too fierce. If I'd listened, got something with modern brakes and . . . But I wanted the Spitfire.'

'Stop it, Joe.'

'I was driving too fast. Not paying attention to the road.'

'Stop it.'

'She was singing. I can remember each lyric, crystal clear. Everything was clear before, just as everything was dark afterwards . . . *Now she's gone and lost forever, awful sorry . . .*'

'Stop.'

'I can't. Not now I've started. I was looking for a tape. A stupid, fucking tape. I didn't see the tree in the road . . . My foot slipped off the accelerator. Jammed on the brake. Earlier that morning I'd bought you this present. A ball, a glass ball. My mum was carrying it in her lap.'

'Oh my God.'

'The car span. Shot off the road. The ball shattered. Tore into her. And when I woke up . . . She was broken, Sam. She was broken and there was no mending her.'

The Bosch boy – Derek to his friends – poked his head out

of the stockroom and looked towards the far side of the bar, where Mr R Nightingale (the name printed on the guy's MasterCard) had taken up residence. Derek had served a few alkies in his six-month career at the Pottery Motel, but this guy was something else. A real pro, he had crawled into the whisky bottle and didn't look like coming out any time soon. The shot glass in front of him barely had time to right itself on the counter before being refilled, drained and slapped down again. Still, he seemed peaceable enough. Probably ruminating on the argument that caused his family to up and leave him like that.

Derek made up his mind. There were no other patrons that night, the agricultural reps having little business here in the height of summer. With the motel manager taking a nap in the back office, it couldn't hurt if he joined Mr R for a chat.

Perching on the neighbouring stool, Derek said, 'How you doing there, Sir? Got everything you need?'

Mr R looked up. He glared, as though Derek had just asked permission to pork his grandmother.

'Pisser of a night,' Derek said, nodding towards the window. 'Still, it'll clear the air.'

'Too late for that, son,' the man grunted.

'Well, I hope it does. I've been sweating so much this last week I smell like a Frenchman's armpit. Anyway, do you want some ice with your whisky, Sir?'

'Ice, you philistine? No thank you,' Mr R smiled. He held up his glass, so that the light ran through the whisky in an oily spectrum. 'I don't want to dilute, to adulterate, one precious drop of this stuff. Nectar, my man, God's own nectar . . . Who the hell are you anyway?'

'Derek.'

'Derek what?'

'Deekwater, Sir.'

'Derek *Dick* water?'

The alkie roared. Derek, used to such reactions, gave a thin smile.

'Sorry, son,' the man said, choking and belching. 'I am. But, Jesus. You poor bastard. My name's Richard, by the way. Here, a peace offering.'

Richard pushed the bottle towards Derek, who stretched across the bar and retrieved a glass for himself. Necking the shot, Derek smiled as he was refilled.

'What do you do then, Mr Deekwater?'

'Work here. Not much else. Live in the village with my mum.'

'Sounds bleak.'

'Bleak about sums it up.'

'Why don't you do something else, then? Go somewhere.'

'Can't leave me mum.' Derek swilled the whisky this time, enjoying the bite as it scorched the back of his mouth. 'She's all crippled up with MS, needs me to look after her. Sometimes I think about leaving her, you know? It's not like we're living in the Dark Ages, even out here. There're services, carers, community nurses and suchlike, and she's got good neighbours. I tell myself this sort of stuff at night, when I'm on my own. It's easier to be selfish at night, isn't it? When there's no-one to hear and judge. You can imagine selfish things in the dark. But I couldn't leave her, not really. Couldn't live with it. If someone needs you, no matter how hard it is, you can't just leave them.'

A hand slapped Derek on the back.

'What was all that about then?' Derek asked, emboldened by the stranger's camaraderie. He nodded towards the deserted table, lit at that moment by a flare of lightning.

'Oh, that? I don't think they liked your starters.'

The drinkers chuckled and chinked their glasses.

'Christ, this is good,' Richard sighed. 'You wouldn't believe it to look at me, Derek, but I used to be quite a credible drinker.'

'Really?'

'Oh, yes. I could drink Peter O'Toole under the table any day of the week. I have the liver to prove it. But my serious drinking days are behind me, and do you know why?'

Derek shrugged and helped himself to another shot.

'Because I love my boys. My sons. They rate me as just about the worst piece of shit you could have the misfortune to step in, but I think the world of them. All right, I haven't been the greatest dad ever, but I've had problems. Just because you become a parent – just because one chunk of spunk hits home – does that mean you're not allowed to have problems anymore? I haven't been what they need, but what about what *I* need? I've given up things for those kids. And you know what else?' Richard leaned in towards his drinking partner. 'I've protected them. They don't realise it, but I've kept things from them. Bad things. My wife, you see, something happened to her. Something terrible. I lived with it, *endured* it, for their sake. And if I had nothing left for them after what I endured, every hour of every fucking day, well I'm sorry. But I did my best. I kept it from them. You think they'd be fucking grateful.'

Richard slammed his glass on the bar.

'But you said they didn't know,' Derek observed. 'How can you expect them to be grateful if they didn't know?'

'You see, logically, I don't, but there's a part of me that thinks: how couldn't they have known? How could they not have seen her for what she was? And, if they loved me, why didn't they understand that I was protecting them? I bore the brunt of the ugliness so they didn't have to see it.'

'And what do you want?' Derek asked. 'Thanks? Understanding? A fucking parade? Sorry mate, it doesn't work that way. If you sacrifice things for someone you love, you don't always get rewarded. Take me and my mum. I feed her, bathe her, sort out the shit that needs sorting. She hasn't once thanked me for it and she doesn't need to. I do it because she's my responsibility. You say you protected your sons? *Whoop*-de-*fucking*-doo. So you should, and if they don't understand or thank you for it, tough shit. I'm just saying.'

Derek could tell that his words had grated. Richard gave him a surly look and turned away towards the light show. White and purple forks shattered the sky, snatched the Fens from darkness and jewelled the rain. The alkie's shoulders tensed and hunched in time with the thunder cracks.

Derek wondered if he had gone too far, flapping his jaw like that. Maybe the guy was about to spin round and deck him.

'You might be right,' Richard muttered. 'But my boys, they're men now, or as good as. I've tried getting close to them, but they don't want to know. I think it's about time I was selfish for once.'

The bulbs behind the bar flickered. Outside, no more than a few hundred yards from the motel, a finger of lightning raked the earth. The crack that followed rang in Derek's ears and made his fillings ache. He was about to ask for another slug of whisky to dull the pain when Richard's mobile rang.

'Hello?' Richard grunted. Then his tone changed. It became timid, almost apologetic. 'Yeah, it's me. How – how've you been?'

Derek yawned and poured himself one last shot. He knew his limit and time was getting on. Soon Jonas 'Jobsworth' McVickery would wake up and, annoyed at the evening's slow trade, start finding him things to do. Glancing idly at his reflection in the mirror behind the bar, Derek rubbed the stubble around his chin. Jesus, he needed a shave – he looked like a fucking Bee Gee.

'Yes. Come down. Tonight. I want to see you,' Richard said. He drained the last of the Jameson's. 'That day in the hotel, I didn't mean what I said. I realise that now. I've missed you so much.'

Lightning dazzled the looking glass. Derek's eyes grew round. In those sudden flashes, he had seen something: a figure standing between himself and Mr R Nightingale . . . A lurking presence . . . Heart racing, Derek glanced down.

There was no-one there.

'That's settled then. Now, you're sure you've got those directions straight? What?'

Outside, the sky erupted. And there she was again. A little girl, standing up at the bar – standing within inches of Derek Deekwater. Her head, reaching just above the counter, was turned towards the alkie. She looked as if she had just walked in from the storm. Wet tangles of hair hung across her face. Behind the hair, Derek could make out the movement of her lips, mouthing silent words. She must have noticed Derek watching, because she stopped and stared into the mirror. Stared directly at Derek Deekwater.

'Yes, that's right. And, Susan, get here as soon as you can.'

The girl's lips moved. 'I will.'

The door to the bar banged open.

'Derek, what the hell's going on here?' Mr McVickery strode through the restaurant. 'Thought you'd help yourself to a bottle, eh? You cheeky little bast . . .'

Only when the motel manager reached the counter did he notice that his ne're-do-well employee had a drinking buddy.

'Ah. I'm sorry, Sir, I didn't see you there.'

'Obviously not,' Richard said, terminating his call. 'So, what's your problem?'

Turning on the oleaginous charm that he had perfected at many a hotelier training conference, McVickery smiled.

'No problem, Sir,' he simpered. 'It's just that we don't encourage our employees to drink while on duty.'

'He's not been drinking.'

'But he looks . . . I can smell it on him.'

'That's probably me,' Richard said. 'Fumes. Anyway, the boy's been excellent. First-class service. Wasted here, of course.'

'There was a girl.'

Richard and McVickery looked at Derek. The kid appeared pale, abstracted.

'You all right, son?'

'Are you ill, Derek?'

Derek stood up. Staggering a little, he pointed at the space between the stools. A pool of dirty water sat upon the tiled floor.

'A little girl. She was standing right here.' He turned back to the others. 'At least, I think it was a little girl. Her face was . . . *horrible*.'

McVickery sneered and shook his head. 'Get a mop.'

Derek backed slowly out of the bar.

When the boy was gone, McVickery stepped behind the counter and cleared away the glasses and empty whisky bottle. This done, he rang the bell.

'Time.'

Richard looked around the empty bar. 'Was that for my benefit?'

'Rules are rules.'

'And what do your rules say about selling me another bottle?'

''fraid not, Sir. Our licence, you see?'

Richard flipped open his wallet and laid two fifties on the counter. McVickery's eyes glistened.

'The Jameson's again,' the alkie said, 'to take away.'

Thirty-seven

Sam took Joe's hand and led him from the car. He was still shaking and, truth be told, so was she. Not that his confession had anything to do with it – to her mind, the death of Janet Nightingale remained an accident, pure and simple. Rather, it was Joe's belief in his own culpability that broke her heart. A momentary lapse of concentration – one split second of recklessness – that was all it had taken for this kid, this almost-man, to bring down a lifetime of guilt upon his shoulders. Sam had to break through that guilt. Had to show him that he could still take pleasure, could still *feel*, without fear or forfeit.

They reached the shelter of the porch. She strained to hear his voice above the gale.

'Bobby,' he croaked. 'I don't want him to see me. Not like this.'

'Is there anywhere we can go?'

Joe looked around. 'The millhouse.'

They sloshed around the front of the house until they reached the mill door. Thunder rumbled and Sam shivered.

Ever since the night of the betrayal, she had always hated storms. Though a romantic at heart, she was not superstitious. Even now, however, some small part of her believed that she had once heard the voice of the thunderheads. That they had told her a terrible secret . . .

Eleven years ago, little Samantha Jones and her parents had been holidaying in the Lake District. Their rented cottage, overlooked by a craggy fell, had stood not thirty feet from the shore of Buttermere Lake. It had been a magical place and, in her memory, those days had been loving and golden.

Sam remembered. Picnics and fishing trips, breathless hikes and sticky-fingered treats. Her mother lavished praise, her father was attentive. Even an occasional scolding was recalled with a rush of nostalgia. And there had been laughter. It was nine-tenths fantasy, but Sam did not care. She pressed laughter into her memories, banging it home like a puzzle piece forced to fit.

Laughter before the storm.

It was the lightning that woke her – flashes filtered orange through marmalade curtains. Sam sat up in bed, listening. The thunder, when it came, sounded muffled, distant. She dared, and then double-dared herself to get up and go to the window. Living in cities her whole life, she had only ever seen lightning caught between rooftops, its fury reduced to that of a penned-in animal. She wanted to see it let loose. She threw back curtains.

An arc of light darted across the sky. The lake, flurried with breakers, flashed in time. Then came the boom as the thunderclouds grazed the fells and darkened the waters below. Another streak, this time branched like an upside-down tree, almost touched the surface of the lake. Then another. And another. Sam jumped in time with the cracks, feeling an urgent need to pee, but unable to tear herself away. Although spellbound by the power of what she saw, its fleetingness terrified her. It wasn't enough just to watch through glass, she must *experience* it.

The girl refused to waste precious seconds pulling on mackintosh and shoes. The storm was waiting. She eased open the front door and stepped outside.

It wasn't cold, but the wind pierced her nightie and the grass was damp. Out on the lake a single column of rain swept north, ruckling the surface as it went. As she watched, the column broke up into sheets and passed over the village, onto the head of Crummock Water and beyond. But the storm had not finished with Buttermere just yet. Colossal black clouds rolled over Samantha Jones. Occasionally, they lit up from the inside and Sam was reminded of spluttering Jack-o-Lanterns. Still they grumbled, still they moaned, and the little girl, tripping towards the shore, held out her arms to them, longing for their tears. She reached the water and span on the balls of her feet.

This time the lightning found its mark. It sparked against the outcrop of Fleetwith Pike. The clap afterwards rang so loud that Sam had been certain the mountain would split in two. And it was now, as this thought occurred to her, that the thunder spoke.

It spoke to her about what she saw in the flashes that followed the first strike: the car, parked a little way down the lane from the cottage. Her father's car, windows steamed, the people inside visible nonetheless. Two people, squashed into the front seat, moving against each other. She had only just begun to sense it in herself, but Sam recognised the kind of passion that motivated them. Repelled, fascinated, she walked towards the car.

Her father, she recognised immediately. The other, too, was no stranger. Aunt Val, her mother's sister, always came along on family holidays.

Sam backed away, her lower lip caught between her teeth. Hidden behind a tree, she listened to the thunder, whose voice rattled deep as it explained everything. Just as later, shivering and sobbing, *she* had explained it to her mother. The terrible secret that, once told, could not be untold.

The next day, the Jones family left the cottage.

Why was she thinking of this now, as she followed Joe into the millhouse? Was it just the storm, or had there been some other trigger? Perhaps Joe's own sense of guilt had been the catalyst that drew the memory out of her.

She watched as he scanned the machinery-littered floor and the low brick parapets – felt him take her hand and lead the way up the wooden ladder – touched his face as they lay down together on the sackcloth that covered the attic floor. And while she experienced these things, she remembered her mother. The crumple of that beautiful face as the secret was told.

Sam leaned into Joe and kissed him, hard and deep.

'I can't.' He drew back.

'You must. You must because . . .' Reasons rose and stuck in her throat. 'Please, for both our sakes.'

Gently, he pushed her away and sat up.

Lightning stuttered against the window. When Sam blinked, she saw the cruciform afterimage of the frame repeated before her eyes. It flickered against the rocking chair that stood in the far corner. Sam felt cold. The dainty little rocker that had once belonged to Alice Daecher. How had it survived the fire?

Sam imagined Alice sitting there, playing, combing her hair. Then, in her mind's eye, she saw the flash of a hand from behind the connecting door. The bottle shattered, the liquid spilled and the fire caught. Flames spread, singeing Alice's frock and smarting the soles of her feet. Yes, Sam could see it, could almost feel the heat of the fire on her own skin. There would be the crackle of roasting meat and the stink of burnt hair. And the screams, of course, as the child staggered across the room towards the window.

Sam saw . . .

Balanced on the ledge, Alice snatched at the air. Painfully

cold air, gulped down into fiery lungs. Everything was characterised by fire now. Every inch of the child's flesh, every sliver of sensation, spoke of burning. Consumed in a ball of flame, Alice Daecher looked down and saw salvation – the water that promised life as it ploughed through the mill-wheel.

Alice jumped.

Sam could see her. The descent into the wheel. The snuffing out of the flames. The buckling and breaking of the tiny body as it wound, up and down, up and down, between a hell of fire and water. Finally, as the child became limp, she slipped out beneath the wheel and into the run of the spillway. Pulverized beyond recognition, Alice swept into the river, flipped onto her front, and floated there in slow circles. What was left of her face stared up into the blackening sky.

Except it was not the face of Alice Daecher.

The river chattered, but Emily Jones was silent. As silent as she had been when listening to her daughter's story. Her expression: utter grief and bewilderment. Emotions that went on to age her horribly as, bit by bit, they undermined her humanity. Sometimes Sam thought her mother had lost her mind. That the secret revealed had let loose a peckish sort of madness that nibbled at the corners of her reason. In reality, however, all that Emily had lost was her faith in love. *Her* love had been betrayed and so her store of it diminished. She could spare none, not for her daughter and not for herself. Without it, she withered before her time.

'How could I keep a secret like that?' Sam asked out loud. 'I had to tell her.'

Did you? The question did not come from Sam's inner voice. It was alien, but still it spoke inside her head: *Isn't it true that lies are sometimes all a body needs to keep itself together? Who cares if the sustenance they provide has no nutrition, so long as the soul that feeds upon them believes in their worth. You took her lies away, Samantha. . . .*

'Sam? What is it?'

She heard him, but he seemed very distant.

You condemned your mother to a half-life.

'Can you hear me? Look at me, Sam.'

She saw him, felt him, as if through a thick gauze.

You tore out her heart and replaced it with a dry, beating husk. You made her empty. Absent. You, Sam Jones, who long for love . . . Where is she, Sam? That woman you crushed? How many years is it since you saw her last? Three? Four? Remember how she would coo over you, her pretty little girl. How she wrapped you up in her arms and smothered you with kisses. All gone, all gone, and only yourself to blame . . . Come to the shadows, Samantha. Descend into the depths of your betrayal.

Sam felt a tug in her stomach, as if a fishhook embedded there was being reeled back in. Something wished to leave her: a dark and finely-textured essence.

Joe kissed her. His tongue slipped into her mouth. Then his lips roamed across her face and neck. Reaching her ear, he whispered:

'Don't be frightened. Whatever it is, I'm here . . . I love you.'

Thirty-eight

Rain ticked against the windscreen, though Richard could no longer see it through the condensation. He lifted the Jameson's to his lips and gulped down three fingers. Tapping the half-empty bottle against his temple, he reached for his mobile and checked the call log for the eighth time. Seeing her number recorded there – *Received. Susan. 23.17* – made him feel warm and wanted. He tried to recall the conversation, word for word, but the booze got in the way. Snatched phrases were the best he could conjure: *Want to stand by my principles but I can't . . . Said I'd never call you . . . Need you, Richard. Need you and love you.* Susan Keele was on her way. The woman who had helped him feel connected to the world during the bleak years of Janet's *Absence*. He had cared very deeply for Susan, but had never loved her. He had used her, and he would use her again. To spite his sons? To feel connected? He wasn't sure of his reasons.

The digital display on the dashboard showed the time as 23.57. From Lincoln it would take an hour at most to reach the inlet of the Wash. He should lay off the drink or chances were he'd be incapable when she arrived. Brewer's droop was not an option tonight. Not when he already ached to touch her, to taste her. His thoughts returned to that afternoon in the Castle Lodge Hotel: the sweat on her back, the sway of her breasts before they were marshalled into the bra. What had possessed him to push her away? He could no longer make sense of it. All he could think of now was the need to fuck and to forget.

He turned the key and the engine gargled into life. Three sheets to the wind, Richard drove the Merc out of the motel car park and headed through Potter's Drake. Signs for non-existent speed cameras, and the plea to 'Please Drive Carefully Through Our Village', passed in a blur. Richard gripped the steering wheel. In all the years of secret drinking, he had rarely driven while the devil swilled in his gut, but he had checked with that jumped-up weasel of a motel manager: there were no taxis operating out of Potter's Drake. McVickery had suggested he spend the night at the motel. When Richard tried calling her to suggest the change of venue, Susan's phone was dead. The thought of her arriving at the millhouse alone, and being confronted by Bobby, was an unnerving prospect. He couldn't risk it. And so he drove through the village, anxious to reach the deserted Fen roads beyond.

Richard hit the country lanes and opened up the engine. Now there was no risk of killing anyone, except himself.

'Big fucking loss,' he laughed. 'Won't be able to move for mourners at that gig.'

He turned on the radio. A selection of modern pap jangled through the speakers. Not knowing the words, Richard hummed along to the tunes.

Lightning strobed overhead and the station crackled. The headlights flickered and went out. The car rolled to a stop.

Richard cursed. He turned the key and gunned the accelerator. Nothing.

And then the stereo blared back into life:

Oh my darlin', Oh my darlin', Oh my darlin', Clementine
Now she's gone and lost forever

Awful sorry, Clementine . . .

Richard stared. If the battery was dead then what was powering the stereo? He tried the starter again. No response, yet still the music played. There was something familiar about the song that fizzled through the static. Had he heard it somewhere recently? Maybe a panpipe version playing in a hotel lobby somewhere? But, no, it wasn't the tune that jogged his memory, it was the words. Words read rather than heard – typed on thin paper, the letters smeared. A photocopy. An official document.

And then he had it. The statement Joe had given to the police. The one in which the boy had blamed himself for the accident. Just before the crash, Joe said that his mother had been singing to him.

Now she's gone and lost forever

Gone and lost forever . . .

Lost. Gone. Absent.

'Janet.' He rested his head against the steering wheel. 'Oh God, Janet.'

'*I'm here . . .*'

Richard sprang back in his seat. From behind the crackle, where the music had once played, Janet Nightingale spoke.

'*It's very dark here, Richard,*' she said. '*Is it dark where you are, too?*'

Richard stabbed at the stereo buttons. The display continued to glow.

'*I did it for them,*' she said. '*Because you're a man and they needed me. I had so little left to give. Please say you understand.*'

Richard pressed the heels of his hands against his ears. In an attempt to drown out the voice, he started humming. Snatches of things – the first few bars of a John Lennon number, a James Bond anthem – anything to refocus his mind. He knew that, if only he could calm himself, the voice would stop.

Blackouts and hallucinations were all part and parcel of the nectar, you see.

Slowly, Richard unblocked his ears. The radio was silent. He took a breath and wrapped his hand around the whisky bottle. It was drained in a single draught. His face looked back at him, slantwise from the windscreen.

'Come on,' he muttered. 'Get a grip.'

He clicked off the handbrake, got out of the car and pushed it to the side of the road. Then he went to the boot to retrieve an umbrella. What he found hiding there made him double up laughing. This really wasn't his night. He had just paid a hundred nicker for a bottle of scotch when, all the time, a half dozen bottles had been lying in the boot. He had clean forgotten about his trip to the supermarket the day before.

Richard picked up the bags, unfolded the umbrella and headed off down the road.

The rain still fell but it looked like the storm was passing. Glimpses of sky could be seen through the clouds. From the east, a sea-scented wind gusted across the fields. With the wind came something else from the sea. It was some way off, but Richard could just make it out.

Mist, thick and grey, ate up the road ahead.

Sam pressed down to meet him. Beneath her perfume he could smell the true, earthy scent of the girl. He breathed it in and glanced down to where his finger brushed her clit. Between groans, she gave him soft instructions.

Joe held her just above the buttocks, his hand tickled by the beads of sweat rolling down her back. She arched and grunted. Eyes open, willing him on, she locked her legs tight around his waist. He leaned forward, encircled a nipple with his mouth and sucked hard. At the same time he felt her pussy tighten around his cock. His balls rode up and he came. A few moments later, she shuddered and their fingers interlaced. Joe drew her to him and they exchanged hot, salty kisses.

Then they lay back upon the sackcloth bed.

'I meant what I said,' Joe whispered.

Snuggled against his chest, Sam frowned. 'Sorry?'

'I love you.'

'You said that?'

A curious expression settled across Sam's features. A look somewhere between apprehension and confusion.

'Of course I did. What's wrong?'

'Let's get out of here.'

With his seed still wet between her legs, she bustled to her feet and pulled on her clothes. Joe followed suit. When they were dressed, he opened the trapdoor and started down the steps.

'Let me go first,' Sam pleaded. 'I just need to get out.'

Joe nodded and helped her down. Balanced on the middle step, he reached back to shut the trapdoor. It was then that he saw the water.

'Joe? Are you okay?'

His eyes remained rooted on the rag bed. A moment ago, those scraps of old sacking had been bone dry. Now, seconds later, they were soaked through. Dark stains spread across the material and murky water trickled from beneath the rags. To Joe's mind, the thought of that filth beneath them while they made love seemed to pollute the act itself.

He slammed down the hatch.

'We need to go.'

As Sam headed down the second ladder, towards the Meal Floor and the door to the outside world, Joe looked back the way they had come. His heart lurched. His body stiffened and braced. It was raining *inside* the millhouse. From the attic boards, a torrent of black water wept across the millstones. Meanwhile, through the window, Joe could see that the storm had abated. Outside it was no longer raining.

He lost no time in following Sam downstairs and through the millhouse door.

All was quiet and still out on the scrub. The wind had died and the thunderheads were fracturing. Bent over, panting, Joe reached for Sam.

'There's something inside that place,' she said.

He looked back. The whitewashed door hung on its hinges, like a drunk clinging to the wall for support.

'Something . . . unnatural.'

His eyes travelled beyond the door. Reluctantly, they followed the lick of darkness back inside the mill.

'Something old,' she said. 'Something bad.'

Thirty-nine

The rain had been more torrential than Joe could have imagined. All across the scrub, water shivered in what looked like the filled footprints of a stalking giant. Birds and reptiles, shaken by the storm, warbled and chirruped in dark, swamp-like stretches. Had Joe known the history of this place he might have reflected that the Drowned Lands had returned once more. But the boy was preoccupied with other thoughts.

Something old. Something bad.

Memories stirred, though they moved through Joe's head like treacle through a sieve. Hadn't he known all along that there was something wrong at Daecher's Mill? It was difficult to be sure. Lately his thoughts had been muddled by so many things. If he wasn't concerning himself with Bobby and the Old Man, there were his feelings for Sam to consider. Most of all there was his mother and the ever-present spectre of what he had done. Yet now disjointed images jogged his conscious mind, as if trying to tell him something. A dead bird on the step. Child footfalls in the corridor. And a figure, at once familiar and horrifying, waiting for him in the bathroom at the end of the hall.

Row, row, row your boat . . . Life is but a dream.

He turned to Sam.

'What did you see in there?'

The effort to remember wrote itself across her face.

'I don't know. Whatever it was, I don't think I saw it *inside* the attic as such, but maybe . . .' she cupped her brow, '. . . maybe inside here. But it all felt strained somehow, as if someone was forcing memories from my mind.'

'What memories?'

Sam shrugged. 'Not good ones.'

From somewhere behind the house, a bird let loose a harsh *aarrk-aarrk*. The call of the bittern rang in Joe's ears.

'The horrible thing is,' Sam continued, 'I felt as if they were taking me. The memories, I mean. Like I was losing myself to them.' She reached for Joe and kissed him. 'You brought me back.'

'I've felt the same,' Joe said. 'At least, I think I have.'

His gaze roamed across the millhouse and dropped down the paddles of the wheel. There was water in the stream, a rill trickling along the spillway.

'Odd things have happened since we arrived here. Not *things* exactly. Not happenings. Feelings, like you say. Experiences that, afterwards, you can't bring to mind. And after each one, you feel a little less whole, a bit less complete . . . Jesus, Sam, this can't be real, can it?'

'Appearances might tell against me,' she said, 'but I'm not very superstitious. I'm not a Goth chick into bloodletting and worshipping mystic forces. The only dark lord I acknowledge is Ozzy Osbourne. But something very bad happened here.'

She looked back at the attic window: a cyclopean eye set into the head of the millhouse.

'Up there, an innocent child was murdered. Burned alive by her own sister. Her guardian. The one person on earth who should have loved her unconditionally. Death has power, Joe, and *that* death . . . Maybe there's some echo of it left in that room. The anger and agony. The sense of betrayal.'

'You're talking about ghosts,' Joe said.

'Not necessarily. Some people believe that an emotional resonance can be left in the fabric of a building. They call it a recording spirit. The soul of the person isn't there, it's headed off to heaven, Nirvana, wherever, but the image of the dead is absorbed into the bricks and mortar.'

'But this isn't a ghost. This is *active*.'

'It was dark thoughts that compelled Muriel Sutton to kill the child. Maybe *that's* the echo. Not of Alice at all, but of the insanity of her older sister. Maybe that's what survived: dark thoughts that draw out the dark thoughts of others.'

Joe shook his head. 'Look, isn't it possible we're seeing patterns in things that aren't there? It hasn't been exactly easy for us since we arrived here. Unspoken crap between Bobby, the Old Man and me. And that bullshit my dad said to you tonight. All I'm saying is, it might just be the result of stress and . . .'

'I don't think that'll work,' said Sam. 'Trying to explain it away. Believe it or not, I don't give a flying fuck about what your dad said. I've heard it all before, and from meaner shits than him. And surely it's just too much of a coincidence to believe that we both had the same kind of experience here.'

'So what are you saying?'

'I'm saying, I don't think that this was the healthiest place for you guys to pick as a summer retreat. I'm saying that what happened here thirty years ago might still be impacting on events today. It's like some kind of emotional sponge, soaking up all the bad things we think and feel. And, even if I'm wrong, don't you reckon your dad's idea of a happy family vacation is dead in the water? Maybe you should think about leaving.'

Articulated by the wind, the house rattled. The whitewashed door slammed shut.

'Smartest thing I've heard in weeks,' Joe said. 'Let's find Bobby.'

Together, they climbed the porch steps and entered the house. The hall was in darkness. Joe flicked the light switch but nothing happened.

'Storm must have tripped the fuses.'

He opened the cubby under the stairs. A pickaxe rested against the fuse box, so he shifted it out into the hall. The tool slipped against the wall and crashed to the floor. The reverberations shattered the queasy silence of the old house. Gritting his teeth, Joe shot Sam an apologetic grimace. He flipped the trips. Lights clinked and buzzed. The darkness retreated into shadows and stole beneath the furniture.

Joe laid a hand on the banister and tilted his head upwards.

'Bobby, you there?'

They climbed the stairs to the second floor and the narrow corridor that led to Bobby's room. Squeezed either side of the door, they waited for a response to Joe's knock.

'Bob, it's Joe. Let us in, will you?'

Silence.

'Look, it's important. We're thinking about getting out. Tonight. We'll leave a note for dad and call him in the morning. Come on, mate, I think we should talk.'

Joe nudged the door. It swung open to reveal chaos typical of a teenager's bedroom. Littering the floor: Warhammer figurines, T-shirts, jeans, knotted towels frowsty with damp, the odd sock worn so hard a hermit crab could make a home of it. The drone of a mammoth bluebottle attracted Joe's attention. Like a despairing lunatic, it beat its head against the window.

'This isn't like Bobby,' Joe said. He walked to the window and gave the bluebottle its freedom. 'He's the neat one. He hates mess. Why do you think . . . ?'

'Joe.'

He didn't need to turn around. Just his name, one soft

syllable from her lips, and he knew that something was badly wrong. He took his time closing the window.

The wardrobe stood behind the door. They had not seen it when they entered. One side was pulled back a little from the wall. It was in this gap that Sam's attention was focused. Joe joined her and together they exposed what lay hidden.

'My God,' Joe croaked. 'Is it . . . ? No. Oh my *fucking* God.'

Sam grabbed hold of him. She guided him back to the bed.

'I'm sorry,' she said. 'But yes, I think it's blood.'

Art rendered in blood.

The painting – for what else could it be called? – occupied three square feet of plasterboard. There was no demarcation of edges, no strict boundaries to frame the picture. Trails of cloud and water reached across the torn wall in varying lengths until, at last, the life-paint from which they had been composed faded. Paint, no longer hot and red, but brown and flaking. In those places where the lines were thickest, the blood had dripped. From the drawn up talons of the birds, for example, and from the bold windows. So much dripping *there* that the effect must have been deliberate, as if Bobby had wanted it to appear that the house was weeping. The millhouse that is, for the main house – the more recent structure – was not depicted. This excision further enhanced the oddness of the painting, though Joe could not fault its overall accuracy. The mill had been captured without detail, but with a keen sense of mood. That his brother could have accomplished such a fine piece of work while dipping his finger, time and again, into some deep wound both astounded and horrified him.

A figure had been placed in the attic window.

Alice Daecher – Joe was sure of it.

'So much,' he murmured. 'He's lost so much.'

'He'll be all right.' Sam rubbed warmth into Joe's arms. 'Look, in some places the blood is older than in others. Bits of it are virtually black. This wasn't all done in one mad rush. He might be hurt, but he's not drained himself. This took time and care. Dedication.'

'*Dedication*? You make it sound like an art project!'

'I think, in a way, that's exactly what it is. And if you ignore the means by which it's been accomplished, it's actually quite beautiful. Like those sculptures in medieval ossuaries. You flinch from them because they're constructed from human bone but, at the same time, you can't help admiring their artistry. All art is about expression, Joe.'

'But what the hell is *this* supposed to express?'

They sat quietly for a moment and examined the different elements of the painting: the three birds caught in mid-flight, beaks agape; the mist roiling behind the house like a dark cowl; the river in full flow, dashing against the millwheel. Each facet conveyed a sense of power unbound.

'What I don't understand is how he knew about Alice,' Joe said.

'What do you mean?'

Joe pointed. 'That figure. I guess it's supposed to represent Alice Daecher. But Bobby wasn't with us when you told me about how Alice died, so how does he know she fell from the attic window?'

'Perhaps your dad told him.'

'I don't think my dad knows anything about it. All he knows is what Gail told us.'

'Gail?'

'Gail Bedeker. She's the granddaughter of the steward you mentioned. The one who accidentally shot himself. After her gran died, old Mrs Sutton let Gail stay at the cottage during the summer and . . . Sam?'

The girl trembled. A sickly grey tinge stole into her cheeks.

'Sam, what's wrong?'

'Gail,' she whispered. 'Gail Bedeker? Christ, Joe. It's *insane*.'

'Tell me.'

'I'll do you one better. I'll show you. Come on.' Sam let out a shock of hysterical laughter. 'Gail's waiting.'

Forty

They went through the house, shouted his name across the scrubland, even searched the knot of trees that overhung the riverbed. Their torches – a maglite from Sam's car and an old rubber flashlight found under the sink – picked out nesting birds and whirling insects.

They found no trace of Bobby.

'Maybe he went that way,' Joe said.

Unable to articulate his fears, he pointed towards the sea. Sam, who after leaving Bobby's bedroom had soon regained her composure, looked into the bank of mist that had settled over the dunes.

'We're just as likely to meet him going towards the road,' she said. 'I think we need to keep a grip on things, you know?'

Joe covered his face with his hands. He breathed between his fingers and nodded.

'Okay,' Sam said gently. 'Let's get going. On the way, you can tell me about Gail Bedeker.'

What little Joe knew was soon related: the Nightingales' accidental meeting with Gail on the road; her brief introduction to the story of Muriel Sutton and Alice Daecher; her inheritance of the family pictures.

'That's odd,' Sam said. 'Why would Mrs Sutton leave her those?'

'Well, I suppose she had more right to them than we did. We weren't even relatives, and at least Gail had known the people in the pictures.'

'I guess.'

'Sam, where are we going?'

'Just a little further.'

They reached the kissing gate and moved on up to the lane. Half a mile or so away, the mist had made incursions across the road. Grey and dense, like liquid concrete, it bridged the dykes and yawned into the fields. The main body of the fret obscured most of the scrub. Soon it would coil and roll across the millhouse, just like in Bobby's picture.

Joe stopped at the hawthorn bushes that surrounded the Bedeker cottage. He took a broken branch from the lane and prodded a gap in the thicket.

'What is it?' Sam asked.

'It's where she lives,' he said. 'Gail Bedeker. Hey, are you okay?'

'Not remotely. Come on.'

Richard walked in a tight halo of perception, while the world around him swirled in obscurity. The mist sweated droplets onto his face, where they ran in the tracks of his own perspiration. His body ached. He needed rest before Susan arrived. She was coming, oh yes, no storm nor fog could stop her. Soon enough she would be racing along this road, desperate to be with him again.

The bag of bottles clinked against his calf, singing in falsetto tones. He had one already open, wedged under his bicep. With the torch in his left fist, bag and umbrella clenched in his right, he found the going cumbersome. He rearranged the cargo and put out his hand. Thank God. The rain had stopped. With no further need for it, he threw the umbrella towards the dyke.

It made no sound. Mindful of the hazard to Susan if it had landed on the road, he slouched off to investigate.

His aim had been fine. The umbrella lay snagged halfway down the dyke bank. Further down, Richard saw that the water level had risen. Since their arrival in Potter's Drake, the dykes and cuts had been dry. Now, with that hour or so of torrential rain, the waterways were back in business. The chuckle of the water's passage sounded strange in Richard's ear, almost triumphant. With exaggerated care, he put down the bag and bottle, dropped to his knee and stared into the water.

Surely it was impossible. Even after such a deluge, the ditch could not be so swollen. He inched forward, his hand catching at clumps of reed for support.

By God, it's running fast . . . running deep . . .

The reeds came away in his hands.

The torch skipped down the bank and plunged into the water. Flickers of light illuminated the depths. Richard scrabbled to keep his balance but the earth slipped through his fingers. His legs cartwheeled behind him, lifting his waist and stomach. His neck cracked as his body turned full circle. There was nothing he could do to stop it. He hit the icy water with a flat smack. The shock of cold took the fight out of him and his head sank beneath the surface.

Bubbles erupted and from down among the bulrush came a soft *pee-wit.*

His gaze swept the coast. On the southern side of the bay, he could make out the brick-red cliffs of Norfolk and, to the north, the huge boulders that marked the Lincolnshire sea defences. He could even see the churning surf. At the breakwater, the skeleton of a half-submerged fishing boat rocked in the turn of the tide. He moved on, over the rain-dimpled sand and back to the rise of the dunes. He saw mollusc shells and coils of rope, driftwood and washed up pop bottles. Each crystal-clear detail confirmed what Bobby already knew. The mist, though it had the flavour of brine upon it, did not come from the sea.

Bobby turned and faced the mainland.

From the earth it reached, from those glinting stretches of water laid down by the storm – a mist of the marshland that touched neither sea nor shore.

'Bobby. Are you ready to play?'

The voice echoed from the doorway. As Bobby approached, he could smell the stench of decay wafting from the mouth of the pillbox. Mingled with it was something stirring and familiar. The intimate scent of the boy he had loved.

Bobby ducked low and entered.

Joe and Sam walked, hand in hand, between the trees. Passing through the lich gate, they huddled together and Joe thought he could feel the warmth of recent lovemaking still on her body. He longed to take her again, even among the gravestones while the dead watched on.

Their feet cracked on the path and padded on the grass. The bulk of the mist had not yet reached here, but an advance guard of grey vapour poured over the wall that surrounded the graveyard. It caressed the tombstones and probed inside the ruins of the church.

Sam had gone on ahead a little. Joe watched as she picked her way through the headstones, stopping occasionally and examining the inscriptions. Finally, she looked up.

'Found them.'

Joe joined her beside a simple stone tablet. Sam tamped down the grass at the base and he read the words inscribed on the granite.

'Jesus Christ. What does it mean?'

'I don't know,' Sam answered. Her voice shivered and she leaned into him. 'You say you met Gail Bedeker, but I'm afraid the real Gail Bedeker . . .'

Her finger traced the dedications, top to bottom.

Rest in Peace
Patrick Bedeker
1910-1971
Loving Father and Husband
Wilma Bedeker
1926-2001
Wife and Beloved Grandmother

And beneath these, hidden by the grass that Sam had flattened:

Gail Anne Bedeker
Died 2001

'She's been here some time.'

Forty-one

An arrow of dark-bellied geese passed over the village. Heading north, the flock swept out across the marshes to their mudflat nests. They honked as they flew and, from the reeds and grasses, their call was answered. A wetland orchestra of waders and wagtails, coot and moorhen *kwoked* and trilled and *kr-k'd* in unison. It was a short-lived symphony. Twilight drew in, and the music of the day gave way to the nocturnes of night creatures. That was the order of things and, although the marshland was a hard, wild place, it had its laws, as immutable as any laid down by Man.

Richard Nightingale, standing at the end of the marsh-path, watched until the geese were no more than flecks in the tobacco-orange sky. Those birds are long dead, he thought, centuries dead. The notion did not upset him unduly – no more than the sensation of water filling his lungs. He felt his death at a distance, only remotely cognisant of the odd stab of pain.

With not much to do but wait, Richard set out towards the village.

Potter's Drake was a cluster of wattle and daub cottages, bordered on all sides by the marsh. Unseen, Richard passed through the community. As he went, he marvelled at his powers of invention. Clever little neurons, firing as his died, really were pulling out all the stops. He could actually smell the dog shit!

And, although he knew that all this was mere illusion – nothing more than chemical explosions from an expiring brainstem – he was grateful nonetheless. A period re-enactment sure beat vistas of hell or – shock horror – the inevitable truth that awaited him: oblivion, nothingness. *Absence*. Nevertheless, he was surprised by this moving tableau. Never a great one for regional history, he wondered from where he had dredged the sights and sounds of a Stuart-era Fenland village.

Never mind, he told himself, just enjoy the ride.

The women went to and fro, bringing in tools, eel baskets and errant children. Although somewhat grimy about the face, and stinking to the heavens, they looked well-fed. Their clothes – simple woollen skirts with shawls over baggy blouses – were reasonably clean. Either he had read somewhere that peasants of old weren't as wretched as popularly supposed, or this was his brain picturing the David Lean version.

He had started watching a group of boys, baiting a cat with a stick, when he saw her. A girl of about ten years old, she sat cross-legged outside one of the circular cottages. She had auburn hair, a shade lighter than the sunset that now singed the horizon. She smelled of the sea and of the peat fire that burned in the house behind her.

To Richard she seemed real. A creature set apart from his imaginings.

This was confirmed by her song:

> *'O, Wo'k as thou wull*
> *Thou'll niver do well;*
> *Wo'k as thou mowt*
> *Thou'll niver gain owt;*
> *For harm an' mischaunce an' Yallery Brown*
> *Thou's let oot thy-sel' fro' unner th' sto'an.'*

The dialect was thick, the rolling tones heavily accented, but Richard understood every word. How could he imagine such a thing?

The girl's hands moved, light and quick. Using a rake made from an axe-head with two bent nails hammered through, she removed plant tangles from the collection of reed and saw sedge at her feet. Then, with a flick of string, she brought the reeds together into bundles of equal length. The pace of her work was breathtaking. Even more surprising was that Richard knew exactly what she was doing. Her father, the reedcutter, had gathered this harvest from the marsh. When dried, the reed would be used as thatching, the sedge, being more flexible, for awkward roof ridges. Richard even knew the names of the tools stacked outside the cottage: the cane sickle, the meak, and a spear for catching eels, known hereabouts as a glaive.

Raised voices carried from inside the cottage. By the way she inclined her head, Richard knew that the girl listened. It was dark beyond the doorway, but the glow of three pipes burned bright as the smokers puffed.

'The delvin's gone too far, you know that, Harold.' This was her father's voice, deep as the Callow Pit. She knew it and Richard knew it.

'That's as maybe,' Harold grunted, 'but there's not a thing under God's sky you can do about it, Stephen Hickathrift. Come on, man, we've tried.'

'Aye.' The reed-thin voice of the third man, Jonah Deekwater. 'We've tried.'

'And not failed yet.'

The girl thrilled at her father's passion and Richard felt his own heart leap. Stephen Hickathrift was a cottar. He ploughed his master's demesne, but he had his own land and he worked it well. By defying his lordship, Stephen had more to lose than his friends, but his sense of justice would not allow him to take the easy path.

'Let me state the case again,' said Stephen Hickathrift. 'More drainin' means more uncertainty. Delvin' changes the land, and land and rights are bound up as tight as fen litter and marsh hay. When all hereabouts is bone dry, where will you fish, Jonah?'

'Where I like.'

'Ah, but will you? With fewer ponds and creeks, there'll be fewer fish for the catching. With the Drowned Lands gone and the meadows sowed, there'll be fewer natural places for hunting of any kind.'

'We'll have to change our ways,' Jonah countered. 'Become year-round farmers.'

'And what's wrong with that?' Harold asked. 'You're a fine plough-hand, Stephen. Wouldn't you prefer that life to wading through the shallows, cutting your hands to the bone every winter?'

'I would not. Don't you understand, either of you, that this is the life we were born to? If we were meant to be year-round farmers, we'd have been raised in Suffolk or some such place. We're Marshmen. Fenmen. Since our Breedling ancestors, our lives have been tied up with the water.'

'Fine words, Stephen, but Sir Giles and his Dutchmen will do as they will.'

'We've hampered their plans before.'

'Those days are over. Wrecking dykes and sluices? It's useless. The people don't have the heart for it anymore. They're compensated by his lordship for their losses and inconveniences. And, now that the Dutch are heading home, the marsh folk are even working on the delvin' theirselves, and getting good pay too.'

'They toil towards their own ruin,' Stephen muttered.

'Aye . . .' Harold hesitated. 'Mayhap they do.'

'Sir Giles has said that, with the marshes dried, the mist will disappear,' Jonah said weakly. 'No more fever. No more fen ague.'

'And no more drownin's neither,' Harold added.

'And farming poses no dangers, I suppose,' Stephen said. 'Look, what I say is this: there's no life a man can live without harm snapping at his heels, but he should live the life he was fated to. We were born of the marsh. A hard parent, no doubt, it sustains us and oftentimes punishes us, but it is at least an honest master. Can you say the same of Sir Giles? We must stand against the delvin' or one day we shall wake to a foreign land. The spirits . . .'

'Come now,' Jonah piped, 'let's not speak of them.'

'They are foolishness,' Harold said, 'and no basis for a man to decide his fate.'

'This is *their* home, too.'

The girl shuddered and dropped her bundle. The dry reeds rattled across the ground.

'How many of the delvers, of the Dutchmen, have vanished?' Stephen asked.

'Drownin's are common.'

'Aye. Very common of late.' Stephen Hickathrift's pipe blazed. 'You try and drive a man from his home, he will fight. Why should the Old Ones be any different? Remember, they were here afore Norseman and Roman. Afore our Lord himself came to these shores. They *are* this land . . . Well, I leave it to you, good friends, but if we do nothing to stop this then, mark my words, we shall suffer as the Dutchmen. The spirits, even the good ones, will turn against us. They will lay a cruel justice at our throats.'

'Nonsense. God is our master and will protect us.'

Stephen sighed. 'I told 'ee: there are older things than Him out there in the marshes.'

From the doorway came the sound of chairs drawing back. Two men, dressed in beige shirts and breeches exited, knocking out their pipes against the lintel. They were followed by a bear of a man, sad-eyed and stooped.

'Been listening, you naughty little boggart?' Stephen Hickathrift laughed.

His daughter nodded. 'They're stupid men,' she said, glaring at the retreating figures.

'Not stupid, just hopeful. Finish that bundle and take it down to the staithe for collection. Then come back and we'll eat.'

Richard followed the girl through the village to the wooden jetty where a few flat-bottomed boats were moored. As they walked, he listened to her thoughts:

She knew that her father was right – about the delving, about the bad things that would come of it. He had no reason to lie to those ignorant men. Everyone knew that Stephen Hickathrift was as fine a farmer as he was a reedcutter. He could plough a field, straight and square. Changing all this to meadows wouldn't harm *him*. Yet still those clog-wearing villeins wouldn't listen. The girl knew that pride was a sin, but she would not apologise for believing her father to be a great man. A man who had the marshes in his blood.

She reached the jetty and laid out the bundles. Glancing down the staithe, she saw that she was not alone. Sally – the maid with the evil eye – sat staring out into the marsh. Mad as a ferret from being dunked once too often in the millpond, she murmured nonsense words that Richard couldn't quite catch.

'Careful now, Sal,' the girl said, 'don't let anyone hear your hexes.'

She laughed, but it was only to mask her fear. Sally, crone-sister of Elspeth, the Isle Witch, had always scared her. Now the girl shuddered as the old woman turned and grinned, runners of spittle slipping between her teeth.

'No stopping it now,' Sally gabbled. 'What must come must come.'

The witch pointed westward, towards the encroaching dykes and cuts.

The girl joined the madwoman. 'My father says there is no God in the marshes.'

'No God,' Sally nodded. 'Will-o-the-wykes with their lanterns. Boggarts and crawling things. Faces 'neath the water. And the Old Ones. Things that have weakened since the crucified-Man came here. Things that have changed, but still endure. But God, Christ-god? No, not him. Only The Lord of the Marshes walks behind the reed.'

'Tid . . .'

'No name. Red is his cloak, grey his beard. His is the mist and his voice, the waters. This is his home. Mean living he will come to, starved to madness. I know madness well, you see? Know its patterns. How it will eat up the Drowned Lands. How it stretches forward to the Dry Times. Good No-Name will be good no longer. Will fight the fading with all the guile and spite of his changed heart. But there is hope.'

'Where?'

'In the water.'

The witch parted her cloak. Her thin hand twitched inside and withdrew a leather stoup or flagon. She offered it to the girl.

'Go to his home. Offer him water. Save the marsh-folk, for a time . . . for a time . . .'

The girl looked back towards the village. The sun had gone and the moon was fat, its light picking out the white daub cottages of Potter's Drake. They looked like moons themselves, she thought. She should go back.

'My father . . .'

'You must do as you see best,' Sally said. 'Best for you. Best for your kin.'

There was a glint in the madwoman's eye, but it was not evil.

The girl walked to the end of the staithe and filled the stoup with water from a clean pond. Then Stephen Hickathrift's daughter hopped into the great man's flat boat. She untied the mooring and took hold of the long oar. Without thinking, Richard stepped off the jetty and joined her. His weight seemed to have no effect on the level of the boat in the water.

As the girl pushed off, Richard glanced back at the madwoman. Impossibly, her eyes seemed to be fixed upon him.

'Oh, yes,' she cooed, 'I see madness right enough.'

The girl rowed out until Potter's Drake was lost behind screens of swaying grass. She ploughed on, sometimes digging the oar so deep her fist touched the water, then skimming the boat through the shallow reed beds. She knew these ways, these secret paths. Stephen Hickathrift had exposed to his daughter the labyrinthine marsh at an early age. Together they had explored it, for, though he knew it well, he seemed to see the place afresh through her eyes. While they rowed and worked, he told her stories. Tales of the Fens and the Carrs. Some he had lost to adulthood (like that of the Dead Moon coming down from the sky and getting trapped beneath the water) but most he still believed.

At the heart of the marsh, the wind moaned. It riffled the reeds and swirled the waters. Richard looked over the side of the boat and saw the sleek body of a vole cut through the depths. It was hard to make out because the water was black and very deep. Overhead, the stars glittered, casting a sheen across the swamp.

The girl stood up. The stoup, which she had clasped to her

breast throughout the voyage, now shivered in her hand. She dropped the oar into the boat. Then she drew a fistful of something from the pocket sown into her skirt and scattered it to the east. She spoke strange words that Richard could not understand. It took him a moment to realise why. It was because they were forgotten; chants so ancient even the girl's father, who had taught her to speak them, did not know their meaning.

With a soft ululation, the girl finished. The wind whipped her hair. The water lapped the sides of the boat. Richard could hear her breathing. She was so very scared.

'Please,' she murmured.

Through the reeds it came, thin and fast. The mist, similar to that which would coat the mill road centuries from now. It trickled across the water and slipped into the boat. It caressed the girl and blotted out the sky. Cloaked in grey, the girl stood fast.

'Tiddy Mun, Tiddy Mun, without a name, is it you that brings the mist?'

No answer. Just the *lip-lap* of the water.

'Tiddy Mun, Tiddy Mun, oldest of the Old Ones, is that your step behind the reed?'

A bird shrieked. Richard glanced around, but the girl's eyes remained fixed on a particular clump of reeds at the prow of the boat.

'Tiddy Mun, was that your voice? And are those your eyes agleam behind the stalks?'

Richard followed her gaze. There was nothing: just reeds and grasses and . . .

Eyes. Dark, shining eyes set into a stone-grey face. It watched the girl in the boat, but its expression remained inscrutable. *Absent*. It was like trying to read patterns in the mist.

'Tiddy Mun,' the girl's voice shook, 'creature without a

name, Lord of the Marshes, we are sorry. The marshmen cannot save your home. Truth to tell, most will not even try. It is our sin. Our sorrow. Our deepest shame. You must know this, and feel it, and know that we are not bad. Please do not harm us like you harmed the Dutchmen. Let us live in our regret and misery. Let the shadows of our sins haunt us. Feed upon *them*, drink them down if you will. That is punishment enough.

'For now, I offer you what is yours.'

The girl held out the stoup. Clean water trembled from the lip of the cup and dribbled into the black marsh.

'A token, Tiddy Mun.'

The Old One did not stir. Its eyes blinked, that was all.

The girl retrieved the oar. She turned away and started to row homeward.

Then she heard it. The voice like the gurgling of a water-hole.

'*They may bring me tokens*,' it said, '*so that I know their shame*.'

When she reached home, the girl told her father what she had done. He did not scold her, but looked long into the fire.

For years to come, the villagers did as the girl bid them. Though the delvers had their way, and the land was long dry, they took their stoups to the heart of the dead marsh and sprinkled the ground. They called on Tiddy Mun and told him of their shame. For his part, the god without a kingdom kept his word. When his tokens were forgotten, however – when their shame went unspoken – he was ruthless. He sickened their cattle, wasted their crops, even took their children. But the day came when the village moved and the Fen was abandoned. Then the god walked alone and, just as the witch prophesied, he starved and went mad.

But he endured, in one form or another: Tiddy Mun, without a name.

Forty-two

Five years dead. Gail Bedeker – the *real* Gail Bedeker – had lain here all that time, while the grass grew and hid her name. As Sam explained how grandmother and granddaughter had died – asphyxiation by carbon monoxide leak from the cottage's heating system – Joe tried to paste the truth over the lies.

'I read it in passing,' Sam concluded. 'Part of my research. It seemed unimportant – to the Alice-Muriel story, I mean.'

'She talked to Bobby,' said Joe. 'Gail, this woman pretending to be Gail Bedeker, she talked to Bobby. He tried to tell me something about her . . . I can't remember. I didn't listen. Jesus, it has to be connected, doesn't it? Bobby drawing that picture and now this.' He kicked the gravestone. 'She must be some kind of psycho. Probably been telling Bob all kinds of weird shit. Warping him.'

Sam shook her head. 'I don't think so. Whatever's wrong with Bobby, whatever made him hurt himself, it runs deeper than some woman whispering in his ear. More likely it has something to do with that kid who died at school.'

'Matt Linton. Yeah, I thought so too at first. But they hadn't been close for a long time.'

'Are you sure about that?'

'No,' Joe admitted. 'The fact is, I don't know Bobby. My own brother does this to himself and I don't have a clue.'

'Well, there's still time to put that right. But now, we have to get your dad involved. He needs to know about Bobby, and about this.'

Sam ran the beam of her maglite across the inscription one last time, as if to ensure that they weren't both hallucinating.

'I'll head straight to the motel. Drive him back again if needs be.'

'You'll have to. It's pretty certain he'll be pissed by now. You sure you're okay with this? After what he said to you.'

'No problem. Like I said, I've heard worse from bigger and uglier than your dad. Well, bigger anyway.'

Richard broke the surface.

Gasping, retching, he dragged himself out of the water and onto the bank. Phlegm-thickened dyke water oozed out of his nose. He flipped onto his side and disgorged what felt like gallons of bile – insects, seedpods and strands of pondweed mixed in. This done, the cold hit home and his skin prickled around his bones. He crawled slowly up the bank, giving the umbrella a vicious kick as he went. When he reached the road, Richard staggered upright.

'Christ. My head.'

His fingers found the spot, soft and tacky, where he had been knocked unconscious. If Richard were a religious man, he would have thanked God that he'd woken before he drowned. As it was, he picked up the bag of bottles, span a cap and took a swig. The whisky spread heat outwards from his throat, but the shaking wasn't going to subside any time soon. He was soaked to the skin, freezing cold and hungry. If he didn't get back to the millhouse soon, then catching a shag off Susan Keele was the least of his worries. Catching double pneumonia would be more likely.

Shirt tails dripping, Richard started once more along the mill road.

Moonlight silvered the mist. This must be like walking through a cloud, he thought. Walking, running, flying through a cloud – soaring over the wattle and daub cottages, beyond the village and out across the marshlands – through the heart of the swamp and the home of the Old One – out, out, out to the mudflat nests . . .

Richard stopped. A flight of geese. An argument between smouldering pipes, waged over a whisky-flavoured fire. A boat, a witch, a stoup and a girl.

The Lord of the Marshes.

A drowning man's dream, it came back to him in its entirety. And, as sometimes happens with dreams, Richard longed for the characters of his invention to be real. The little girl and her father, even Mad Sal and the villeins. Not because they were wonderful or clever, but because they had seemed so vivid. He felt cheated by the fact that they were *not* real.

'Nuts,' he whispered to himself. 'You're fucking nuts, mate.'

But the admonishment did not change his mood.

Many thoughts occurred to Richard as he completed the last half-mile. He wondered why the car had stopped; why he had not drowned in the dyke; whether he would ever reach Daecher's Mill or if he would walk on through the mist forever. The tremors were back and the cold became unbearable. He was just about to drop when he reached the kissing gate. Barely conscious, Richard slogged the last few metres up to the house.

'Who's here? Joe? Bobby?'

His greeting met with silence. Even if they were here, why should they answer? He had only a vague memory of the things he had said to Samantha Jones, but he knew they'd been bad. Guilt stirred, but the anger that had dogged him through the mist stamped it down.

Dreams of a steaming bathroom, whistling radiators and a hot shower evaporated when he opened the bathroom door. The pipes were leaking and the pressure was gone. He turned on the shower. The water hit his outstretched hand like blades of sleet. Throwing off his clothes, he rubbed himself dry on the threadbare weft of an old beach towel. Then he went to his room and tugged on a couple of T-shirts and a pair of slacks.

Back downstairs, he paused by the windowsill where he had left the bottles. More drink was a bad idea. He needed hot milk with honey, not scotch, but the bottles were whispering again. *Chink chink*

While he drank, Richard watched his son and the Jones girl cross the scrub. Sure enough, her stylish little Volkswagen was parked outside. How the hell had he missed it? They reached the car and exchanged a few words. Christ, she was pretty. Probably even beautiful beneath all that makeup. Richard's imagination ran on. Self-loathing finally put a stop to his erotic daydreams, but not before he looked down to find his cock tenting his slacks. He turned away from the window.

And then Richard heard something that swamped all other thoughts and feelings.

The tinkle of a bell.

He must have imagined it. He was ill. Auditory hallucination brought on by . . .

Ting. Ting-ting-ting.

He dropped the bottle. It didn't smash, but rolled in a wide circle, sloshing tides of whisky from its mouth.

Tinggg-tinggg-tinggg

The boat rolled: he could picture it, water spilling over the sides, the prow turning east as the tide changed. And the little girl, red hair stuck to her brow with sweat. The oar in her hand dug deep as she propelled the boat homeward. She looked fierce and determined, but the warning bell tolled. Stephen Hickathrift's daughter was in danger.

Unbelieving, but desperate to help, Richard followed the sound of the bell. He didn't have far to go – only ten steps or so, through the door and into the study. His eyes were wide as he dropped to his knees and put his ear to the floorboards. He laughed. She was here, of course, rowing her boat beneath the house.

Richard went to the hall. He found the pickaxe lying there, as if someone had left it out for him. And, indeed, why not? He grabbed the tool and returned to the study. Then he listened, just to make sure he wasn't losing his mind. But no, there it was again – the trill of the bell. He stood beside the wall that separated the study from the porch outside. Feet planted wide, axe raised, his hands slipped. He tightened his grip on the haft.

'I'm coming, honey,' he said. 'I'll help you.'

The axe head buried itself between the boards. Richard tore it free and brought it down again. He watched as the neatly laid flooring came away in chunks. Again and again, he powered the axe, tearing apart his son's careful labours. He forgot about the girl, about the need to reach the tinkling bell. Instead, he took joy in destruction. With each stroke, he thought of Joe sanding the wood, fitting the tongue and groove, loving the work of restoration, just as Richard himself had loved the art of it many years ago.

Whistle – *Joe and his girlfriend.*

Crack – *Joe and his grief.*

Tear – *Joe and his martyrdom.*

Wrench – *Joe and his stupid, selfish dream.*

Exhausted, Richard slid down the wall. The pickaxe slipped

from his hand. Knees drawn up to his face, he surveyed the wreckage. What would Joe think when he saw it? Poor Joe, whose grief and guilt and martyrdom were needless.

Something caught Richard's eye. A glimmer from beneath the ravaged floor. He reached into the hole. He expected to draw out a tiny bell, but instead found something equally strange: a lapel badge with pin. He held it up to the light, cleaning off the surface dust with his thumb. That was when he saw the colours – red, white and black – and the infamous insignia. But what was it doing here?

Then he remembered Gail Bedeker's story.

Guido Daecher had wept when he heard of the Night of Broken Glass. Kristallnacht. The first Nazi pogrom against the Jews. Now Richard wondered: had the old man wept tears of sorrow or of joy?

Forty-three

Joe broke through the hawthorn. He emerged into the garden, spitting out leaf membrane and spider web. There was no light in the cottage windows. With the ground shrouded in mist, and the moon visible only as a faint yellow disc, Joe found his path to the cottage a difficult one. He stumbled a half dozen times and once caught the toe end of his trainer in a rabbit hole.

Reaching the door, he knocked and waited. After a brief interval, he started to move around the side of the house. A metallic rattle brought him up short. Joe knelt down and ran the chain through his hand. A dog leash.

The year before Silas Sutton died, the dog attacked little Alice. Caught her outside the millhouse and very nearly tore her throat out . . .

Joe went from window to window, wiping peepholes in the grime. All the rooms were empty, filthy. In fact, the whole cottage looked deserted. Had the woman posing as Gail Bedeker really stayed here, he wondered. When he came to the master bedroom, his question was answered. On the floor lay a mattress, a sleeping bag, a green Gore-Tex jacket, a paraffin stove and a couple of tins of beans. Who was this woman? A squatter? When they met her that first day, had she simply spun a tale in order to spend the summer in this rat hole? Perhaps, but that didn't explain how she knew the history of Daecher's Mill. No, she *had* to be familiar with the family, the area.

Joe pressed his face against the glass. These questions about 'Gail' were important, but there was something far more vital. He had to find out what she had told Bobby. Although Sam was no doubt right about the depths of his brother's problems, Joe felt sure that this impostor had, in some way, warped the kid. If only he had listened to Bobby that morning . . .

'I saw that woman yesterday, Gail Bedeker. In the millhouse. She told me things about this place. Weird things . . .'

Joe's eyes fixed on the white sheet in the fireplace. It covered a stack of oblong frames. Of course – the family portraits Muriel Sutton had left to Gail Bedeker . . . But wait. That didn't make sense. Muriel would have known that Gail was dead. After all, Gail had been buried only a stone's throw from the millhouse. Not only that, but the girl had died in the cottage *with* her grandmother. So why would Muriel leave family pictures to a dead woman?

Joe picked up a rock from the garden and broke the window. The lock was a simple catch, and he was soon up and over the ledge.

The Bedeker cottage reeked of damp and dry rot. Joe spluttered on the stench. He looked around the mottled walls, decked with tenantless webs and hollow cocoons. There was an emptiness here, as if the soul of the place had been torn out. Joe crossed to the fireplace and plucked the sheet away. A cloud of dust flew into the air. When it settled, he saw that there were three pictures in all, and one tattered photograph album. In the grate lay the charred remains of the other dozen or so pictures missing from the walls of the house. He took the surviving portraits to the window.

By moonlight, Joseph Nightingale examined the late Gail Bedeker's inheritance.

The first picture showed a couple, arm-in-arm. It was posed, probably in a studio. The pastel shades of their clothes and the backdrop had saturated the print, bleeding the colour from the subjects' faces. The groom was a huge man, blonde hair severely parted. His bride looked gnomish beside him. The portrait itself had been well-preserved in a sturdy frame and behind thick glass. Joe turned it over. In the bottom right corner he found an inscription.

Guido and Mariah Daecher. (Poppa and Mama-their wedding 23rd June 1939)

The second picture was a family group. Joe recognised the Daechers, although husband and wife looked a little older around the eyes. Arranged in front of the house, Guido stood while Mariah sat on the porch steps. A baby, no older than a few months, rested in Mariah's arms. At first, Joe thought that the sepia tint of the composition had obscured the child's face. On closer examination, however, it appeared that the oblit-eration had not been accidental. It was a cigarette burn, he was sure of it. The inscription on the back:

Poppa, Mama and Me. Spring 1945.

Joe turned to the last portrait.

He saw the face staring out at him and dropped the pic-ture.

Me

The glass cracked. The frame splintered.

Joe tried to make sense of what he saw. Eventually, he admitted defeat and, with shaking hands, picked up the por-trait.

A woman. Late twenties, early thirties. She stood in the long grass that grew on the far bank of the extinct river. She was smiling and, although not pretty, her delicate features were compelling. In her hand she held a ball and a cricket bat. A child's red rubber raincoat was slung over her shoulder. Her eyes were grey-green. She wore a sequined scarf.

The inscription told Joe who she was:

Me. Taken by my darling Silas in the Heavenly Summer of 1970

Muriel Sutton. But Joe knew her by a different name. Gail Bedeker.

Forty-four

She found nothing on the dial. From end to end, all through the FM and AM bandwidths, just crackle and white noise. She needed something to listen to; music helped her think. There must be an explanation for all this. A thread to tie together seemingly disparate mysteries: her experience in the millhouse; Bobby's gruesome painting; the resurrection of Gail Bedeker. It frightened her to think that there was *no* rational answer.

Sam toed the accelerator. The car crawled along at a steady ten miles an hour. The fog lamps glared, but illuminated only a few feet of road. Then, quite suddenly, the Beetle came out of the mist. The radio whistled. It found a local station and the tones of Corinne Bailey Rae melted through the speakers. Sam span the dial. She heard Radiohead, Eminem, The Kinks, a phone-in about EU agricultural subsidies, a catchy number from The Feeling. Finally, something other than the hum of the tyres and the dark tread of her thoughts.

Sam slammed on the brakes.

'What the hell?'

She pulled over and got out of the car.

Her maglite played across the windscreen of the Mercedes. She approached the driver's door and tapped the glass.

'Mr Nightingale? Are you in there? It's Sam, Samantha Jones.'

No answer. She tried the handle and found it locked.

What was going on? If Richard Nightingale had driven out here, why had he abandoned the car? Sam took a quick look around. No punctures and, from the outside at least, the Merc appeared to be in good condition. It was probably a simple breakdown, but something Joe had said worried her: *It's pretty certain he'll be pissed by now.*

She went back to the Beetle and took the mobile from the hands-free mount. She dialled Joe.

'Sorry, there is a fault. Please try later . . . Sorry, there is . . .'

Sam dropped behind the steering wheel and reached for the ignition. She had to tell Joe about finding his dad's car. No doubt the old bastard was back at the house right now, but what if he'd fallen arse-over-tit into a ditch? She'd never forgive herself. The key turned. Nothing. Sam tried again. Zip, zilch, nada. She flipped the bonnet and checked the engine. Everything looked fine. Shaking her head, she glanced over at the Merc.

'Weirder and weirder, said Alice.'

She wrapped a scarf around her neck, put the mobile in her pocket and locked the car. Then, maglite in hand, she faced the mist.

It lay across the road in a solid wall, spreading east to west over the fields. She had driven through mist like this before, and it always gave her the heebie-jeebies. Sense dictated that it should taper out, not just stop dead, but often, driving across The Wolds, she had emerged suddenly out of a dense bank into the crystal clear night. This seething mass before her was no different.

Still, she hesitated. Her research into the stories that had unfolded in this place came back to her. The tragedy of Mariah Daecher and her baby, lost in the marshes. The strange deaths of Guido and Silas and Patrick Bedeker. The murder of Alice

Daecher at the hands of her own sister. Research undertaken to bring her closer to Joe Nightingale; to give her an excuse to be with him. Pathetic, and yet he hadn't laughed at her or, much worse, sent her away. He loved her and he needed her help.

'Here goes,' Sam said. 'Down the rabbit hole.'

She stepped into the mist.

Richard was scared, though his fear came in flashes. When it made itself felt, it bowled through him like a cyclone across a dusty plain. Other emotions – anger, dread, frustration, self-pity – anaesthetized by the liquor, were whipped up to the forefront of his mind. That was when he would reach for the bottle, spin the cap and cork the storm.

The world beyond the window had vanished, eaten by the mist. Only the porch lamps shone through, like a burst of incandescence in the dimness of a Turner painting. The wind had died. A blanket of stillness settled over the house, disturbed only by the chink of the chime on the porch, but even that sounded distant and unconnected. A remnant of the outside trying to make its voice heard.

Richard put the bottle to his lips. He drank with the hunger of the alcoholic, not through thirst, not to get drunk, but to feed the beast.

'You won't make old bones, Richard Nightingale,' he muttered. 'You're finished. She'll get here, look at you, and she'll think, "what the hell am I doing with this saddle-bagged old bastard? Bet he can't even get it up."'

To keep his mind from such thoughts, Richard cast an eye over the objects he had arranged on the windowsill. Eleven items in all, fished out from beneath the floorboards. He nudged the first with his little finger and the fear-cyclone began to howl again.

Item:

1: A Nazi Party lapel badge. Dusty. Scratched.
2: Volume 1 of Attabers' Young Persons Encyclopedia: Aadvark to Cromwell. Payment Plan for 1988/89 slipped inside cover page. Dog-eared.
3: A silver compass. Glass cracked.
4: A selection of religious pamphlets, notably the Jehovah's Witness newsletter, The Watchtower. Badly water damaged.
5: A school exercise book with a torn sticker on the front: 'GEOGRAPHY. Thomas Ray Jenn Class 4B'.
6: A dog's name tag. 'Shamus. If found return to Bedeker Cottage'.
7: A leather bandolier, inscribed 'F. Harringdon'. Holster empty, two shotgun cartridges in the pouches.
8: A St Christopher, gold and silver plate with the familiar iconography on the front.

A bizarre collection, deliberately hidden. The items had been dropped into the old hatchway then pushed, probably with a stick, through the broken ventilation brick and into the space beneath the porch. But why? The question could barely register with Richard. He was deafened by the cyclone. Too confused, too afraid, by the last three items he had brought up into the light.

9: A rabbit's foot. In poor condition, rubbed almost bald.

There was no mistaking it. It was the same totem that George Cuttle had dropped in Richard's office. What was it doing here? Had Cuttle come back to the house of his late client and buried it under her floorboards? If so, why? There was no point wondering, Cuttle was dead. And, in any case, the other items were even more disturbing and difficult to explain.

10: A Rolls Royce key fob. Solid silver.

Richard knew it well. Hadn't the Confection King dangled it in front of his face often enough? To Richard, the fob symbolised everything that was David Tregennis: ostentation, avarice and a genuine concern about the size of his cock. That meant David had received his message. The King must have turned up while the Nightingales were out and had a good look around the millhouse. The place to which his daughter had fled in order to escape him. Tregennis must then have dropped his key chain in the study and, somehow, it had slipped between the floorboards. Except that was just too much of a coincidence, wasn't it? That the key to David's manhood extension ended up with Cuttle's rabbit's foot and the rest of this weird shit?

Taken in conjunction with the last item, the coincidence was impossible.

11: A Scotch-brand cassette tape.

Richard's hands shook so badly it took three attempts before he could open the box. He immediately recognised the writing on the tape (*Mix Side A – Mix Side B*) as his own, bold and youthful. No need to read the sleeve, he remembered the order of the tracks: Wham, T'Pau, The Petshop Boys, Madonna, Rick Astley, Bananarama, Prince and Genesis. Even Los-fucking-Lobos. On side B, he'd included a few of his own favourites, in the hope of educating her musical palate: Ray Charles (the ABC years), The Eagles, James Taylor, Bob Dylan and a few tracks from the 'Rubber Soul' album. She had never listened to these, of course.

'Pearls before swine,' Richard mumbled.

He used to say that to the woman he loved, and afterwards feel like the most self-righteous prick ever to walk the Earth.

Now all he felt was small and afraid.

This was Janet's mix tape. The one he had put together the summer they met. The first gift he had ever given her. He couldn't rationalise the feeling in his gut but, to Richard, its presence here was an act of blasphemy, like taking a holy relic into a brothel. Still, finding it inside the house was perhaps not wholly impossible. He had worked out for himself that Janet had come here, and Gail Bedeker had confirmed that suspicion. Wasn't it conceivable then that Janet might have brought the mix tape with her? Yes, it was conceivable. In fact, it made perfect sense: a young girl, alone and afraid, clinging to her love token. But why, and by whom, had the tape been buried? It was the inexplicability of the thing that frightened Richard Nightingale.

Someone was coming down the stairs.

Richard shrouded his discoveries behind the curtain. He slumped into an armchair and swallowed a quarter-litre of scotch straight. Through the study door, he watched a shadow slip across the wallpaper. It was followed by a pair of legs flashing between the banisters.

Richard gagged. He rocked forward and threw up down his shirtfront. Spots of blood stippled the vomit. His spine arched and his teeth clenched. As the tremors faded, he slouched back into his seat. His brain was on fire. Darkness fought against him and he saw everything in bursts of light.

A boy in the doorway. Bobby. His son. Second born. Precursor of *The Absence*. Bringer of the empty days. Bobby: scared, white, speaking. Pleading. Blood. Bloodbloodblood*bloodBLOOD*. Not in the puke, not *his*. Dripping. No, more than dripping. Running. A flood.

Bobby Nightingale, the Crucified-Man.

'Help me. Dad, please, help me.'

Laughter – drowsy at first, then as hard as flint. But not Bobby's. Whose then?

His own, of course.

'Don't. Don't laugh. Please, Daddy, help me. I need you.' Bobby reached out. 'The shadows are coming . . .'

Forty-five

Joe couldn't take in what he was seeing. The revelation of the portrait would not submit to reason. It was confirmed, however, by the photograph album he held in his hands. The face of a dead woman passed in a blur as he riffled the pages. Muriel Sutton, nee Daecher, sometimes with her husband, Silas, sometimes alone. And, once or twice, with that pale little sister of hers, the girl who possessed an inexplicable air of deformity. A description had been written beneath each picture: *'Silas and Me on the beach, Summer '71', 'Me on the porch, '70', 'Me and Alice, picnic, '72'.*

'Me'.

Joe tried again to marshal his senses. Why did the woman posing as Gail Bedeker so resemble the young Muriel Sutton? Even the costume and look was the same: the scarf and the plain dress, the salt-and-pepper hair tied up at the back. He paced the cottage and found no answers, and so decided to return to the millhouse.

The mystery followed him across the scrubland and into the house. Only when he entered the study did it fall away. What he saw there drove all other concerns from his mind.

Vomit-stained, Richard lay semi-conscious in an armchair. Standing before his father, arms outstretched, his blood raining on the floor, Bobby begged for the Old Man's help.

Joe approached his brother. Gently, he took the boy by the shoulders. Bobby shrugged him off. The kid knelt down and reached out to his father. The act reminded Joe of films and pictures he had seen of beggars pleading for alms.

'Please, Dad, help me. I'm bad. I've done bad things. He – he won't leave me alone. Up in my room, in the pillbox, in the attic, he's there. He tells me to come with him now. Says they're waiting for me. In the dark. In the shadows.'

'Bob, come upstairs,' Joe said. 'Let's get you cleaned up.'

'Dad, I need you . . .'

The Old Man laughed. The sound gurgled out of him, throaty and warm. Joe had never heard anything so chilling in his life. He felt Bobby fall back against him, as if the kid had been physically struck. Joe caught hold of his brother. His fingers slipped in the hot flow of blood.

'Come on,' Joe whispered.

He led Bobby out of the study. Halfway up the stairs, he looked back. The Old Man was slumped in the chair, his eyes rolled white.

Joe steered Bobby to the bathroom and washed his cuts. Angry and deep, they looked as if they had been reopened at least twice. A stringy goo wept into the sink, but there was no gangrenous smell. Even so, the wounds would need stitching. For now, Joe cleaned them with disinfectant wipes and applied bandages. During all this, Bobby didn't utter a sound. He just sat on the edge of the bathtub and stared into space.

'Okay, mate,' Joe said, 'you wait here. Won't be a sec.'

Downstairs, Richard hadn't moved from his chair. At first, Joe thought that his father might have suffered a stroke. Saliva hung from his bottom lip and his face looked as if all the muscles had been removed. His backside had dropped off the armchair, but he held himself up with an arm slung over each rest. A bottle of scotch, reduced to dregs, remained clenched in his fist.

A little afraid, Joe knelt beside the chair and slapped his father's face. A grunt. A shiver. Joe repeated the slap. This time, Richard blinked.

'Dad, can you hear me? Where's the car?'

'What? Eh?'

'Bobby's hurt. He needs to get to hospital. Where's the car?'

'Bobby's hurt? Who's hurt him?'

'He's hurt himself. Hey. Wake up, you arsehole.'

This time, Joe didn't pull the slap.

'What? What the fuck?'

'The – car. Where's – the – car?'

'Car? Not here. What? It stopped. Fucked, Joe. The car's fucked. Leave me alone.'

Richard waved his son away and buried his head in a cushion. There was no point in further questions. At least the semblance of normal conversation had convinced Joe that the Old Man wasn't ill. He got up and started back towards the hall. At the study door, he stopped. In helping Bobby out of the room, he hadn't noticed the wreckage. Now he saw it and his face burned.

'What have you done?' He turned back to his comatose father. 'I . . . I worked hard. I *tried* so hard.'

His protestations sounded weak. He swallowed hard and kicked at the splinters. The boards that he had placed and sanded lay in pieces at his feet. Where smooth joins had once held, there was now a gaping hole. Joe pushed his toe into the breach. He felt pain, as if he had delved into a wound cut from his own flesh.

'Couldn't I have it?' he whispered. 'Was it too much?'

There was no answer. The vandal went on sleeping.

Joe went to the door. 'We're going now. I'm taking Bobby to the hospital. But before I go, I just want you to know how badly you've fucked this up. Fucked *us* up. Goodbye, dad.'

They crossed the porch and took the steps, one at a time. Joe guided his brother, ready to catch him when he stumbled. The kid seemed strong enough to walk, but Joe was already debating the wisdom of leaving the house. A glance at those red-flecked bandages decided the matter. If the bleeding continued Bobby could be in serious trouble.

Joe stopped a few feet from the house. He took out his phone and tried 999. Yet again, he heard the bleeps that told him there was no signal. He waved the phone about, in the vain hope of picking up a bar.

'We'll have to move out a bit further,' Joe grumbled. He looked up into the grey canopy that blotted out the sky. 'Maybe it's interference from the mist.'

'Sounds convincing,' Bobby said. 'Yeah, the mist, I'll go with that.'

Joe managed a half-smile. 'You gonna be okay?'

Bobby's features twisted, but he didn't cry.

'Okay,' Joe said, 'let's get to the road. Worse comes to worst, we'll have to make it to a phone box. Can't be more than a mile or so.'

The brothers walked on.

They had gone some way when Joe glanced back. He could still see the glow of the porch lamps, swaying to and fro, like fairies lost in the mist. *Jing-jing, jing-jing* went the fairy-voices, and though he knew it was the call of the wind chime, he shivered. He remembered that part of Sam's story in which Mariah Daecher had been taken back to the Hyam farmhouse. There, on her deathbed, she had spoken of little men and changelings, of creatures that stirred in the mist and in the waters.

Joe turned his thoughts to the road ahead.

Blood-red capillaries floated before Richard's eyes. He waited until the study came into focus. First he saw the dustsheet-covered chairs pushed up against the wall. Then the door, the window and the hole in the floor. He yawned and stretched. Darts of pain prickled along his spine. His bones ached and his liver wept.

Headlights pounced through the mist. Richard could hear the rub of tyres, the squeak of the axle, as the car bounded across the uneven ground. The headlight glare fell across him, like a searchlight trained upon an escaping convict. Then darkness, almost complete, returned to the study. From outside came the putter of a familiar engine. A car door slammed.

She had arrived: Susan Keele, lover, comforter, guardian of his sanity.

Click-clap, click-clap. Her footsteps on the porch boards. *Clunk.* Her suitcase dropped. *Clun-clun-clun.* Her knock upon the door.

Grunts and curses did little to ease his passage out of the chair. Upright, his chest tightened and his legs almost collapsed under him. He kicked the bag of bottles into the hole in the floorboards. Glass shattered, but Richard was too busy righting himself to care. One hand on the door jamb was enough to stop him keeling over, but sudden verticality didn't agree with him. The room started to move, the ghostly chairs spinning in a demented, spectral Morris dance. It was too much. In the same moment, he felt his bladder empty and his stomach shunt the last of the bile up into his mouth. He leaned against the jamb and squeezed, but it was too little too late. There was no stopping the exodus.

The front door opened.

'Richard? Are you here?'

'No. *Na-rrghhh*. Su-Susan. Wait.'

'Richard, what is it? Are you all right?'

'Susan, stay there. I . . .' His insides spasmed, but there was nothing left. He spat a mouthful of something black and green onto the floor. The last of the swamp water: *feed upon it, drink it down, if you will . . .*

The hall light came on.

'Susan, I said . . .'

Richard felt the muscles throb and this time his legs did give way. He crashed to the floor, cracking his nose against the door as he went. Pain roared across his face. When his sight returned, he saw her standing over him. A beautiful and somewhat frightened woman.

'Jesus Christ, Richard. What have you been doing to yourself?'

The question was enough. Richard gave way. His insides parched, he could summon no tears. Arms encircled him and hands cradled his head.

'Hush. Hush now. It's going to be all right. I'm here, Richard. I'm going to take good care of you.'

Forty-six

'We should've reached the road by now,' Joe said.

He ran his torch over the scrap of ground at their feet. Pools rippled the light. Since leaving the house, they had sloshed through dozens of these sucking, clutching puddles. Water was everywhere, and what ground remained was dissolving into a mire. Off to the left, Joe could hear the babble of the river.

'It doesn't want us to leave,' Bobby said.

Joe turned to his brother. 'It?'

'The house. The millhouse. Her.'

'Gail Bedeker?'

'Yes . . .' Bobby shook his head. 'No. I don't know.'

Joe stopped. 'What did she say to you? That morning in your room, you tried to tell me something about her. Think, Bobby, what was it?'

The boy shivered. Blood dripped from his fingers. Joe followed the trail back to its source and saw two red islands staining his brother's shirtsleeves. Questioning the poor kid like this was crazy. Joe needed to get him to hospital, and quick. If only the mist would lift, if only he could get a signal on this piece of shit phone.

'I'm sorry,' Joe said. 'Come on, let's get going.'

Bobby didn't move. Joe turned the torch on him.

'She told me a story. Asked me to think long and hard about

it. I was supposed to tell someone, someone who could help . . . But I only thought about myself.'

'Doesn't matter. We can talk this out later. You're not well, Bob, you need help. I'm sorry I didn't see that sooner.'

Bobby stared at his brother. He brushed Joe's hand from his shoulder.

'You've seen it, haven't you?'

'Right now we need to get you to a doctor.'

'You've seen my painting.'

Joe nodded. Over the sound of the river, the water birds screeched.

'Did you like it?'

'Shit, Bobby, what's wrong with you?'

'I think it's one of my best pieces,' Bobby grinned. 'My "Calling of St Matthew". My "Starry Night". I did the foundation sketch at home, before I'd even seen this place. How did I do that, eh? Draw the millhouse, the river?'

'I don't know.'

'Well, if you think that's weird, how 'bout this: without knowing it, I painted my picture on one particular bit of wall. A wall that wasn't a wall, but a doorway. The entrance to another world.'

Bobby laughed. It was high-pitched and Joe heard something like madness at its ragged edges.

'Not a bad bit of composition, though. Birds caught in flight. Nightingales maybe. Sometimes I thought I'd run out of paint before I finished it.' Bobby looked down at his arms. 'But it kept flowing. It never stops. I want it to stop.'

Joe shook his brother. 'Bobby. I can help you.'

'Oh, Joe. I don't want this to sound mean, but *you* can't help me. You can't even sort out your own fucked up life, let alone mine. I heard you, you know, after mum died. The crying and the things you said in your sleep. Loads of times, I thought about shaking you awake and telling you that you were wrong. It wasn't your fault. She died. Shit happens. But you know why I didn't? Because part of me *did* blame you. And it wasn't a small part, Joe. She was my mum. The only real parent I ever knew, and you took her away from me. Whatever punishment you were suffering in your dreams, I thought you deserved it.'

'I rarely dreamed, Bobby,' Joe sighed. 'The dreams were the least of it. What you heard, the crying, the talking, most of the time I was awake.'

And so it had been said. Joe almost felt relieved.

'We do bad things, don't we?' Bobby said. 'But what you did, it's nothing. I can beat yours hands down.'

'Bobby . . .'

'You have some responsibility for mum's death. One life on your conscience. But mostly it was an accident. What I've done wasn't an accident. In no way shape or form was it an accident. A boy killed himself and it was all my fault.'

'Matt Linton.'

'He came to me. Asked for my help. There was this guy at school making his life a misery. A shit-souled bastard who liked to hurt people. He was dragging Matt down, making every second of every day a living torment. I don't know if you've ever been bullied, Joe. I was, in my first year, before I learned how to take care of myself. But even then I was only bullied a bit, nothing like what Matt had to endure. People say it's something everyone goes through, like it's a rite of passage. Do you know what, though? Being bullied, day in day out, without a sliver of mercy: it's the hardest, darkest part of childhood. It strips you of dignity and rubs you raw. There's no end to it, either. It's with you even when school's over and the bully goes home. I saw what it was doing to Matt. Saw the desperation in his eyes. The dread and the honest-to-God terror. You know what I did to help him? Nothing.'

'It wasn't your fault he died,' Joe said. 'If anyone's to blame, it was the kid that bullied him.'

'"Being bullied". It sounds so pathetic,' Bobby continued. 'But what it means is being tortured. Being degraded until you feel worthless, less than dog crap on the pavement. Being a slave to some bastard's sadism. He was terrified, Joe. That's what people don't understand. These kids are scared for their safety, for their *lives*. And it's all right for adults to say they'll get over it, that bullies can't really hurt you. Adults know the larger world, but a kid's world is small. There are tyrants in those small worlds, Joe, and Matt had met one of the worst.'

The boy was rambling. Through loss of blood, tiredness, Joe wasn't sure. He just knew he had to get him to a doctor. To achieve that he would have to calm Bobby down.

'Mate, listen to me. If this is true, then maybe you were wrong not to help him. But – Hey, are you listening? – Matt wouldn't want you to blame yourself. He was unhappy and that was why . . .'

'I loved him.'

'Of course you did. He was your bud.'

'No, Joe. I *loved* him. And he loved me. And I let him die. My shame, my rejection put the razor in his hand.'

Blood dropped into the pool at Bobby's feet and billowed into clouds.

'We played games, you see? Kissing games.'

Tears rolled down Bobby's cheeks. The marsh birds called out in tight unison.

'Bobby, I don't know why . . .'

Joe stopped. He had heard something. A car. A door opening. Then, from out of the mist:

'Joe? Are you there? Can you hear me?'

'It's Sam. Hey! We're here! Sam, Bobby's hurt!'

'Where are you? I can't see you.'

'Down here.' Joe waved the torch about. 'S'no good. She won't be able to see us from the road. Stay here, Bob. Call out, so I can find you again.'

Bobby caught hold of Joe's arm. 'Don't leave me.'

'Look, I promise, I won't be a minute. Shout for me, yeah? I'll come back.'

'But there's something else. I thought it was justice for Matt. Please, Joe, I have to tell you what I've done.'

'Bobby, we have to get you to a doctor. Then we'll talk.'

With the torch clamped under his arm, Joe adjusted Bobby's bandages. The bleeding appeared to have stemmed for the time being. Then, managing a carefree grin, Joe set off in search of Samantha Jones.

Bit by bit, he disappeared, until there was just a hint of movement and the faintest glow of torchlight. Then he was lost to the mist.

Wait, he had said, but Bobby knew there was no point in waiting.

'Justice for Matt Linton. Punishment for Kelvin Hope. Hope trapped in the millhouse. They want me, Joe. The darkness and the shadows and the girl.'

Alone, Bobby started back across the scrub.

'We deserve this place.'

Forty-seven

Richard wiped an oval in the steamed bathroom mirror. He saw bloodshot eyes, skin tinged yellow, a general unhealthy glow. Overall, however, not too bad – and considering he'd polished off almost two bottles of scotch, fucking miraculous. He wrapped a towel around his waist and headed for the bedroom.

'Feeling better?'

Save for bra and knickers, Susan was naked. She lay across the bed, her head propped up on one hand. Richard's eyes focused on those full lips and then slipped down her neck to the heavy chest. Nipple erect, the lower breast rested on the mattress while the cleft between her tits glistened. Richard could already taste the salt of her sweat on his tongue. His cock stirred. Maybe in response to that twitch of the towel, Susan parted her legs, ever so slightly. The dark delta of her sex pressed through her panties. Richard dropped his towel and went to her.

Pinioned beneath him, he felt her wriggle and remove the bra. He went from kissing her to planting his mouth on her breast. He sucked and tickled, moving his lips only to pinch a nipple between thumb and finger. At the same time, his other hand slipped across her tummy. His fingers crabbed over her knickers, nails grazing the thin material. Usually she went wild when he did this, but there was no murmur. Maybe she was punishing him, making him work for his supper. Well, that was fine by him. He moved across to the other breast. Not a moan. Not a whimper. It was time to pull out the big guns. Tongue tracing the contours of her midsection, Richard slid down and pressed his mouth and nose against her vagina. He breathed deeply, taking in her scent. Her musk. Her warmth . . .

Except there was no warmth. And the smell was different.

'You're afraid of love, Richard Nightingale.'

He sat up. Between his legs, the tip of his cock shrank and bowed.

She smiled at him. Susan Keele didn't smile like that.

'You were afraid to love me and you're afraid to love your sons.'

Richard got off the bed. He grabbed the towel from the floor and covered himself. He no longer wanted to be exposed before this woman. This stranger.

'You won't love them because you think that, if you do, they'll leave you. Go away and never come back. Just like Janet.'

'Shut up.'

'Except she didn't go away, Richard. She was *here* all along.'

'I said . . .'

'Just like those boys of yours. They'll join her soon. They'll return here and be fed to the shadows.'

Return here. What did she mean? Where had the boys gone?

Then Richard remembered. Garbled sections of what had gone before: Joe shouting at him ('arsehole', 'bastard') and Bobby, hurt and bleeding. Christ, had he done that? Made the kid bleed? He remembered that time in Bobby's bedroom, the way his hands had itched to punish the boy. To go on punishing until his son understood the meaning of pain.

'I have to go,' Richard said. 'I need to borrow your car.'

'There is no car.'

'But I heard it. I saw the headlights.'

The woman's head canted. The corner of her mouth dropped. That pose. Thousands of pounds worth of whisky had never subdued the horror of it.

'I have to go,' Richard repeated, his voice unsteady. 'My kids need me.'

'They've needed you for a long time,' she said, the words gargled from a slack lip. 'Why start caring about them now?'

Richard edged towards the door. 'I do care. I've always cared. I kept things from them. Bad things'

'Bad things are part of life, Richard.'

'No. Not like that. Not the . . .'

'*Absence*? Poor Richard. Your desire to keep them safe has delivered them to this place. You wanted to protect the love they felt for their mother, and you've destroyed the love they should have felt for you. You wanted to safeguard your sanity, lest *The Absence* was passed on to them, but all you've done is squander what little time you had to share. Because there are no more chances left. Your opportunity to be a father to Joe and Bobby is gone. *The Absence*, the shadows, whatever you choose to call it, is ready for them.'

Susan's hands went to her face.

'It's ready for you, too.'

The lights flickered and went out. What little heat there had been in the room ebbed away. Richard's skin turned to gooseflesh and his breath billowed in grey twists. The figure on the bed sat very still, its eyes shining through the darkness. Richard backed up to the door and wrenched at the knob. It wouldn't turn.

'What's the matter, darling . . . ?'

The voice changed. Richard recognised it at once. Not wanting to look back, but unable to resist, he turned.

Moonlight dappled the form of Janet Nightingale.

'. . . tired of kissing me already?'

She opened her mouth. Slivers of glass fell from between her lips. *The Absence* blunted her features; robbed them of emotion, of any hint of humanity.

Richard pressed his back against the wall. He told himself, over and over, that he was not seeing this. It was the drink, a blackout, a breakdown. The hallucination paid his protestations no heed. It went on fixing him with its blank expression. Went on accusing. No, this did not feel like a dream. The smell of damp and sweat, the firm floor beneath his feet: it was all substantial. Real. And, ironically, the most *lifelike* part of the whole thing was the figure on the bed. Janet, who now reminded him of his crime.

Richard tore at the doorknob. It came away in his hand and fell to the floor. He cried out at the sound of it hitting the bare boards.

Something was happening. Janet's eyes rolled and she vomited a stream of glass into her lap. In the same moment, her face shifted. Like thick needle-heads working through leather, a dozen or so spikes or spurs pushed out from the skull beneath the skin. Except, in this case, Janet's flesh was more pliable than animal hide. The elasticity was amazing. The skin stretched two full inches, forming a series of vein-etched, conical tents. Then, with a wet splitting sound, the shards broke through.

Blood burst from the head. It splattered the floor and the window. The light outside shone through, coating the room in a pinkish haze. Richard felt warmth on his lips. He wiped a hand across his mouth and it came away spotted red. For the second time that night, he pissed himself.

'It knows, Richard,' Janet said, her face a slick ball of blood and glass. 'It knows what you did.'

Flesh hung from the half-exposed skull and steamed the air.

The light from the window died.

Darkness.

'The shadows are here.'

Forty-eight

Bobby studied the living painting in front of him and gave a crooked smile.

The mist, frozen mid-swirl, had cleared above the house. The stars shone down, like diamonds laid upon a black velvet cloth. The sky wasn't exactly right. In his ink and charcoal original the heavens had been indistinct. Likewise, in the blood version, the one he now thought of as definitive, the sky was unfinished. Otherwise, however, the scene spread before him was an exact replica of what he had etched upon the Bristol board and the back of the attic door. There were the two-dimensional trees to the left of the millhouse, and here the puddles made by the rain. True, he couldn't see the sea in the background, but he could hear the thrash of the waves. They sounded angry, as if they wanted to break over the dunes and take their rightful place in the picture. The house itself was just as he had envisioned it: a network of disjointed lines, suggesting a structure without real substance. The only parts of the building to have definite shape and solidity were the windows and the little whitewashed door.

Bobby looked up. Of course they were there; the picture couldn't really exist without them. He stood beneath the birds and marvelled at his own skill. He could make out the feet, drawn up to their breasts, and their yellow mouths, slightly agape. Three nightingales caught mid-flight, on course for the hazy heart of the house. That was where they were destined to roost.

The paper entrance of the millhouse opened, like a door on an advent calendar.

'Come inside, Bobby.' Matt Linton's voice echoed. 'We're waiting for you.'

Blood fell from the birds' wings and ran down Bobby's face. They started to sing, but it was not the melodic call of the nightingale. Instead, a gravely *pee-wit, pee-wit* emanated from their beaks. The trees, the mist, the house, everything started to run, thick and red. There was no choice left to him.

Bobby stepped into his painting.

Joe shouted himself hoarse, but no-one answered. He had gone in search of Sam and the road but had found neither. Mindful of Bobby's injuries, he soon gave up and retraced his steps, only to discover that his brother had vanished. There was only one thing left to do. He must go back to the house and wake up the Old Man.

He cut through the puddles, taking them at a run. His feet, already cold, froze at the touch of the water. Again, the distance across the scrub seemed unusually long, as if the land beneath his feet had been stretched out. But perhaps his senses were playing a trick.

What he experienced next could not be put down to imagination.

His torchlight reflected in the windscreens, mirrors and tail-lights. He stopped dead. All thoughts of Bobby, Sam and his father were relegated to some deeper level of consciousness, as the surface of his mind tried to grapple with the scene laid out before him. He walked between the vehicles, observing details without taking in the complete picture.

They were parked in a single line: four cars, two

mountain bikes and a scooter. Layers of dust coated their bodywork, though some were more neglected than others. The first he came to was a 1950s Citroën DS, the famous shark-nosed model. The front passenger window was rolled down and Joe stuck his head inside. Vintage car smells – old leather, greased metal and stale tobacco – filled his senses. The gear knob was worn shiny, as were the buttons on the 8-track player, but the car had the air of something treasured. A packet of Opal Fruits sat on the dashboard, its wrapper torn into a curling tongue. Religious pamphlets lay scattered on the back seat.

The next car was a B registration Mini Mayfair, mint-blue with a cracked headlight. The interior was a mess: brown paper sandwich bags, empty Smith's Crisps packets, Styrofoam cups, stains on the upholstery. Rust had gone to work on the wheel arches like a pack of moths on a winter coat. Inside, Joe saw stacks of encyclopaedias sealed in plastic. A permit stuck to the windscreen claimed designated parking for 'Mr A. Pye. Bay 17'.

Joe glanced towards the end of the line. What he saw there made him hurry past the next few vehicles: two 21 gear, full-suspension mountain bikes, a green Range Rover estate, a neat little Lambretta scooter.

He put out a hand and touched the bonnet of the Rolls Royce. The Wraith II had been an embassy roller before being privately sold to the Confection King. Records came with the sale, detailing which VIPs it had conveyed during its time On Her Majesty's Service. Diana and Charles had driven in this very car on a state visit to Paris. Joe remembered what his grandad had told him on one of the infrequent visits he and Bobby had made to the Tregennis estate: 'If her and that Arab had been driving in *this* beauty that night, they'd still be here now. MI5, CIA, God himself wouldn't have been able to touch 'em.' Then the old guy patted the black, bullet-proof bodywork and smiled a satisfied, almost orgasmic smile.

Grandad Tregennis' Rolls Royce. A fit of giggles bubbled in Joe's gut. He gave full vent to it, roaring until tears streamed down his face. This was well and truly fucked up. The laughter made him feel weak and he dropped the torch. It hit the floor, blinked twice and went out. He bent down to pick it up.

Overhead, a trio of birds broke through the gloom and were swallowed again in the blink of an eye. Joe didn't see them, but he heard the flap of their wings and their night cries. It was not those brittle screams, however, that killed his laughter.

It was the voice, rolling out of the mist.

'*Row, row, row your boat gently down the stream . . .*'

Joe left the torch behind.

Slowly, the mist fell away and the millhouse took shape. At first, he saw it as a wavering hulk. Then the windows and doors found their form and stared out at him with blockish, sightless eyes. Next came the porch and the chimney. And finally the finer details, like the lamps and the wind chime. The tinkle of the chime acted as an accompaniment to the woman's song.

'*Merrily, merrily, merrily, merrily . . .*'

She stood in front of the house, looking up at the attic window. The attic in which, not two hours ago, he and Sam had made love. Those fumbles and caresses seemed unreal, part of a forgotten world. What was now real to Joe was a collection of impossible things: dead women impersonating dead women, disembodied voices, phantom cars.

'*Life is but a dream.*'

The woman turned.

'I sang that to your mother, Joseph,' she said. 'It calmed her, as she held you in her arms.'

- *Interlude* -

The Last Guest: Tommy Ray Jennings
Made Absent on 13th May 2006

'. . . the search continued today for missing schoolboy, Tommy Ray Jennings, who disappeared while on a school trip. In a fresh development, the police have interviewed local woman, Muriel Sutton. Mrs Sutton, sixty, is the owner of Daecher's Mill, the only inhabited property within a five mile radius of the area in which Thomas was last seen. We pass over now to Paul Simms, who is standing outside Potter's Drake Primary School. Paul.'

'Jane, as you may remember, on Monday the thirteenth of May, ten-year-old Thomas Jennings left this school to visit a farm owned by local man, Oliver Hyam. It was the kind of outing organised by schools up and down the country every day. Tommy and his classmates were taken to visit farm animals and later spent the afternoon picking flowers for a geography project. Sometime after lunch, Mrs Ainsworth, headmistress here, did a headcount and found that Tommy was missing. A full-scale search swung into action but no trace of the child has yet been found.

'Early on, it was established that Tommy had been in a state of distress for some weeks prior to his disappearance. In April of this year, he had been firing his father's air rifle in the garden without permission. Unfortunately, there was an accident. Tommy severely injured his baby brother, Jasper, blinding the child in one eye. Counselling had been provided, but Tommy had difficulty coming to terms with what he had done. Since then, he has run away from home on a number of occasions, but always returned within a matter of hours. The police believe, however, that this maiming of his brother might account for his disappearance.

'One further development: we learned today that Detective Inspector Innes, the man heading up this inquiry, has interviewed local resident, Muriel Elizabeth Sutton. Mrs Sutton was tried and convicted thirty-four years ago for the murder of her little sister, Alice Daecher. In a case dubbed "The Fenland Horror", Alice was burned to death in an upper room of the Deacher millhouse. Mrs Sutton was later found insane by a jury and committed to an asylum for sixteen years. Now, Inspector Innes has been keen to point out that Mrs Sutton was *not* interviewed under caution. Indeed, he said the lady was most upset by the news of the disappearance and insisted that the police search her house. Daecher's Mill is a disused millhouse, full of old machinery, and Mrs Sutton was worried about Tommy having gotten into the building and injuring himself. A full search was made, but no sign of the boy could be found. The police have stressed that Mrs Sutton is *not* a suspect in this investigation, and was interviewed purely because her house is the only local residence. In fact, it is believed that Muriel Sutton is very frail and could not be considered a danger to children . . .'

Muriel Sutton turned off the radio. She looked at the figure of the boy standing in the doorway. One hollowed out eye bored into her.

'I didn't bring you here,' she said weakly. 'I wouldn't do that. Not to a child. You came while I was sleeping. *She* found you on the porch. She . . . I didn't . . .'

Pitiless, the eye stared.

'I'm tired,' Muriel sighed. 'Too tired to do this anymore.'

From above came the sound of the rocker. That never ceasing creak, up-and-down, up-and-down. She was weary of it, soul-sick.

'What can I do? How can I stop it? I've tried, God knows I have. Please, just let me die. Let me curl up and . . .'

The boy glided towards her. In his hands, he held out a tattered exercise book with 'GEOGRAPHY. Thomas Ray Jenn Class 4B' printed on the cover. Muriel took it from him. She saw the ghost of a smile crease his features. Then the blankness washed over him again, and he was lost to grief and blindness.

'Shadows,' Muriel whispered. '*Her* shadows. If I brought the boy here, then maybe . . . No, I cannot. He's innocent.'

She glanced up at the ceiling. The rocking continued, swift and steady. Could she do it? To Alice, to that poor family, still reeling from their loss? She had no choice now. The creature had grown strong while she weakened with every passing day. What would happen here when she was gone?

No, the shadow of the schoolboy must be the last to ever enter this accursed place.

Muriel Sutton went to her bureau, took out a pad of note-paper and started to write. In her dying hour, she completed the document that would draw the Nightingales to Daecher's Mill.

Forty-nine

'Who are you?'

'I think you know who I am.'

'Muriel Sutton.'

The woman nodded. Here it was confirmed: the truth told in the pictures from the Bedeker cottage. But what was the nature of that truth? In this place, where the real and the fantastical seemed to exist, side-by-side, could Joe be sure of anything? He reached out to touch her.

The woollen sweater felt soft between his fingers. He gripped her arm. Flesh and bone. Warmth emanated from under her clothes.

'But you're dead,' he said. That shivery laughter returned to his voice.

'You have to calm down, Joseph. We don't have much time.'

Joe rubbed his palms together. He couldn't accept this. He needed something solid and vital to concentrate on. Bobby was hurt and he had to find him. He marched towards the house.

'You're wasting your time,' said Muriel Sutton. 'Your brother's gone. *She* has him.'

Joe stopped beneath the shadow of the porch. Reflected in the study window, he could see the dead woman and the fog banked up behind her. His breath steamed the glass and condensed into droplets. A spectrum of light glinted in each. Could he dream such detail?

He retreated back to the scrub.

'Okay,' he said. 'I'll listen.'

Muriel nodded towards the house. 'It's important for you to understand what happened here,' she said. 'The only way for you to do that is to hear the story in its proper order. Its real beginning may be too far back for anyone to truly know. Prehistory, perhaps, when our ancestors sat around their fires and created religions from the natural world. I told someone recently that the story of this place is the story of water. It shaped the lives of generations until, one day, Man imposed his will on the landscape. He fenced it in and made himself a desert. He thought he could do that and there would be no consequences.'

Muriel Sutton gazed into the mist. Something in her expression told Joe that she was looking beyond the veil. That she could see the scrub and the dykes, maybe even the road and the faraway glow of the Fen towns.

'But I have no knowledge of those times,' she said. 'I'm restricted to more recent history. My father came here just before the war. Guido Daecher, he . . .'

'Your father came here. Met your mother. Settled,' Joe said. 'They had you and then Alice came along. She was born out there somewhere, in the Fen mist. Your mother died hours later, babbling about spirits and . . .'

'Changelings. Yes. My father was never the same after that night. He became morose, depressed.'

'The death of his wife.'

'It was more than that. I think he had done things before leaving Germany. Things that haunted him. Now, with this child by his side, he couldn't escape them. He bore with it for five years and then, one day while working in the mill, his mind gave way. A massive stroke they said, but there was blood on his hands. Nowhere else, just on his hands . . . After that, I was alone in this place, with only the Bedekers and my sister for company. I loved her, but I couldn't bear to be near her. Dark thoughts, you see?'

'She brought them out of you.'

'Yes. Although, to begin with, I couldn't remember those waking dreams.'

'Why didn't you get out? If you really believed all this, why not put her into care?'

'Because she was my sister.'

'But you wouldn't go near her. She was inhuman.'

'No. That was where my mother was wrong. She called her child a changeling. Do you know what a changeling is, Joseph?'

'A baby taken by fairies and replaced with one of their own.'

Muriel nodded. 'That's right. But Alice was not a changeling. She had not been swapped at birth, she had been . . . reduced. Infected. Taken over by a parasitical darkness. Nevertheless, I saw it sometimes, the humanity behind her eyes. Part of her was just what she appeared to be: a little girl.'

'Please,' Joe said, looking up at the attic window. 'My brother.'

'The story won't be hurried. Five years after my father died, I met and married Silas Sutton. Two years later, Alice killed him.'

'Your husband committed suicide.'

'I held him as he lay dying. The things he told me.' Emotion choked her voice. 'She had shown him the darkness inside himself and he couldn't live with it. Few can.'

'And so you murdered her.'

'I locked her in that bloody attic and set it on fire. She died . . . God, *how* she died.'

'And while you were in the asylum, you had the upper floor of the millhouse partially rebuilt. Why?'

'Because Alice told me to. She followed me to the madhouse, whispered in my ear for sixteen long years.'

'Your sister's soul came back to you.'

'That other spirit was strong. It had lived without form for centuries and could do so again. Except, when Alice died, something happened which it hadn't anticipated. It too had become infected. Alice survived with it.'

'So she stayed with you in the asylum. And when you came home?'

'She – It – was waiting. But in the interim, the Spirit had weakened. Alice had fed off me for sixteen years. Rich food, sweet meats: the guilt one feels for murdering a little girl. But perhaps the flavour of that remorse was beginning to pall.'

'I don't understand,' Joe said. 'Why *did* you go back? You knew it was waiting.'

'It would have followed me wherever I went. In any case, wasn't it just punishment for me to relive my crime, over and over? Remember, I hadn't just murdered a monster. But now we come to it: your part in the story.'

Joe's mouth dried up. 'You said something about my mother.'

'Yes. This was where she escaped to. I told your father that I found her wandering on the beach. Not true. I found her in *there*.' Muriel pointed to the attic window. 'It was the night of the Fifth of July, 1988. Eighteen years ago tonight.'

'No.'

'Seeking shelter, your mother broke into the millhouse. She toiled up to the Garner Floor. Something called to her, you see? It calls to all who come here. There, alone in the darkness, she started giving birth to a little boy. Except she wasn't alone. *It* was with her.'

Joe felt small in the shadow of the house.

'No,' he repeated. 'No.'

Muriel did not listen. Her eyes took on a distant, glazed aspect.

'I heard her screams. So did Wilma Bedeker and her granddaughter, Gail Anne. We found your mother . . . There was so much blood, and you, half out of her. I told Mrs Bedeker to run back to the cottage and fetch towels and blankets. I knelt down beside Janet and took her hand. "Look," she hissed, and pointed. It was then that I saw the figure in the shadows. She was there, sat upon the little rocker my father had made for her. A smile cut across that ruined face. I saw straightaway what it meant. Your mother could see it too. She was screaming: "No, it couldn't have you, no matter what". And then Alice spoke, and offered what I imagine It offered my mother all those years ago. A trade. A life returned if half of it was forfeited. I didn't understand until I glanced down at you. You were blue, Joe. Eyes shut. Not breathing. From beneath the chair, a pool of black water formed and spread out towards us. I stood up and faced my sister.

'I told her I would do anything if she let Janet keep you. It didn't listen. The water, that black baptism, continued to roll across the floor. With it came the threats and promises of a creature desperate to be whole again. That was when I first saw the true nature of the thing. It was insane. Something ancient beyond reckoning, that had once been vital and worshipped. For years, it had wandered alone, forgotten, until madness overtook it. I had spent sixteen years in an asylum and, believe me, I knew madness when I saw it. There was no reasoning with the thing. I even tried to appeal to Alice – to that sliver of humanity – but perhaps she too had lost her mind.

'The water touched your mother's feet. There was only one

thing I could do. If you were dead, my actions couldn't hurt you. I bent down and tore you out of her. My hand grabbed at the scythe nailed to one of the support posts. I used it to cut your cord. Blood gushed from your mother, a tide that held back the black water. Through the trapdoor, I could hear Wilma Bedeker coming up to the Stone Floor. I shouted and passed you, lifeless as I thought, through the hatch. As I helped Janet to her feet, the thing behind me shrieked. There isn't a sound like it, except perhaps the call of the marsh birds.

'Somehow, I got Janet down the steps and out of the mill-house. We followed the Bedekers to their cottage. Halfway across the scrub, I looked back and I saw her – my sister – raving at the window. A creature hungry for life . . .

'Once inside the cottage, I saw to Janet while Wilma and her granddaughter looked to you. Gail. Sweet little Gail Anne, who died before her time.' Muriel looked in the direction of the Bedeker home. 'Janet kept calling for you. I tried to calm her. Obviously, there was no hope of you surviving. And then we heard it, and both laughed. We heard you cry.

'"Good old fashioned remedies and common sense," Wilma said, lifting you out of the sink. You were steaming from the hot water. Steam caught in the glow of the fire: it looked like a halo of light. Wilma put you in your mother's arms, and then set about cleaning up Janet. It was strange, but we never thought of calling a doctor. Doctors and their medicines were from the outside. This birth was not of that world. While Wilma worked, Janet took my hand. She was trembling, holding you tight against her breast.

'"She took something from me," Janet said. Her face creased as she tried to explain it. "My – my shadows. Please, I need them back." I told her to hush, but she couldn't. And so I sang to her. A nursery rhyme. *Merrily, merrily, life is but a dream.*

'She stayed with us for a few days, this bright, beautiful

young woman. In that short space of time, I think I grew to love your mother. She was like the sister I should have known. But she was right about the shadows – her shadows – she *had* left them behind.'

'I don't understand.'

'Her guilt. Her grief. Her remorse. I've known only two people to have had these things exposed to them, frankly and in the full light of day, and survive the experience. The rest have been trapped, inside their guilt and within the walls of the millhouse. Your mother and George Cuttle are the only ones to have escaped. Cuttle because he was allowed to leave. As a lawyer, as a representative on the outside, he was useful to Alice. To us. But your mother escaped because of my intervention and her own strong will to protect her child.'

'But she left part of herself behind, that's what you're saying.'

'Yes. And an important part, too. She sensed it almost immediately; something taken away from her. You see, Joe, guilt and grief help to define us. Perhaps more than love and joy, these shadows tell us who we are. They give us a moral grounding and inform how we behave towards others. Without guilt, we are less than human. I saw the change in your mother. The effort it took for her to put on a show of being whole. Sometimes I would come into a room to find her sitting in a chair, standing by the window, except she wasn't there. Her face betrayed her incompleteness. She recognised this in herself. I remember our last conversation before I drove her to the Salvation mission in Peterborough. "I am like that poem," she said, "that haunting poem by John Donne. Richard loves that poem . . . I am reduced, Muriel. I sense within me the parts of my soul that are now dry, pitiless. That thing . . . *It has ruined me, and I am rebegot, of absence, darkness, death; things which are not.*" As she spoke, that new creature – rebegot – appeared before me. It was a horror of emptiness. Of absence. And then, in the blink of an eye, Janet was back, and I saw the effort it took to be whole scored upon her face. "I *will* be a complete person," she said. "For my baby, if for no-one else."'

'She wasn't there,' Joe murmured. 'That's what my dad said. After Bobby was born, she wasn't there.'

'Perhaps the strain became too great. With two loved ones, she could just about keep up the pretence, but three? Maybe she had to choose who got to see the mask and who was left with what lay beneath. Her children came first.'

'Dad. Oh, Jesus.'

'She left her demons here and her angels suffered.'

Joe looked up to find tears running down the dead woman's face.

'You did love her.'

'Very much.'

'Then why did you bring us here? Her children.'

'After your mother left, I was alone again with Alice. I had betrayed her. Robbed her of life for a second time. So I went up into the Garner Floor and poured out my guilt for her to feed upon. Only this time, it wasn't enough. She was weak after her exertions and my shadows were a thin gruel. She pleaded with me to bring her tokens. Shadows. Food.'

'You didn't. . . .'

'She was my sister'

'A parasitical darkness. And if the host faded, then Alice died.' Joe glared at the woman. 'She was a monster.'

'She was a little girl. The little girl I had murdered once already. I couldn't do it again.'

'And so you brought her shadows. Victims.'

'Not at first. To begin with, I locked up the millhouse, ignored the cries and the threats. For months after your mother left, I lived with the torment. And then Alice mustered enough strength to drag herself into the house. She stood by my bed, weeping, saying she was afraid to die.'

'Why didn't you pack up and leave? If she was so weak, she might not have followed.'

'I did, dozens of times, but would you leave your brother alone to starvation and death? No, I always came back. And, finally, I broke. Three months after Janet left, taking what little happiness she had brought with her, I reopened the millhouse and fed the shadows. A little man, fat with sin, came to my door one night selling encyclopaedias. She took him and was satisfied for a time.'

'But he wasn't the last.'

'Oh, no. He was unpleasant enough, but not the rarefied sustenance she was used to. Remember, she had fed on the remorse of a child-killer. And so, yes, I brought others. Six more, at intervals, over the years. Until the last, little Tommy Jennings, showed me a way out of the nightmare.'

'You killed them.'

'They're not dead. They're just lost inside their own dark worlds. That's what It does, this neglected god, makes the hell of our conscience real.'

'But why?'

'Because It has nothing else. Once It had the water to keep It alive. Then the tributes of the people who had betrayed It. Then only Its waning superstition. But It has changed. It is Nature wronged by humanity; warped, transformed, made petty and spiteful. Many old gods changed, Joe, through the arrival of Christianity or the destruction of the world that had created them. Pan became the Devil, while the fairies, dark once, now adorn picture books and bedroom wallpaper. It was change or die, and the Lord of the Marshes chose change. The tributes were given through a sense of guilt and he got a taste for it.'

'But you've brought others here *since* we arrived. My grandfather.'

'He came of his own free will. And, yes, I took him to face himself. I did that for Janet, because I remembered what she had told me about her father. Some people deserve such punishment.'

'What did he do to her?'

'Nothing you need to know.'

'But the others. Innocent people.'

'No-one is innocent, Joe. If they were there would be no shadows.'

'You still haven't answered my question,' Joe said. 'Why did you bring us to this place?'

'Because of you, Joseph. Because of what you are. Because you can stop this thing. Now. Tonight.'

Fifty

'How can I stop any of this?'

Muriel Sutton walked towards the house. Bones cracking, she eased herself onto the porch step. Weariness washed over her and the truth of her years could be glimpsed behind the mask.

'With your gift,' Muriel said. 'You must have recognised it in yourself, Joseph, as others must have too. You feel an affinity for their sorrow, don't you? Their remorse.'

Bobby's accusation came back to him: *bad things happen and you prod and prod until it all comes tumbling out . . .*

'That is your birthright. It was given to you, albeit unknowingly, by the spirit that infected my sister.'

'I don't understand.'

Once again, Muriel Sutton's eyes took on that glazed, faraway look.

'Your mother was sleeping. I had just put you down in a fruit box cradle lined with blankets. Not a murmur, such a good baby. I was dozing myself when Wilma Bedeker came into the room. Little Gail was with her, clutching her granny's hand, eyes as round as saucers. She was your first playmate.'

'We found her grave.'

'A gas leak,' Muriel said. 'Though sometimes I wonder . . . Wilma took me to one side so that Gail couldn't overhear. She told me that she had seen Alice looking over the edge of the trapdoor as I helped your mother down. I don't think Wilma believed my story of Alice's true nature until she saw her that night. Up to that point, I think she subscribed to the belief that I had lost my mind after Silas died. Even though, the year before, old Patrick Bedeker had shot himself.'

'It wasn't an accident? He was running with the shotgun.'

'There was no stumble, no misfire. The bullet hole was clean and angled square under his jaw. My opinion is that Bedeker met with Alice outside the millhouse and she showed him sights he couldn't live with. The dog was with him and, confused by its master's actions, attacked the thing it sensed was responsible. Wilma had always thought it a shame that poor Alice had had to witness the accident. But then seeing her that night, after sixteen years of laying flowers on the child's grave . . .

'Wilma told me what had happened in the millhouse when I passed you through the hatch. "Black water," she said, "came dripping through the floorboards. It dribbled on the bairn's head. Not so strange, you might think; jus' dirty rainwater from that bust roof. But this weren't no normal water, Missus. It went into the little one's mouth and eyes. He didn't choke or squint it out, no indeed. He swallowed it and absorbed it, like tears running backwards."

'A week later, Gail Anne came to us as we sat in Mrs Bedeker's kitchen. She looked half scared to death. Her granny took the child on her lap and asked what the matter was. "The baby," she said, her voice tiny. "We was playing peek-a-boo and he was holding my finger. He didn't mean it, granny, I know that. But . . ." She burst into tears. "He made me think of naughty things. Spite-ish things that I sometimes think on my own. About the girls who tease me at school. I never did nothing to none of them, but sometimes I'd like to." That was when I knew what you were.'

'I'm not like your sister,' Joe said.

'No, you're different. Do you know how I knew that, even then? Because you cried. Alice never uttered a sound in her life. After she died? That was another story. But *why* were you different? You'd been baptised with the same black water. My guess was that your mother hadn't consented to the creature's arrangement. But its pledge – the water, the spring of its powers – had been offered. You took a diluted form of those powers, so weak you didn't even realise you possessed them.'

'Even if this is true,' Joe said, 'what do you want me to do?'

'What I could not. I want you to destroy my sister and the thing keeping her alive.'

'For Christ's sake, how?'

'By using what *It* gave you.'

Muriel pointed. In front of the millhouse door stood a collection of oddments and knickknacks, arranged as if for some bizarre garage sale. Considering the things that he had heard and witnessed that night, these items should not have surprised Joe. Strangely, however, they struck him as the maddest part of the whole thing. What on earth did they mean?

He turned back to Muriel.

'Why didn't you tell me all this straightaway?' he asked. 'As soon as we got here?'

'Would you have believed me? You had to come at this gradually, Joseph, surely you see that?'

'But you've put my family at risk.'

'It was the only way. I worked hard to deceive Alice as to the true nature of my plan; setting up the inheritance, bringing you back here. I convinced her that, if you returned, she could complete her possession. Perhaps she will, if you aren't strong enough.'

Muriel rose to her feet and hobbled towards the mist.

'Good luck, Joseph Nightingale.'

Joe swept a hand over the collection. 'I don't understand any of this. What am I supposed to do with these things?'

'That's for you to decide.'

'Wait. Tell me why you came back. How you came back.'

'I stayed to keep an eye on you. Guide you. I didn't expect you to find Gail's grave or the family pictures Cuttle had stored in the cottage. I should have burned them all, of course, but the memories captured there weren't all painful. As to how I came back, don't you remember your bedtime stories? Fairies can grant impossible wishes. This?' Her hand swept down her body. 'It's a reward for a lifetime of dutiful service. To make me as I was the last time I was happy. But like hers, it's a half-life of no real substance. A curse. I can't feel the sun or the wind. Cannot leave this place. But she - *It* - can make things real. Guilt is not an illusion, remember that.'

She was half-lost in the fret when Joe asked his final question. 'What will happen to you?'

'I don't know. Nothing is certain and not everything can be resolved. To be honest, I no longer care. If hell awaits me, it is no more than I deserve. My deeds are black and my sins must find me out.'

Those bright, damp eyes looked at Joe one last time.

'Goodbye.'

Joe went to the millhouse.

He stood for a moment or two, passing an eye over the dozen or so items lined up beside the door. Finding no sense in them, he gathered the bits and pieces together. He put everything into a plastic carrier bag that itself contained a couple of bottles of scotch. The same brand his dad had been drinking that evening. Partway through the collection, he stopped. It wasn't so much an epiphany as a stumbling realisation, made unsteady by doubts and questions. If the whisky was his dad's, the Nazi lapel badge might have belonged to Guido Daecher. Then there were his grandfather's car keys and the same encyclopaedia and religious booklets he had seen in the Mini Mayfair and the Citroën DS. Perhaps all these things were the belongings and keepsakes of those that had entered the millhouse. That would mean Richard was inside. Joe felt sick but managed to hold it down.

The last item looked like a piece of litter. About to toss it, Joe paused. Not seeing anything that reminded him of his brother, Joe had come to the conclusion that Bobby had not returned. That the kid was safe. But the empty Dr Pepper bottle in his hand told a different story. Of course, it *could* have been left by anyone at any time. The thought was cold comfort. Joe remembered his brother in the rear seat of Sam's car, quiet as a mouse as he sipped his drink. No, there was no doubt: the bottle confirmed Bobby's presence in the millhouse, but that wasn't the only tale it told.

Joe fingered the glass tube that poked from a hole in the bottleneck. It was discoloured grey, as was the inside of the bottle. At the base, the plastic was wrinkled and charred. A few loose granules rattled inside. How long had Bobby been using this shit? Joe didn't have a clue. He felt the pain of that admission and dropped the makeshift bong into the bag.

He got to his feet and grasped the handle of the millhouse door.

Tremors shivered the woodwork. They fizzed through the metal handle and chattered into Joe's hand and along his arm. It felt like an electric shock and he jumped back onto the path. At the same moment, a blade of light pierced the attic window. Like a lighthouse beacon, it blazed through the mist.

The millhouse shuddered. Brick dust puffed out from

fissures in the walls. The windows clattered in their frames. A roof tile sang past Joe's head and shattered on the ground. He had barely enough time to step back before five more rained down. Below this crashing, grumbling cacophony, the boy could detect another sound. It was the voice of a chimera, something put together with scientific artistry from ancient sources. While the house roared, Joe walked to the sluice bridge, following the rumble of wood and metal.

The river was in full flow and the millpond, once a bone-dry crater, now swirled with dark water. The water pressed into the channel of the headrace and, through the gate, its power was realised. Gushing against paddles, it span the millwheel at a terrific pace. A fine spray leapt into the air and doused Joe's face, but he hardly noticed. His attention was focused entirely on the wheel. No longer a broken limb, its axle lay steady in the moorings. The voice of the wheel thundered and shook the house to its foundations.

Joe hung fast to the handrail. He breathed deeply and tried to stay calm. It wasn't easy. He had never been so frightened in his life, not even on the night his mother had died. Part of him wanted to flee, to set off back towards the road, leaving Bobby and the Old Man behind. He knew, however, that the mist would not let him go. That he might walk miles, only to find himself once more in the shadow of the house. And even if it were possible, could he live with two more deaths on his conscience?

Joe left the bridge and entered the millhouse.

If the wheel was the mouth of Daecher's Mill, then the Meal Floor was its throat. Thrown back and forth between the walls, the noise from outside resonated here at an even deeper pitch. Joe's ears ached fit to bleed. He scrambled up the ladder onto the first floor. Here the sound was different, one of stone rather than wood and water, though equally deafening. The huge slabs of the millstones had been placed together. Powered by the wheel, they pummelled the grain that fell from the third level.

The Garner Floor.

At the top of the ladder, Joe put his shoulder to the trapdoor. It gave easily enough. He looked back the way he had come. Beaten out of the grain, flour dust billowed across the Stone Floor. It spread like the mist that had enveloped the world outside. In fact, it was virtually identical. Perhaps . . .

Bobby's screams tore through the house.

Fifty-one

The screaming stopped.

As Joe pushed against the trapdoor, his position in relation to it flipped through ninety degrees. The sensation unbalanced the boy. With the doorway now no longer above, but directly in front of him, Joe stumbled through it and into a familiar room.

It was not the Garner Floor of the millhouse.

The tiles beneath his feet gleamed under an application of industrial bleach. Backpacks, football boots and sweat-stained school shirts hung from the changing benches. Blocks of lockers stood along the walls. Joe ran his hand over their dented doors. They felt solid, not dreamlike at all. His head reeled.

Then Joe heard something that focused his thoughts.

Steam rolled out from the shower room, and with it, a sound like the murmurings of a maltreated dog.

'Bobby?'

Joe stepped into the showers. His face ran with reformed water. Through the steam, he could make out the rough shape of a boy slumped against the wall.

'I'm here, Bobby. Speak to me.'

It is illusion, Joe told himself, nothing more. It can't hurt you. But he knew that wasn't true. Within these walls, illusion was real and deadly. He had to be careful; to question whatever he was shown. He might walk into the steam – the mist – the flour dust – only to find that this cowed form was not his brother. That it was part of his own guilt-dream, in which he would soon be lost.

Yet the voice sounded so like Bobby's.

'I'll come with you now,' it said, nasally. 'We'll be together and you'll forgive me. We'll . . .' after each word came an intake of breath, signalling sudden but expected pain, 'play – kissing – games.'

Joe darted forward.

'Bobby, don't. I'm here.'

Joe's mouth clamped shut. He saw what his brother had done and stumbled against the wet, weeping wall. He didn't cry out. There was no air left inside his body. He just stared and abhorred every detail. The thing that shivered under the shower was a mass of red. No matter how much water rained down upon it, the boy kept his bright, brilliant colour. A quote from *Macbeth* – a text Joe had studied for his English A Level – mangled in his head: 'who would have thought the poor bastard to have so much blood in him?'

'Bobby?'

Bobby's mouth fell open, dribbling gore over teeth and lips.

'Too late, Joe. I've done it and I'm glad.'

The boy held out his hands. In his right palm lay the implement of his mutilation: a broken glass pipe, like the one in the Dr Pepper bottle. Flesh adhered to the jagged end. The other hand offered up the nose that Bobby had hacked from his face.

'Why?' It was the only question worth asking. The only question left.

'I told you why.'

Mucus poured from those serpentine slits.

'And I told you,' Joe said, 'Matt wouldn't want you to blame yourself. He . . .'

'It's punishment, Joe. Justice. And you're wrong, he *does* want it.'

Bobby's gaze moved to a point beyond where Joe stood.

Matthew Linton appeared from out of the steam clouds. He gave Joe a cursory glance as he passed, his eyes the only moving part in a vein-marbled face. He dropped down beside Bobby and kissed his friend's forehead. Fascinated, repulsed, Joe watched as the dead boy's neck gaped open. The kisses moved down to Bobby's cheek and then across to his ruined nose. Matt's tongue played there, slipping in and out of the slits. Ecstasy: that was the expression which replaced anguish on Bobby's face, and now he returned the kisses. His mouth pressed into Matt Linton's fatal wound. His lips met thick cartilage and knuckles of exposed backbone.

Joe couldn't move. Couldn't speak. Could only watch.

They parted and smiled, like lovers. And then, from nowhere, Matt brought out the razor. He took the glass tube from Bobby's palm and replaced it with the blade.

'No,' Joe whispered.

Bobby clenched the haft and brought the razor up to his neck. It shimmered there, reflecting the lower side of the boy's jaw.

'No. Please, Bobby, don't.'

Bobby's eyes shifted between his brother and his soul mate: both implored, but only one held out the promise of salvation. The struggle did not appear to be a difficult one.

Joe murmured, 'God, please don't let this happen.'

But God wasn't listening.

Bobby swept the razor across his throat. It tore clean through his windpipe. The wound hissed like a deflating balloon. Joe sprang forward. He tried to catch hold of the razor, but his fingers passed through it. What he felt instead was a rush of blood on the back of his hand. He glanced down to find his skin unstained.

I'm not here, Joe thought, I don't matter.

Punctured, the carotid artery made a firework across the wall. Flares dribbled from the main burst and snaked down the tiles. Bobby dropped the razor. His fingers went to the wound, exploring, perhaps even trying to close it up. His mouth fell open, but the air whistled out of his neck and robbed him of expression.

'Shhh, shhh,' Matt Linton comforted.

He kissed Bobby and they bled together.

Unable to help his brother, Joe turned away. He staggered back towards the changing room. Blinded by tears and steam, he reached for the wall. Instead of meeting tile, his hand brushed against hard, pitted stone. The ground no longer slipped underfoot, but echoed. The sultry air was replaced with a dank chill. Joe opened his eyes.

Bobby's world was gone.

Joe now stood in the darkness of a different shadow.

Fifty-two

Joe stood at the foot of a huge column. Colours danced across the limestone and the dark marble shafts of the pillar. On the flagstones of the floor, a motley carpet twinkled. Joe turned and faced the source of the light. He immediately recognised the stained glass window.

Depicting the Calling of Samuel, the window's lower medallion was crowned by two snapshots from the life of Christ. This was the Teaching Window, dedicated to the mathematician and grandfather of computer science, George Boole. Joe remembered it from countless school trips. He'd even written a project on Boolean algorithms, using a photograph of the Samuel scene for the cover. But if this *was* that window, then . . . He looked out between the pillars. There was the Nave and, up ahead, the Crossing. But what was he doing here, in the North Aisle of Lincoln Cathedral?

He knew every inch of this place, although he had not set foot in the Minster for almost two years. Aside from those school trips, he had visited once with his dad. He had been only five years old, but he remembered that time vividly. They had walked around for hours, Richard pointing out details that his young son had struggled to grasp: how the aisle arches had been constructed to give the nave a greater sense of light and space; the cleverness of using Purbeck marble to accentuate the flow of the piers; early examples of purely decorative ribbing in the choir ceiling. 'Art in stone,' his dad had called it. To be honest, Joe had been more interested in the story of the Lincoln Imp, sitting at the top of its column, ready to come alive and make mischief. His little-boy-brain had wondered why God allowed a demon to run amok in His house. He had asked his dad, and Joe remembered how the Old Man's face darkened.

'He seems to suffer a lot of unnatural things, Joseph.'

'But at school they say He is A'mighty,' Joe had said. 'If he is, then he could stop a stupid stone monster.'

'Perhaps he can't be bothered.'

'But if a monster was going to get you, and you prayed hard, then God would have to stop it, wouldn't he? In't that the law?'

'Prayer can't take away all the monsters.' Richard held on tight to his son's hand. His tone was bitter as he took in the majesty of his surroundings. 'After your brother was born, I prayed. I prayed and prayed and no-one answered.'

'Were you 'fraid of monsters, daddy?'

'Not monsters. I was afraid of . . . Absence.'

Then Richard looked down at Joe, whose brow had creased.

'"Absen"? Like absen*t* in the school register? What does "absen" mean?'

'I hope you never find out, son. I pray to God you don't.'

A faint mechanical ticking brought Joe back. He stepped out from behind the pillar.

Burnt rubber, petrol, and the smell of the forest wafted through the church. His heart jarred as the fiery light strengthened through the stained windows and flooded into the Nave. Keeping his eyes rooted to the floor, Joe walked out into the central aisle. He recognised the smells, of course. Just as he recognised the *tuck-tuck-tuck* of the nearside wheel as it span in slow evolutions.

'Why here?' he whispered to himself. It made no sense.

Smoke poured from beneath the crumpled bonnet of the Triumph Spitfire. Crashing through the altar table, the car had wrapped itself around the last pillar before the Crossing. Although it was dark at that eastern end of the Nave, Joe could make out the vehicle's spinning wheel. The Spitfire lay on its side, pivoted as it had been on the night of the accident. This time, however, there was no bracken beneath it; the passenger side hung in midair without any visible support. The wheel slowed to a stop. With a final petulant hiss, the steam from the radiator evaporated. Everything was still.

It should look comical, Joe thought: the flame-red car smashed against a pillar of one of England's finest cathedrals. The incongruity of it made him think of that Dada painting of the Mona Lisa sporting a devil moustache. Except the car's presence here wasn't artistic or funny, it was grotesque. Not only because it shouldn't *be*, but because Joe couldn't understand how it represented *his* shadows. Surely that was what he was supposed to be seeing: a hell of his own making. He asked himself the question again, 'Why here?' There was no answer, and so he walked on towards the wreck.

He reached the third column when the Spitfire's bonnet let loose a violent prang. The sound echoed from stone to stone, until it aged and died between the ribs of the ceiling. By degrees, silence returned.

Joe followed the tyre tracks until he reached the car's back bumper. He rested a hand on the boot and let his chin sag to his chest. Autumn leaves rustled from under the car and chattered around his feet. A low wind moaned through the darkening church.

Joe moved towards the point of impact. Again, a surprise awaited him. The last pillar of the nave – around which hung the devastated nose of the car – was unlike the other columns.

Whereas they were smooth, this pillar had a ridged, organic trunk. In fact, now he came closer, Joe saw that it was not a pillar at all. It was a tree. The oak tree from the woods. Sprouting out of the floor, it reached up to support the cathedral's vaulted ceiling. He took a moment to run a finger through its knots and whorls.

Then he turned and faced what he had done.

'I'm sorry.'

The words wheezed out of him like a breath exhaled after a punch to the gut.

Through the shattered windscreen which framed her, Joe watched his mother die. Her breathing came in gasps. Her left hand plucked spasmodically at her chest. Shards of glass peppered her face and one brutal splinter lay embedded in her throat. Just as he remembered, hair covered her eyes in bloody curtains. All thoughts of Alice Daecher and the millhouse left him. His mother was dying again and no therapist, no counsellor, not even Samantha Jones could convince him that it wasn't his fault. He had killed her as surely as if he had cut her throat. Not only that, he had damned Bobby and his father to grief and shadows. He . . .

He was there, in the driver's seat, unconscious but breathing. But that didn't make any sense. If these were *his* shadows, he should be taking an active part. Standing here, watching, he was just an observer, as he had been in Bobby's nightmare. And the question persisted: why *here*? Why not in the woods, where his mother would come alive and punish him, just as Matthew Linton had punished Bobby. The only answer was that these were *not* his shadows.

Footsteps echoed down the Nave. A shadow fell across the car and halted. The footfalls quickened to a run as Richard Nightingale caught sight of the wreck. He didn't seem to be puzzled by his surroundings; his attention was focused entirely on the Spitfire. Joe shouted his dad's name, but Richard did not respond. As he ran, the Old Man gripped the mobile phone in his hand.

Of course, now Joe remembered: after the accident, he had dialled home and Richard had answered. His dad must have searched the woods and found the wreckage . . . Only that wasn't how it had happened. The emergency services had got an anonymous call reporting the accident. The police had told him that the ambulance guys were the first on the scene. But if his dad had got there first, then . . .

Horrified, Joe stood back and watched.

'Joe? Joe, can you hear me?'

Richard pulled open the driver door and slapped his son's face. 'Joe' from Richard's imagining (or was it memory?) groaned. Richard's fingers went to the boy's neck and sought out a pulse. Relief washed over the Old Man's features. Then he checked Joe's shoulder injury, grimacing, but clearly not too concerned.

'Thank Christ,' Richard murmured. He started to dial 999. 'What the hell happened here . . . ?'

Richard cancelled the call.

He had caught sight of the pincushion face of his wife, prickled with glass. Slowly, he replaced the mobile in his pocket. His eyes darted left and right, as if suspicious that he was being observed. Then, after checking Joe's pulse a second time, he closed the driver door. With little, shuffling steps, he moved around the car to the bust passenger window.

'Janet?'

Richard took air through his nose and kicked the wheel arch. He stalked away down the Nave, running fingers through his hair. The mobile was taken out again, flipped open and stared at.

'Fuck. Fuck Christ.'

Richard thrust the phone back into his pocket. He marched up to the car and put his head through the passenger window.

'Are you there, Janet? Please, just tell me you're there and I'll call an ambulance. I want . . . I want . . .' Richard's face contorted. The emotion could not be mistaken. It was grief, agonising and full-bodied. 'I need you to be in there, Janet. My Janet. My love. My *love*. My world. Tell me you're still there. I miss you so much.'

His hands shook. His face twisted. Richard parted the curtain of hair that obscured his wife's features. The cry he let out resonated through the chamber.

Joe gasped. He longed to reach out and comfort his father – this desperate, broken man.

Before Richard let the hair fall back into place, Joe caught a glimpse of what had been revealed. It was a face composed of nothingness: features without the context of colour or expression. There wasn't even the ghost of humanity that often haunts the faces of the dead. It was soulless. *Absent*.

Row, row, row your boat.

Joe remembered that one time when the mask slipped and he had witnessed the horror that lay beneath. The mask that she had kept in place for him and Bobby. The mask she never wore for her husband, who had been forced to live with *The Absence*, day after day, year after year. For the first time, Joe began to understand his father – the drinking, the difficulty he found in emotional attachment – and, in understanding, Joe saw what Richard was about to do.

'No, dad. Please, Jesus, no!'

The Old Man had withdrawn from the car and was standing against the tree. Caught in the glare of the headlights, he looked horribly pale. Trails of snot ran from his nose. He wiped the back of his hand across his lips, then buckled over. Vomit flushed through his fingers. When he recovered himself, he went back to the car and ducked his head into the window. He touched the glass shard embedded in his wife's neck. It was a good two inches in width and stuck close to a beating artery. He pinched it between forefinger and thumb. Though his entire body shook, he kept a firm hold on the splinter.

He said . . .

'I love you, Janet.'

. . . and tore the shard from her throat.

Joe looked away. He heard his father's screams and sobs, even the guttural gush of blood. The world around him darkened. The smells of the cathedral, the forest and the accident disappeared. He felt the stone floor beneath his feet soften into timber beams. From below came the roar of water and the voice of the wheel.

He was back in the attic room of the millhouse.

'Welcome home, Joseph Nightingale,' said a watery voice. 'Did you like the things I showed you?'

Fifty-three

Fingers grasped the arms of the chair. Bare feet pushed and bumped against the floor. To and fro, back and forth, the little thing rocked.

'Poor boy,' it said, head inclined towards Joe. 'Poor, darling boy.'

Then it laughed. The hair covering its face parted a little, showing glimpses of the fire-blighted features beneath. Its nose lay flat against its face, the nostrils melting into the upper lip. The lower lip had been stripped down and a set of teeth jutted forward, giving a horrible idea of the skull beneath the skin. Side on, the left portion of its mouth, between cheek and jawbone, was gone. In that cavity, Joe could see a long tongue sprout out from its throat like some slick reptilian head.

So it had kept those scars from the death of Alice Daecher. Perhaps that meant Muriel Sutton was right: part of the creature was still human. Joe sent up prayers that this *was* the case. He made a tighter fist around the bag of oddments and forced himself to take in the rest of the figure. Leaves shivered in its hair and in the folds of its clothes: an assemblage of tattered rags that might well have included a red rubber raincoat once upon a time. Its legs, arms and hands ran with black water, which trickled to the floor and collected around the chair. Up and down, the rockers seesawed through the gathering pool.

'I want you to stop what you're doing to my family,' Joe said.

The head jerked sideways. A single dark eye fixed on him.

'Family?' again, that derisive laughter. 'I'm not doing anything to them, my child. They make their own shadows.'

The thing pointed to the far corner of the room.

Lost in their own worlds, Bobby and Richard huddled together. As Joe watched, he saw the fear leave their eyes. Their faces slackened and emptied. It was as if a painter, dissatisfied with a portrait of human misery, had taken an alcohol-soaked rag to his work. Bit by bit, he rubbed away until all that remained was the blank oval with which he had started. Soon that was all that Bobby and Richard would be: absent templates upon which emotion would never be painted again.

Rebegot

Joe knelt between them. He wanted to bring comfort, to wrench them from their shadows. He tried to shake his brother out of the trance.

'It's no good,' came the voice. 'They can't hear you. Too much of them has already been garnered. Let me show you.'

Richard and Bobby's mouths snapped open. Their stomachs contracted and their shoulders hunched. Bowed over, they spewed their shadows into the air. Oily with guilt, the shades coiled and twisted across the room. From the corner of his eye, Joe saw the figure in the chair hold out its hand, as if conducting the darkness. The shadows followed her/his/Its orchestrations and fed themselves into a raised wooden box. This was the bin which siphoned grain to the millstones downstairs. Joe watched as the dark deeds of his family were garnered, ready to be ground and refined, turned into foodstuff for the thing in the chair. Then, left empty, Bobby and Richard would wander alone through their nightmares.

'Usually I take my tributes quickly, greedily,' the thing said, 'but Muriel was right. Your family are special. Your shadows are so *rich*. I wanted to savour you.'

Trails of guilt and grief continued to chatter into the box. Joe felt weak. Tired. He asked, 'Why do you do this?'

'Because it is what I am owed.'

'Have pity.'

'Why should I have pity for those that abandoned me? Left me to rot in their dry, dry world.'

'That was centuries ago. These people – my family – didn't hurt you.'

'Man abandoned me. Forgot the water. Forgot the tributes. But *I* remembered. Remembered the guilt in their eyes for taking my home, for turning to the new god. The god of stone and shame. My church was in the fog, behind the reed and in the deep, deep waterholes. I kept the fevers from their door, called up the wind to fill their sails. I promised neither damnation nor salvation. I asked only for the marshes, but the Flesh delved deep and pledged a cupful of water in its stead. I did not judge. I took what was offered. But soon even that was gone. Long years I roamed the Dry-Lands, and I remembered that look in their eyes. If not water, then guilt would sustain me. I would be changed. Rebegot.'

'And you were,' Joe said slowly. 'Reborn inside a human child.'

'Why don't you leave them, Joe?' the creature smiled. 'They're lost anyway. And even if you could save them, why should you? A brother who pours poison into his veins. A father who allowed you to suffer the guilt of your mother's death. You're a family that inflicts pain upon each other, day after miserable day. Why not let the shadows have them?'

'And you'd let me go?'

The thing nodded.

'I don't believe you. I know what you really want: me. These poor bastards,' Joe indicated those draining faces, 'they're just a party trick.'

'She told you.'

'Muriel told me a lot of things.'

Joe plunged his hand into the plastic carrier bag. He brought out the first volume of Attabers Encyclopaedia.

'How you tried to strike a deal with my mum.'

He crossed the room and, keeping his gaze away from that ravaged face, placed the book in front of the rocking chair.

'How the black water "christened" me, and how that left you drained.'

The silver compass joined it.

'She told me about the people she brought here.'

Then the Nazi lapel badge, the Rolls Royce keys, the religious texts, the bandolier, Tommy Jenning's exercise book.

'Those sorry souls you fed on, just to keep something alive that should have perished years ago. But most important of all, she told me what you were.'

'What is this?' the creature asked. There was fear in its voice.

'You're a forgotten god.' Joe caught sight of the name carved into the stone. '*Tiddy Mun* . . . But you're something else, too. You're Muriel Sutton's sister. You're a human child. And when children do bad things . . .'

Joe laid the last of the items – the makeshift bong and the whisky bottles – at Tiddy Mun's feet.

'They say sorry.'

The rocker halted. The shadows pouring into the bin froze. While the house trembled, and the stone wheels ground, the girl stared at the artefacts arrayed before her.

'Alice, can you hear me?'

A murmur, a flutter of breath. Again, Joe saw that melted face.

'Do you remember the people your sister brought here? These were the things they left behind.'

Tiddy Mun shook its head, 'Their shadows were mine to take.'

'But they weren't *yours* to take, were they, Alice? Why didn't you stop him? Did you just watch as he took what he needed? Did you see the fear in their eyes? Did you hear their screams and pleas? You should've helped them. Why didn't you?'

With each accusatory question, Joe's self-hatred deepened. He was blaming a child for these crimes. A child murdered by its sister. An infant that, in any case, had never truly lived, and that must have witnessed unequalled horrors during its short existence. Could it even sense shame and guilt? And, if it could, what kind of monster would dare to condemn it?

'You killed your mother, Alice. You burst out of her and you took her life.'

'She gave it willingly.'

'Your father, too. Do you remember showing him things? Things so bad his mind buckled under the horror of them? And then there was Silas Sutton and Mr Bedeker. And Muriel. In the asylum, back at the house, you fed off her for years. And like a good sister, she let you feed.'

A human, child voice broke through. 'Please . . .'

'No, Alice, you have to hear this. You've been a very bad girl. After my mum left, you were weakened. You'd given away some of your power and needed to feed. But Muriel's shadows had grown thin, and so you sent her out to bring richer meats to your table. These people,' Joe swept his hand across the collection, 'not innocents, perhaps, but *people* nonetheless. Flawed human beings with their own lives and hopes and miseries. You took those things away from them. Hollowed them out and imprisoned them. How does that make you feel, Alice Daecher?'

The little girl stood up. With mangled fingers, she clawed the hair back behind her ears.

'Bad. It makes me feel bad.'

Joe saw what fire and water had made of the child. His soul balked at the devastation. Fearful of what he had done, he called out to her.

'Alice.'

But Alice didn't hear him. She was staring at the objects from the bag. Suddenly, her mouth dropped, exposing the skeletal jaw. Her entire body lurched forward and her eyes went glassy and wide. Like a stream of sewage it came, the dense shadows of a life lived darkly. There was a potent, cloying odour to it that set Joe spluttering. The smell filled his head with voices that scraped like knives behind his eyes. He watched as the ribbon of darkness spilled out of the girl. It hit the ground and twisted around the collection. Then, spiralling upwards from each keepsake, it began to sculpt itself into shapes. Human forms that gathered around the child.

'I'm sorry,' she cried.

A fat man made of smoke regarded her with blank eyes.

'I didn't mean to hurt you.'

Not one of the figures responded. Not the plain young woman nor the elderly preacher; not the stick-thin boy nor the pig-tailed girl. Not David Tregennis nor Kelvin Hope. Silently, they closed in around her.

Joe heard the whimpers. They carried over the drone of the shadows, which both invited and accused. She's just a child, Joe thought, and I'm damning her. He started forward.

Muriel Sutton's words came back to him: *I want you to destroy my sister and the thing keeping her alive . . . by using what* it *gave you . . .*

The shadows parted. Spilling into each other, the cloud snaked across the room and poured into the garner bin. Below, the millstones chomped hungrily upon the soul of Alice Daecher. Joe looked across to the rocking chair. Slumped there in a tattered, autumn-red coat sat a tiny, fleshless skeleton.

'Joe?'

It was Bobby. The shadow-river had vanished from his mouth. Joe rushed to the far corner of the attic and helped the boy to his feet. His eyes were weary, ringed with brown circles, but humanity shone through. He hadn't been entirely lost. Bobby nestled his face in the crook between Joe's neck and shoulder. Dry, heaving sobs rattled through him.

'It's over,' Joe said. 'Come on, we need to see to dad.'

Between them, they lifted Richard upright and rested him against the wall. His eyes remained tight shut. Joe slapped his face and was rewarded with a low murmur. The Old Man looked just that: aged, spent. The boys carried him to the trapdoor.

'I'll go first,' Bobby said, 'take the weight.'

'Are you strong enough?'

'Joe, I just want to get out of here. Now.'

Joe nodded. He threw back the hatch.

A cloud of flour dust burst into the attic. It boiled in the square of the trapdoor and obscured the Stone Floor below. Joe tore strips of cloth from his shirt. He tied one around his father's face and threw another to Bobby.

'Here, put this over your mouth.'

His arms wrapped around Richard's waist, Bobby descended. The ladder groaned under the weight of two. Sweat sprang out on Bobby's face and ran into his eyes. He adjusted his grip on his comatose father. Then, with only his head above the cloud, Bobby let loose a frightened yelp. He had lost his footing. The kid tumbled into the dust. Joe, who had been using both hands to help support the Old Man, could do nothing to help his brother. The sudden dead weight was too much and Richard slipped through his grasp. A rumble and crack sounded from below.

Joe squatted over the trapdoor.

'Bobby? You okay down there?'

No answer. Joe started down the ladder.

The fourth rung had snapped. Joe's foot went through it, but he managed to stay upright. His eyes narrowed into slits. Wheezing as the dust filled his throat, he looked around for Bobby and Richard. They were by the little window, Richard propped up against the wall while Bobby tried to raise the sash. Illuminated by moonlight, and covered in flour dust, they looked like a Victorian engraving of lost souls. Aside from a cut to Richard's head, they didn't appear to be hurt.

'Let's just get out!' Joe shouted.

Bobby pointed at his ears and shrugged. The roar of the millstones was deafening. Joe pulled off his mask and mimed escape through the second trapdoor.

'Can't,' Bobby mouthed. 'Locked.'

Joe shook his head, disbelieving. He retied his mask and went to the trapdoor. Taking hold of the metal ring, he tugged upwards. It refused to give. He examined the ring more closely. A padlock had been clamped at the base and fastened to a hoop of metal in the floor. Only someone already inside the millhouse could have fitted the lock. He looked around for a key but could find nothing amid the debris.

Joe went back to the window. He was about to suggest smashing the glass, when a voice gurgled out of the mist. It was rich and malevolent and spoke as if from the depths of a well.

'Nightingales take wing and fly, but gods can pluck them from the sky.'

Fifty-four

The voice came from that area which housed the mechanical heart of the mill. There, in the semi-darkness, amid metal, wood and rough-hewn stone stood something older than the oldest component of this primitive machine. The parasite of Alice Daecher. The weaver of shadows. Spirit of the Marshes, twisted by madness into a new and darker form.

It looked pale, almost translucent. In fact, Joe swore he could see the spur wheel working behind it. Covered in filthy, straggling hair, it was difficult to make out the features. All that could be seen was its eyes and mouth, running with thick, black sputum. Bobby's hand sought out his brother's and squeezed. Joe felt fear scrape along his spine.

The thing reached out. Between bird-like talons it held a single match.

'I die,' it said, '*You* die.'

'The dust,' Bobby said. 'Gail told me. Jesus, Joe, the flour-dust in the air. It only needs a spark.'

Tiddy Mun nodded. 'We'll burn together. Unless . . .'

The creature looked at Joe.

'What does he mean?' Panicked, Bobby switched to the little man. 'What the fuck do you mean?'

'Stay with me, Joseph,' said the spirit. 'We shall weave new shadows. And the darkest, bleakest of them shall be your own.'

'No.'

Joe and Bobby looked down at the man slumped against the wall. Richard repeated that simple denial.

'No.'

The boys helped their father to his feet. Suddenly, the Old Man turned and rammed his elbow through the window. Then, in quick succession, he ran his arm around the frame, clearing the splinters of glass. It was the action of seconds but, when completed, Richard's shirtsleeve was soaked scarlet. He gritted his teeth against the pain.

'Go,' he instructed. Before the boy could protest, Richard had lifted Bobby onto the sill. 'Jump.'

'Dad, no.'

'For Christ's sake, Bobby, we don't have time to argue. Just jump.'

It took only a glance for something profound to pass between father and son. Then the boy was gone.

'Joe, you next. Quickly.'

'I can stop this,' Joe said.

'You're my son. Now, do as you're told.'

Richard grabbed Joe by the scruff of the neck and forced him up to the window.

'Pathetic heroics from a dissolute father,' said the voice of Tiddy Mun.

The spirit moved the match to within an inch of the millstone. One strike and the place would ignite. They would burn like Alice Daecher had burned all those years ago.

'I killed my wife,' Richard screamed. 'I killed her and I was glad to do it.'

The match hovered innocently above the spinning disc. Tiddy Mun had frozen. Hungry eyes turned towards Richard Nightingale.

'I hated what she'd become, what *you* made of her. She was

so bright, so loving, so full of beauty. And then she was nothing. *Absent*. For years, I lived with that absence. It twisted me, curdled my soul. It drove me to women, to drink, to the brink of fucking insanity. But did that give me the right to take away the mother of these boys? Of course not. I was selfish, mad with hurt and grief. There hasn't been a minute since that night that I haven't felt the guilt of what I did. Oh, I chose to ignore it, to block it out, but it was always there. But do you want to know the worst of it? I murdered my wife and let my son shoulder the blame. I allowed him to believe that it was *his* fault. So feed on that, you son of a bitch.'

Tiddy Mun gorged himself on the promise of this shadow. His eyes glazed, his mouth slavered.

Richard span around. He took Joe's face in his hands and kissed the boy's forehead.

'I love you, son.'

Joe clung to his father.

Then he felt a blow to the chest. His fingers slipped through his daddy's hands. He tumbled through the air, screaming and crying.

When he hit the ground, every bone in his body jolted and his lungs contracted. He rolled onto his side and squeezed the trapped air from his throat. Lights danced behind his eyes and pain reddened his thoughts. Something was broken. Dazed, he struggled to his feet and screamed like a child woken from a nightmare.

Fire exploded from the window. The aftershock knocked Joe ten feet back onto the scrub. The roar resounded in his ears, but through it he heard something else. Groaning, splintering: the death cry of the great wheel as it cleaved off the side of the millhouse and crashed into the river. Through dimming eyes, he watched as this miracle of ancient engineering shattered into its constituent parts.

His gaze tunnelled. Orange tongues filled his view. From somewhere far away, he could hear Bobby shouting his name. He tried to answer but found that he had no words. Darkness had swallowed them. A complete darkness, where shadows had no place.

With a thankful heart, Joe Nightingale abandoned himself to it.

Epilogue

- Nine Months Later -

The minds of everlasting gods are not easily changed.

The Odyssey, Homer

Joe ferreted in his pocket for change. His shoulder hurt. It had been a year and a half since the accident, but he still experienced the odd twinge. Strange really, that such a minor injury should continue to trouble him. In contrast, the fracture he had sustained to his leg the night of the Daecher Mill fire had healed without much fuss.

A pretty nurse walked past. Joe sensed her sizing him up but didn't turn around. He was a taken man, after all. His fingers closed around a fifty pence piece. He fed it into the drinks dispenser and made a selection from the pictured buttons. The machine clanked and gurgled. Powdered hot chocolate and scalding water spewed in the general direction of a plastic cup. An automated voice instructed him to:

Enjoy your . . . HOT CHOC-O-LATE

'Cheers, mate. But maybe, next time, I can get the black coffee I asked for, yeah?'

Joe pinched the superheated cup between forefinger and thumb and took his drink to the X-ray department waiting room. He collapsed onto a plastic bucket seat and popped a couple of paracetamol. Jesus, he was tired. Every time he dozed, however, a thrill of anxiety jolted him awake. He glanced down at his watch and counted the last few seconds: Four, three, two . . . And. Yep. Twenty-seven hours straight. Surely this wasn't normal. He should go back to the nurses' station and start asking questions. Not much point, though. Experience taught him that he'd get the same old answer: 'No sense in rushing these things needlessly, Mr Nightingale. Why don't you go home and get some rest? We'll call you straightaway if there's any change.'

Joe started reading the NHS notice board for the fourteenth time. He was now an expert in recognising the signs of meningitis, the importance of a healthy diet and how to check for testicular cancer.

His eyes fluttered. Sleep took him.

Joe hadn't dreamed much since the fire, but when he did the dreams weren't good. Mostly, he saw his dad, perching him on the windowsill like a parent sitting a child up on a table and asking for a kiss. He would feel Richard's arms close around him; feel that fatherly warmth emanate from the man. And then the words would come. Words made powerful by the fact that they had seldom been spoken.

I love you, son.

This was the only good bit of the dream. He knew what came next, but still it horrified him. Strips of flame broke out across his dad's face. They stitched together to make a flickering cowl. Features melted into each another. The mouth formed into a fiery 'O' and the smell of burnt flesh filled Joe's senses. He twitched in his sleep, desperate to escape . . .

'Hey, Joe. Wake up, man.' Bobby let go of his shoulder. 'Bad dream again, huh?'

'Hmm? Yeah. Just the usual.'

'Do you want to talk about it?' Bobby asked. He took the seat next to his brother.

'No, it's cool. Cheers, though, Bob.'

They sat in silence for a moment. Above the unmanned X-ray department desk, the appointments clock ticked away. The harassed tones of a junior doctor, swearing at his pager, echoed down the corridor. Joe was partway through a heart disease information sheet when exhaustion finally shattered his nerves. He doubled over and wept. Bobby said nothing, just rested a hand on Joe's back. They stayed like that for a while.

'Where've you been?' Joe asked. He wiped the tears from his cheeks and sat up.

'Seeing dad.'

'Was it okay?'

'Yeah. I tidied up a bit. Talked, you know?'

'That's good. Did you take the flowers I got for him?'

'Course. . . . You should go see him, Joe.'

'We made our peace, Bobby. In the end. Anyway,' Joe put an arm around his brother's shoulder, 'you know I'm no good with cemeteries.'

'I put those bluebells on the grave, too. The ones you bought for mum. It looks nice. So, no news yet?'

'Nope.'

'I still can't believe it. Even after nine bloody months. You know what, you've actually done something you can be proud of, dick-face.'

'Thanks, cock-knocker.'

The brothers grinned at each other.

'Well, she better a get a shift on,' Bobby said. 'My installation opens the day after tomorrow, and you guys better be there. I'm really shitting it now. Mr Fleet's invited a few art dealers up from London. Big fucking cheeses. Might even be able to sell a few pieces.'

'Bobby, that's great.'

'Yep. And when I become a millionaire, I might even invest

in that tin-pot restoration business of yours. I'd want a good rate of return, though. Just because we're brothers doesn't mean you can shaft . . .'

'Mr Nightingale?'

The nurse tapped Joe on the shoulder. The banter with Bobby had momentarily driven cares and worries from his mind. Now they flooded back. His heart raced. There was something in the nurse's expression that Joe didn't like.

'What's happened?' Again, he felt Bobby's hand resting on his back.

'It's over,' she said.

Joe jumped up. He pushed past the nurse and ran headlong down the corridor. The sound of his boots pounding the floor meant that he didn't hear the calls for him to wait and listen. The long stretch of the children's ward passed in a flurry of colour. He had spent hours wandering this hall, a perma-grin plastered across his face. He knew by heart every clown and giraffe, every giant and Father Christmas, every rollercoaster and glitter-sparkled night sky. Once or twice, he found himself tearful, imagining a future of bedtime stories and finger painting. A future he couldn't wait to be a part of.

He burst into Delivery Room C.

A screen had been put up around the bed. Outside the curtain, that snooty doctor they had met on arrival conferred with a senior nurse. He caught sight of Joe and came over.

'Ah, Mr Nightingale. Yes, now I'm sorry we couldn't find you.'

'Is she okay?'

'Your partner's fine.'

'And the baby?'

'There were no complications with the labour. But . . .'

Joe started forward. The doctor caught hold of his arm but Joe threw him off. He ran to the curtain and tore it back.

Sam was sitting up in bed, the gown she had been given on arrival hitched up to her knees. She looked pale and scared. A nurse, her face a picture of concern, spoke comforting words that she obviously didn't believe. In Sam's arms, something tiny lay cradled in a blanket.

Joe felt sick. This wasn't right. The finger-painted future dissolved before his eyes. Sam looked up at him and made clutching gestures with her hand. He took hold of it and squeezed.

'Joe, there's something wrong with her. Our baby girl.'

The doctor said over his shoulder. 'Nothing wrong physically. She seems healthy. We're just going to do a few tests, that's all.'

From behind, Joe heard Bobby enter the room. He was asking the senior nurse questions.

'It's okay, Sam,' Joe said. 'Let me see her.'

Sam turned her face away and Joe felt her shame.

'We'll love her,' he said. 'Please, Sam.'

He bent down and kissed the mother of his child. Then, very gently, he took the baby from her. There seemed no weight to the thing at all. It lay still in his arms and, for a moment, Joe wondered whether there had been a mistake. Surely this child was dead. Then he felt a little kick against his chest and his heart filled up. It was going to be all right. There would be stories and finger painting after all.

'She hasn't cried,' Sam said, grief-stricken. 'Why won't she cry?'

Joe looked down at his first-born.

The features were frozen, like an alabaster mask. There was nothing there at all: no hunger, no yearning for warmth and comfort. As he looked, a dark tear dribbled from the corner of its left eye and ran into the folds of the blanket.

Joe screamed.

He went on screaming long after the baby had been taken from him. He felt his mind lose its anchor and cast itself adrift. Upon the surface of a black ocean, he saw only one thing: his daughter's face. The sight stayed with him long into the night, as he tried desperately to read something from the features. The barest sliver of human emotion. But there was nothing, not even shadows.

Only *Absence.*

Author's Note

It was during the turbulent 17th Century that the drainage of the Lincolnshire Fens began in earnest. Despite fierce resistance from the indigenous population – the so-called 'Fen Tigers' – the schemes of wealthy landowners progressed and, within decades, an ancient way of life had been made all but extinct. Much of the rich mythology of the Fen country also seemed to dry up with the landscape. Old practices died out and memories faded...

This story takes place during the blistering summer of 2006 – the hottest summer since records began in 1659. It was inspired by the beauty of the Lincolnshire watermills at Cogglesford and Claythorpe, and by the poetic, but largely forgotten, folklore of the Fens.

Acknowledgements

My love and gratitude go to my grandmothers: Vera Sanford and Lillian Hussey. I'd also like to acknowledge the following for their friendship and support: Scott Newby; Edward Tong; Paul Clark; Andrew Clarke; Luke Wilson; Tom & Emily Cunningham; Joseph D'Lacey; Mathew Riley; Lee Casey; and Simon Appleby. As ever, I owe a huge debt of gratitude to all at Bloody Books, especially Kat Josselyn, Anthony Nott and Simon Petherick. The research materials for this book were difficult to come by, and so my heartfelt thanks go to the ever-resourceful librarians at Skegness Library.